"Ingenious and witty . . . as if Terry Pratchett at his zaniest and Larry Niven at his best had collaborated."
—Roland Green, *Booklist*

"Fresh and imaginative. From a plausible yet startling invention, McCarthy follows the logical lines of sight, building in parallel the technological and societal innovations. 'Our Pick.' I wanted to visit this Queendom and meet these people."
—Mark Wilson, *Science Fiction Weekly*

"Humor and SF seem an unlikely pairing, but Wil McCarthy does his best to make the marriage work in his newest novel . . . worth reading, and it's a good sign for McCarthy's future that he's willing to experiment with new styles." —*Science Fiction Chronicle*

"A fairy tale [with] . . . the most delicious superscience since Larry Niven's *Ringworld*. Stylistic diversity and hard scientific rigor blended with panache and striking imagination. McCarthy works hard to draw out pathos and character development. Genuinely exciting—a wonderful hoot."
—Damien Broderick, *The New York Review of Science Fiction*

"The author of *Bloom* once again demonstrates his talent for mind-expanding sf. Vibrant with humor, drama, and quirky ideas. Highly recommended."
—*Library Journal*

"I don't recall the last time a book made me laugh out loud. I did so here on page 146, and at the book's end I did so again . . . though my eyes were moist as well. McCarthy has created a story here that is distinctly Asimovian in flavor, though his voice is very much his own." —Ernst Lilley, *SFrevu*

"Prepare to use your grey matter. [McCarthy] fills his pages with lovingly rendered descriptions . . . but it is the strength of his scientific imagination that really shines through." —Rob Williams, *SFX Magazine (UK)*

"A most dazzling future. What follows is a mind-spinning struggle that recalls a Henry Fielding novel of manners, Michael Moorcock's epic sagas and the cosmic free-for-alls of Doc Smith. There's fascinating science aplenty, mad scientists, robots running amok . . . What more could you want?" —Terry Dowling, *The Weekly Australian*

"A decidedly odd but enjoyable mix of mannered, decadent comedy and far-out physics. I liked and was even prepared to believe in [it]." —David Langford, *Ansible (UK)*

"A wonderfully off-kilter space operetta, best described as a sophisticated version of those golden-age serials of the '30s populated with slightly mad scientists who happen to have total mastery of nanotechnology and black hole physics." —Netsurfer Digest

"McCarthy's satirical humor and mastery of the hardest of hard science—he actually is a rocket scientist—are just as much in evidence here as in his earlier novels. It's lots of fun." —*Netsurfer Digest*

"Strong world-building enhances the witty and satirical tone of THE WELLSTONE (4) by Wil McCarthy. It's a wildly inventive and entertaining soap opera, disguised as futuristic science fiction, which forces us to question our ideas of human utopia." —*Romantic Times*

"Examines the downside of immortality [and] manages to work some pointed satire into what is actually a very good adventure story." —*Chronicle*

"Inventive and often funny, with a dark undertone, reinforced by a downright grim prologue and epilogue, that lends a certain *gravitas* to the theme." —*New York Review of Science Fiction*

LOST IN TRANSMISSION

"A gas." —*Entertainment Weekly*

"Explores the bumps on the road to utopia in a story that stands on its own within the world of this highly inventive series." —*Denver Post*

"Very cool." —*San Diego Union Tribune*

"Imaginative." —*Kansas City Star*

By Wil McCarthy

TO CRUSH THE
MOON
Being the Final Volume in the History
of the Queendom of Sol

WIL McCARTHY

BANTAM BOOKS

TO CRUSH THE MOON
A Bantam Spectra Book / June 2005

Published by
Bantam Dell
A Division of Random House, Inc.
New York, New York

This is a work of fiction. Names, characters, places, and
incidents either are the product of the author's imagination
or are used fictitiously. Any resemblance to actual persons,
living or dead, events, or locales is entirely coincidental.

Bantam Books, the rooster colophon, Spectra, and the
portrayal of a boxed "s" are registered trademarks of
Random House, Inc.

ISBN 0-553-58717-X

Printed in the United States of America
Published simultaneously in Canada

www.bantamdell.com

OPM   10   9   8   7   6   5   4   3   2   1

To Michael Barnstijn and Louise MacCallum
for their tireless patronage of
the arts and sciences

TO CRUSH THE
MOON

acknowledgments

With special thanks to Anne Groell for buying into my madness, to Deanna Hoak for taming it, to Hayden Green Mountain for the view that inspired this multivolume story, to Rich Powers and Gary Snyder for serving as vital sounding boards and bullshit detectors, to Bruce Hall for editing as though he were autistic (I mean this in a good way), and to Cathy for, well, everything.

The third part of this volume is drawn in part from twenty-year-old doodlings in the margins of the Computational Fluid Dynamics notebook I used at CU Boulder in 1985. Ah, Boulder. The title and a bit of the Lune imagery come from a dream I had during the same period, in which I held and examined a paperback book by that name, apparently written by myself. I'd like to thank Chun-Yen Chow and Scotty Cassut for inspiring these, and Richmond T. Meyer for the offhand remarks and critiques that have been cooking in my back brain ever since. More recently I had the pleasure of discussing the physics and biology of the squozen moon with Jack Williamson, and with Hal Clement (Harry Stubbs) shortly before his death. I'm grateful to both for their enthusiasm and support.

That these silly ideas have actually wormed their way between the covers of a book is literally a dream come true, so in addition I'd like to thank you, the reader, for indulging me in this way. You rock.

The ideas behind parts one and two have also been a long time building, and owe their cohesion in large part to Gary Snyder, Shawna McCarthy, Mike McCarthy, Vernor Vinge, Scott Edelman, Shelly Shapiro, Chris Schluep, Anne Groell, Stanley Schmidt, Bernard Haisch, Richard Turton, and Sir Arthur C. Clarke. I am their imperfect messenger; hold them blameless (well, mostly blameless) for any errors you encounter in these pages.

in which a city's gates
are breached

The skirmish at Timoch's gate is little recorded by conventional history—a minor engagement of Silver and Yellow and Stealth Gray, lost in the shuffle of much larger events. But a great deal of subsequent chaos turns on it, as an avalanche is said to turn on a single pebble. Regard it, then, as a moment of critical change which makes all the rest of it possible. It begins like this:

In the two hundred and first decade of the death of the Queendom of Sol, an ancient man finds himself trudging across the plains of a strange world. His escort—half a dozen armed men nearly as ancient as he— have already led him from the base of a bluff called Aden very nearly to the walls of a city called Timoch. And although the man has been to this world before—has lived here, wept here, bled and sweated here—he's never seen either of these places. Indeed, he's not even sure they existed when last his bootheels trod this gray, powdery soil, for he has spent a great many years . . . away. Asleep. Ensorcelled.

The world's name is Lune, although it was once called Luna. The man's name is Bruno de Towaji; he was once called "King." See him now in your mind's eye: a body incapable of frailty, wrapped round an ancient soul. His frayed, yellow-white hair extends to his shoulders in a kind of fan shape—very thin on top. His teeth are chalky nubs in a jaw as sturdy as ever. His skin—liver-spotted and yet still flushed with youth—is not so much wrinkled as *creased*. As if he's been folded up in a drawer somewhere.

Which is not far from the truth. Not nearly as far as Bruno would like.

"In decades past, the oldest towers were still enlivened. Programmable—faced with wellstone," says Bruno's primary companion, Conrad Mursk, pointing at the city with young-old fingers as the group crests a hill and looks down upon it. "They had diamond cores and deep foundations. Survivors of the Shattering, yes, very old and very grand. But twenty years ago there were some strange malfunctions, and Imbrians can be painfully superstitious about things like that. So, in the Year of the Lamb the buildings were torn down at great cost. The high towers which remain are of poured concrete over an iron lattice—a technique dating back to the Old Moderns of pre-Queendom Earth."

And that seems a strange thing to say, for Mursk is no architect. Hasn't been for a long, long time. Instead, he has passed himself down through the ages as a kind of soldier. Indeed, the guards accompanying the two—five men-at-arms as frizzed and ancient as Mursk and Bruno themselves—call him "General Radmer" when they call him anything at all.

"Let's not tarry here, shall we?" says one of them.

The men are angry, for this old leader of theirs—whom they clearly adore—has dragged them through one battle already, and is urging them now to Timoch, where they were once—and perhaps still are—considered criminals.

"Too much metal down there," says Sidney Lyman, the nominal leader of this ancient band. His tone is disapproving as he glowers down at the city. "How can the glints resist? There aren't soldiers enough—nor walls, nor glue—to hold them at bay forever."

Ah, and that's the other problem: this war of theirs. Not of these men—these Olders—in particular, but a war belonging to the entire world of Lune. And it's going badly, and as near as Bruno can determine, this places the *entire human race* at risk.

He glances up at the Murdered Earth, visible as a puckered distortion in the evening sky. The sun has set behind the mountains here, but the sky is still bright, alive with clouds of fierce orange and yellow. And behind them, the tortured rainbow of sunlight refracting around the centimeter-wide fleck of hypercondensed matter that was once the world—the one and only world—of human beings. It is, in truth, a tragically beautiful sight.

There is a Murdered Venus as well, and a Murdered Mars—crushed into black holes virtually indistinguishable from Earth's—and Bruno has no reason to suspect the other planets, especially the gas giants, have been spared in the years of his exile. That leaves only the moons and asteroids and planettes, many of which had still been thriving in the Iridium Days—the last days Bruno can still remember. But given the tendency of economic depressions to isolate vacuum habitats, slowly choking off the energies and machineries of their air supply, it's doubtful any could have survived this long. That leaves only the planettes, which of course have problems of their own, and cannot retain atmosphere indefinitely without maintenance. Surely a great many of them have failed already.

And that leaves only Lune, that greatest of planettes, that living world squozen from the lifeless mass of

Earth's primordial moon. Squozen by Conrad Mursk, in fact, at the command of Bruno de Towaji.

"Well, it's really no problem of ours," adds Sidney Lyman. He points an elbow in Bruno's direction, forcefully enough that Bruno half expects a Palace Guard to materialize from the ether to restrain him. But the Guards are dust now, like the Queendom of Sol itself, and Lyman goes on. "We'll get this Ako'i fellow back inside yonder walls, then scurry like hell to reach the veils of Echo Valley in time for sunset."

Which isn't saying much, Bruno muses, considering that sunset—judging from the angle of the sun and the shadows of the trees—is still a good thirty-five hours away. The days are long here.

"He's not going 'back' to Timoch," says Conrad Mursk. *General Radmer,* Bruno reminds himself. *Not Mursk. They call him General Emeritus Radmer.* And I am Ako'i. "He's going *to* it."

"Ah! A first-timer. A virgin in the hallowed ancient halls of that mausoleum of a city. Come now, Ako'i, one cannot dwell this long on Lune—" A thought seemed to strike him, then. "Oh, but you've been on Varna! Marooned, cast away. For that long? Since before there was a Timoch? Since the Shattering itself?"

"Possibly," Bruno grumbles, hoping to leave it at that. Tellingly, Lyman and his men have not recognized the husk of their old king. They don't know his name, his crimes, his many failures, and he prefers it that way. "Ako'i" isn't a name at all, but a Tongan epithet, something like calling a man "perfesser" or "genius" or . . . or "de Towaji," yes. Perhaps they would forgive him if they knew, but what matter? Perhaps Bruno might have forgiven himself, had he *been* himself these many, many centuries. But that doesn't matter, either. He is here as a figure out of history, to correct a historical mistake. Or to try, anyway.

They pass through a field of grazing, bleating sheep with gold-colored wool and curiously oversized heads. Then there are rock walls topped by wooden fences, leading down into a broad expanse of fresh-mown corn stubble. Soon, they find themselves on an actual road, paved with a smooth, continuous sheet of what looks like diamond or zirconium or some allotrope of silicon carbide. The surface is flawless, but to Bruno's eye something about it conveys a sense of tremendous age. On one particularly sharp curve, a mound of dirt has spread from the roadside to cover part of the road itself.

Bruno first mistakes the pile for a construction project, and then a termite mound of the sort that had once been common on the savannahs of Africa. But on closer inspection there is something almost crystalline about it: straight lines and flat surfaces. And the "termites" themselves are large and of curious design, with angular body parts of clear and superabsorber black and translucent, glassine blue.

"What are these?" he asks, pointing.

"Termites," Lyman answers, with no detectable irony.

"They're a bit . . . modified, yes?"

"No more than anything else around here. It ain't a natural world."

As the city draws near, Bruno can see that the walls surrounding it are at least as recent as the termite mounds out on the plains. They're flawless—not in the manner of wellstone or diamond but in the manner of freshly poured concrete which hasn't had a chance to weather. For all he can tell, they might have been poured yesterday.

"Those damned walls," Radmer is saying. "My goodness. They may indeed protect the city for a time, though not in the intended manner. The iron over which the cement was poured will be...tempting. The enemy may find it easier to dismantle the wall than to breach it and sally through. Every gram of it makes them stronger, while the people inside grow hungry. Not exactly the delay the City Mothers might wish for, but they're hardly in a position to choose."

Radmer's manner of speech does not much resemble Conrad Mursk's. Nor, really, does his face. A lot of time has passed here.

"Bloody valets," one of the soldiers says, making a heartfelt curse of it. "Bloody glints."

And Bruno doesn't know whether to laugh or weep at this, for the armies of doom are quite ridiculous, and the swelling of their ranks can probably, if indirectly, be blamed on himself. Who set this stage, if not the king of all that preceded it?

Damn and blast. If dying were easy he'd've done it long ago. He *had* tried. But there had been nothing on the planette Varna capable of extinguishing this robust carriage of his, and to die of hunger or thirst required more concentration than he'd been able to muster. Every time his attention wandered, he would find his belly full of turnips and spring water. And in the aching solitude there, his attention did nothing *but* wander.

Finally, they arrive at the gates of the city, and Bruno sees the gate and wall are much smaller than they'd looked from a distance. Not more than four meters high, possibly as little as three. The men upon the walls, with their burnished iron helmets, their rifles and bayonets, are quite a bit shorter than the grizzled old men who've escorted him here.

"Ho there," Radmer calls up to them. "We require an audience with the Furies."

"Oh wonder! It's a band 'f Olders," one of the guards

calls down contemptuously. "We'n't seen y'r like here since th' troubles begun."

"There ha'e al'ys been troubles," Radmer calls back, with a rising contempt of his own. "My name is Radmer, and you will open this gate."

"Y'all c'n have audience with my arse, Mr. Radmer."

"E'en if your arse were a magistrate, m'boy, I would have to decline. I will see no guard, no City Mother, not even a senator. I'm here to speak with the Furies."

Bruno finds it difficult to follow this exchange, for accent and inflection so clot the guard's voice that his might almost be another language entirely. This "Radmer" has spoken Queendom-standard, Tongan-inflected English up to this point, but with the city guard he speaks in the city dialect. Flawlessly, as near as Bruno can detect.

"He doesn't know you," Lyman says to Radmer, in Queendom-standard tones of quiet indignation. Then, to the man on the wall, "Groveling in the dust is where you should be, maggot. This is *General Emeritus Radmer*, who turned back the armies of Red Antonio and saved this pathetic city of yours, when your grandparents' grandparents could not. More than that, you glob of phlegm, he carved the very world upon which you now stand, whose air you now stink up with your putrid excuses."

The man is not impressed. "Y'all Olders 're all Gross High Mucky-Muck of someorother, close as I can figure. And 'f this man built the world, then he be a god, and should need no 'sistance o' mine."

"Good point," Lyman says, sounding approving for the first time this day. "You have wit enough to call us Olders. Have wit enough, then, to realize we *request* your help for the sake of decorum. And we'll open the gate, if you will not."

Radmer holds up a hand at waist level—a gesture which commands silence. And Lyman—reluctantly—obeys.

"We dare not tarry out here," Radmer says to the guards. "I bring with me an item of great strategic value, and the Glimmer King's scouts have found us already. You do know they're here, yes? Soon the hills will be lousy with them. If you turn us away, O morbid child, I daresay you won't last the week."

Glimmer King. Is that what they're calling Bruno's son these days? His only child, his greatest error? If indeed Bascal Edward de Towaji Lutui is (a) alive, and (b) responsible for all this mad suffering—Bruno has heard only Radmer's suspicions on the subject. But those were enough to draw him here, to this unreal place. A father's disappointment—and atonement—run as deep as his love.

"If he turns us away he won't last the minute," Lyman says, drawing his sword. And a sense washes over Bruno yet again, that he is living in some hell of his own creation, for the sword in Lyman's hand could well be a figment of fevered dreams. Ancient, yes. Sharpened and sealed with a film of epitaxial diamond. The weapon has a wicked point, and a basket hilt to protect the wielder's hand, and in between there is . . . nothing at all. Nothing to parry, to grasp, to see flashing in a deadly arc. In showing it off to him, Lyman had called it an "air foil," and had declined to estimate the number of deaths it had inflicted at his hand, and the hands of other soldiers before him.

Ploughshares into swords, alas. That wasn't what mass-stabilized wormholes were *for*.

But Bruno's musings are cut short when someone up on the wall cries "Bandits!" and hurls down a wooden spear tipped with barbs of iron. Of course it bounces harmlessly off the marble-gray cloak of one of the Olders—Brian, his name is—who picks it up quietly, examines it for a moment, and then breaks it calmly over his knee.

And suddenly everyone is fighting.

"Inviz" was mainly a fashion statement in Bruno's day, one of many geostat patterns that seemed to hold stationary while your clothes and body swirled around them. In set theory terms, inviz was the special case of geostat in which the display pattern matched the background pattern. But in the hands of an artful dresser it became something more, something beautiful. A complement to the other nonspectral colors—superblack and superreflector, wellwood and glowhoo, animorphic and animimetic and the ever-popular c0untərsənsə. How he misses those! How he misses the fops and dandies who strutted around in them, with hardly a care!

But on the wellcloth cloaks of Sydney Lyman's band, stealth inviz is just another instrument of murder. The Olders lift their hoods and vanish, or nearly vanish, leaving only smudges in the air and dancing shadows on the ground. They must be wearing speed boots and wall-hugging gecko gloves as well, for in what seems no time at all, the air is shimmering on top of the wall itself, and the guards there are dropping their weapons, dropping their helmets, staggering and falling in disarray. Struggling vainly with unseen assailants.

"Harm no one!" Radmer commands, and it occurs to Bruno to wonder whether he's speaking to his own men, or to the city guards, or to the world of Lune itself, with a frustration that borders on despair. *Here is a man,* thinks Bruno, *who knows combat all too well, and loves it not at all.* He feels a moment of pity, for the earnest young man who had long ago dreamed himself a builder, just as Bruno had dreamed himself a physicist. But the moment passes, for this whole world is like a nightmare, and there's a great deal Bruno doesn't know. He'll take nothing for granted, and he feels—perhaps foolishly—that nothing can truly surprise him, or move him. He's beyond all that.

Old-fashioned cast iron bells are ringing up on the wall now—alarms from the guards close enough to observe the fray but not close enough to be caught in it. Still, the gate—a simple affair of welded steel bars and plates—swings slowly open on squealing hinges, and Radmer strides casually into the city. Not waiting to be summoned like a dog, Bruno trails close behind.

The city within could have been clipped straight from Bruno's Old Girona childhood: an environment of stone and brick and heat-trapping colored glass. A cluster of hundred-story towers stands anomalously at the center, ringed by artful moats and bridges, but few of the other buildings are more than six floors high, and (per Radmer's warning) none seem enlivened. Between them, streets of diamond and cobblestone and muddy gravel slope gradually down toward the seashore.

And on the streets are crowds of dwarfish, big-headed men and women dressed in drab spectral colors. Fluttering gray shadows cling beneath their chins and eyelids, the undersides of their arms. Reactive skin pigment—an adaptation generally used for shedding heat. These people are Eridanians, he thinks at first, but on the heels of that he notices other engineered features as well: the six-fingered, dual-thumbed hands of Sirius, a hint of the thick, trollish skins of Barnardean extremists. Also the occasional head of translucent blue-green hair—a photosynthetic adaptation that had started right here in Sol System, under the very nose of a disapproving Queen Tamra.

At the moment, these strange, patchwork people are

scurrying back or fleeing outright, their eyes wide on the opened gate. "Olders!" some of them cry.

"What are they?" Bruno asks quietly.

"They call themselves 'human beings,'" Radmer answers without irony. "They're the people of Lune."

"Ah. Well. What do they call *us*, then? Olders?"

"Or bandits," Radmer agrees, "or *indeceased*, which is an unkind word indeed. But our numbers have faded over the centuries—especially here in Imbria, which is a hard nation to inhabit in secret. They sometimes hunt us, so we try to keep out of sight."

"Some of us do," says Sidney Lyman, materializing suddenly at Bruno's side. He glares pointedly at Radmer. "Others don't ever learn, no matter how much misfortune they bring down upon the rest of us. These 'humans' go through spurts of curiosity and outreach, seeking us out as historical reference works, which is fine except that it lays the groundwork for the next round of bloodletting. Know thy enemy, eh?

"And of course it's worst for our own children. Immorbidity doesn't breed through; if they stay with us, we watch them grow old and die. We're like statues to them, unbending, wearing down on a timescale they can scarce perceive. But if they join the mainstream of human society, they do so as tall, five-fingered freaks. There aren't even ghettos for them, not anymore, so the freak show never ends. Many of them *do* become bandits, in the times when relations are poor. And our dear Radmer here is always stirring things up."

"*Was* always," Radmer says. "It's a habit I'd long abandoned."

"Until these lucky days," Lyman answers, with more than a hint of bitterness. "Now you've gone all the way to Varna, braving radiation and vacuum to bring this . . . gift to the Imbrians. How very noble of you."

"I like to think so, Sid. Really. If *this* civilization falls, what do you think will succeed it? Another Queendom? Another dark age? Do you really want to find out? Most of the time, the people of this city give little thought to our existence, except as characters in ancient songs."

"But now they need us, in your opinion," Lyman mutters. "Even if their own opinions disagree."

"Yes," Radmer says simply. Then, "I asked you to bring me this far, Sid, and you've done it. I won't ask any more. In fact, I'll invite you to leave before things get any worse."

"And abandon you here for lynching?"

Radmer laughs humorlessly. "I've been here a hundred times, Sid, and they haven't managed it yet. I'll be fine."

"Meaning no offense, sir, but I think we'll wait here a minute and see what happens."

"Hmm. Well. Suit yourself."

And presently, as if called forth by this exchange, a new set of guards appear—first a dozen, then two dozen, then a hundred strong. They're dressed all in yellow, and in addition to rifles and swords they carry, here and there, the elongated wormhole pole-arms which Lyman has called "air pikes." A few of them, Bruno notes with surprise, are quite obviously female.

"Ah, the Dolceti," Lyman says, in almost welcoming tones.

"This is more serious," Conrad murmurs to Bruno. "The nation's elite guard, trained in blindsight through the channels of fear. Don't underestimate them."

"I hadn't," Bruno says, meaning it. He has no idea what any of these terms mean, or what anyone here might be capable of. Blindsight? Channels of fear? The name "Dolceti" itself is suggestive; it's about as unTongan a word as human mouths can utter, and assuming it descends from some species of Latin or Greek, it might mean "sweet" or "pleasing." It might also mean "pain" or "chop" or "deceit," or even "whale."

"You lot are under arrest," says one of the Dolceti—not obviously marked as a leader but certainly carrying himself that way. His dialect is not quite as impenetrable as the wall guards' had been, though it does sound forced, as though he's dredging up some ancient tongue he'd learned and half forgotten.

"Y'all near c'rect," Conrad Mursk says back to him, in what sounds to Bruno, again, like flawless Lunish. "We're t'be escorted to the Furies."

"On whose authority?" the Dolceti wants to know.

"Mine," Radmer answers calmly. "As Third Protector of Imbria."

That sends a ripple of surprise through the guards. "You're Radmer?"

"I am. Are you the captain here? Is Petro dead already?"

"Petro retired twenty years ago, when the haunted towers came down. I'm the captain, yes."

"Well, Captain," says Radmer, "I'm afraid we don't have much time, for the enemy's scouts are in yonder hills already, and will soon pin you against the sea. Come now: close the gate and do as I ask."

At that, the Dolceti captain moves with amazing swiftness, drawing a short sword—an ordinary one, though an air foil hangs at his side as well. In an eyeblink, he leaps forward to lay the iron blade across Radmer's neck. "I take no orders from—"

But Radmer has stepped aside, not quickly but at just the right moment, with the ease of long practice. Centuries of practice—millennia. He's out of reach, untouchable. Then, with no greater urgency, he tosses a nearly full canteen at another Dolceti, whose rifle is aimed exactly between Radmer's eyes. The guard doesn't flinch, but he does swat the projectile aside with a viper-quick motion, letting his rifle waver for a second. Which gives Radmer enough time to draw his blitterstick without seeming to hurry.

Intended mainly for use against robots, a blitterstick—or blitterstaff, or blitter-anything—is an ungainly and rather cruel weapon to turn against human flesh. Rarely lethal, its shifting wellstone patterns—caustic and thermally abusive, alive with pseudoatom disassembly brigades—leave puckers and burns and worse disfigurements which, in a medically impoverished environment like this one, must surely be permanent. But Radmer's only other weapon is a pistol, far more lethal.

What happens next strikes Bruno as something like a chess opening: no one attacks, but everyone glares and sidesteps, aims and tenses, lining up for a kill. The drop of a feather will set them off, but neither side is crass or undisciplined enough to *engage*. Not first, not in cold blood. The Dolceti outnumber the Olders ten to one, though, and from the looks on their faces they seem to think it will be enough. To penetrate the diamond weave beneath a soft Queendom skin? To shatter the brickmail and impervium of faxborn Queendom-era bones? Probably not, but they can still drag a man down and pinch his nose shut until he smothers. And they seemed prepared to.

"Always a pleasure, coming here," Radmer says. "The Imbrians of Timoch are such a fine, appreciative people."

For a moment, Bruno toys with the idea of unveiling his true identity. Perhaps the shock value will defuse this situation, and get the Olders inside without bloodshed. Then again, he would be a figure as remote in the Imbrians' past as Aristotle and Alexander were in his own. Would they believe him? Would they recognize his name, or understand its burden of significance? Would they even care?

He is spared any further thought on the matter when a voice from atop the wall calls out *"Glints!"* in a tone that registers panic across all possible dialects. Bruno turns, looking back across the sloping plains he and Radmer have just crossed at considerable peril. And indeed, yes, the enemy is still at work out there: he sees the unmistakable glints and flashes of sunlight on superreflective impervium. Less than five kilometers away. Less than *two*.

Behind him, a ripple of concern passes through the Dolceti.

"You must attack," Radmer says, simply and without fear. "They're only scouts, but they're *right here*, barely a rifle's reach from your capital gates. And if they report back, the Glimmer King will know I've been to Varna and back in a sphere of brass. He'll know I came *here* afterward. Assuming he doesn't know it already."

"Varna is in outer space," the Dolceti captain replies, as if to a child's bad joke.

"Aye," says Radmer. "I had to launch from Tillspar, over Highrock Divide. All I can say is, thank God for pulleys. You might be interested in my catapult, by the way; properly cocked it can bombard any point on this planette's surface."

"You lie," says a voice in the crowd somewhere.

"Do I? For what purpose?" Radmer's tone is patient. "The enemy is *that* way, friend, and if you swear this man's safety"—he points at Bruno—"upon all that is holy and dear, then I will fight at your side to defend these ill-forged walls."

The captain is angry but not stupid; he considers the offer, considers the evidence before him. "What's special about this man?"

"Wisdom," Radmer answers. "And if you will not pledge his safe conduct to the Furies, then you'll have *two* enemies, and no friends, and soon no country to defend."

"Very diplomatic," the captain grumbles, then steps forward to offer his hand. "I'm Bordi, grandson of Petro."

The two men shake on it, prompting Sidney Lyman to mutter, "You'll be the death of me, General. But I'll not let you enter this fight by yourself."

"Nor I," says the Older named Brian, and the others grunt in assent.

"Natan," says Bordi, gesturing sharply to one of the taller Dolceti. "Stay here, you and Zuq. Guard this Older, this font of wisdom, until I return."

And with that, the Dolceti are off and running in a hooting, jabbering mob that quickly settles into three perfect V formations, like flights of geese. Not to be outdone, Lyman's Olders follow on their springy well-leather boots, quickly overtaking the Dolceti, leaping right over the "human beings'" oversized heads and dashing out in front, to form a smaller, faster V of their own.

"Be safe," Radmer says to Bruno, not in a kindly way but as a command. Then he, too, is sprinting toward the enemy.

Bruno still carries Radmer's binoculars, and they're of ancient design, wellstone lenses and all. He lifts them to his eyes now, and can clearly resolve the enemy squad: another group of twenty, moving rapidly toward the city on feet so dainty and small that a baby girl's ballet slippers could easily fit them. They carry no energy weapons or projectile throwers, and except for the swords, and the black iron boxes affixed to the left sides of their gleaming faceless heads, they could easily pass for Queendom-era household robots. Valets, yes. Scullery maids. But already Bruno knows, from bitter experience, how fast and strong and remorseless these impervium soldiers really are. Delicate killers, bent on some demented form of world domination for this unseen Glimmer King.

"If 'ts metal they want," says the Dolceti named Natan, "I say let 'em have it. Right through the ocular sensors and out through the box. *Bap!* I want to be *out there*, old man, not wiping your withered old nose."

"Your captain must have great faith in you," Bruno says, trying for some reason to be kind to this man, who seems little more than a figment of his senile imagination. Thus far he's been driven forward by curiosity alone—a desire to see this thing through to the end, like a play. None of it feels real.

"Fester these *robots*," Natan spits. He might use the word "devils" or "child molesters" in milder tones.

"They were once our servants," Bruno says to him, because he's not sure Natan even knows this.

"Really?" says the younger Dolceti guard, Zuq. He's shorter, with light green hair underneath his yellow cap. "Well thank you very much. We've nothing but your Older mess to live in, and this really contributes. Thanks for the Shattering, too, and the Stormlands. And for Murdered Earth while we're at it."

"You're welcome," Bruno says dryly. His grief burned out a long, long time ago, and if he starts bogging himself down now in pointless guilt, then where will it lead? Whom will it benefit? "If you had seen the Queendom in its heyday you'd understand. It seemed worth any price. Truthfully, it still does."

Yes, and *there* is a damning indictment, for he and Tamra had built, in the words of Rodenbeck, "a house of collapsium and straw." And they knew it at the time. How could they not? It took a lifetime of determined self-deception to ignore the generation problem, the population problem, the limits of mass and energy and physical law. What had they been thinking?

But then, in all fairness to himself, what could he, Bruno de Towaji, have done differently? He didn't create the Queendom; he was conscripted by it. And he hadn't known—couldn't have imagined—how thoroughly his early discoveries would rewrite the human story. Once collapsium was out of Pandora's hands, into the ham fists of Prometheus, Bruno had been as hard-pressed as anyone just to keep up. Perhaps if he'd guessed the future better, or raised a gentler child, or succeeded in his later research...

"Well," he says, suddenly glummer, "if my apology helps, then be assured you have it. We've left some terrible messes behind."

"I can't understand your prattle, old man," says Zuq.

"Maybe you should shut up," Natan suggests.

And in spite of everything, Bruno finds his neck growing warm, for no one has spoken to him like that since his earliest days at Tamra's court, and rarely then. Even the megalomaniac Marlon Sykes had been polite—often deferential—toward his fellow declarant-philander. Well, usually.

He waves a hand at the yellow uniforms, and in his best professorial tone he advises, "Overconfidence is the chief failing of elites, boy. The robots will have no trouble finding you in these canary suits."

"We don't hide from our enemies," says Zuq. "Our enemies hide from us. That's not overconfidence, it's psychology. And my rank is 'squad leader,' not 'boy.' This is *Deceant* Natan."

"Well," says Bruno, "'old man' isn't my rank, either. I won't invoke ancient titles that mean nothing here, but I was fighting robots when the Queendom itself was young."

And so he was. They'd made him king for it! But the Dolceti's point is taken nonetheless: he isn't a king here, nor a soldier, nor even a guest. If anything, he's a sort of commandeered munition, hauled from the mothballs of history and pressed back into service. He can't really imagine what knowledge Radmer thinks he possesses, to turn the tide of this war. His Royal Override has already failed to halt the enemy's advances, though in fairness to Radmer it did give them pause. They do carry within them some vague memory of the old allegiances.

Bruno raises the binoculars again, and sees to his mild surprise that Lyman's Olders have already engaged the enemy, with Radmer and the canary-colored Dolceti not far behind. The robots fight well—they fight *perfectly*, with the fluidity of dancers and the cool precision of clockwork. Their swords flash in elaborate sweeping arcs, as if spelling out glyphs in the afternoon air. But oddly enough, the Dolceti are faster. And the Olders are certainly more cunning, and anyway the robots are—for once!—badly outnumbered.

One of them manages to raise an antenna—the robotic equivalent of a scream for help—but it's quickly cut down by the swords of human beings. The mast is a telescoping wand of impervium, theoretically unbreakable, but it isn't all one piece, and everyone seems to know where to hack, where the vulnerable joints are. Meanwhile, the box on the robot's head explodes in a hail of metal bullets. The other robots are down just as quickly, and the only casualty Bruno can see is a single Dolceti guard, holding her throat while a spray of blood jets between her fingers, turning her yellow tunic bright red. She looks calm, but she'll be dead within the minute.

And Bruno takes this as a bad omen indeed, for if twenty robots can strike a blow against the elite guard of this world's strongest nation—with Queendom technology assisting, no less!—then what will happen when the robots return in their hundreds of thousands? In their millions? Radmer has been right all along: without a miracle, the city of Timoch doesn't stand a chance.

Damn Conrad Mursk anyway, he can't help thinking. This isn't the first time the boy has swept into Bruno's life, turning everything on its head. Even in the days of the Queendom, Mursk had always had an uncanny talent for trouble.

book one

the
barnardyssey

chapter one

in which the arrest of a drifter proves troublesome

The ship had seen hard use over long years; her sides were streaked with burns and gouges, with dead spots where the hull's wellstone plating had given out, leaving man-sized squares of inert silicon. She was one of the old starships, no doubt about that: a round needle thirty meters across and seven hundred and thirty long, capped at either end by a faintly glowing meshwork of blue-green dots: the ertial shields—essentially a foam of tiny black holes, emitting weakly in the Cerenkov bands. The ship was otherwise dark, her running lights extinguished. There was no sign of her photosail; the compartments that should hold it were open to vacuum, their doors torn away. The streaking patterns suggested this had happened long ago.

But the worst of the damage looked slightly less ancient: a round, meterwide hole punched through the portside hull of the ship, just in front of the engines, and out again through the capside in a shotgun-patterned oval large enough to admit an elephant. Interestingly, there were some intact pipes and ducts visible through the hole, running right through the path of destruction.

These were shiny in the middle, and looked duller toward the hole's edges, as if they'd been grafted in place after the accident. Structural damage to the hull itself was minimal; the hole edges looked almost cauterized, suggesting the projectile had been very small and moving very fast—a sand grain flying through at 1% of light-speed. The actual damage had been done by heat, and by plasmified hull material entrained in the particle's wake.

The fact that the ship was tumbling end-over-end at 2.06 revolutions per second also supported this theory. Getting that much mass moving that quickly required a substantial momentum transfer.

"Visual contact," said Bruno de Towaji into the microphones of his space suit helmet. "Running lights and station-keeping thrusters are inactive, but there are signs of . . . well, perhaps not life, but activity at any rate. *Something* on that ship survived the accident, at least briefly. The severed plumbing between the reactors and deutrelium tanks has been repaired."

Here in the hundred and thirtieth decade of the Queendom of Sol, Bruno himself was aboard the grappleship *Boat Gods*, which had its own ertial shield and its own deutrelium reactor, plus gravitic grapples whose use would be illegal for 99.9999% of humanity. With these, Bruno could grab on to anything—moons, planets, the sun itself—to pull *Boat Gods* around the solar system. The grappleship was tiny as such things went, but its interior was nicely appointed, and filled of course with breathable atmosphere. Bruno's space suit—actually a set of full battle armor, with high-domed helmet and thick wellcloth shielding all around—was strictly a precaution.

The starship whirled in his view like a fan blade, like a dizzying wheel of enigma and peril and his own damned confusion. Irritated by the blurring motion, he switched to a snapshot view that updated every five seconds. And in one of these frozen views, in bold red letters affixed to the ship's port side in some ancient chemical paint he read: QSS NEWHOPE. Which made sense on the one hand, for this ship had come out of the constellation of Ophiuchus, just off the Snake Holder's right shoulder. And *Newhope* was the name of the ship that the Queendom of Sol had launched, long ago, to Barnard's Star, which lurked invisible to the naked eye in precisely that location. The first of the great colony ships, yes. But on the other hand it made no sense at all, because the Barnard colony had been silent for hundreds of years—presumed extinct—and the QSS *Newhope* had been reported destroyed hundreds of years before that, in some sort of freak collision during an ill-advised sun-grazing maneuver.

"Target identity confirmed," he said. "She's QSS *Newhope*, apparently out of Barnard. Carrying what? Carrying whom? This makes no sense."

And while Bruno had always loved a good mystery, this one was a bit too personal, for his own son had been a passenger onboard this ship. Had been the King of Barnard, just as Bruno was, now and always, the King of Sol. And though it be foolish—there was no reason to suspect his exiled progeny had escaped the colony's fall—the sight of those words on the hull of the ship were enough to bestir in Bruno a pathetic sense of hope. For he loved his pirate, poet son as dearly as any father must.

What must it be like in there? Could anyone have survived? Those repairs had probably been carried out robotically, and in an ordinary spaceship that centrifugal tumbling would produce, what, almost six thousand gee at the fore and aft ends? Enough to crush a human into broth, to rend any possible hull or superstructural material. Even impervium—that strongest of wellstone substances, that perfect arrangement of quantum dots and confined electrons—should have given way long ago.

But this wasn't an ordinary spaceship; it was an ertially shielded *starship*. Even sweeping sideways through the ether, those ertial shields would have a deadening effect on the space around them. Absorbing and destroying the vacuum's delicate resonances, yes, clearing a bubble of supervacuum and greatly reduced inertia. And the so-called centrifugal force *was* inertia, nothing more.

Were there habitable, ertial spaces within the ship? Were there safe (or quasi-safe) regions where he could dock, for search and rescue purposes? Mathematically speaking the situation was appallingly complex, but here before him was a cheat, a peek at the answer, for QSS *Newhope* had not flown apart in a haze of carbon and silicon and black-hole hypercollapsite. Having been a professor and a laureate and a declarant long before he'd been a king, Bruno knew something of these matters, and though he declined to slog through the formal calculations, it seemed to him that attaching at the center and poking around would be safe enough.

And if not—if he destroyed himself—*Boat Gods* would simply withdraw, and print a fresh copy of him from its onboard fax machine. Or perhaps it would be flung away in ruin, and a fresh Bruno would have to be printed on Earth. Either way, it promised to be an interesting ride.

"Attempting a docking maneuver," he informed Traffic Control. For all the good it would do them; by the time they received the signal, he'd already be dead, or several hours into his rescue. *Boat Gods* and *Newhope* had encountered one another in the vast, cold wastes of the Kuiper Belt, where the sun was little more than a bright star, and the waste-ice dredging of a few dozen unpiloted neutronium barges was the only activity in some sixty thousand cubic light-hours of space. Civilization was a long way off.

Anyway, survivors or no, if he could stop this ship or change its course there was profit to be made, for the hypercollapsites used in ertial shielding were among the most valuable commodities in existence. And God knew the cash would be useful! Bruno would fax himself back home and return with the Queendom's finest salvage teams. And then the derelict, stripped of any special spacetime properties, could be vaporized by any superweapon his navy (or rather, his wife's navy) preferred.

Nor was this some trifling bureaucratic matter, for QSS *Newhope* was, alas, on a direct collision course with the sun. Her navigators, setting out from Barnard over six light-years distant, had done their job too well; aiming at Sol and driving their error sources to zero. So, in thirty-two days' time the derelict *Newhope*—moving at 2,500 kps, nearly 1% of the speed of light—would come screaming into the Inner System, passing the orbits of Mars and Earth and Venus and Mercury and then plunging (if grazingly) into the photosphere of their mother star.

The results would not be pleasant; the sun would escape destruction—probably—and the 90% of Queendom citizens nestled beneath bedrock or planetary atmospheres should be safe enough. But the flares would be colossal, and the Vacuum Cities' billion-odd residents would have to be evacuated as a precaution. And there was *no bloody place to put them*. Ergo, the naval response.

But first an investigation, hmm?

How the lords and ladies of Tamra's court had struggled against that suggestion! Or rather, against his doing it himself, without assistance.

"Dear," Queen Tamra had said to him, intruding upon his study in the way she almost never did, except in times of real trouble. "There's a tumbling starship on a collision course with the sun."

"Hmm?" he'd said, looking up from the equations and sketches on his desk. His mind was bursting with wormhole physics; he barely heard her. He barely noticed the storm outside, lashing rain and tattered palm fronds against his windows while the waves hammered the beach below. He was close—he was *close*—to understanding the dynamics of the throat collapse that had destroyed every one of his test holes. And this was as important politically as it was scientifically, for a functioning wormhole would solve nearly all of the Queendom's problems. Nearly all!

But Tamra knew this, and would not have broken his concentration without good reason. She could have printed an alternate copy of him from the palace archive, and given *it* the news, and let the two of him reconverge later on in the day. For an ordinary emergency, she'd've done exactly that.

Ergo this was no ordinary emergency, so with some effort he processed her words. "A starship, you say? One of ours?"

"Presumably," she'd answered testily, for no bug-eyed aliens had ever been detected out there in the void, whereas Sol had sent ships out to a dozen and one colonies. Still, the king could be forgiven his surprise; none of those ships had ever come *back*. "It's traveling out of Ophiuchus."

"Ah, the Barnard Express! Any sign of our boy?"

Unhappily: "No. The ship appears to be derelict; perhaps her crew is in storage. But Bruno, she's ertial, and on a collision course with the sun. Thirty-nine days from now."

"Ah. I see." Bruno nodded at that. As a young man not yet to the century mark, he'd made his greatest fame by rescuing the sun from the fall of the first Ring Collapsiter, which would surely have destroyed it. He rose from his chair. "Well, I suppose I have work to do."

At this, Tamra simply rolled her eyes. "Your swashbuckling days are over, darling. We have a meeting with the navy in fifteen minutes."

And this was true; he'd been king for eleven hundred years, whereas he'd been a swashbuckling hero for barely more than a decade, and only then by accident. Declarant-Philander Bruno de Towaji! It seemed an improbable history now, even to him. Before that he'd been a teacher, a drunken lover, a layabout courtier, and a wilderness hermit. Ah, but like everyone in the Queendom, he had the immorbid body of a twenty-five-year-old; his soul might grow old, but his physical self could not. Was he less capable of heroism now? Surely not! So he had dutifully attended his meetings, dispensing judgments and calculations and recommendations while his wife faxed herself to the navy's flagship, the QSS *Malu'i*—Tongan for "Protector"—and ordered her seat of government temporarily transferred there.

And yes, it might be the job of a woman to manage a fleet in time of disaster, and to rule over a Queendom in times of peace, but surely it was the job of a man to rush forward willy-nilly to survey the scene ahead of her.

"Let the navy handle this," his courtiers had urged as he finalized his plans. "Your Majesty, we need you *here*." Which was blatant flattery and foolish besides, for he was first and foremost an inventor, and impatient—after all this time!—with the fussy details of governance and the inane formalities of court. The courtiers and ministers needed him more as a symbol than as a living, breathing human, and what could be more symbolic than this?

"The navy hasn't the proper expertise," he'd answered.

For that was true; almost no one in the Queendom truly understood the mathematics of ertial shielding.

"Then let the navy transport you," they'd urged, as he fitted himself into his space armor, flexing and testing the joints one by one.

"They haven't the speed," he answered, for indeed the fastest interplanetary vessels were the ertial grapple-ships, and none were faster than *Boat Gods*.

"It's bad for the Queendom if you're hurt or killed," they'd tried, as he'd powered up the ship's systems and rolled aside the hangar roof to reveal, in a shower of loose palm fronds, the bright blue sky left behind by the storm.

"I've made my backups," he told them sternly. "If anything happens, restore me and await instructions. That's a command, good sirs and madams, from your king. Even from Earth, from these very islands, I can reach this mystery vessel three days ahead of the navy's best picket boats out of Neptune, and *five* days ahead of Her Majesty."

"May I come?" asked Hugo, his own pet robot, who'd been emancipated for more than a millennium but still chose to remain at home, learning how to be alive.

"Not this time," Bruno told him. "I can't spare the mass."

"But Sire," his manservant Adelade said cannily, "who's to develop the wormhole in your absence?"

And that had almost stopped him. Almost. But if there was one thing he'd learned about the hard problems of physics, it was that they often yielded when the body and mind were otherwise engaged. And he missed this derring-do, and feared that his people—even his own servants!—thought him no longer capable of it. And anyway, blast it, saving the sun was *his job*. Not Tamra's.

Almost as an afterthought he'd said to Adelade, "Will

you take stewardship of the Earth, please, until Tamra's or my return?"

"Er, well..."

"There's a good fellow. Mind the impending holidays."

He'd closed his hatch then, stoked his reactor, fired up his sensors and hypercomputers. Engaged his gravitic grapples, yes, latching them on to the crescent moon and yanking himself right off the Earth.

And in a rare moment of perspicacity, as the stars came alive around him and he wheeled the ship for a new, more distant grapple target, he had muttered under his breath, "Oh, yes, my friends, this vagabond heart lives on, smothered in census figures. None among you can refuse me now! Surprised though I am to say this, sometimes it's good to be the king."

chapter two

in which a revolution is halted

There are moments for musing. Not moments of truth, but moments *before* the moment of truth, when the mind squirts sideways, time stretches, thoughts race. Insights leap across the gray matter like fleeing deer. For Bruno it went thusly:

Given the Nescog, that glittering network of black-hole matter which linked every part of the Queendom to every other, he could step through the print plate of the fax machine behind him and, in a few hours' transit time which he himself would not perceive, step out through an equivalent plate in the palace foyer back on Tongatapu. Or anywhere else! The bulk of this journey would happen, alas, at Einstein's lightspeed, although ring collapsiter segments—long, thin tubes of collapsium with high-speed supervacuum inside—would shave a few minutes off it here and there.

Ah, but with wormholes in place of collapsiters, the journey could be instantaneous! Not just to Earth, or to any other corner of the Queendom, but to the stars themselves. To the failed and failing colonies scattered among the nearby stars and dwarfs. Bruno and Tamra had sent too many young men and women out there to their *deaths*. Their *deaths*! But it was an error on which they could still, in some small measure, make good. If Bruno could just build a damned wormhole.

The whirling fan of *Newhope* expanded in his view, and expanded some more. Belatedly, Bruno pulled up a schematic of the ship from *Boat Gods'* library, and then sketched an outline of the entry and exit wounds upon its hull. Presumably, the projectile had been stationary, at least in comparison to the starship's own large velocity. And that meant *Newhope* had not been facing forward or backward at the time, as she should have been for safety's sake, but rather broadside to the dust and debris of interstellar space. Oops.

So what had happened? From *Boat Gods'* myriad sensors, a story began to emerge. The accident had occurred hundreds of years ago, the ship taking first a freak hit to its forward ertial shield, slightly off-center. The shield was hard to damage, and would have absorbed almost all of the kinetic energy, releasing it over several minutes as a blue-green flare of Cerenkov photons. A survivable event, yes. But compressive interactions had probably sent shockwaves and electrical surges all up and down the hull and superstructure, stunning the wellstone and preventing the navigation safety lasers from receiving power.

This much at least, the starship was designed to handle. But it had gotten unluckier; the collision tipped it slightly, and before the nav systems could recover or the lasers could vaporize it, a second particle—probably larger—had struck, and the resulting plasma had flashed straight through the hull at near-relativistic speed, sending her into a wild, chaotic tumble while her fuel supply squirted away into vacuum. And without its deutrelium the ship's reactor had run down, and the ship itself had gone to sleep, perchance to wake at some future date.

Well, with any luck, that day was now at hand.

Bruno adjusted his grapples and set about the task of attaching himself to the center of the tumbling ship. The rest should be easy enough; *Boat Gods* was outfitted with a universal airlock and augmented with the Royal Overrides which guaranteed Bruno access to, and control over, any enlivened device designed or constructed in the Queendom of Sol. Which included QSS *Newhope* herself, yes. And although the starship had no matching airlock—no hatches of any kind in the region of concern—the mere feather-touch of his grapples stirred piezoelectric voltages in the wellstone there, bringing it to some weak semblance of life.

The ship exchanged handshakes and data packets with the airlock, accepted an automated welcome-home message, and requested an infrared beam from which it could draw additional power. Then, more fully awake, it prostrated itself before the Royal Overrides, and agreed to allow itself to be damaged. And although the tiny hypercomputers inside it would not pass a self-awareness screening, and were at the moment no more collectively intelligent than a frog, the wellstone did express a sort of relief at finding itself, after all this time, among properly enlivened programmable materials rather than the mere metals and ceramics of the Barnard colony. It was good, apparently, to be home.

Bruno felt a moment of dizziness as *Boat Gods* pulled itself toward the whirling baton that was *Newhope*. But he had, at various times in his youth, found himself trapped in the ertial supervaccum of a ring collapsiter, or standing on the windblown surface of the very first neutronium-cored planette, or falling into a hypermass somewhere. Hell, one of him had fallen into the sun itself, and never returned. A bit of spinning wasn't going to stop him!

In the last few meters of closure, *Boat Gods* itself began to spin. And because it too was ertial, it matched the rotation of *Newhope* in no time at all, and with almost no sensation.

The airlock knew its business, too; once the two hulls had kissed, it commenced tearing an opening in the well-stone plates of *Newhope*, shuffling the atoms aside into a sort of docking collar. From the inside of *Boat Gods*, this activity sounded like the crack of billiard balls followed by a light rainfall. And when it came time to leave, the airlock could just as easily pull the atoms back again, restoring *Newhope*'s wellstone to something very like its original condition.

Bruno had invented this technique long ago. Bruno had invented a lot of things. Why, then, must something as truly useful as a wormhole generator elude him? Perhaps he *was* getting old and slow, alas. He didn't even throw off his safety harness and fling open the airlock to see what lay behind it. Instead he studied his scans again, more intently.

The results were not encouraging; living people would show up as hot spots, of which he detected none. They would require atmosphere, of which he detected none. This was not surprising; at 29 Kelvin—barely above the four-degree cosmic background—every gas but helium would have condensed out as liquid or settled as a frost. But he didn't detect liquids, either; the ship's crew compartments had leaked or been deliberately evacuated. There might of course be *stored* human beings in a temporary fax buffer somewhere. These would show up as dense charge patterns in a wellstone matrix, and he found a few of those behind a structure that might be some sort of low-quality print plate. But over hundreds of years the cosmic-ray flux would have scrambled much of the data into total nonsense. If those were human patterns, the people they represented were dead. To survive the journey, any stored human images would need to reside in shielded memory cores, of which Bruno detected none.

What he did detect, in the cargo pods attached to *Newhope*'s midsection, just aft of the crew quarters, were cylindrical masses of water ice, roughly three meters long and one meter wide. Thousands of them; tens of thousands. The ice was shot through with complex organics which he couldn't identify from here, and by tuning his sensors to a calcium channel he was able to pick out fine, solid structures within the cylinders. Human skeletons, surrounded by greasy envelopes of frozen human flesh, drowned in ice-filled tubes of glass and metal.

Twenty-five thousand frozen people. Interesting. Troubling. There would be a lot of bureaucrats busy on this one.

Freezing was not considered a lethal event in the Queendom of Sol, any more than heart failure or drowning were lethal events. A few people had even been reanimated after *hundreds of years* of cold storage. This was one of those "civic-duty" things Tamra had enacted in the Queendom's earliest days—hunting down from the Age of Death all the frozen and mummified and pickled bodies which might conceivably be restored to life. Most of these efforts had been pro forma, mainly an archaeological exercise with little chance of *medical* success, but a few—twenty or thirty, Bruno thought—had been resurrected, and were brief celebrities in that heady time when anything seemed possible. Look, look! We can bring history itself to life!

Ah, but there were limits to human achievement. Painful limits, as Bruno and Tamra had learned through the blood and toil of their exiled subjects. Projects could fail; lives could end. Whole star colonies could suffer economic collapse so severe that the air tankers stopped running, their scattered habitats suffocating one by one while the Queendom stood helplessly by. Indeed, whole civilizations could lurch from seeming health to agonizing death in less time than the signals took to reach Mother Sol. Theirs was a hard universe, which granted no clemency.

In many cases, the only "survivors" of a colony's demise were those who had managed, by hook or by crook, to have a summary of their neural patterns transmitted back to the Queendom. Hardly more than interactive mail—just a few petabytes, or a few hundred petabytes. They were not people, though they sometimes believed they were. But their transmission consumed precious energy and transceiver time which an ailing colony could ill afford.

And even if they were people, didn't the Queendom have enough already? Was there room for more? Copy-hour restrictions had been tightened and retightened, to the point where most individuals—even those who'd once sent whole herds of themselves out into the world—counted themselves lucky to be plural at all. The waiting list for a birth license was now *five hundred years long*. And yet the cities grew taller and wider every year, encroaching not only on the precious primordial wildernesses of Earth, but the invented ones of Mars and Venus, which were far more delicate. *Half the population* was living in caverns and domes, dreaming in vain of fresh air. Should these very citizens be expected to fund the creation of an expensive new person from the tatters of a dead one?

So the messages remained, for the most part, in the limbo of quantum storage, against the day when resources might exist to birth and house them properly. If, indeed, such a day could be expected at all.

And here before Bruno was a similar question: what were the rights of a frozen, cosmically irradiated corpse from outside the Queendom? Doctors would have to be consulted before any decisions were made here—certainly before anything was vaporized by the navy. But why had someone gone to the trouble of bringing these corpses here, across the vastness of interstellar space? To be resurrected? Had the Queendom of Sol become a kind of afterlife, a dream of heaven for the children of the colonies?

Alas, there was almost nothing else onboard this ship. She was oversized for the job, her crew quarters mostly empty. The only other feature of note was a much smaller cluster of bodies—four, in fact—just forward of her engine control rooms, in a space that looked like a workshop or laboratory of some kind. For what? For whom? This ship had seen heavy modification in its long years abroad.

The chamber was not far from Bruno's own docking site. And presently, the sound of rain ceased; the burrowing airlock had gently punched through. Bruno threw off his restraints and rose from his couch.

"Sire," *Boat Gods* said, in a basso voice rich with gravitas. "You'll want your helmet on."

"Ah!" Bruno said, eyeing the transparent, nearly invisible dome tucked under his arm. "So I might! I'd've opened this hatch on hard vacuum."

"Hardly, Sire." The ship could not truly be offended, but it managed to sound that way. It would not have allowed the hatch to open.

"Well," Bruno said, popping his helmet in place and listening to it crackle itself sealed, "do please open it now."

"Aye, Sire."

It would take a steady, hundred-kilowatt feed to wake up *Newhope's* higher functions, and given the level of cosmic-ray scrambling and the long absence of functioning maintenance routines, the wellstone was inclined to take this process very slowly indeed. Still, unseen and unsensed by Bruno, the starship's running lights came on, and its interior began, gradually, to warm.

When he stepped through the hatch, the head- and taillights of his battle armor came on automatically, casting pools of glare and gloom around a wedge-shaped compartment—a crew cabin—covered in frost, unused, undisturbed by anything but his own featherlight footsteps, crunching faintly against the jags and spines of frozen atmosphere.

By now, the wellstone's awareness was no longer limited to a handful of lightly powered hull plates. Indeed, almost the entire structure had come alive, and was slowly charging itself, rearranging its electronic structure, becoming a proper starship hull and skeleton once again. And in its newfound powers the starship remembered its manners, and produced a soft yellow glow from the cabin's frosted ceiling.

"Ah. Thank you," Bruno said, though it wasn't clear whether the ship could actually hear or understand him yet.

Bouncing lightly along the hoarfrost-crackling floor, he moved to the cabin's only exit. He smiled, for here was an actual *door*, not some temporary aperture but an actual plate hung on mechanical hinges and enclosed within an actual door frame. There was even a little knob or handle which, if he recalled correctly, one had to turn in order to release the latching mechanism. He grasped the handle, turned it, and with delight felt something click and release between the door and its frame. He pushed, and felt a sort of crunching through the wellcloth of his armor as the frost-sealed door broke free and swung open. Marvelous!

Bruno himself had grown up in Old Girona, before the Queendom, at the very peak of the Catalan love affair with ancient habits and technologies and social mores. The Sabadell-Andorra earthquake had of course smashed that daydream—and Bruno's own parents, and thousands of other human beings besides. It was the last great disaster of Old Modernity. But before then he had turned his share of doorknobs, uncorked his share of glass bottles, even knotted his shoes to his feet with laces of hand-woven cotton! He was careful not to overromanticize those days, but he wasn't above the occasional reminiscence.

Outside the cabin was a circular hallway, linking six similar cabins around the ship's circumference, and in the center of the floor was a steep ladder leading both up and down. Bruno had been on this ship once before, touring it with Tamra after its christening, but that was a thousand years ago, and bore no resemblance to the scene before him now. Nevertheless, from his scans he knew that the four corpses of interest, and the laboratory which held them, were two levels aft from this point. So he mounted the stairs, wrapping a hand around each rail, and glided down.

This proved a mistake, however, for the "gravity" at the bottom of the first flight of stairs was more than three times what it was at the top—very nearly a full gee! He staggered under sudden weight, collapsing to his armored knees at the bottom. The sensation of spinning was also more pronounced here. Picking his way around the staircase, he took the next flight more cautiously.

Two centimeters of wellcloth space armor massed twenty kilograms all by itself, with the solid helmet adding another two or three, but fortunately a properly designed suit would stiffen and relax in response to its wearer's movements, lightening the burden. Carrying its own weight, as it were, and in heavy gravity it would do its best to carry *your* weight as well. God bless the stuff.

This level had the same circular corridor as the one above, but with only two hatches instead of six. Bruno chose one, and on the other side he found a ring-shaped chamber far less tidy than the rest of the level. Its floor was littered with hand tools, with dead wellstone hoses and sketchplates, with other items he couldn't immediately identify. The air had frozen over these tumbled implements, and afterward nothing had moved. For centuries.

There were six support columns holding the floor and ceiling apart, and by these landmarks he circumnavigated the chamber, noting the position of the four corpses in their coffins of glass. And then, approaching one, he felt a dizzy wash of déjà vu.

"I know this man," he muttered, and felt in his bones that he had said this before, on another spaceship somewhere, contemplating some other frozen corpse. During the chaos of the Fall? Life was long, and like any bounded system with finite variables it *must* repeat itself periodically. No matter how improbable the event.

Unless Bruno was badly mistaken, this crystallized starman had been a privateer during the Children's Revolt. A revolutionary, a confidant of Prince Bascal, and later a builder of orbital towers on the face of Planet Two, better known as Sorrow.

"He is Senior Commander Conrad Ethel Mursk," said a quiet voice in Bruno's helmet. "First Mate of the QSS *Newhope* and First Architect of the Kingdom of Barnard."

"Ah, so you're awake," Bruno said to the walls and bulkheads around him.

"Aye, Sire," replied the QSS *Newhope* in some radio frequency or other, and in vaguely feminine tones. By tradition, machines had an accent of their own which set them apart from human beings, but the Barnardean *mechsprach* was slower and breathier than the Queendom's own—almost comically so. "You honor us with your presence."

"Us? Are these people alive, then?"

"These four were," the ship said, "when I froze them after the accident. They were my crew."

"Ah." Curious, that. A crew of four for an entire starship?

"However," the ship continued, "since reviving them is beyond my capabilities, the answer to your question rests upon your definition of the word 'alive.' There are bodies in my cargo pods as well, who died and were frozen before the journey began. So I will answer, guardedly, that four of these people are alive, and twenty-five thousand are dead but presumed recoverable."

"I see. Thank you." Bruno was about to ask for further clarification when he felt a hand on his shoulder.

"Gaah!" he cried, spinning in surprise and alarm. One did not expect to be *touched* onboard a ghost ship! But as he wheeled around, dizzy against the ship's own spinning, what he saw behind him was no ghost or zombie but his own wife, Queen Tamra-Tamatra Lutui, in her own suit of space armor—royal purple trimmed with gold. She didn't look happy, and flanking her on either side were an equally unamused-looking admiral and a burly midshipman, both in navy black. And behind *them* were a pair of superreflective Palace Guard robots—a reminder that Bruno himself was here, against laws and traditions and the insistence of his staff, without his own two guards. It had taken a Royal Override to dismiss them, but Tamra's override trumped all others. Were these two for him?

Blast.

"Hello, dear," he tried saying.

She crossed her arms, nodding once inside her helmet. "Darling. *Malo e leilei*. It was very kind of you to bring an active fax portal and network gate here. It saves us all kinds of time. Why, we can fax here directly from *Malu'i*, still en route."

"Ah. Well, er, you're welcome."

"Were you planning on telling me any of this?"

"I told the house staff," he said. "And Traffic Control." But that sounded weak and plaintive in his ears. She might be the Queen of Sol, but he was the king, and her husband, and a grown man who had *invented* this sort of mad ertial errand during a time when all of humanity hung in the balance. "If you're here to help, why don't you send these navy lads down for about fifty barrels of deutrelium and some labor robots? On my personal account, if budgets are a concern. I'd like to fire up the reactors and halt this damned spin."

Tamra favored her husband with a glare, then turned to the admiral. "Do as he says, please. And bring qualified assistants who can help him bring this vessel under control."

chapter three

in which the consequences of immorbidity are lamented

A trip through the fax was the treatment of first resort for any ailment or injury, but the Nescog morbidity filters were meant to repair the living. Clever algorithms examined the genome, along with its appendices and parity blocks, in a large enough sample of cells to screen out any accumulated mutations. Then, based on this corrected blueprint the system extrapolated what the body ought to look like—allowing of course for undocumented cosmetics—and then compared that ideal with the scanned body image itself, rearranging the cell structure as appropriate. All damage and signs of aging were wiped away in the process, rendering the subject "immorbid."

This much was traditional, and nearly as old as the Queendom itself. Under their own strange forms of duress, though, the ailing colonies had piled whole suites of additional "healing" onto the process, weaving protective meshes and brickmails throughout the body, filling the cells with wellstone-fiber networks and organelles adapted from alien microbes. Even inserting active programs into the genome, to fight back disease and aging among individuals too poor to have regular fax access.

Via Instelnet radio downloads, the Queendom had imported some of these techniques as either quality-of-life enhancements or cost-cutting measures, so Bruno was no stranger to exotic biomods. But even so these four star voyagers' bodies were something else altogether; something foreign, alien.

Two of the four were former Queendom citizens whom Bruno had known personally before their Barnard exile: Conrad Mursk and Xiomara Li Weng, the latter being *Newhope's* captain. The two were lovers if Bruno recalled correctly, although Xiomara—"Xmary" to her friends—had nearly been Prince Bascal's instead. Or so it seemed to the prince's father, several paces removed from the actual intrigue. At the molecular level, though, neither of them much resembled their original childhood patterns.

The other man also checked out as a Queendomite: one Yinebeb Bragston Fecre, who had played a major role in the Children's Revolt, prior to the founding of the colonies. The fourth body was female, and matched no Queendom records.

"Eustace Faxborn," *Newhope* said of her. "Custom printed in the Barnard colony, one hundred standard days prior to this mission's departure."

"Custom printed?" Bruno asked. "Not born, but created for some particular purpose?"

"She is the bride of Yinebeb Fecre."

"Ah."

A barbaric custom, that: the crafting of "adults" specialized for...well, various purposes. Honorable marriage was one possibility, but by no means the only one.

At any rate, the legal status of the citizens was clear enough: they were entitled to revival. For the twenty-five thousand actual corpses the opposite was true; they were legally dead noncitizen strangers. Any revival would be an act of charity—of foreign policy, essentially. And this Faxborn woman fell somewhere in the ambiguous middle.

Alas, it seemed a moot point, for all four of the bodies were, according to *Boat Gods*' fax machine, either not human or else irreparably damaged and in need of archival replacement. And since there were no archives available—no buffer copies or formal backups—the four would need that rarest of Queendom services: live medical attention.

So the four bodies were shipped to Antarctica, whose landscape was dotted with small hospitals experienced in the treatment of accidental whole-body frostbite. But the doctors there objected to the extensive radiation damage in these "corpses," and in the end a team of specialists had to be faxed down from the moons of Jupiter, where radiation accidents were commonplace, and up from Venus, where genomic engineering was both high art and science.

All of this was charged to King Bruno's accounts. No private charity or government agency seemed prepared to take charge of these people, for fear of an implied obligation to care for their thousands of shipmates. Even if those revivals were free—which they surely would not be—the housing costs alone would be considerable. There weren't that many vacant apartments in the whole of Earth!

As for *Newhope* herself, the navy guided her—bodies and all—into a parking orbit in the lower Kuiper Belt. There to remain, like the Instelnet message-ghosts, until some brighter future should happen along.

"Appalling," Bruno said to his wife as they lounged that night in their bed on Tongatapu. "Have we not wealth enough?"

"It's more a matter of space," she reminded him. "If

we're to have any wilderness at all, we must contain urban growth on the habitable worlds, and our own children—natural-born humans with no sins on their shoulders—must have the first pick of what growth we allow. Or do you propose a Queendom without children? I confess, I can't see the point of *that*."

"Mmm," Bruno grumbled. "No one volunteers to die anymore. To make a bit of space."

"Would you?" the queen asked with a bitter-tinged laugh.

"No," he admitted. Not while the wormhole project remained incomplete. Indeed, he had *dozens* of incomplete projects which held the promise of a better life for all. "But we must do *something*, you and I."

"Yes," she agreed, taking his hand. "We must. This trickle of refugees has begun to add up. We could almost fill a city."

"A floating city?" he suggested.

She made an unhappy face. "Not another one, dear. Please. The oceans need to breathe."

"The oceans are vast. One more won't hurt."

"But a hundred more," she said. "A thousand more. Where does it stop? Why don't you revive your Lunar program instead?"

It was Bruno's turn to laugh, stroking Tamra's hand against the wellcloth sheets. "It was you, my dear, who ordered a halt to it. Too many displacements, you said. Too much economic disruption, including the loss of one of history's greatest landmarks. And you were right: sparsely domed though it may be, the moon is proud home to *four million people*. Where shall I put them?"

"On a floating city," she said, and sighed. "It's like a puzzle. Slide one piece and the others have to move. To make an opening, you've got to close one. And yet, the alternative is death."

"So say the Fatalists," Bruno chided. "Do they lack imagination? Do we? 'Everything has an end,' they insist. 'Let's engineer it, peacefully and with love.' By which they mean the vaporization of innocents, the sabotage of shielded archives. Bah! I say everything has a *solution*, and we've only to find it."

Tamra kissed him firmly. "And I, my darling, say that everyone must sleep. Come, let's have a bit of darkness."

And suddenly, for no discernible reason, Bruno knew just what to do about his wormhole problem. "Egad!" he said, grabbing for the sketchplate he theoretically kept on his nightstand for moments like this. But theory and practice were only lightly acquainted; the sketchplate wasn't there. Bruno searched the area for a second or two, but the idea was hot on the tip of his brain, and though his fatigue had vanished he was nevertheless terrified he would fall asleep or suffer some distraction, or that the idea would simply trickle away before he could record it.

In desperation, he slid to the floor and began scribbling there with his finger. The wellstone, long accustomed to such behavior, responded with trails of black obsidian in its surface of faux bleached wood. These rough figures arranged themselves into elegant numbers and symbols as the king's finger raced ahead. "There's a long axis," he muttered. "Indeed, indeed. Where the mass distribution falls away as a function of Z, it drives an instability in X and Y. But it needn't! We shall present the spherical opening with a *cylindrical plug!*"

Her Majesty Queen Tamra was also accustomed to these intellectual fits and spasms—her husband's renowned mind was anything but linear—and she knew better than to disturb him in the midst of one. Indeed, she watched with sleepy interest for a few minutes as the obsidian equations spread upward along one wall, and were joined by holographic diagrams: spheres and cylinders surrounded by a forest of right triangles.

"*Two* spheres," Bruno said to himself. "They're one and the same—the real and imaginary component of a single object—but to an observer that's not evident. How could it be? And the observer's viewpoint is *valid*, yes? Or relativity be damned. Two positions in real space, connected by a line. By a *cylinder*."

The queen was no mathematician, but she'd seen enough of her husband's work to know he was trying—vainly trying—to sketch out some four-dimensional object or relationship in a 3-D image.

Fortunately their bedroom was a suite whose outer chamber could be sealed off from both the outside world and the bedchamber itself. And so, sighing, the Queen of Sol stooped to kiss her king upon the shoulder, then dragged her blankets from the bed and stumbled off to sleep on the couch. For the one message she could read clearly in the walls, albeit implicit, was, *This will be a long night, dear. Don't wait up.*

When Conrad Ethel Mursk opened his eyes, he was astonished to see something other than the afterlife. There were no angels, no clouds, no twinkling stars, and certainly no God or devil waiting to judge him. Instead, there were green walls and white examination tables, and a young-looking woman with copper hair and eyes the color of jade, dressed in powder-blue medical pyjamas.

"I'm not dead," he said, and was surprised by the clarity of his voice. He sat up, and was surprised by the pull of gravity. Not grav lasers or spin-gee but *planetary gravity*. Then he charmingly added, "Where the hell am I?"

The woman was fiddling with controls of some sort

behind Conrad's headrest, and in sitting up he had placed his viewpoint only centimeters from her torso, so that she appeared mainly as a pair of breasts. Still, he caught her smile.

"Welcome back, Mr. Mursk. How do you feel?"

"I don't know," he said, pausing for a moment to take stock of himself, to feel his body up and down for numbness or injury. "I suppose I feel all right, all things considered. Is this Sorrow?"

She chuckled. "This is Earth. More specifically, Frostbite Trauma Center in the city of Glacia in Victoria Land, Antarctica."

"Oh," he said, digesting that. "What year?"

She told him, and he heard a low, pathetic groan escape from his lips. He'd been gone a long time—so long that the numbers barely made sense. A thousand years? Forty childhoods? Fifty thousand episodes of *Barnes and Manetti*? The Queendom he knew was ancient history. And so was he.

"Shit," he said. "Wow. How's my crew?"

"All fine," the woman assured him, now stepping back to give him a view of something other than her chest. "We've woken you last, since your reconstruction was the most difficult."

"I was burned," he remembered suddenly. "The coolant lines blew out. There was this swarm of damage-control robots, just pouring out of the fax machine, draining the mass buffers, hustling us down into storage and trying to stop the air leak. But the ship was coming apart, and somebody had to be last in line. I remember thinking, *We tried. We did our best, but this is where it ends.*"

"You were fortunate," the woman said. "It could have been a lot worse."

"Hmm," he answered, mulling over the sheer obviousness of that. "It seems I'm in your debt. Or someone's. What about the passengers? We had twenty-five thousand in cold sleep."

Her expression shifted, and he had the sense she was choosing her next words carefully. "Well, yes. It should be possible to recover most of them at some point. But sleep is a generous term here, don't you think? Some of those people were already partially decomposed when you froze them."

"It was a rescue mission," Conrad said vaguely. And right away he could see how stupid his plans had been, how pointlessly optimistic. The Queendom of Sol *could* help his countrymen, yes; it had the wealth, the technology, the notable absence of psychotic leadership and sociopolitical collapse. The Queendom of his dreams would have done exactly that. But the Queendom of the real, physical universe had problems of its own—didn't every place? A pile of dead colonists would be a curiosity at best, an unwelcome intrusion at worst.

"I'm an idiot," he said. And it was true; he'd come all this way on the theory that a faint hope was better than none. But if the faint hope didn't pan out, then it was as good as none. Or worse.

"I doubt that," the woman answered, offering him a handshake. "Angela Proud Rumson, Doctor of Medicine and Extrapolative Cosmetics."

He examined her hand for a moment—it looked absurdly soft, like she'd never used it—and then shook it. It *was* soft.

"Conrad Mursk," he said, and was about to add a title or two of his own. But what was the point in that? What status did he hold here? What he said instead was, "Refugee."

"Very pleased to meet you."

"Can I see my friends now?"

Angela Proud Rumson's smile was reserved. "Tomorrow, if you please. They've gone to their temporary quarters already, and I'm expected to hold you for observation. Test drive the old nervous system, make sure we've done all the wiring correctly. Shall we say twelve hours?"

chapter four

in which fatalism is confronted by action

Perhaps the event at *Newhope's* lonely drydock was inevitable. Certainly, its cargo of dead human flesh invited public commentary: *Are we responsible for these lives? For their premature ending, for their mere existence? If so, then aren't these corpses likewise culpable in the demise of the Barnard colony? Do they then deserve a second chance, at our expense?*

Or: *Why'd they send us their bodies at all? Why not just their heads, their brains, their memories? If the medium is the message, this message stinks. Where exactly did we sign up? To salvage putrid alien flesh simply because it's dumped in our laps is to play the chump.*

Or: *A species of promise was made in the Queendom's banishment of morbidity—a statement of ultimate equality before God and Nature.* Thou shalt not die. *This was affirmed in the Fall, and has thereafter formed the defining aspect of our societal character. Such pains as result are ours by choice, and by example we endure them gladly, ever mindful of the alternative. That these folk are the get of our own miscreants is beside the point; by definition, any justice must exist for all comers, or it be no justice at all. Dare we, my brothers and sisters, choose death for those who have come in search of life?*

And it was this, more than anything, which inflamed Fatalist sentiment, for if the so-called "right to life" could not be waived for the long-dead corpses of nonhuman noncitizens, then it could not be waived at all, and the Fatalist cause was utterly lost. But by its very nature, Fatalism could not take an armchair view of these matters.

Shall we imagine a deathist philosopher and Fatalist general? Call her "Starquake" or "Dark Cloud" or "Shiva." Shall we imagine her followers, in their dozens or hundreds, or perhaps even thousands? Shall we describe the terrifying Death persona they crafted and physically instantiated, to loom cadaverously in their midst and remind them of their supposed duty?

This much is certain: a group of individuals held a meeting. Enormous care was taken to conceal their identities, as well as the meeting's location. In theory this was both possible and legal, for the Queendom was not a tyranny. But it was astronimically *difficult*, for by its own nature the Nescog must store buffer images of the people passing through it; must log their movements and enforce their copy-hour limits. Too, nearly everything under Sol's light was made from wellstone, or from other forms of programmable matter, and *its* nature was to record the commands—even subtly implied commands—that washed over it every moment of every day. Indeed, the universe itself was a witness to all of the events within it, and like any witness it could, with the proper inducements, be compelled to testify. And then, of course, there were the participants themselves, human and therefore corruptible.

To gather a "cluster house" or secret assembly from all corners of the solar system, whether virtually or in the flesh, and to leave no trace of having done so, was a work of great cleverness of which only a few thousand citizens were capable. And for *no one* to blab or squeal or accidentally invite a government informant would require not only an improbable degree of dedication, but also a meticulous attention to matters of psychology and logistics. Indeed, from this and other circumstantial evidence we may suspect that at least a few of the participants came from the highest echelons of bureaucracy and law enforcement, for such meetings had been going on for centuries, and none had ever been discovered.

The list probably also includes the most prominent and vocal right-to-death pundits and commentators of the day, as well as convicted murderers who had outlived their hundred-year "life" sentences. Surely *they* felt that life could be taken without consent, for some higher (or lower) purpose. Too, there may have been workers from the assorted and largely bygone deathist industries—the morticians and hospice orderlies, the coffin designers, the groomers and protectors of Earth's historical graveyards. These were the people most displaced by the death of death, and also those most inclined, by general disposition, to see some value in its return.

But it must be said that the Queendom government, following this same line of reasoning, applied particular scrutiny to these individuals without ever turning up a single conclusive lead. "Vast conspiracy" is an oxymoron in any era, but despite this movement's scope and influence and funding, it held successfully to the shadows of a nearly shadowless society. From this we may conclude that the conspirators were in fact the *cloistered copies* of our suspect individuals, secretly created without their progenitors' knowledge. Imagine our Shiva—officially deceased, perhaps a victim of the Fall—selecting the most trustworthy of her living friends, hijacking their fax traces and printing unauthorized copies. Briefing and drilling them, yes, scanning their loyalties in a hidden cavern somewhere and killing off the ones who presented even the slightest security risk. If five captains—call them the Reapers—each found five lieutenants, who found five sergeants, who found five corporals and privates and orderlies, then an army of thousands could be assembled in as little as six months. Across the centuries of known Fatalist activity, we can only guess at the true scope of their operations.

Still, in the absence of evidence we may safely imagine our Shiva banging her gavel or drumhead, calling the attendees to order. We may then suggest that words were spoken in praise of death, for death was an integral component of the "natural cycle" which dominated their philosophy. If they (or their progenitors) did not choose death for themselves, it was because their lives were necessary for the advancement of the *cause* of death—a higher-order effect. The *reasonable* deathists were long in their graves; these were diehard visionaries, and this much at least can be said in their favor: they were more likely stout game theoreticians than cowards or hypocrites. They knew what they were doing, and they did it well.

Little is known of their religion, although the public writings of the pro-death movement argue for a variant of the dominant animism: a megapantheon of small gods or *kami* ruling over the mundane articles and processes of life, both natural and technological. And a single God, yes, who either rules over these *kami* or is, in some information-theoretic sense, generated by them. An afterlife—involving both reincarnation and divine judgment—is strongly implied. Drum music apparently played a symbolic or therapeutic role, along with more obscure rituals. "Grounding and awareness techniques" and "energy circles" and "silent cheering" were enlisted to generate "an atmosphere of support and appreciation and joy." That these phrases are difficult to reconcile with the movement's coercive violence is, one assumes, a failure of our own empathy; the Fatalists clearly viewed themselves as heroes rather than villains.

In any case, we shall suppose that under the guidance of Shiva and the Stygian glower of Death, certain motions were proposed, debated, amended, and voted affirmative.

"We have a direct action opportunity," Shiva may have said, "which combines the salubrious traits of an open target, a high symbolic value, and a higher-than-usual alignment between public sympathies and our own cause. We have carried too much for too long, we few, but this is energy work for the soul of Humanity itself. Power originates in freedom of movement, and the love that flows in this circle must be channeled outward in a strong and coherent way. Can you feel the presence of the Whirlwind? He is storm and revolution and fire, lord of wild transformations and sudden, chaotic change. Great forces are gathering here; great deeds will flow through this space and into the physical Queendom. Nature herself feels enraged at the continual violation. Our natural ally, Entropy, held long at bay, grows stronger and more insistent, and Rage rises over her sister Compassion. *They will dance*, comrades, with ourselves as their avatars."

Or perhaps it went nothing like that. Perhaps there was no Shiva. But certainly there was a Death, for he was physically present among the *Newhope* strike force.

This much is a matter of historical record: fifty days after the delivery of QSS *Newhope* into her parking orbit, a nameless inertial fusion boat, stealthed, without running lights or identity beacons, appeared some three thousand kilometers off the boot of *Newhope*'s docking cradle, and matched velocities with a hundred-second blast from its motors. The boat then fired a cable lanyard which wrapped itself mechanically around *Newhope*, and shortly thereafter, nine space-suited figures emerged bearing rectangular wellstone bricks of unknown programming and purpose.

They were accompanied by Death, who apparently needed no space suit, and whose black cowl had been programmed to swirl about him in a picturesque and unvacuumlike manner. The precise nature of this Death figure is not known, but he (or it) appeared skeletal within the robe—in some images, starlight clearly showed through the chin and neck vertebrae—and his movements showed a humanlike purpose and articulation.

If the strike team had intended the mere destruction of *Newhope*, they needn't have visited in person. Any bomb or missile or long-range energy weapon would have served, although to be fair, *Newhope* was reported to have survived at least one space battle. She *was* a tough old ship. At any rate, whatever plans the boarding party might have had fell apart moments after their debarkation, when the fax machine on *Newhope*'s docking cradle flickered to life and expelled both a platoon of vacuum-capable SWAT robots and a trio of human commanders.

This much should be said in favor of the Queendom authorities: they had little success in tracking or isolating or even comprehending the Fatalist organization, but they were masters of pattern recognition, and knew a tempting target when they saw one. The platform was a light-hour and more from the nearest naval or Constabulary outpost, and so would have had to wait *two* hours for a response to any distress signals it might have raised. But the docking cradle itself was intelligent and primed for trouble, as was the starship within it, and the troopers, along with other weapons, had been pre-positioned in its fax buffers and instantiated at the first sign of disruption.

In his deposition, Constabulary Captain Cheng Shiao said of the encounter, "Upon exiting the fax I established my bearings and took measure of the alleged intruders, of whom there were ten, clad not in stealth or inviz but simple optical black. On the citizens' frequencies I pronounced them under arrest on suspicion of trespassing and read them their rights, which proved to be a formality when they opened fire with mass projectors. This was not unexpected, and although our armor was struck by multiple projectiles—five-gram impervium wirebombs accelerated to several hundred meters per second—the attackers' aim was such that no serious damage was inflicted at that point. Our suits were not breached, and the SWAT robots were not disturbed from their duties."

In the recorded testimony, Shiao sits very straight in his chair. His expression is placid, as though he finds his own story interesting but not upsetting. The other voice belongs to Hack Friesland, the Kuiper Belt district attorney, not visible in the frame.

"Did you fire back?"

"No, sir. I issued an order that the attackers were to be taken alive at all costs, on account of their distinctive nature. Observing two of them at close range, I noted that beneath the helmet domes their heads were hairless and earless and very pale, with two apelike nostrils taking the place of a normal human nose. Their eyes were gray and somewhat oversized. There is no direct evidence linking this attack with any known group, but these features are typical of suspected Fatalist operatives, who are believed to be disposable copies of the actual organization members, downloaded into physically and genetically identical bodies to baffle our investigators. The popular term for these avatars is 'ghoul.'"

"We're aware of the terminology," says Friesland. "But how did you expect to capture one?"

Shiao's testimony continues, "The attackers' weapons were recoilless, sir, but as the projectiles obviously were not, we were forced to rocket ourselves upstream through a hail of them. We did succeed in overpowering nine of the attackers, although under the effects of sustained fire, four troopers and both of my sergeants were disabled. I later learned that they were killed. However, the nine attackers were in fact restrained."

"But not arrested."

"No, sir. At this point, a voice on the citizens' frequency cut in, shouting, 'All hands abort! Abort!' And the faces of the attackers I could see fell immediately slack. There is a particular look on a human face, sir, when the animating consciousness behind it is erased. The lights go out, so to speak; there's nothing ambiguous about it. Later scans showed that these individuals' brains, skulls, and even their spinal columns and stomach nerves had been subjected to a complete quantum wipe. Similarly, all information in the bricks they carried was summarily destroyed.

"Our sensors can be quite astute, and some small fraction of these data were eventually reconstructed in spite of the attackers' best efforts. We know, for example, that one of the attackers ate tea cakes on at least one occasion. Unfortunately, very little was uncovered that proved useful to our investigation."

"I'm sure the physical damage to the evidence didn't help?"

"An excellent point, sir. With the engagement apparently over, we would have called fresh robots from the fax, shipped the bodies to a Constabulary lab for immediate analysis, and moved in to search the suspect vessel on probable cause. That would be standard procedure.

However, the vessel's fusion reactor initiated a cascade overload, resulting in a kiloton-class explosion which scattered the physical evidence, obliterating some of it beyond hope of reconstruction. *Newhope* itself had grown the proper shielding, and was minimally damaged. I did not know any of this at the time, but I suspected it, as my helmet dome went superreflective and I was aware of a sharp physical impulse, very much like striking the ground after a fall. I felt my body tumbling, and when it was recovered six hours later, the autopsy revealed I had died shortly thereafter, from a combination of blunt trauma and gamma ionization. I recommended myself for disciplinary action, sir, but was refused."

"That's in the record, yes. Do you have any regrets about the encounter?"

"Many. Most notably, the skeletal figure was not apprehended during the scuffle, and no trace of it could be found afterward. This, too, is typical of our encounters with presumed Fatalists. We have yet to develop an effective tactic for arresting them."

When asked what he did with the Medal of Conduct he'd won for his heroism, Captain Shiao replied, "It's against regulations, sir, to wear such adornments on duty, or to wear them at any time on a garment other than a Constabulary uniform. There is one that I sometimes bring with me to state functions; this particular medal I placed in a locker with the others for safekeeping. It's a great honor to serve the Queendom in this way, for the Fatalists are *breaking the law*. The awards themselves are of secondary importance."

And when asked if he expected to die himself someday, Shiao frowned in thought before answering, "Permanently? Irretrievably? That would be a gross dereliction of my duties, sir. Unless a qualified replacement were found ahead of time, I should do my best to remain alive.

However, if it happened that my services were no longer required, I suppose I'd consider terminating my life voluntarily, as an act of community."

In response to this remark, Shiao's wife Vivian, the beloved Director of the Constabulary, is reported to have offered a colorful rebuttal which history, alas, does not record.

chapter five

in which innocents are imperiled

The doctor, Angela Proud Rumson, turned out to be only the first of a tag team of nonthreatening female civil servants paraded through Conrad's room. There was P.J. the environmental technician—who thoughtfully interrogated him about the conditions of his "native" Planet Two. Was the light too bright for him here? Would he prefer a chlorine atmosphere?

"It was called 'Sorrow,'" Conrad told her, "and I wasn't born there. I'm from Ireland, originally."

"Oh, how nice," she said, sounding surprised.

"It wasn't that much dimmer than Earth, just . . . yellower. And the chlorine was never more than a trace gas."

Again, surprise. "Fatal concentrations, I thought."

He shrugged. "To a regular human lung, sure, but it's a minor biomod. I barely noticed it after the first couple years. The biggest difference between P2 and Earth is the length of the day; P2's is a *lot* longer. And that's not something a sane person would miss."

And when P.J. was gone there was Lilly the nurse, and then Anne Inclose Ytterba, who was apparently some sort of famous historian.

"You want to know about life in the colonies?" he asked.

"Very much so," she said, "but I've been asked to hold that conversation for another time. Right now I'm here to brief you on the past thousand years."

Which turned out to be a really short conversation; the population of Sol had quadrupled, and nine of the thirteen colonies had gone offline and were presumed extinct. Nothing else of any real import had happened.

"We lost contact with Barnard in Q987—three hundred and three years ago. The circumstances were curious; there had been talk of a budget crisis, and then a cemetery crisis. No details were offered, and in your King Bascal's final announcement no mention was made of them. The next message—the colony's last—was from something called the 'Swivel Committee for Home Justice' announcing that King Bascal had abdicated his throne, and that the Instelnet transceivers were being temporarily shut down to conserve energy. This occurred on schedule, and no further transmissions have been received from Barnard since that time."

"So they might still be alive?" Conrad asked, reeling under the news. He'd been born into a world without death, and the grim toll of life on Sorrow had never seemed normal to him. It was, fundamentally, the reason he'd braved the rubble-strewn starlanes once again: to bring thousands of children to a place where "dead" was a medical condition rather than the end of a universe.

"They might," she agreed, "although the so-called budget crisis was really more of a food crisis. The population had just passed the one million mark, but the fax economy was declining asymptotically to zero, and agricultural production had not fully taken up the slack. Think of it as an energy shortage, if you prefer; insufficient conversion of sunlight into food."

"The soil there was worthless," Conrad said, with a tinge of bitterness. "Never enough metals. No matter how much organic mulch you throw down, plants *just won't grow* without trace metals. But you can synthesize food in a factory, right?"

"And they did," Anne agreed, "from air and ocean water and metals mined from the asteroid belt. But all that takes energy, too. Sunlight and deutrelium, and the technology to exploit them. To function smoothly, Barnard's economy needed more people than it had the resources to support."

"So they died."

"The ones you knew, yes, very probably. I'm sorry. At the time of last contact, the average lifespan of a Kingdom citizen was just a hundred and ten years."

"Jesus," Conrad said. He had socks older than that.

"Still," she offered, "Sorrow's air is breathable. There's water to drink, and *some* vegetation. It just grows slowly. By most estimates, using nothing but human labor the planet should support roughly one person for every twenty fertile acres. And it's a big planet, right? There's no telling what's happened up there, but I'd be astonished if there weren't someone still alive. Possibly hundreds of thousands of someones—the great-grandchildren of the people you knew and loved. They may even be happy."

"Hooray," Conrad said, managing in his distress to make an insult of it. *The world you've left behind is gone. Everyone you know is dead.*

Anne didn't appear offended, but the interview was over; she began the process of gathering her things. "I don't blame you for being upset, Mr. Mursk. I'm sure I would be. But most colonies aren't as lucky. At Ross and Sirius and Luyten, they didn't *have* the cushion of a habitable planet to fall back on. When their economies failed, the air trade failed with them, and most of the communities died out within a year. Maybe someday we'll travel there, to find vacuum-preserved corpses by the hundreds of millions. A field day for people like me, I'm sure, but nothing alive. Nothing contemporary."

"Nothing decomposed," Conrad said. "You could just wake them all up."

"Except for the radiation damage," she answered. "The way I hear it, you were barely recoverable yourself. If we left right now to rescue them, those people *might* have a chance."

"But the Queendom of Sol has its own problems," he finished for her, "and isn't going anywhere."

"Unfortunately, yes. But consider this: *you* got out, along with thousands of your countrymen. And in light of recent events, there's little doubt *they'll* be revived. If the Fatalists hate you that much, most people will find some reason to love you."

"What recent events?" Conrad asked, not liking the sound of that. "What Fatalists?"

Anne Inclose Ytterba, already stepping through the doorway, turned to offer him a look of sudden sympathy. *Now* she felt sorry for him. "Didn't you hear? You're all the targets of a secret society's deathmark. It seems you're emblematic of everything they've ever struggled against, and they want you expunged."

"Really?" Conrad wasn't exactly a stranger to conflict; he'd shot his way out of Barnard, and before that he'd been in the Revolt. If people would just *be nice*, just look out for each other and share the wealth along with the problems, he'd've lived long and peacefully without complaint. Hell, if life were short he'd've been happy enough to take over his father's paving business in Cork, living and dying in the county of his birth. But rare indeed was a century without conflict, and this far-wandering Conrad Mursk had already slogged his way through the darkest hours of more than one. Shamefully, he held himself responsible for dozens of deaths—many of them permanent.

But his enemies, numerous though they were, didn't usually take the trouble to swear out a formal deathmark. That was something one expected of Old Modern robber barons, or cartoon characters. The illegality of it paled in comparison to its sheer absurdity. They want to do *what*?

"We just got here," he said to her, a bit defensively. "What could we possibly have done?"

And here Anne the historian cocked her head and laughed a strange little laugh. "You're *breathing the air*, Mr. Mursk. Tsk tsk."

After that charming encounter, Conrad enjoyed a few hours of darkness and sleep, and then another visit from still another civil servant: Sandra Wong the social worker.

"Look," he told her, before she'd had a chance to say very much, "I just want to get out of here. I want to see my wife." He was standing at the window, peering out through the frost and into the polar darkness. Except for the faint, shining curtains of aurora australis hanging over the wellstone lights of Victoria Land, it looked just like the view from *Newhope*'s observation lounge. The same damned stars, a bit less vivid. He hadn't seen a *sky* in hundreds of years, but it was winter here; dry and cloudless. The sun wouldn't be up for months.

"I understand—" Sandra began.

"I'm not sure you do," he said, turning to glare at her. "We were in a terrible accident. We had to freeze ourselves, without any guarantee we'd ever be revived, and I haven't seen her since. You people have been kind, and you *offer every assurance* that she's fine, just fine. But since when is that a substitute for . . . for . . ."

"Warm flesh and a smile?" Sandra asked, looking down at her sketchplate and nodding. "I'm your last visitor, Mr. Mursk, and my job is to process you back into Queendom society. Technically speaking, you're still a prisoner."

"Eh?"

"For your role in the Children's Revolt. You *were* banished, yes?"

"Oh, that. Yes." It seemed such a long time ago. But these people were immorbid, and forgot nothing. Time passed for them like a kind of dream, a river without end.

"As your caseworker, I've filed a temporary motion to reinstate your citizenship with full privileges. This means, among other things, that you're entitled to draw Basic Assistance. It's not much, but it should get you on your feet until you're able to find employment. What's your area of specialty?"

"Uh," Conrad answered brilliantly. Specialty? He'd kicked around from one profession to the next, mastering few tangible skills. Life in the colonies was like that; there was always more work to do than there were people to do it, and no one was really qualified. You just grabbed urgent-looking tasks and did them, and then you grabbed some more, and just kept on like that. Until you died. But how could he explain that to someone like Sandra, who'd probably had fifty years of schooling before her first lowly apprenticeship?

"Architect," he finally said, for lack of anything better to attach his name to. He'd been First Architect of the Kingdom of Barnard, for whatever that was worth. A laugh, here, probably.

Indeed, Sandra's expression was primly amused. "Architecture is a *field*, sir. I need a specialty."

"You *need* one?"

"Every citizen needs one. If nothing else, it may win you Appreciator status, which would boost your assistance level."

Conrad frowned. "You mean I'd be paid to walk around admiring buildings?"

"In a sense, yes."

"Would I have to write anything?"

Again, that flicker of amusement. Sandra was trying not to smirk, not to condescend; she seemed like a nice person, and certainly her profession was one of understanding and tolerance. But Conrad was just too damned ridiculous: not just a refugee but a *bumpkin*, from a place so backward it had collapsed and died in its own filth, without building so much as a teleportation grid. Architect, indeed.

"Sir, that would make you a Reviewer. I'm not sure you've got the background for that."

Ouch. "Hmm. No, I don't suppose I do. I became a revolutionary *because* there was nothing else for me here. All the good jobs were filled with people too competent to ever leave them. And that was a long time ago. Today, I'm a thousand years more foolish!"

A faint smile acknowledged the joke, but then she said, "There's nothing wrong with being an Appreciator, sir. It's honest work. Most people don't have the eye for it."

"Hmm. Well. I suppose I'm flattered, then."

"I do need to put something down for your specialty. Shall we say, residential architecture?"

"Oh, I've *done* residential," Conrad said. "Single- and multifamily. Also industrial, civic, monumental, and certain infrastructure projects, including roads and tuberails. But lots of people were doing that. The only *specialty* I can claim is in transatmospherics. I once built an orbital tower a thousand kilometers tall."

Sandra the social worker blinked at that. "Personally? With your own two hands?"

It was Conrad's turn to laugh. "Yeah, I'm magic. I had a crew, miss. Twenty-five men and eleven hundred robots."

She blinked again, then glanced down at her sketchplate and said, "Specialty: transatmospheric architecture with supervisory experience." When she looked up, the condescension was gone. "You may qualify for more than Basic Assistance. It could take a few weeks to sort out, though."

"I'm a patient man," he said, "except where my wife is concerned. For that matter, I wouldn't mind seeing my parents, whom I haven't laid eyes on in a thousand years. And the sky, the *wind*. I tried to go outside, here, but the door wouldn't open. It said I'd freeze to death in ten minutes. I said I'd be back in two. I've lived on polar caps before. But as you say, I'm still a prisoner."

"We'll be on our way in a few minutes," Sandra assured him. "But first, shall we talk about your wardrobe options? The right appearance could make a big difference in your prospects."

Conrad laughed again, pinching the hospital gown he'd been wearing since before they revived him. "Are you saying this is the *wrong* appearance? I'm shocked. Miss, we wore clothes in the Barnard colony, too. Give me a fax machine and I'm sure I can work something out."

"You'll have access to one," Sandra said cautiously. "You won't own it."

"Good enough," Conrad said. And then, with a burst of wonder: "I'll be able to travel anywhere in the Queendom, won't I? I can eat whatever I want, and I'll never get sick or geriatric again. I'll be immorbid. I'll be *rich*."

Sandra shook her head at that, and dutifully burst his bubble. "Don't get your hopes up, sir. You'll be living on Basic Assistance, in a Red Sun emergency shelter in one of the hottest, wettest climates on Earth. You'll be in the bottom percentile for personal income, with sharp travel and plurality restrictions."

"Plurality!" Conrad chortled. "I can make copies of myself. I can be twins, triplets!"

"You can be twins," Sandra said, "but it just means your energy budgets will go half as far. There's no way of knowing how long you'll be on assistance, sir, and you need to prepare yourself for the reality of it."

Conrad *was* a patient man, and a kind one, but this went too far. He'd had enough of these self-important children telling him what to do, what to think. "Miss," he said coolly, "have you ever walked out of a blizzard with a broken collarbone? Have you spent a *hundred years* aboard a starship, or fought off a team of angry asteroid miners? I once watched my best friend's daughter cut in half, while her image archive was permanently erased. I've stood knee-deep in the rot of a failed ecology, and handled a city's worth of corpses. I've betrayed the trust of a king, and lived. So don't tell me about hardship, all right?"

"I'm . . . sorry," she said.

And before she could say anything else he nodded once, trying hard to squelch his anger. "Thank you. Your apology is accepted. Now take me to my wife, *please*."

chapter six

in which a community is overrun

Faxing from one place to another had been a perfectly ordinary feature of Conrad's youth. He'd done it several times a day, with no more thought than he'd give to stepping through an ordinary doorway. Sure, the body was destroyed and then reassembled as an atomically perfect copy, but what of it? The atoms in your body were temporary anyway—constantly churning, moving, departing and being replaced. This thing called "life" was just a standing wave in a flowing river; it endured across the smaller patterns that came and went. Only a deathist would obsess about the higher meaning of it all.

But that was a long time ago. Conrad had last seen a medical-grade print plate in the autumn days of Sorrow, and the last person to step through it—Princess Wendy de Towaji Lutui Rishe—had paid a high price, dying elaborately from an undiagnosed glitch in the system. Even that memory felt remote, far removed from this time and place, but its lessons lingered in the bones. Sandra led Conrad to the nearest fax machine with no further difficulty, only to find him balking at the threshold of the gray-black, vaguely foggy-looking rectangle of its print plate.

"Are you all right?" she asked.

And what could Conrad say, who'd just gone on about his impatience, his courage in the face of hardship? "I'm . . . fine, thank you. It's just been a long time since I traveled this way."

"It doesn't feel like much," she said, shrugging. "Just a little tingle as you go through."

"I know, dear, but there's more to it than that. I've been to the stars and back, and I've lost little bits of myself here and there along the way. One grows . . ." Cautious? That was hardly the word for a man who'd defied martial law, who'd stolen Barnard's single most tangible asset, who'd plowed a course through rubble fields and smacked head-on into trouble, bringing his closest friends along for the ride. "One *thinks* about these things more and more. Right and wrong, life and death, freedom and servitude. Every decision kicks up these *consequences* that follow along for the rest of your life. Which is forever, right? It sometimes pays to take a moment and think."

Sandra had apparently seen her share of wackos on the job, and took this comment with equanimity. "I can arrange for other transport, sir. If your beliefs require it, I may even be able to waive the associated fees."

"No," Conrad said, for his eagerness outweighed his caution by several orders of magnitude. "I'm done thinking. Let's go."

But still, he let Sandra walk through the plate first. It was like watching someone step through paint; the surface parted around her with a faint crackle, and a glow not unlike the southern lights in the cold Antarctic sky. She shrank into it and was gone. Well, here was the heaven he'd bought for Sorrow's dead; taking a breath, he stepped in after her.

And truly, there was no real feeling to it. It was a bit

like falling and a bit like drowning and a bit like a static shock all over his body, but mostly it was nothing much. Stepping through paint would at least have been cold and sticky. And there was this to be said for the process: on the other side there was sky.

He came through, right behind Sandra, in an open-sided, glass-domed atrium the size of a soccer field. There were no trees, but there were people sprawled out on blankets, as in a park. And like a park, the dome's floor was covered in short grass of a green so bright it hurt Conrad's optic nerve. There was nothing like this in Barnard; Sorrow's vegetation favored dark browns and ambers, with the occasional splatter of deep olive, under a sun much redder than Sol. The skies of Sorrow ranged from aquamarine to yellow-gray, and its clouds were hazy or feathery or even *striped* as the warm, slow jet stream skipped on and off of the cooler, denser layers underneath.

But the sky here was as blue as the grass was green, with the yellow-white sun shining brightly through an arch of puffy cumulus clouds. Did the soul ever forget this stuff? Did the body, independent of the intellect, feel the allure of its natural home?

"Oh my," said Conrad, his eyes agog, his heart aflutter.

And almost as quickly, with his first few steps, he felt a sort of brightness in his own body as well. His flesh had been optimized by the best morbidity filters the Barnard colony could devise, and Barnard was (or rather, had been) the clear leader in that field. He was *very* difficult to injure—on *Newhope* it had taken a propylene glycol explosion, the boiling liquid jetting out so hard it had smashed him right through a wellmetal railing. And he'd survived even that, long enough to get down to the cryo tubes.

And for the same reasons, his body aged slowly. In the

colony's waning days, when Conrad and Xmary had stolen *Newhope* and spirited away the frozen dead, Barnard's elite classes had spoken half-seriously about *outliving* the coming dark age. Hoarding the last of the medical-grade faxes, they planned across the millennia while the proletariat lived and died around them. According to some of the models, a single optimization might carry a careful person through a thousand years of life. Or more. Ah, but Conrad and his fellow traitors had been *so long* on that ship, that damned, cramped tower of a ship. With limited exercise, limited stimulation, an industrial-grade diet of recycled organics and minerals. Ordinary human beings would surely have cracked under the strain. They were *a hundred and forty-six years* into the voyage when disaster finally struck, and Conrad, without realizing it, had felt every day of that in his bones!

But the Frostbite Trauma Center had lifted those years away, and now that he was out in the world, in the fresh air and sunshine, he felt light as a pillow and springy as a sapling. Indeed, he'd last felt the tug of Earth at the age of twenty-five—absurdly long ago—and being back here now made him feel almost that young again.

"We're near the ocean," he said, for the air smelled of salt. Not the grotty acid smell of Sorrow's lightly briny oceans, but something cleaner and heavier. Almost edible, a kind of stew. And then, feeling a slight rolling motion in the ground beneath his feet, "We're *on* the ocean. A floating platform?"

Sandra nodded. "This is *Sealillia*, an emergency shelter owned by Red Sun Charities and deployed in times of crisis. I think the last time it was used was during the Amphitrite habitat failure on...one of Neptune's moons. I forget which one. Twenty thousand people came streaming through these fax portals"—there were three of them here, side-by-side along one edge of the grassy field—" and stayed here five weeks."

Ah. Interesting. "This place can hold *Newhope*'s passengers, then."

She grimaced slightly. "Well, in principle. Right now there's a bit of a squatter problem."

Indeed, there were two dozen people sprawled out on the grass, wrapped in blankets and apparently sleeping. This was no real surprise; open real estate with any sort of facilities access—such as the fax machines here—had attracted the indigent even on Sorrow, where indigence tended to be fatal and therefore self-limitingly rare. But as he stepped over one of the sleeping bodies, he saw a woman with painted nails and wellgold earrings, her immaculately coiffed hair only slightly smooshed by its contact with her pillow. A hobo-ish backpack lay at her feet, but she was outwardly young and certainly well dressed, in a peach-colored wellcloth pyjama adorned with moving circles of metallic gold. Her blanket was the reverse: circles of peach roaming a cloth-of-gold surface.

The others around her, men and women alike, looked comparably respectable, though they seemed inordinately fond of wellgold jewelry. And that was interesting, because the indigent people of Conrad's time had been hairy and smelly, antisocial and unadorned, and that wasn't the sort of fashion that ever went out of style. The ones in the old days were mostly men, too, whereas these people were about a fifty-fifty mix.

"They're overgrown children," he said, recognizing their type at once. Here were fully ripened citizens of, he would guess, anywhere from twenty to a hundred years of age, who could not for the life of them find the employment, the wealth, the *respect* accorded a true adult. And how could they, when the self-appointed adults of the Queendom refused to grow old and die? The positions of power and influence were all filled long ago, before the colonies were founded. That was *why* there were colonies. That was why there'd been a Children's Revolt to inspire their hasty founding.

"Yup," Sandra agreed. "They just show up. Tired of living with their parents and too poor to afford places of their own, they just sort of drift around the Earth like a vapor, condensing on any flat surface."

Conrad laughed; he hadn't realized his caseworker had a sense of humor under that bureaucratic exterior. He realized suddenly that the mere fact of her being an obstacle in his path, and a tool of the government he'd once rebelled against, did not in any way prevent her from being a likable person.

She laughed as well, but then added, "It's only funny until the eviction crews show up. The Amphitrite evac was fifteen years ago, but Red Sun is required to maintain a state of readiness. It *needs* this place for the next refugee crisis, whenever that may be. Probably you guys; probably soon."

"And the kids can't use it in the meantime?"

"The kids have a way of messing things up, Mr. Mursk. The platform spends most of its time folded up somewhere—probably in the waters off Tonga—to prevent exactly this from happening."

"Hmm. Well. How big *is* this thing?"

Instead of answering, she led him off the grassy field and out through one of several arch-shaped openings in the dome. As they approached a railing, he saw that the dome was built atop the die of a circular plinth or podium two hundred meters across, which sat in the center of a six-petaled raft of some gray, cementlike material. Covered end-to-end in black-roofed, three-story wellwood dormitories, *Sealillia* was a kilometer-wide flower on the surface of a featureless ocean. Around it was a low ring, projecting half a meter out of the water; the sea outside was blue and nearly waveless, but within the ring the water was distinctly greenish in hue, and teeming with laughing, splashing humans in various states of undress.

"It's a model city," Sandra answered finally. "Larger versions dot the equator from Galapagos to Kiribati, where hurricanes fear to tread. Probably twenty million people altogether. At the moment, I believe we're a thousand klicks north of the Marquesas, or forty-five hundred northeast of Tonga."

"Fascinating," Conrad said, meaning it. Nothing of the sort had been necessary in his own time. In fact, he suspected it would've been illegal, as there was a push at the time to shrink the Earth's population and expand its wilderness areas, by pushing people off into space. Apparently, this hadn't gone well. Still, he wasn't here to admire the scenery, or even the architecture. "Where are my friends?"

"This way," she said, pointing, motioning for him to follow as she approached the staircase that ringed the central plinth. "They've got a pair of apartments in Building One."

If that was Building One there at the foot of the stairs, then Conrad could see right away that something was going on; there were kids everywhere, but here they were *clustered*. Here they were all facing the same direction: toward a second-floor balcony on which three people stood. Xmary, Feck, and Eustace.

Conrad's heart leaped at the sight—they looked fine! In fact they looked *beautiful*, much better than they ever had onboard the starship. Over the years of that bitter journey Eustace in particular had grown into a fine, clever, resilient woman, with no way to express or define herself except in terms of the mission. But there she was,

standing out over a crowd of strangers like she'd been doing it all her life. Xmary, by contrast, had started as a so-
cialite and become a spacer mainly by accident. *She*
looked even better, even more at home, even more
smugly pleased with herself. Mission accomplished!

The three of them were dressed in wellcloth togas
of superabsorber black—"sun cloth" it was sometime
called, for it could absorb and store many kilowatt-hours
of solar energy, and then release it at night to warm the
wearer and light her way. Their hair had been cropped
close, in a way that gracefully emphasized their age
somehow. Conrad felt immediately self-conscious about
his own unruly mop, but at least he had combed it. At
least he'd let Sandra pick out a pair of pants and a shirt
for him—plain, but tasteful.

"If you insist on putting yourselves in harm's reach,"
Xmary was calling down to a crowd of hundreds, "you
should at least prepare yourselves for what's to come.
That's just my advice, but you'd do well to listen. You
need to study this group's tactics. Does anyone here have
combat experience?"

No hands went up, although many a nervous foot was
shuffling on the cement.

"What's she doing?" Sandra asked quietly, turning a
funny look on Conrad.

"Preparing a defense," Conrad said, as though it were
the most obvious thing in the world. Which of course it
was; if they truly had been marked for death, then he and
his friends had best gird their loins for battle. And with
these young'uns hanging around, there were only three
options: evict, recruit, or watch them die in the crossfire.
Drowned, most likely; the easiest thing to do with a
platform like this was to sink it with all hands aboard,
then pick off the survivors as they swam. Would Fatalists

discriminate between targets and bystanders? It seemed unlikely.

"But that's the Constabulary's job," Sandra protested. "Or the local police for this jurisdiction."

"Then where are they?" Conrad asked. "If they want to help, that's fine, but we're not going to sit around waiting." And then it dawned on him that that was *exactly* what Sandra—what the Queendom authorities and probably the Fatalists themselves—expected the refugees to do. He laughed and said, "In the colonies, miss, one learns to take care of problems as early and as thoroughly as possible."

"But—"

Whatever she was about to say, it got cut off when Xmary noticed Conrad at the back of the crowd. Her stern face brightened immediately, and she whooped, then put her hands on the railing and vaulted over.

The crowd fell back a step, gasping. The fall was only four meters, and Xmary's bones and joints were woven through with wonders. She could fall twice that far without serious injury. On Earth, with its higher gravity and thinner atmosphere than Sorrow, the terminal velocity was higher as well, but if she didn't mind a repair trip through the fax she could conceivably survive a fall from *any* height. So could a squirrel; there was nothing especially miraculous about it.

Nor was Xmary particularly reckless, or athletic, or consumed by the need to show off. She just didn't like to waste time. Especially now that they were off the ship, and time actually *meant* something again. She wanted her husband! The real irony was that Barnard's morbidity filters had been exported to the Queendom; most of these kids were probably as indestructible as she was. Had they never tested their limits? Did they even know what was inside them?

In any case, they parted like water as Conrad's wife fell toward them, her toga flapping up, clearly exposing her navel, her black underpants, her navy tattoo. She landed heavily on her sandaled feet, dropping into a crouch with one hand down in front of her and the other up in the air, for balance. "Hello, darling," she said, grinning.

"Hi there," he returned, stepping up to offer his hand. "I like what you've done with your hair."

The kids enjoyed that; their silence fell away into cheers and hoots and catcalls. They liked it even better when she rose to a standing position, reached for the ruff of Conrad's shirt, and pulled him in for a kiss. Then, pulling away, she looked around and addressed them all again. "Let's reconvene in an hour. Right now I have more pressing business."

And who, in an immorbid society where hormones raged in young and old alike, could fail to understand *that*? With a smile so wide it must have hurt, Xmary took Conrad's hand and pulled him toward the building's entrance. The crowd cheered.

"But weapons are *illegal*," Sandra Wong was say-ing. She was in one of the apartments—Conrad's, apparently—standing primly while Conrad and Xmary, Eustace and Feck sprawled on the bed. A dozen of the kids, whom Xmary had identified as potential leaders, sat on the tables and chairs and floor, watching the exchange with interest. Sandra gestured at the small fax machine built into one of the walls. "This thing won't even *print* them for you. And why should it?"

"Anything can be a weapon," Feck pointed out reasonably. And Conrad had to smile, because Yinebeb Fecre—

aka Feck the Facilitator—had improvised his way through more sudden skirmishes than Sandra could possibly imagine. Like Conrad, he had sent his share of bodies to the Cryoleum, and to the even more final crematorium of Barnard's stellar furnace. "We could stage an impromptu golf tournament. I don't know about you, but my aim with a golf ball is pretty good. I suspect our collective aim, with hundreds of golf balls, is even better."

"But why would you *do* such a thing?" Sandra wanted to know.

"To stay alive?" Feck suggested.

"But your patterns have been safely archived. Everyone's have. All you'd be doing is disturbing the crime scene, making it harder for the authorities to determine what happened."

"We're supposed to let them kill us?" Eustace Faxborn asked, more in confusion than genuine horror. "We're supposed to trust our lives to a backup system that we haven't personally tested? I'm sorry, miss, that's nonsense."

Eustace had spent virtually her entire life aboard *Newhope*, trusting nothing, testing everything, and fixing whatever she could. She was a no-nonsense kind of gal; when their nav solutions were corrupted and they'd suddenly realized they were drifting into a dust shoal, she'd hardly batted an eye. When the nav lasers were overwhelmed, and then damaged, and then ground to dust themselves, she'd shrugged and run diagnostics on the ertial shield. And when the ship was holed and tumbled and coming apart, she'd simply called out, "Cryo tubes," because that was the final backup. When all else fails, leave a good-looking corpse.

"There's no law against self-defense," Xmary told Sandra Wong. "I looked it up. In fact, under *maritime* law, which applies here, you're even allowed to defend a stranger's life 'with all necessary force and means.'"

"But that's crazy," Sandra said. Like Eustace, she seemed more perplexed than upset at the misunderstanding. "I think each one of you needs to consult with your own caseworker and hash out an activity path that leads away from violence."

Xmary was about to object, but really, Sandra Wong *was* the ranking authority here. And while Conrad had no particular awe for authority—he'd led his share of mutinies and rebellions over the years—he did at least know enough to work with them, until such time as you were working against them.

"That's probably wise," he said to Sandra, and was satisfied with the surprise on her face. "Could I trouble you to send for them? We have no intention of breaking the letter or spirit of the law; we just want to present our enemies with a discouraging target."

He sat up and looked at the kids assembled here, feeling for a moment that he could barely tell them apart. Here in the Queendom, modifying your mind or body required an alteration permit, and those were hard to get. As a result, these were some of the purest humans he could recall ever seeing.

It was too bad, in a way; Conrad was used to reading people's character in their bodyforms. Troll? Centaur? Self-created jumble of anatomical talents and handicaps? Gorgeous human of near-mathematical perfection? Here they were all just kids, and to the extent he could read them at all, it was in their clothing and posture, their coloration and adornment, their facial expressions and manners of speech. And these things were easily changed, easily imitated. They didn't require the bodily commitment that even, say, backward-bending knees would require.

More or less at random, he singled out one of the young men seated on the table. Like many of his fellows, the kid was shirtless—clad only in a pair of loose trousers and a thrice-looped wellgold necklace that flashed improbably in the room's dim light. But his skin was chlorophyll green, lightly striped with darker tones, and Conrad liked that, taking it as a sign of personality.

"You," he said, "what's your name?"

"Raoul Handsome Green," the kid answered.

"Handsome Green? Really?"

"Yes, sir. That's the name my parents gave me."

"Hmm. Good one. And when did they give it to you? How old are you?"

"Fifty-one, sir."

"Do you have a specialty?"

"I do. I'm an art appreciator. Mostly Late Modern photography, although I admire the painting and sculpture of that period as well."

"Hmm. I see. But you have other skills, right? Can you swim?"

"Yes."

"Hold your breath?"

"Sure. For five minutes, maybe . . . I dunno, maybe six or seven minutes."

"Really? Good," Conrad said. "Very good. Why don't you find some other swimmers and go print up some gill-diving gear? If we're attacked, I'll bet you four-to-one it comes from underneath."

Raoul Handsome Green had no response to that.

"Is something wrong?" Conrad asked him.

At least Raoul's face was expressive; his look combined the sullenness of a frown, the helplessness of a shrug, and the pointed amusement of a smirk. "I don't know how to do those things, sir. Who do you think I am?

Who do you think *you* are? We don't become interstellar heroes just because you walk into a room."

There were scattered sniggers at this from the other kids.

"You're all staying here illegally," Feck pointed out, fluttering his hand in annoyance. "What I would say is, who's taking care of you if not yourself?"

"There are libraries here," Conrad said, "right? You can pick up a block of wellstone and start asking questions. They still teach that in the schools, I assume? Research?"

Raoul shrugged. He wasn't going to commit to an answer one way or the other.

"Anyone else?" Conrad tried.

It went on like that for a while, and Conrad eventually decided there were three separate problems here. First there was the obvious ignorance of these people. He found this personally disgusting and offensive—how could they look themselves in the mirror?—but in all fairness they simply had no practical experience. Doing *anything*. Nor did they need any in the eternal lives the Queendom had mapped out for them.

They were drowning in knowledge, but actually absorbing some, actually learning a skill, was something they did for amusement, not for money or survival. Their minds simply didn't work that way. Of course, they'd all been born on Earth. If this conversation were taking place in a Lunar dome or asteroid warren, a planette or a spin-gee city in interplanetary space, he might have better luck. Presumably, ignorance could still be fatal in places like that, and would be discouraged.

Secondly, though, there was the problem of authority. Conrad and Xmary didn't have any. They had surprised the crowd with their leaping and prancing, and yes, their status as returning star voyagers did carry a certain shock value. These kids had never met anyone like them; nobody had. They were clearly impressed. But it didn't mean they would *listen*.

And there was a third problem which perhaps over-shadowed the other two.

"Maybe the platform *needs* sinking," one kid suggested at one point.

"I'm happy to risk my life," said another. "And I don't even have current backups."

"What point are you trying to make with this self-defense crap?" asked a third, with genuine puzzlement.

And finally Conrad understood: *these kids were death-ists*. Not Fatalists, perhaps, but not the sworn enemies of Fatalists, either. The philosophy of random mass murder did not strike them as obviously wrong. "There are too many people," they'd said several times already. "There's no purpose for any of this. Maybe there used to be, but we've never seen it."

And it was a strangely difficult point to argue with; Conrad had groaned under the same burdens in his own youth. The answers had been different then, but the questions had not. And yet, life—any life—was full of challenges. Could it really be so different here?

"You may feel a greater urgency," he suggested, "when death is actually imminent."

chapter seven

in which certain difficulties
are unmasked

"Your Majesty," said Reportant Bernhart Bechs to the Queen of Sol, "this seems an awkward time for the king to be absent. Did you ask him to leave a copy behind?"

"No," she said, not only to Bechs but to the other reportants here, clustered around her and her Palace Guards in a buzzing hemispherical swarm. Ordinarily her personal press cordon was set at eighty meters, with strict acoustic volume limits to discourage uninvited chitchat, but this was a press conference. Typically these would be handled by her press secretary or by some crisis-specific bureaucrat, but there was a lot going on this week, and she had dozens of copies working all across the solar system. Printing out one more was hardly a bother, and people were burning with curiosity anyway, so she had generously permitted the paparazzi to approach within ten meters of her physical person, and to ask—within the bounds of decorum!—anything they wished.

"The king," she went on, "does not divide his attention when matters of science loom large. He is cloistered at his workshop on Maplesphere, and will remain there until his experiments are complete."

"Does that mean weeks?" Bechs followed up. "Years?"

Bechs was, at the moment, a four-winged news camera only slightly larger than the queen's pinkie nail. Strictly speaking this wasn't necessary; they were in Chryse Downs Amphitheater on the northern lowlands of Mars, and Bechs' physical self—one of him, anyway—was in a rental office just a few kilometers away. He could remote this bug; there was no need to *be* it, to run a shadow of his brain within it. Too, he was among the most respected reportants in the Queendom, and would be welcome at her side in his own human body. But old habits die hard, and Bechs was an old, old man. He was accustomed to interviewing Her Majesty in this way, and she, for her part, always recognized his signature wine-red cameras.

"Weeks, most likely," the queen said. "If his problem is tractable he'll solve it, and if it isn't he'll move on to something more immediate. It's possible he'll uncover new principles requiring much more detailed investigation, but if so he will delegate the problem—at least temporarily—to his technical staff. He's aware that I have pressing tasks for him here, and he won't lightly refuse."

"Is it the wormhole physics again?" asked another of the cameras.

"I don't discuss my husband's work," she reminded. But her tone was indulgent, for when Bruno retreated to Maplesphere, which happened three or four times each decade, he generally returned with treasures: the back-time processor, the quantum screw, the popular word-cypher game known as "Nickels." Nothing could match the twin bombshells of his early career—collapsium and ertial shielding—but he remained the most inventive soul in a population of one hundred and sixty billion.

Tamra would never blame her subjects for being curious about his current interests.

"What's happening with the Barnard refugees?" asked someone else.

"The four living crewmates remain in Red Sun custody," she said. "No decisions have been made about the others."

"Has the attack on *Newhope* accelerated the timetable for their revival?"

"I repeat," she said, less patiently than before, "no decisions have been made. Whatever we finally do here will set a precedent for all time hereafter. There is no reason to enter into it hastily."

"What about radiation damage?" another reportant demanded, somewhat angrily. "You can't leave them out there forever."

"Steps are being taken," the queen assured. "Whatever status these people are finally accorded, we will treat their remains with utmost dignity."

Meanwhile, another Bernhart Bechs camera had found its way to *Sealillia*, to interview one Conrad Ethel Mursk. It would be the climax of a series; Bechs had already profiled the other three, whom he thought of as the Captain, the Comedian, and the Cactus. He'd even interviewed the ship itself.

In a lurid, voyeuristic sense, the Cactus was by far the most interesting of these; Xiomara Li Weng and her jokester second mate, Yinebeb Fecre, had been born in the Queendom and exiled in the Revolt. They'd had real lives, if sad ones, whereas Eustace Faxborn was *created* specifically for the interstellar return mission, stepping live and whole and nearly adult from a Barnardean fax machine. This custom had been commonplace out in the colonies, where—strange notion!—there was a chronic shortage of human beings. But in the Queendom this was considered one of the the basest possible perversions.

Especially since people named "Faxborn" were, for the most part, sexually active from the word go. Indeed, if the refugees' accounts were accurate—and Bechs had no reason to believe otherwise—Eustace Faxborn had married the Comedian shortly before the bloody surprise attack that was the mission's unauthorized departure. She'd begun less as a member of *Newhope*'s crew than as part of its life-support system: a living sex robot for the otherwise lonely second mate. In this sense, she'd done quite well for herself, and Bechs was careful to say so in his profile.

"You could run that ship by yourself," he'd said to her in the interview, echoing the words of the Comedian. "You could fix any subsystem. You've a quick mind, and quick hands to go with it, for you've been using them all your life."

He'd meant it in the best possible way—most of his viewers had no such practical skills, and admired them greatly—but her reply was characteristically prickly: "*Newhope* ran for five hundred seventy-eight years without any crew. After the accident it repaired itself with no help from me. It's smarter than a human being when it needs to be."

Which was partly true and partly her own sort of modesty, but mostly it was an uncomfortable and vaguely hostile evasion. The Cactus seemed at ease only when reciting facts, or describing the emotions of others. Her own self, her own feelings, were a troubling subject she didn't care to examine. And why should she? She'd lived her life in a microcosm, with only two other people besides her husband. Plus the ship itself, yes, which could spin out robots and specialized personality constructs to suit any whim or need. But it wasn't human.

"I regret the accident," the ship had said to Bechs in its own interview, conducted at distance over the Nescog voice channels, with hours of signal lag between question and answer. "I was aware of the divergence in the navigation solution, but I was unable to formulate a response. I failed to realize the debris shoal was within our position envelope, and failed to imagine the resulting collision. I was caught off guard."

"What *did* you imagine?" he'd asked in response.

And the ship had replied: "Very little, sir. Imagination is an inductive trait, and difficult to mechanize."

Of course.

At any rate, Bechs had buzzed and flitted his way back here on the news that the ship's first mate—the captain's husband—had finally been released from hospital. Bechs would round out his story and then rerelease the whole thing, with commentary, to a curious public.

Unfortunately, several dozen other reportants had beat him to it; he found Mursk seated at his apartment's tiny dinner table, swatting angrily at a cloud of them.

"Shove off, parasites. I'm done. I'm *eating*!"

And so he was: fax-fresh plibbles and bran flakes, steaming blood sausage and curried potatoes, with miso soup and the nutrient paste known as "mulm," which Bechs had never seen eaten by anyone but navy crews and merchant spacers. It was far more food than a human stomach could hold, and there were three nearly full beverage mugs in front of him as well. Here was a man who hadn't *tasted* for decades. Not enough, anyway, or not the right things.

But still the cameras pestered him, spitting out questions, stepping all over each other in a haze of white

noise. Most people had no idea how to run a press conference, even if they'd called it themselves.

"Welcome back to civilization," Bechs said to him,
raising his voice above the din. He could do that; he had
a special volume license, along with other privileges. "You
do realize, I hope, that you can order these cameras outside? They can't invade your home, nor peer through
your windows, without permission."

"Ah!" Mursk said. "Then my permission is revoked.
Off with you pests. Off!" To Bechs he said, "Thank you."

"Quite welcome," Bechs assured him, while the others buzzed sullenly away. "I wonder if I could speak with
you when you're finished, though. I've already interviewed your friends, and I'm hoping to round out my set."

"You're Bernhart Bechs," Mursk said.

"Yes."

"I remember you from when I was a kid."

"Do you?" Bechs was surprised, and pleased. "That
was a long time ago."

Mursk laughed. "You're telling me? But you did that
thing on the history of Europe, and the one about the
plight of juvenile commuters."

"God, I barely remember it myself. When can I return,
Mr. Mursk? I don't mean to trouble you."

Conrad looked down at his food, then up again at the
maroon bug that was Bechs. He seemed disappointed.
"You know, truthfully, I'm already full. What would you
like to know?"

Conrad Mursk turned out to be very nearly an ideal
interviewee, whose life story could, Bechs sensed, fill volumes of its own. Nearly everything Bechs asked was met
with a long, detailed answer which neither rambled nor

lacked a point. A longtime spacer, Mursk had as much vacuum lore as any of his crewmates—and quite a bit more than Eustace Faxborn. But unlike the other three, Mursk had done a lot of additional things with his life, spending more than a century of it on the ground, and decades more on the sea and on the ice of Planet Two's small polar cap.

He was never a politician—he made that abundantly clear—but he had nevertheless been a member, if unofficially, of King Bascal's inner circle. He'd been remotely consulted on several occasions by the King and Queen of Sol, and seemed to have been present at almost every major turn in Barnard's history.

"I'm a trouble magnet," Mursk said at one point. The admission seemed to sadden him, which only heightened his aura of thoroughness and thoughtfulness. If he had a single great fault, it was a kind of self-doubt that bordered on self-loathing. To hear him tell it, he'd done little good in his life. Still, Bechs sensed through these deep layers of modesty and guilt that nearly every calamity had involved his *attempting* to, often against terrible odds.

"Our departure helped collapse the Barnardean economy," he would say. Or, "I shortened the Children's Revolt through an act of blatant treachery." Or, "I never convinced the government to soften its punitive measures, and in terrorizing the miners into ending their rebellion I gave my de facto approval to their indenture."

But from these statements Bechs extracted the unspoken corollaries: *I've risked my life to preserve innocents. I know when to cut my losses. I know how to broker a deal. I am unspeakably interesting.* Bechs could have questioned this man for days, for *months*; but as fate would have it, the two had only been talking for twenty or thirty minutes when a commotion rose up outside. Not the buzz of reportant cameras but the actual shouting of live human beings, transmitted through the paper-thin, almost tent-like wellstone of the dormitory shelter.

"Excuse me," Mursk said, a look of worry blooming on his face. He rose from his chair and moved to the wall, murmuring "Window" to it just as though he'd been in civilization all his life. And when the window appeared, he said, "Oh, brother."

Conrad had been expecting trouble since before he'd even arrived here, and he'd spent much of his time huddled at a library in the apartment's wall, learning what he could about Fatalist tactics. But what he saw outside was a surprise nonetheless. There was an attack of sorts under way, but the invaders coming down the staircase were not gray-skinned Fatalist ghouls or skeletal Death avatars, but ordinary men in blood-colored jump-suits trimmed with white.

Conrad had spent time in four different Barnardean services, and had a fine eye for uniforms. These were neither military nor medical; they looked more like a mechanic's coverall than anything else. They had names stenciled in black across the left breast, but no indications of rank or functional specialty. Indeed, the only insignia was a white rectangle on each man's left sleeve, bearing a blood-red circle surrounded by five outward-facing triangles. A sunburst, highly stylized.

Conrad counted twenty men, two of them with bullhorns and *all* of them carrying objects he recognized immediately: contact tazzers, capable of dropping any human being in his or her tracks with the merest brush of their business end. The tazzer was a humane weapon as such things went, but the people who'd actually been struck by one—Conrad included—tended to give them a wide berth. In the words of the poet Rodenbeck, "Being tazzed is like being stepped on by an electric elephant."

The other surprise was that the half-dressed kids at the bottom of the stairs—nearly a hundred of them— were holding their ground rather than falling back or scattering.

"What's happening?" Bechs asked, buzzing up beside Conrad for a look.

"It's the Red Sun eviction team," Conrad answered. Then, in a much louder voice: "Feck! Xmary!"

He stepped out onto the balcony, prepared to vault over its railing as Xmary had done, or at least call down advice to the children and warnings to the Red Sun security. But the surprises just kept on coming.

"We are not taking names," said one of the bullhorn carriers in an amplified but outwardly reasonable tone. "No one here will be punished. We simply request that you vacate these premises so they can be put to humanitarian use."

But the kids—boys and girls alike—were forming up into battle lines as though they'd been training for it all their lives. Their wellgold necklaces and earrings flashed and flickered in the sunlight, not merely reflecting but in some way *modulating* the glare. Passing notes in class, oh my, in their own secret language. Did they feel it as taps upon their skin? As nerve inductions? As sights or sounds?

They couldn't change their bodies, but clearly they could use their brains. And whatever they were passing, whatever they were saying to each other, the Red Sun workers seemed oblivious to it until it was too late, and their fate was sealed. When the mob had self-assembled into five clean ranks, they rushed their attackers. Silently at first, as rows one and two launched into motion, but then rows three and four let out an ululating yell, while row five raised its fists in defiance.

Nor were these kids afraid to absorb some hurt; the first two rows were sacrificial, simply throwing themselves against the Red Sun line—in some cases right up against the tazzers. This put the Red Sun workers off balance—literally—so that the third and fourth lines could sweep them off their feet, wrenching the tazzers from their hands. This was also sacrificial, as most of the kids involved went down twitching and grunting. But the fifth line swept over them without opposition, taking up the tazzers and hurling them away, without even bothering to use them against their owners.

Instead, the Red Sun people were hauled up by their armpits and threaded into cunning arm- and neck- and headlocks that made optimum use of the strengths and weaknesses of human anatomy. The guards, like everyone else, must be terribly hard to injure, but against overpowering *leverage* they had little recourse.

"Here now!" one of them said.

"This activity's unlawful," tried another.

But more kids were streaming into the area, and the ones already here were finding their voices. "We're not hurting anything! Why are you on us like this? Leave us the hell alone!" And then, in a rising chorus: "Into the drink with you! Swim for it! Swim for it! *Swim for it!!*"

"Excuse me," said the camera of Bernhart Bechs, buzzing down for a closer view.

Conrad didn't know what to feel. Barely fifteen seconds after the first commotion, the kids were dragging their captives toward the platform's edge, at the juncture between two of its flower petals, and they really were going to throw them in the water.

"Stop!" he shouted after them. "There are . . . there . . . shit. There are smarter ways!"

But nobody was paying attention to an old man's babbling, and if he jumped down there to intervene, in all likelihood he'd just be going for a swim himself. Damn! Whatever faults these kids might have, helplessness was clearly not among them. And Conrad had seen this all before, had *lived* it all more than once—the anger, the spontaneous order and chaos, the pent-up need for action. *Alas, Utopia,* Rodenbeck had written in the wake of the Children's Revolt, *thou retreatest from immorbid grasp as a cricket from fractious children.*

And yea, verily, Conrad could feel it in his bones: the dream of a better life never ended, even when all sense said it should. And so the Queendom of Sol—forged with the loftiest of intentions by the best minds in history—was poised, once again, at the brink of revolution.

"Eternal life," Conrad observed though no one was there to hear him, "is a tuberail car that won't stop crashing."

chapter eight

in which old haunts are revisited

Perhaps Conrad should have stayed. Perhaps he should have brought his negotiating skills to bear, and brokered some sort of agreement between the squatters, the platform's rightful owners, and the Constabulary who'd come pouring out of the fax gates a few minutes after the fighting had ended. Perhaps he should have let himself care. But in fact he did none of these things. Feck and Xmary knew the squatters better than Conrad did, and had also enjoyed more extensive contact with the Queendom bureaucracy. In some sense, they'd begun the negotiation process well before the actual skirmish—before Conrad's revival had even begun—and he didn't feel like playing catch-up.

Hadn't he done enough already? Didn't he have his own needs and wants? Indeed, far from helping Xmary help the kids, he tried to seduce her away.

"This so-called Basic Assistance is pretty hefty," he said. "We can go places, do things. You've spent your life on spaceships, dear, and on worlds that might as well be spaceships. But here's a place that offers wonders beyond the dreams of Barnard."

They were sitting side-by-side on the steps outside the park dome, enjoying the night breeze off the ocean while the crowds chattered and shouted behind them.

"Sorry," she said with a sheepish look he could just barely read in *Sealillia*'s night-light glow, "but the rest of us are already broke. We retraced our old footsteps in Denver and Tongatapu. Went to the moon, took a submarine ride. We've been here two weeks; we blew through our monthly allotment in one."

"So get some money from your parents."

She put her head on his shoulder and sighed. "They won't see me, Conrad. They're still livid about the Revolt."

"Really? A thousand-year grudge?"

"You don't know my parents."

"Hmm."

"Anyway, I think we can make a difference here. We should get back inside."

"I'm sick of making a difference," Conrad said, scanning the night sky for some sign of the moon, which he still hadn't seen. "When I built the Orbital Tower, I felt like I was making a real contribution to Sorrow's future. Not like a stadium or an apartment building; this was something that *really helped*. But it wasn't enough; it didn't save the colony. And everything else I try just ends up . . . I don't know. It wasn't so bad on the ship, but we're among human beings again. And the thing about human beings . . . I just . . . It seems like wherever I go, people are fighting. And I can't help them, and I can't make them stop. Can't I be tired of that? Is that okay?"

"Sure," she said, hugging his arm. "For a while. But every now and then you poke your head up at just the right time, and it *does* help. Sometimes fighting is the right thing to do. We can get by without you here, so yes, go on ahead. Spend your allowance; have some fun. Just don't turn your back when you *are* needed. There's no point living forever if you don't use yourself as a positive force."

He made a smile she couldn't see. "Aye, Captain."

"I mean it, Conrad."

"So do I." But then he scratched an eyebrow, cleared his throat and said, "If we all did that, all across the Queendom and throughout the colonies, a hundred and sixty billion people using their lives as a positive force ... That seems so overwhelming. How can everybody help everybody, when we're crammed together like this, or dying out among the stars? I don't know *how* to use my life."

"Well, not by throwing people in the ocean."

And that, at least, they could both agree on.

He had been to every corner of Barnard system, had crossed every millimeter of the space between Barnard and Sol. Twice! He knew the land and seas of Sorrow from pole to pole, and he had radioed personality snapshots to a dozen other worlds, and gathered back scores of self-aware replies which he'd folded back into himself. He was quite possibly the best-traveled person in history. But Saturn's rings were a sight unequaled in the colonies, and Conrad had never seen them with his own eyes. So that was where he went first.

And God damn if it wasn't the most stunning sight his eyes had beheld since the first time he'd seen Xmary naked. From a hundred thousand kilometers above the seething cloudtops, at a latitude of twenty degrees south, he found himself looking "up" at a ring structure that filled the center of his view, leaving only the edges black.

The planet itself was more striking than either of Barnard's gas giants, Gatewood and Vandekamp. Unlike those blank turquoise spheres, Saturn's blonde atmosphere was broken into subtle bands of light and dark whose edges blended together in little swirls and ripples that were probably the size of Earthly continents. Some of the lighter bands were split by very thin ribbons of dark, snaking north to south and back again, and a few of the dark bands were home to brunette specks and ovals that were darker still: storms, shearing and growing out of the boundary ripples. In his sailing days, Conrad had been a student of Sorrow's weather, and had seen patterns like this in the thermal maps of her currents and trade winds. But not right there in the sky, all at once.

Even the limb of the atmosphere was interesting; against the blackness of space he could easily pick out three separate cloud layers—call them blonde, brunette, and redhead—floating above the general murk. You saw nothing like that when you were this close to Vandekamp, and at Gatewood it was too damned dark to see anything at all.

Conrad had seen—not personally but through the eyes of a holographic avatar—tidally locked planets like Gammon and Wolf, whose surfaces were as banded and stratified as any gas giant's atmosphere. The sun never rose or set; the melting point of water was a geographic location. That was kind of pretty, if inconvenient for the inhabitants. But for sheer visual impact it was nothing compared to the Eridanian world of Mulciber, where clouds of tin spilled as rain into quicksilver oceans, in countless craters smashed down by cometary impact. From its dusty moon—the only safe place to view it—the planet looked like an iron ball decorated with hundreds of circular mirrors.

Conrad had seen his share of ring systems, too, but here was the true majesty of Saturn; its rings were *young*, still nursing their original complexity. He could barely take his eyes off them. According to the hollie windows in the dome of the observation platform, each of the three main rings was wider than the Earth, and the innermost one began almost exactly one Earth diameter away from Saturn's visible edge. These were nice amaze-the-tourist facts, but from this vantage point Conrad couldn't really tell where the "three" rings were supposed to be; he counted at least a hundred, of so many different colors and thicknesses and brightnesses that they each, like mountains or oceans or cities, seemed to have a distinct character all their own.

The observation platform itself was interesting, too. He shared it with five other gawkers who'd come through the fax at the same time. And to keep them all from barfing in surprise as they sailed out through the print plate, there was gravity; not from a finicky graser but from actual Newtonian mass. Within its soap-bubble dome the platform was a flat triangle of diamond sitting atop another flat triangle, with a neuble's worth of neutronium squashed between them. A billion tons of matter: a fifty-fifty mix of protons and neutrons, with a haze of electrons shimmering around them, giving the substance a pearly appearance. The heart of the structure was, in essence, a single gigantic atom, pressed flat and oozing superfluidly into the corners of its prison.

Conrad had come to see the planet, but as the minutes stretched on, he found his attention drawn more and more to the floor beneath his feet. He'd learned a fair bit about neutronium during his brief tenure as a gravitic engineer, and had been fascinated by its liquid qualities. The theory of it all was far beyond him, but he'd gotten surprisingly far by thinking of neutronium as a kind of oil, impossibly slippery and impossibly dense.

There were whole *worlds* of this stuff out there in the wider universe: neutron stars. Atoms the size of Earth, with the mass of two or three suns, held together not by nuclear forces but by their own enormous gravity. In his more romantic moments, he sometimes dreamed of seeing one up close. What would it look like? What color would it be? If immorbidity meant anything at all, surely he must someday have the chance to find out?

In any case, between the extremes of hydrogen nuclei and neutron stars lay the man-made neuble: a two-centimeter atom held together by pure human stubbornness. They had only two uses: they could be squeezed into the tiny black holes from which collapsium was made, or they could be exploited architecturally for their intrinsic gravity, which was considerable.

In free space, the pull of an ordinary spherical neuble could break a person's back, could fold a person's limbs around itself in a bone-snapping, rib-crushing embrace that admitted no hope of escape, or even breath. He'd heard of accidents like that, where it took a team of specialists and superstrong robots a week and a half to pry the body off. Not for any sentimental reason, but because *burning* it off could ignite or destabilize the diamond shell, releasing the tremendous pressure it enclosed. *Bang*.

For this reason, neubles were rarely encountered in free space, and the builders who employed them were *very* careful about surrounding them with protective structure. Their gravity fell away rapidly; two and a half meters away it was Earthlike, and at twenty-five you could barely feel it. Squashing one flat like this was a neat trick that spread the mass and gravity around, allowing you to get closer without getting killed. But it also struck Conrad as surprisingly risky for the staid old Queendom of Sol; he'd only ever heard of *circular* platforms being fashioned in this way. Squares and triangles had a nasty habit of concentrating stress at the corners.

"How old is this platform?" he asked the wall.

And one of the hollie windows replied, "A very intelligent question, sir. It has been in service as a tourist destination since Q20."

The very earliest days of the Queendom, in other words. "Huh. And who designed it?"

"Declarant-Philander Marlon Sykes, sir."

Ah. A man so comfortable with risk that he'd very nearly destroyed the sun, very nearly murdered the king and queen. He *had* murdered thousands of others, if incidentally, and he was a torturer, too—a closet sadist exposed only at the very end of his days. The Queendom had never imposed a death penalty, but in Sykes' case it had made something close to an exception, firing him off into the void at the speed of light, in a cage of collapsium that sealed him off forever from the universe of decent people.

A difficult man to admire, yes, but Conrad had studied architecture, and that was a subject one simply could not discuss without frequent invocation of that accursed name. Sykes had invented superreflectors and a hundred other common things, and was responsible for some of the most striking and innovative structures in human history. Including, arguably, the Nescog, which had been built amid the ruins of King Bruno's original collapsiter network. Bruno had designed the Nescog as well, but he'd had Sykes' own Ring Collapsiter, ill-fated but undeniably ingenious, to draw upon for inspiration.

"Hasn't anyone complained?" Conrad asked. "Aren't people afraid to come here? Why not just build a new platform?"

"Excellent questions," the hollie window congratulated him. "I don't have the information here, and the speed of light is such that I may not locate it for several hours. But I will research these issues and forward the results to you."

"Um, okay. Do you need my name?"

"I have your name, sir," the window informed him proudly. "It's an indelible part of your fax trace, and also encoded in your genome."

Ah. Of course. Conrad had grown up with all this, and it was slowly coming back to him. There was something vaguely unsavory about it—he'd never been crazy about machines that watched his every move, talked secretly among themselves, and also enforced such laws as they were able to. In what way did that advance the causes of freedom and human dignity? But at the same time, he felt a part of him melting with relief. On Sorrow there was no backup, no supervision, *no help*. If you got into trouble, you got yourself out or you died. Conrad and his friends got out; Bascal and *his* friends had apparently died. But no more. Here, that kind of death simply wasn't possible.

But Conrad's parents were Irish, and in spite of his best efforts they had managed to imprint him with a certain degree of superstition. He had seen a ghost once, no shit, and he looked around now, suddenly realizing all the other tourists had filed away without his noticing. He was here alone with the machines, on a platform designed by the very cleverest of history's monsters.

"I think I'll go to Denver," he said to the fax machine, and hurried to fling himself through the plate.

But Denver, where arguably his own involvement in the Children's Revolt had begun, was all wrong. Most of it hadn't changed at all; the old skyline was still there, instantly recognizable. The streets were still bursting with children—for this was a Children's City—and with buskers and athletes and *pedestrians*, for this was also an Urban Preservation District where short-range faxing was severely discouraged.

But though the old Denver was still visible beneath, today the city had a *lot* of extra grown-ups pushing their way through the streets of downtown, and a lot of robots scurrying daintily through morning errands. And the downtown district itself lay in the deep morning shadow of six enormous towers—not orbital towers, but simple pressurized stratscrapers capable of holding a million people each. Taller than the mountains to the west, taller even than the Green Mountain Spire which had once been the city's signature landmark, they . . . they ruined it. They made the city look small and artificial and old.

"How long have those been there?" he asked a passerby, pointing up at the monstrosities.

"Huh?" said the man, looking for something out of the ordinary and not finding it. His breath steamed in the October air.

"The towers," Conrad said, huddling into the warmth of his wellcloth jacket again, for he had not been cold in many decades. "The big ones. How long?"

"Oh, a long time. Hunnerds of years," the man said. Then, looking Conrad over, he brightened. "Hey! You're that feller from Barnard, aren't you? Returned from the stars to back here whence you were born."

"I am," Conrad admitted, "though I haven't been to 'whence' yet. I'm from Ireland."

"Eh? Well, welcome back to society, just the same. Does it feel good? Does it feel right?"

"I don't know," Conrad answered. "I only lived here for twenty-five years. I've been gone for a thousand."

And yet, those twenty-five loomed very large in his memory. At the time, they'd been one hundred percent of his life's experience, whereas Barnard, even at the end, had never been more than ninety percent. And hell, thinking back now it didn't *feel* like much more than half. A lot of important things had happened to him out there—shaping his character, informing his judgment—but the *trajectory* of his life had been determined here. Literally: right here on this very street, on a warm July night, with the Prince of Sol at one elbow and Ho Ng—a man Conrad would one day murder—at the other. Denver was the crucible to a lifetime of rebellion; the cannon from which he'd been fired.

"It looks smaller," he said. "It feels crowded and weedy and gone-to-seed. But that's a funny thing, because nothing has really changed. Aye, and maybe that's the problem."

"Well, good luck to yer," the man offered, grabbing and pumping Conrad's hand, then dropping it and moving on.

Ireland *should* be the next stop: a ritual visit to his parents, whom he loved and missed. They had raised him well enough; his vagabond life could hardly be blamed on anyone but himself. But this was a funny thing, too, because where Denver still felt recent to him, his life with Donald and Maybel Mursk seemed impossibly remote. And those had been the *same time*.

So he didn't feel quite ready. He needed to steep in the thin dry air of Denver awhile, before he could face the damp chill of Cork. Instead he found a seat in a nearly full restaurant, where the wellstone was working overtime to cancel out the crowd noise and leave each table in its own bubble of quiet. Eventually a human waiter appeared, and offered him a choice between ten different meals. Conrad selected the least Barnardean of these—a spicy egg sandwich with blue corn chips on the side—and settled back with a mug of bitter red tea.

The waiter just laughed when he tried to pay. "The walls know, sir. Who you are, what you can afford. Food is free, right? The door wouldn't open unless you could pay for *service*."

Ah. And service didn't come cheap. Not here, not anywhere. He asked the wall, "Excuse me, um, hello. How much money have I got?"

And the wall answered immediately, in that fast, clipped accent of Sol's machines: "Twenty-seven trillion dollars, sir."

Wow. There must have been some mean price inflation here in the Queendom, because the last time he'd been here a trillion dollars was enough to pay ten thousand workers for ten thousand years.

"That's to three significant digits, sir. Do you require greater precision?"

"Uh, no. Thanks. But how much is my lunch? A few billion?"

"No, sir. Two hundred and six dollars, sir."

"Two hundred? Dollars? But that would mean . . ." He was rich? He: an exile, a vagabond who'd rebelled against two governments? He'd had money for a while in Barnard, but he'd squandered it all on secret schemes and silly interstellar messages. And even if there was a bit left over, what value would a few Barnardean dollars have here, when Barnard itself was just a dream? He'd had a Queendom bank account as well, holding trivial sums when he'd departed, but even compound interest couldn't account for such an explosion. In an immorbid society, interest rates were very low indeed!

"I'm afraid you've made some sort of mistake," he told the wall. "My name is Conrad Ethel Mursk. I'm a refugee."

"Possibly, sir," the wall agreed. "But your bank records

are quantum entangled with the physical universe, and thus incapable of error."

He laughed. "Are they, now? I've never seen a system incapable of error. Where would I get so much money?"

"It isn't my place to know, sir, but I can find out for you."

"Um. Yeah, okay. Do that."

Why not? He was intrigued. And half a minute later, the wall answered, "Sir, the greater bulk of payments into your account have been from Mass Industries Corporation, with a minority share from World University. I also detect one deposit from the Office of Basic Assistance, in the amount of one thousand dollars."

Conrad mulled that over. Mass Industries was King Bruno's neutronium company, whose dredges gathered up the stray dust and gravel of the solar system and squeezed it into billion-ton neubles. Conrad had once helped to hijack one of their ships, but that was the closest he'd ever come to a business relationship with them. And his connections with World University were even more tenuous than that.

"That doesn't make sense," he said.

"I wouldn't know, sir. I'm just a wall. Two messages have just arrived for you, sir. Shall I play them?"

"I don't know. What are they?"

"The first comes from Ring Observation Platform Two. Seven hundred eighty people have complained, sir, and the number who are afraid to go there is not known. The platform—the only one of its kind—remains in service as a historical landmark. The other message is a request for a job interview on Maplesphere at your earliest convenience."

Job interview? Already? Hmm. Maybe that Appreciator thing had come through. "That's odd. What's the address?"

"Maplesphere *is* the address, sir. Just speak it to any fax machine. Would you like to hear the complete message?"

"It sounds like I just did. All right, look, I'm going to eat my breakfast, and then I'm going to visit my mom and dad. Hold my calls, if you would, until further notice."

"I will inform the network," the wall said dutifully. "And I must say, sir, it's been an honor working with you."

"Likewise," Conrad said, unsure whether to grumble or chuckle at that.

The meeting with his parents, when it finally came, was sadder and louder than he'd expected. He didn't fax straight to the house, but to the northern edge of downtown Cork, which lay in the late-afternoon shadow of another million-body stratscraper, and had pedestrian and robot crowding issues of its own. Nothing else had changed, although the landscape seemed tired somehow—the leaves a bit droopier, the grass and hedges just as orderly as ever, but in some way less emerald. Here was a place that had simply been walked on too much.

And yet, and yet, his hairs stood at attention, craning their follicles for a view. He knew this place as he'd known few others: in his bones. And Donald Mursk's roads were in excellent repair, and in his soft Queendom shoes Conrad followed them home without difficulty.

Or rather, to the place where his home should be. But the trees and hedgerows were gone, replaced with a smooth low carpet of grass, and the *house* was gone, and the tall, skinny mansion that took its place sat twenty meters farther back from the road. Egad. It had never occurred to him that his parents might have *moved* in the millennium he'd been away. But he walked up just the same, and the house said to him, "Master Conrad! You are *most* welcome, sir. Do come in, do. Your mother is leaping from her chair as we speak, and while your father is away, I'm printing a fresh copy of him to meet with you."

Indeed, Conrad was still an arm's reach from the gray front wall when a wooden door appeared in it with a crackle of wellstone, and immediately swung open to reveal Maybel Mursk, who flew out weeping and laughing. "My son! My son is here!"

Conrad's father was not far behind, and when the hugging and backslapping and handshaking were done, and they were dragging Conrad back inside, he couldn't help a wash of guilt. "Come on, now. Mom, Dad, I barely wrote to you."

"Sure," his mother said, "and we missed you all the more for that. Sit down! Sit! Can I get you a drink or something? We've found a fine beer that we're quite fond of these past two centuries. Oh, look at you. *Look* at you! Not a boy any longer but a fine, proud soldier."

Conrad should have taken that in the spirit it was meant, as a pure compliment. But surely he *looked* the same as ever, a fit twenty-five, just as Donald and Maybel Mursk surely looked, to their own eyes, too young to be the parents of a grown adult. Much less a thousand-year-old. They'd been born into a morbid world, expecting to live a childless life and die before the century mark, poor and ignorant. Conrad, like immorbity itself, had seemed a constant source of amazement for them. "Look," they would say, "we have a boy who rides a bike! Look, he's a space pirate now! Look, he's a thousand years old and returning from the stars!" Conrad's only "soldier" time had been as a security thug in the Royal Barnardean Navy, pushing around the miners and 'finers and wranglers of interplanetary space. It was a period in his life he'd just as soon forget, and even the thought of it had the power to bring out what venom he possessed.

To his shame he blurted, "That's a bit presumptuous, Mom. You knew me for two decades out of what, a hundred and twenty?"

And of course his mother started crying at that, and his father said, "Oh, now, what do you go and say a thing like that for? Breaking your poor mother's heart. Have you had any children yourself? Well, then, I don't expect you know too much about it. You pour your *soul* into a child, lad. How could you not? And it doesn't pour back. It wanders off. It gets surly and insults its mother. Now come on, you, tip a glass with us and we'll speak no more about it. You owe us the tale of your many adventures, and don't think you'll escape from here without it. I don't care *how* old you are; in this house you'll listen to the pair that gave you life."

And then Donald Mursk started crying as well.

in which a self-deceit is exposed

When the Mursk boy finally showed up, Bruno was elbow-deep in wormholes. Not literally, of course—he'd lost more than one arm that way already—but in the figurative sense; he'd scratched self-solving calculations on nearly every flat surface in his study, and was no closer to a meaningful answer than he had been twelve hours ago. Bah. He *hated* ceding his concentration to outside disruptions. If he didn't, he'd be at home right now, basking in the company of his dear wife! But he was old and wise enough to recognize an empty rut, and when Mursk announced himself with a toppled chair and a clatter of spilled sketchplates, Bruno's irritation was leavened with relief. It was time for a break, yes.

"Hello?" Mursk called out, from the cottage's small atrium.

"Hello," answered the voice of Hugo the Robot.

"Excuse me," said Mursk. "Is this Maplesphere?"

"I don't know," Hugo answered flatly. And why should he? He wasn't part of the systems here, nor a guest, nor precisely a resident. If he was anything at all, he was a dim-witted friend or a particularly intelligent and loyal pet.

But the answer did seem to throw Mursk for a moment.

"This is Maplesphere," Bruno called back, then allowed his chair to raise and flatten and dump him on his feet. "Door," he said to the scribbles on his study wall. A rectangular seam appeared and, almost too quick to see, filled in with knotted oak shod and hinged in black iron. The door creaked open, revealing a vaguely disheveled young man, framed in a ray of sunlight.

Today's fax filters could clean and straighten and press the clothing of a body in transit, could scrub the toxins from every corner and give the DNA a thorough proofread. A glow for the cheeks, a twinkle for the eye . . . They could even compensate, to some extent, for lack of sleep, and restore the mental and physical equilibrium that a night on the town had depleted. But Bruno was the son of a restaurateur, and had been a shameless drunk for three decades of his early childhood. He'd given that up even before the people of Sol had made him their king, but one never really lost the eye for it.

To the very slight extent that Queendom technology permitted, Conrad Mursk was hung over.

"Welcome," Bruno said with mild amusement. "I see you've met Hugo."

"Good God," Mursk replied blearily, looking Bruno up and down. He was amazed, yes, to find himself face-to-face with the King of Sol. This was a common reaction among the commoners, and elicited no surprise in Bruno himself. He barely noticed such things anymore, although truthfully, when one was summoned to Maplesphere one ought to expect an encounter with its sole inhabitant.

"I thought this . . ." Mursk stammered. "I was asked . . ." He glanced out the window, at the round, shady curve of the planette: a miniature world domed over with the blue haze of a miniature sky. Something in the view seemed to stabilize him. "What is this, about a fifteen-thousand-neuble core? Three-hundred-meter lithosphere? Those sugar maples run their roots deep. You must have the lining layer about four meters down from the surface."

"Four and a half," Bruno agreed. He stepped out into the daylight and then quickly thought better of it. However perfect his eyes might be, strong light still made them ache when he'd been working too long. He retreated to the study instead, motioning for Mursk to follow. "Clear off a chair and sit, if you like."

Mursk's eyes ran along the floorboards, taking in the zero-elevation curve where floor met wall. On a planette this small, a surface could be either "level" like Bruno's floor—hugging the shape of the ground—or "flat," pleasing the eye but spilling and rolling every loose object into its center. Mursk opened his mouth as if to comment, but then noticed the scrawled equations and came up short again.

"Wormhole tensors," Bruno said apologetically. "An arcanum even by mathematical standards. I've been tempted, these past three centuries, to recast general relativity in matrix notation, just to make sense of the damned arithmetic."

Having no response to that, Mursk shrugged blankly and cleared off a seat. "This is a job interview?"

"It is," Bruno confirmed. And though a part of him squirmed with impatience, with the burning need to get back to his equations, he had other curiosities which burned even brighter. He'd known this lad who'd known his son, and he would wade through any pleasantries necessary to get the full data dump. *What had Bascal really done out there in the colonies?* And yes, in truth Bruno was hungry for company as well. He could always put a copy of himself back to work if necessary. "But there's no hurry. I thought we could chitchat, you and I."

"You want to know about Bascal," Mursk said, with no particular emphasis.

"I want to know about everything."

"He was a good king," Mursk lamented, examining his fingernails as if the dust of Sorrow might still somehow be lodged there. "He really was, for hundreds of years. A builder, a visionary. He foresaw the economic collapse, long before anyone else did. He took steps to avert it, then to mitigate it, then to ride it out. But apparently it was bigger than he was."

"You were friends," Bruno prodded.

"The best. No matter where I went or what I did, I always ended up in his dining room. It's hard for me to think that won't happen anymore."

"But you and he had your differences, yes?"

"Philosophical," Mursk said with a dismissive wave. "We all have differences. Your son was a brother to me, and we squabbled like brothers."

Bruno shifted in his chair, feeling it adjust beneath his weight. Was this refugee telling the full truth? Was he telling King Bruno what he thought King Bruno wanted to hear? With a sudden stab of impatience, he stood up again. "Come with me, lad. We'll have a walk around the planette."

"I've seen planettes before," Mursk said, though he stood and followed Bruno out.

Maplesphere was a large world as such things went, and Bruno used little of its space except as, well, space. On the far side, the obligatory lake was small, crowded by trees. Bruno's maple forest covered half the remaining land area, blocking the view of the too-close horizon, making the pocket world seem that much bigger. The trees also damped reverberation, so that the daylight squawking of a bluejay would not disturb the nighttime slumber of a squirrel on the world's other side, which after all was only a kilometer's walk away. Even the miniature "sun"—a fusion-powered sila'a or pocket star—was only forty kilometers distant.

"A laser-cooled tropopausal barocline," Bruno said, pointing up at the cloud-strewn sky, "allows this world to retain a nitrox atmosphere, without heavy nobles cluttering up the gas balance. The weather itself serves as a backup system, cooling the upper atmosphere so its molecules have a harder time escaping into space. Moist air rises, radiates its heat to the vacuum, and then falls as rain. Maplesphere is the rainiest planette ever created, and thus the most meteorologically stable."

"Interesting," Mursk said, with apparent sincerity.

"Alas, 'most stable' does not mean 'actually stable.' Day by day, year by year, the planette loses gas to the wilds of space. Without replenishment, I'd have a pure vacuum at ground level within two hundred years. If the power failed, I'd have it much sooner than that. And as the colonies have shown us, sooner or later the power always fails. If civilization is to ride out its gloomier moments, we'll need a larger class of planette—one that can hold its atmosphere indefinitely."

"Is this place serviced by tankers, then?" Mursk asked.

"Rarely. I've designed a tertiary system which is capable of bleeding mass from the neubles at the planette's core."

"Hmm. Clever." They passed from the cottage's grassy meadow into the green gloom of the forest itself.

"Lad, I want you to level with me. No sweeteners, no half-truths. You fled the Barnard colony with guns blazing, in the midst of what proved to be a total collapse. What happened?"

"A disagreement."

"With Bascal?"

"Aye, with Bascal. Who else? He was in charge, Sire. Of everything." Now Mursk was angry.

"Gently," Bruno said, fearing he might not get an answer at all if he pressed too hard, or in the wrong way. "It's all in the past, and I'll not prosecute misdeeds which took place outside my dear wife's jurisdiction. You understand? The chips have fallen; the cards are on the table, and I call. I just want to know."

Behind them, the sun set through the branches and canopy of the forest. On the world's other side—currently its night side—it was the crickets, not the birds, that chirped. Such was life on a planette: you could walk to any time of day you liked.

"People were dying," Mursk said. His tone begged no forgiveness, offered no apology. "Your son's plans were rational, but they weren't humane."

"And yours were," Bruno said.

"Aye. But not rational. And not loyal. Your son put his faith in me, and I betrayed him."

Bruno could hear the pain in Mursk's voice, and he supposed it was all true; this man did love Bascal Edward de Towaji Lutui. As a friend, as a brother. As a traitor—squirming under the bootheel of oppression—loves his country and his people. Bascal had always been, in his father's sad opinion, more a user than a developer.

"Sometimes opposition *is* loyalty," he offered, though it must be cold comfort indeed.

"Maybe. You should know, Sire, that there's a partial copy of Bascal in *Newhope*'s comm archives. Not a whole person by any means, but a valid memory nonetheless. I promised him that when we got here, I'd transmit it back to Barnard."

"Promised him? Even after he tried to erase you from the colonial sky? My goodness. Lad, the worst evil is the kind we feel fondly toward. I understand your reluctance to condemn him, truly. But you must be honest with yourself, and with me. Do you know who *my* best friend was?"

"Marlon Sykes," Mursk answered, for every schoolchild knew this.

"Correct," Bruno said. "And as you say, we fought as only brothers of the spirit can fight. With absolute conviction, with love and honor and hatred. To the death." And even after all these centuries, the wound still felt fresh, still brought an angry mist to Bruno's eyes. Rational and inhumane, indeed! Marlon had been a brilliant creator as well as a villain, and if the two traits could have been separated somehow, then perhaps Bruno might not have pulled that switch, and sent his friend packing in a *cage de fin*, on a one-way journey to the end of time. But the *damage* that hidden monster had caused—the sheer scale of it—boggled even Bruno's imagination. Some offenses simply overflowed the dams and levees of any possible compassion.

"That must be quite a load for you to carry, Sire," Mursk said to him, as starlight broke through the trees.

"Quite," Bruno agreed. And they finished the walk in silence.

"I don't know anything about wormholes," Mursk admitted. "You're making them? Here?"

Seated once more in his comfortable study, Bruno spread his hands. "Trying to, yes."

Sensing an appropriate moment, Hugo appeared with a pipe and lighter, which Bruno accepted gratefully.

"Thanks, old thing."

"You're entirely welcome," Hugo answered, sounding

truly pleased with himself, albeit that stale, arithmetic sort of pleasure to which emancipated robots were given. "May I walk around the yard a bit?"

"You're supposed to do as you please, my friend."

"It pleases me to serve," Hugo said, and wandered off.

With the ease of much practice, Bruno ignited the home-grown, home-cured weeds in the pipe's ceramic bowl, and drew a puff of their smoke into his mouth. The natural drugs involved, passing through the tissues of his cheeks and into his bloodstream, were mild and crude and beside the point. It was the anachronism of the act itself that Bruno savored; the loops and whorls of rising smoke connected him to Einstein, to Edison, to all the great thinkers of the Mortal Age, of whom he was the last. Connecting him, indeed, to the fireside musings of primal humanity itself.

"What are they for?" Mursk asked. "You intend these wormholes as a substitute for fax gates?"

"Ideally, yes. There may yet be time to prop up these failing colonies, if I can just—"

"Make it work?"

Bruno laughed around the stem of his pipe. "Yes, make it work. Clever lad. Alas, I fear I'm not up to the task. These old chalkboards are getting white."

"Eh?"

"Chalkboards. Blackboards. Ah, what do you children know?" The cloud around him thickened with his huffing, and he waved it away. "In the tradition-heavy wilds of Catalonia, where I cut my first set of teeth, the last vestiges of the stone age lingered very nearly until the rise of the Queendom. A chalkboard was a slab of hard, dark slate onto which you would scribble with little cylinders of soft, white chalk. Really! We had one in every classroom, every kitchen. You'd erase the board with a rag, you see, and write in a new batch of lessons or chores or ingredients. But sometimes you'd misplace the rag, and you'd have to scribble around the margins of what you'd already written. If you let this go on long enough, eventually the board would get so white with scribbles that you couldn't read it anymore. And so we learned: too much knowledge is as bad as none at all. We forget how to forget. But this lesson itself seems to have fallen from our collective memory. Our civilization grows too brilliant to brush its own teeth.

"At any rate, yes, I'm battering my head against this problem, and what progress I've made has been more tantalizing than helpful." Bruno didn't generally present his works-in-progress—too embarrassing—but in a sudden fit of hospitality he added, "I can show you, if you like."

"Sure," Mursk said, shrugging. "It sounds kind of fundamental to our future."

This irritated Bruno. The lad meant well enough, surely, but a king could grow very tired of his people's unreasonable expectations. "Only if luck is on our side, lad. The universe is under no obligation to please our petty whims, and I have failed many times to throw a harness round its neck."

The trick with a pipe was not to puff on it too much, lest its smoke turn sharp and acrid—or too little, lest it fade to the dull flavor of ashes. But Hugo was back again, this time with Bruno's ashtray, which he whisked onto the desk in front of him before dancing back out of the study again with too-quick, too-perfect fluidity.

"Nice robot," Mursk said, with less than total conviction.

"He saved my life once, in battle. He's quite brave." Bruno set the pipe down in the ashtray and began tapping at his desktop controls. "Now, the first trick in wormhole dynamics is to develop your standing gravity wave very, very rapidly. It's not at all like collapsing a neuble into a black hole. Second, you've got to dump in twice as much power as theory predicts you ought to. I'm still figuring that one out."

While he spoke, the writing vanished from every surface, zipping into archive space. Glittering green-black bullseyes took their place on two opposite walls. The lights dimmed, and though it wasn't apparent from here in the windowless study, the sun itself dimmed as well, focusing fully eighty percent of its output in a single strand of violet laser. Bruno's eastern photovoltaic array, hidden away in a forest glade, took the beam head-on and fed its power directly into the gravity lasers. The air in the study began to shudder, then to twirl itself into fist-sized eddies that popped and lashed their way around the room.

"The third trick," Bruno said, raising his voice above the hiss, "is to ram a cylindrical mass through the wormhole throat, to stabilize the two openings." Leaning, he dragged a half-meter iron bar out from under his desk and held it up for Conrad Mursk to see.

"Is this experiment safe?" Mursk wanted to know. The air devils were whipping at his hair, driving him back, blinking and puffing, against the door frame.

"Not particularly," Bruno called back, "but your image is archived in my fax buffer."

And then the time for talk was past, for a pair of rippling distortions appeared like lenses in the air between the two men. The spherical wormhole mouths: each displaying a funhouse-mirror view of the photons striking the other. Their instability was apparent even to the naked eye; they wandered and quivered, orbiting one another in a slow spiral that would, within seconds, bring them swirling together in a flash of canceling energy.

Bruno's initial tests had taken place in vacuum, ten kilometers from Maplesphere and with the trillion-ton mass of the planette between himself and the relativistic action. It was only by accident—literally—that he'd discovered the radiation of a wormhole's collapse was non-lethal. Or not immediately lethal, anyway; the flux of photons and virtual particles would surely wreak lasting havoc on a body with no access to fax repair.

"Watch!" he instructed, hefting the bar and jabbing it at one of the holes.

There was no preferred direction of travel between the two wormhole mouths; each point on one sphere—or vector through it—corresponded with a point or vector on the other. Bruno's aim wasn't bad, but even a glancing blow would have done the trick. The bar slid silently and effortlessly into the nearer sphere, its far end emerging just as cleanly from the other. The two halves of the bar were pointing in wildly different directions, but within moments the two mouths were sliding and rotating into the minimum-energy configuration, wherein the bar was straight. They missed on the first swooping pass, and again on the second, but the oscillations tightened until suddenly the vectors locked.

The spherical distortions vanished. The whirling air devils quieted. The bullseyes faded from Bruno's walls, and his equations returned, and the lights came back up, and the sun resumed shining, and somewhere in the distance a bird chirped uncertainly.

"Jesus," Conrad Mursk said.

"Indeed," Bruno could only agree. He held up the bar for Mursk's inspection. The two ends were perfectly intact, not damaged in any way, but the distance between them was more than twice what it had been. And the center of the bar . . .

The center of the bar wasn't there at all. Or rather, the center existed in two places. The bar existed in two halves, with half a meter of empty space in between.

Bruno waved the thing around, demonstrating to a goggle-eyed Mursk that the metal was in fact contiguous; each end moved with the other, just as though it were all one piece. Because it *was* one piece. It just had a gap in the middle, a kind of elongated four-dimensional wrinkle.

"The state of the art," Bruno said, "in mass-stabilized wormholes."

A string of quite astonishing curse words tumbled from Mursk's gaping mouth, and Bruno had to remind himself that the lad was, among other things, a sailor.

"Forgive me, Sire," Mursk added finally. "I've just . . . I've never seen anything like that before."

"Nor I," Bruno said, "until a few weeks ago." He tossed the bar behind him, clanking onto the heap with the dozen or so others he'd created thus far. "And it's certainly not what I had in mind. We need *tunnels*, from one point in space to another."

Mursk thought that one over. "Can you drill through the center of the bar? Make a hollow tube of it?"

"One would think so," Bruno told him. He tugged at his beard, mulling and fretting over it. "But every attempt thus far has pinched off the wormhole, cutting the bar in half. Nor have I been able to prop the throat open with wellstone, or wood, or any other material. There's something about the crystal structure of a solid metal, or the free electrons roaming through it, that allows the wormhole throat to stabilize. Something *mysterious*, you see? With the unified field equations in hand, it should be possible to derive any result, to describe any physically demonstrated system. But the math can be unimaginably complex, and it's not always clear how to express a physical system in those terms. I've tried to approximate this one by various methods, but so far nothing has come close to describing what we see here."

"And you think *I* can help?" Mursk asked, sounding surprised and perhaps even vaguely offended.

The question surprised Bruno as well. "With this? I think perhaps you could," he said carefully, not wanting to drive off this man whose services he hoped to secure, "with your background in gravitic engineering."

"My what?"

Mursk seemed genuinely puzzled. Had there been some mistake? Bother it, Bruno didn't need yet another digression! But just the same, he pulled up a window on the surface of his desk, while the desk tilted itself toward him to improve the reading angle.

"Have I erred in some way? Your name came up at the very top of my search. Have I perhaps summoned the wrong Conrad Mursk? No, here it is: according to your employment profile, you invented the 'pinpoint drip' style of matter condenser."

"The what?" Mursk frowned for a moment, and then seemed to have a dull epiphany of some sort. "Oh, that. Squeezing neutronium with a small black hole, right?"

"And pumping it," Bruno agreed, "and storing it in a metastable reservoir until there's enough to neubleize. It's quite a clever invention, which has streamlined our mass dredging operations considerably. Do you have any idea how much money you've saved me over the years?"

"Not I," Mursk said, with a sudden laugh. "That machine was invented by Money Izolo, in the wake of an industrial accident on Element Pit. I had nothing to do with it."

Nothing, eh? Bruno prodded harder. "I examined the patent document myself, lad. There was an Izolo listed as coinventor, but your name appeared first. You also built a . . . Gravittoir, was it? A system for pulling heavy payloads off a planetary surface?"

If anything, that suggestion made Mursk uneasier

than the first one had. He cringed and fidgeted. "I didn't build it myself, Sire. I mean, I headed the team..."

And here, seeing what was going on, Bruno summoned his most regal glare and turned it full-force upon Conrad Mursk. "False modesty," he said, "is a form of lying, and I have very little patience with it. I'm going to ask you some questions, and I require you to answer simply and truthfully. And if I have reason to doubt your answers, lad, I will copy your brain and dissect it alive until I find what I'm looking for. Is that clear?"

In point of fact, Bruno would do no such thing, and indeed he wasn't even sure it was possible. But he saw that Mursk really *had* lived in a tyranny, for he believed it at once, and looked afraid. And Mursk really had rebelled against that tyranny, too, for on the heels of his fright he swelled with such anger that the cottage summoned a Palace Guard to glide up silently behind him. Just in case.

"Very clear, Sire," Mursk said tightly.

Bother it. Why had the people of Sol made an inventor their king, who could scarcely maintain his end of a civil conversation? Bruno adored the people of Sol, and he understood exactly why they adored his wife, their first and only queen. But he had never understood their love for *him*, and feared at times that it was nothing but spillover. If Tamra loved him then so must they, by extension if not by inclination. But Conrad Mursk had been away for so very long.

Bruno had learned, through long bitter practice, never to retract or apologize for anything he said. A king simply wasn't permitted this courtesy. But he did soften his stance, adding, "The labors of coercion are never as useful as the labors of willing gift. There are still assaults in the Queendom, every now and again, and I often suspect their perpetrators have simply never felt the touch of kindness. For if they had, then the fumbling of a cornered victim could hardly measure up. Here's what criminals fail to understand: in a civilized world there is nothing left to steal. There are no goods or commodities they can carry away with them, nor services of value they can commandeer. Even a *beggar* has better odds than a thief."

"Meaning what?" Mursk demanded, relaxing only slightly.

Bruno spread his hands. "I want your help. Not with wormhole dynamics, if that's what you're thinking, but with a project whose distractions threaten my delicate concentration. I need to be free to retreat here to Maplesphere at any time, so I dare not manage this project myself. And in this queendom of third-order specialists, I dare not turn it over to an unqualified leader, for my terraformers know nothing of gravity. My graviteers know nothing of DNA. My architects and planette builders are craftsmen, unacquainted with the needs of a large project, and my megaproject managers know nothing about anything. I need generalists, of a sort which Sol has simply stopped producing. On Sorrow you built the Orbital Tower, yes?"

Bruno could see Mursk contemplating some hedge around the correct answer, but in the end all he said was, "Yes. It's one of the few things in my life I'm unequivocally proud of."

"Aha. And you discovered the wellstone substance known as Mursk Metal?"

"Um. Yeah."

"Well, then, you may be interested to know it's a key component of today's gravity lasers. You've also personally operated a variety of construction equipment, from bulldozers and cranes to neutronium barges and asteroid bores. True?"

Reluctantly: "True."

"And you've worked as both an ecological engineer and a climatologist?"

"Well, a wildlife surveyor and a weather station monitor."

"All right, fair enough. But on a world in the midst of terraforming operations. Indeed, you've lived most of your life in extreme environments. Spaceships, polar wells, desolate alien landscapes. Would you agree?"

"I . . . suppose."

"And you've been the captain of a ship."

Mursk balked at that one. "What? Oh, an *ocean* ship. Yes. But only for sixteen years."

Bruno tapped a thumb on his desk, feeling himself grow restless again, impatient with this young man's aggressive modesty. He needed yeses, not maybes, if they were to finish this quickly. But he pressed onward, reading his way down the profile. Fortunately the thing had been assembled by hypercomputers delving back into Queendom records and archived Barnardean transmissions, for if Mursk himself had written it, it would be all of ten words long. "Good. Now, you were present at the *Sealillia* riot a few days ago. Ordinarily I wouldn't hold that against you, but given your history . . ."

"We were bystanders," Mursk said, with convincing irritation. "If those kids had listened to us, it would have gone very differently. Peaceful protest, maybe. I don't know."

"So you tried to organize them? Pacify them for their own good?"

Defiantly: "Sure."

"That's good," Bruno said, looking up briefly to meet the boy's gaze. "Most people wouldn't. Now, if I understand your records correctly, you were briefly in charge of the entire planet of Sorrow?"

"Um. Well, *very* briefly, yes. Before the terraforming had started, before we'd done much of anything. There were only a few hundred people orbiting it at the time, and no one on the surface."

"There will be a few thousand on this project," Bruno said to him. "Perhaps ten times as many as you've previously managed. Would this present a problem for you?" Then he thought better of that phrasing, and amended, "Do you have some intellectual or emotional defect which would prevent you from attempting it?"

"Uh, well, I don't think so. I mean, I could certainly try."

"Then you're hired," Bruno said.

And suddenly Mursk was backpedaling, taking back some control over the interview. "Hold on, now, I haven't agreed to anything. You haven't *told* me anything. Location, duration...I suppose pay rates would be good to know. I'm trying to imagine a job for which my name comes up first, and I'm sorry, but I'm blanking. What exactly is this project?"

And here Bruno smiled, because he knew he had his man. "It's a terraforming, lad. We're going to crush the moon."

chapter ten

in which worlds are critiqued

In a crazy-ambitious kind of way, Conrad could see it made sense: the moon was too small and light to retain an atmosphere of its own. But the moon's gravitational attraction—like that of any object—dropped off with the square of the distance from its center, so that compressing the surface down to forty percent of its current elevation would sextuple gravity's pull there. Yielding an Earth-normal gravity of 1.00 gee, and ensuring that the atmosphere was truly stable, even over geological spans of time. Talk about terraforming!

Fortunately Luna did not lack for oxygen, and as for the light metals which life required, why, Luna's crust was richer than any of the colony worlds—richer even than Earth itself. For organic molecules to exist, there would of course need to be a huge importation of hydrogen and nitrogen and carbon. But once this was done it would be possible to construct a soil so deep and so fertile that the new world—with a surface area equal to that of China or Australia—could easily support a billion people even at a colonial-or-worse level of technology.

Moreover, thanks to conservation of angular momentum, reducing the moon's diameter would also speed up its rotation, so that its "day" would shorten from 29.5 Earth days to a more hospitable 4.92 days. Indeed, Conrad immediately suggested crushing just a wee bit less, so that the day would work out to exactly 5.00 Earth days, or 120 hours. He'd had his fill of goofy clocks and calendars on Sorrow, and the decrease in surface gravity that would result—a mere 0.02 gee, according to Bruno's office wall—would inconvenience no one.

"An excellent suggestion," the king said, with approval and relief in his voice. "I see we're in good hands. In any case, the way is paved for such an endeavor by the engineering of large planettes, by the terraforming of Mars and Venus, and of Sorrow and Gammon and Pup. And in truth a squozen moon is more suitable than those colony worlds in a variety of ways. Locked tight against their red-dwarf stars, those three are metal-poor and radiation-rich, and their days are very long. We can do better by design than by astronomical accident. But I forget myself. I don't have to tell *you* this, who have seen it all firsthand."

He was leading Conrad toward the fax gate, and at first Conrad assumed he was being dismissed. Bruno had what he wanted—a leader for this bizarre project—and now he was getting back to his own work. But apparently, the sales pitch wasn't over quite yet, for the king murmured something to the fax gate and stepped right through it alongside him.

They came out on a warm, windswept mountaintop under a sprawling canopy of stars. This was some kind of scenic overlook at a mountain's summit: a flat, circular depression lined with a wellstone emulation of the surrounding rock. A winding stone staircase led downward, to a cluster of wellglass buildings ringing the mountain farther down. There were no other peaks in view, and a few hundred meters below the buildings was a layer of cloud that hid the ground, making it impossible to tell how high this mountain was.

Not very, Conrad thought at first, from the dry thickness of the air and the dim, twinkly look of the stars. Must be close to sea level, or even . . . But no, the air was *too* thick, and didn't smell right, and it occurred to him suddenly that this was *Venus*, not Earth.

Nor was that his only surprise. The fax had produced two Palace Guards along with the bodies of Bruno and Conrad—one in front of them and the other appearing behind as they stepped away from the print plate—and when Conrad turned his head and saw them he nearly yelped out loud. He shouldn't be surprised to find the king traveling in the company of his royal bodyguards, but there'd been Palace Guards in the Barnard colony as well, and in the events leading up to the Children's Revolt, and they had certain . . . unsavory associations for Conrad. That hulking silhouette was a symbol of danger, of impending unavoidable pain.

A curse rose unbidden to his lips, and though he managed to keep it silent, his heart rate jumped. Damn!

"Venus," Bruno said, spreading his arms as if he owned the place. Which he did, Conrad seemed to recall, as majority shareholder or some such. "The day is long here as well—fully twenty-eight hundred hours from dawn to dawn—and this world is also a geological nightmare which periodically liquefies broad swaths of its own crust. There is no way to curb its immense volcanic activity, its immense and continual outpouring of carbon dioxide and sulfuric acid. Thus, terraforming has become an unending process, which will never make anything but the highest mountaintops habitable to humans unless we engineer a special Venusian strain."

That'll be the day, Conrad thought, for the Queendom, unlike the colonies, expressly forbade biomods until they'd been thoroughly studied and vetted, their full consequence plumbed. "Tinkering produces monsters," the Queen had said on more than one occasion, "who cannot grasp the humanity they've lost. Can the fall of the colonies be completely unrelated to this truth? If we're to be free and happy, it's necessary that we avoid such self-destruction." Rather an extreme position, Conrad thought, but there you had it.

"Anyway," Bruno said, "the sun is damnably hot here during the long days. As a result, people venture outdoors mainly at night, if then. And does this not undermine the very purpose of terraforming? Immorbidity does not imply omnipotence, alas. We were ambitious in ever thinking this place could be tamed by such as we."

"Maybe Venus could be crushed," Conrad suggested. "That would speed up its rotation. You'd have to remove a lot of mass to keep the gravity tolerable, but you could make a moon with it. Hell, you could get two viable planets out of it, and if you set up the eclipses properly they'd shelter each other from the noonday sun."

"Ho!" Bruno chortled dryly. "What have I pulled from this hat of mine? An architect of worlds, indeed! Your ambition does you credit, lad, but there isn't money enough in all the universe for a scheme as mad as that. If you can imagine such a thing, I'm actually running short of funds. I, yes! I've built thirteen starships out of my own pocket, and each of them cost as much as the entire Nescog and provided not one penny in returns. Some corners of society may be richer for the investment, but I myself am not.

"My coffers have slowly recovered from the shock, but your squozen moon will set me back a thousand years. Think of the energies we must deploy, the masses we'll shift! And here you speak to me of lifting half the weight of a planet, against the planet's own gravity, and then crushing it all! That's twenty times the project you have before you, lad, and the project before you is the largest since Marlon's Ring Collapsiter."

He paused a moment, though, tugging his beard and pinching his chin, and finally said, "Still, the suggestion has merit. Someday, perhaps. Meanwhile I have more to show you, for Venus has not been our only disappointment."

The fax took them next to a low hilltop overlooking a village in the middle of a rusty plain, with steep red cliffs rising up on either side, just beyond the horizon.

"Savage Mars," Bruno said, "turns out to have none of Venus' rages and sorrows, and in truth human beings have discovered no gentler world anywhere, except the Earth. He needed a bit of air, a bit of warmth to get him going again, but Mars never forgot how to live. Thriving, though, has always eluded him, for he's a scarred old soldier whose energies are long spent. The warmth of Sol touches this place with a quarter of its Earthly intensity, and the core of the planet is dead and cold and solid. Nor is there enough heavy hydrogen in the poles for economical fusion. So deutrelium is imported, and solar power stations throughout the Queendom beam their energies here. Without this input, this net inward flux of foreign energy, the cities of Mars would grind to a chilly halt. It's a fine world for poets and dilettantes, gardeners and gamers, but *industry* must look elsewhere for its shelter and comfort."

The king eyed Conrad curiously. "Unless you've, er, got some suggestions for this place as well?"

Conrad shrugged. He wasn't exactly a font of spontaneous genius. He said to the king, "There's always tidal heating, right? On Sorrow it was the only thing keeping the core molten. If Mars had a large, close moon . . . Well, wait a minute. Imagine a *water* moon, larger than the planet itself, with no solid surface or center. It doesn't weigh as much as rock, but it could still exert a strong tidal force. And it would act as an enormous lens, gathering light from the sun and heating up. It would radiate in the infrared, and Mars' gravity would pull it into a teardrop shape that should direct more than half the emissions toward the planet. Right?"

"Hmm," Bruno said, thinking about that. "Possibly. But would it be stable over geologic time? I suppose it might!"

"Or we could move the planet," Conrad added lamely. "Closer to the sun."

The king laughed at that. "I see thinking small is not among your faults. Long ago, I'd thought to give the squozen moon project to Bascal, but in truth he was never suited. He was a political creature, and started a revolution instead."

So did I, Conrad answered silently. For he was just as guilty as Bascal, or nearly as guilty, in getting the Children's Revolt moving.

"And he clawed his way to the stars," Bruno mused, staring down at the village and the red desert plains beyond it, "through *my* pocketbook. And there he met his end."

At that poignant sentiment, Conrad asked, "Sire, what will you do with the image of Bascal? The one in *Newhope*'s memory?"

"I don't know," the king answered. "If my son is dead then this thing, this recorded entity, must be more a caricature than a copy. We could overlay it on his childhood fax archives and see what happened, but . . ."

"But tinkering produces monsters?"

"Indeed. And so does hardship, of which you had plenty out there in the dying colonies. I'm sick with guilt about that, lad, and I'm not eager to compound my past errors. Some people are more inclined to monsterdom than others. But I do mourn for the little boy, the Poet Prince who used to putter around Tongatapu on that noisy little scooter of his. What a happy lad, what a joy to behold! Already containing within him the sprouts of wickedness, or poor judgment. Even before the time of *Newhope*'s departure, he'd become a stranger to us. A dangerous one."

"You're going to let him die? Your own son?" Conrad couldn't help feeling a little bit horrified, after he'd gone to the trouble of preserving that damned message. If it was the *only* record of Bascal's adult life . . . God, it must be a wrenching decision. If it were up to Conrad, what would he do?

"We don't know his fate," the king said sadly. "We only suspect it. And this so-called cousin of his, this Edward Bascal Faxborn, is an alternate expression of the boy I raised. 'King Eddie of Wolf' they call him, in tones of true friendship. I've never met the man outside a self-aware transmission, but is he not also my son? A better version? A different set of choices?"

The king moped for a few seconds, the Martian breeze twisting in his long hair. "Someday, perhaps, when we've universe enough to contain him, we can dare to unleash that spirit again. But for now I suspect we're better off leaving him where he is. If it's a kind of murder to postpone his resurrection, I'll invite you to join in the conspiracy. Will you do me the favor, Architect, of forgetting this conversation? I don't want his mother finding out."

Conrad's next stop was Luna itself—specifically the small domed city of Copernicus, nearly dead-center on Nearside, which was to be the site of his temporary headquarters, until by his command the ground started shaking and cracking and falling in on itself and the surface became uninhabitable.

"How exactly do we accomplish this?" he'd asked the king, for there were already detailed cross-sectional blueprints of the squozen moon, showing exactly where the surface must lie, and how the dense subsurface must be layered in order to maximize the world's utility to its future inhabitants. Toxic metals were to be buried deep—the moon had an excess of nickel and arsenic—and useful ones were to wrap the planette like foil, in layers easily accessible from surface mines. Deeper, a third of the way down to the core, there'd be a layer of di-clad neutronium supported by pillars of monocrystalline diamond.

"How?" the king asked, as though the question had never occurred to him. "I should think *you* would tell *me*."

Fortunately, there didn't seem to be any huge hurry; Conrad was given two hundred years to complete the task, and a budget of trillions to get it started. Still, Bruno's tour around the solar system, ending back in the remoteness of Maplesphere far out in the Kuiper Belt, had been a long one. Subjectively they were gone for just a few minutes, but the speed of light was the speed of light, and most of the Nescog was incapable of exceeding it. Invisibly, the journey had chewed up nearly a day in transit times, during which the evacuation orders had been broadcast to Lunar citizens, along with Conrad's name and face.

As a result, his materialization in the Copernicus town square was greeted by no small number of shouts and dirty looks from the hundreds of people assembled there. Ah, yes: the *people* of Luna.

The moon's gravity was too low for the planet-born and too high for the space-born. Too high also for practical low-gee manufacturing, and the place couldn't compete with Mercury for solar energy, or with the asteroids for mineral accessibility, or with *anyplace* for remoteness from the traffic lanes and comm chatter of Earth. So industry here was even scarcer than on Mars, and with no carbon or hydrogen of its own, Luna wasn't exactly a garden spot.

And yet, in Conrad's day it had ironically been one of the most expensive places to live in all the Queendom. As a result, it attracted a small population of fierce eccentrics who loved its vast lifeless spaces, its laissez-faire attitudes, its quaint little crater-domed towns. People who could afford to pay! Lunatics, yes, who looked down on the crowded Earth with thumbed noses. Oh, how *happy* they would be at the news of their eviction!

"Developer," one woman called out to Conrad as he exited the fax. On her lips, the word was definitely a curse. "Trillionaire! Dirty robber baron," said someone else.

Looking around, Conrad decided that the Lunar domes, too, held a lot more people than they used to. The only uncrowded place he'd yet seen was Maplesphere itself—hardly representative of society as a whole.

"What's wrong with the moon we have now?" demanded a red-haired man in reedy tones. And with a shock, Conrad realized he was looking at humanity's greatest playwright, Wenders Rodenbeck, who had penned such classics as *Uncle Lisa's Neutron* and *Past Pie Season*. Under other circumstances, Conrad would have been pleased to shake the man's hand, to sit down with him over a mug of hot tea and chitchat about the ways of the world. But Rodenbeck—a noted opponent of terraforming—had brought an angry mob with him, and Conrad figured this might not be the best time. In a glance around the square, half a kilometer beneath the town's domed roof, he could even swear he saw the hooded, translucent figure of Death out there at the back of the crowd. When he looked again, though, the apparition was gone.

"I didn't start this project," Conrad called out to the

mob, for all the good it would do. "Your king has simply hired me to take a look at it, to alleviate the crowding problems and provide a home for billions."

That went over well. The crowd groaned and shouted and cursed.

"Listen," Conrad said. "You'll be compensated for the fair value of your property here, and as far as I'm concerned you can continue to occupy it for as long as it's safe—probably several years, while we're getting the project logistics in order."

"Go back to Barnard!" someone shouted, and Conrad answered angrily, "I wish I could, sir. How very rude. How many of *your* friends have died forever?"

Presently, a group of men in heavy but helmetless space suits pushed their way to the front of the crowd, and Conrad, fearing violence, briefly wished the Palace Guards were here. Or at least the local police, who on Luna were renowned for their courage and skill. But the leader of the men said to him, "Mr. Mursk, I'm Bell Daniel, the president of Lunacorp Construction."

"You're hired," Conrad said at once. "Your first assignment is to find me an office, away from this mob." Then, thinking about it, he added, "It might also be a good idea to start digging a hole."

"Um, okay. What sort of hole, sir? How deep?"

"All the way through," Conrad told him.

Only much later would it occur to him that he had missed his chance to see the moon—the old, the *original* moon—in the skies of Earth, before King Bruno's proclamations had begun the long, slow process of crushing it.

"Call Xmary," he told the wall of his new office, just as soon as he stepped inside. The network took a few fractions of a second to figure out whom he meant, and the light of his signal itself took a second and a half to reach the surface of Earth. But presently her face appeared, framed against clouds and sky, green grass and oceans.

"Conrad," she said, "where have you been? Three days you've been gone, and no message?"

"Sorry," he told her. "A lot has happened. It turns out I'm a trillionaire. Also I met the king, and I have a job. Oh, and my parents say hi."

Xmary nodded impatiently. "That's nice, dear. *We're* under attack."

chapter eleven

in which death comes wrapped
in cellophane

So was Conrad, as it turned out. He heard a really loud noise, like a glass battleship crashing down outside his building, and a moment later his ears popped, and his building's exterior doors and windows were closing and vanishing, locking the place down.

"I'll call you back," he said to his wife, then rushed to find Bell Daniel.

Fortunately, Daniel was caught just this side of the front door, and was sealed in rather than out. "The dome came down!" he shouted in the overloud voice of a deafened man. "Blew up and came down. I've never seen anything like it. It's the Fatalists, sir—I saw Death outside, with his arms up in the rising air and the falling wellglass. There were space suits, too, stealthed in inviz. That was *before* the dome broke."

Conrad uttered a curse that even Barnardean spacers considered obscene. Fortunately, Daniel didn't hear it, and everyone else in the building was shouting and running around, or trying to call out on the Nescog. Or fleeing toward the fax machine, yes, but already the early arrivals were turning back, fleeing elsewhere.

"The Nescog is down!" someone said.

And that was impossible. It would take a *huge* calamity to bring down the entire network—even the shock fronts of a supernova would take hours to reach the solar system's remotest corners—and the fact that these people were all still standing here put sharp upper limits on the violence of what might've happened. But you *could* cut off a planet's access to the network. Conrad had done this himself, during the Children's Revolt, and he imagined a sparsely populated world like Luna could be serviced by as little as a few hundred hardware gates. How difficult would it be to smash them all?

"Window," he said to the wall in front of him.

"Not authorized," the wall replied.

"Excuse me?"

The wall cleared its imaginary throat. "Regrettably, sir, I'm observing disaster protocol, and am required to maintain a superreflective exterior. There could be hazardous radiation outside, or bioinformatic viruses, or visual imagery which could damage you psychologically. I'm incapable of allowing any harm to come to you, sir."

"Override," Conrad told it impatiently.

"Not authorized, sir. I can be overriden only by badged emergency personnel, government officials, and members of the royal family."

"Yes?" Conrad snapped. "Really? Because I'm the chief architect of this fuffing planet, and I need to look outside."

"I have no way to confirm that, sir." The wall now sounded uneasy, and willing perhaps to hedge its bets. "Would you settle for a low-resolution cartoon, assembled from sensors on my exterior surface?"

Conrad waved a hand. "Whatever. Yes. Show me what's out there."

Without further ado, the wall produced a hollie of the

buildings outside, rendering them as hypersmooth, two-color fantasies. Broken walls were shown as stylized zig-zags, and the shards of wellglass littering the streets were little isosceles triangles of translucent white. The worst of it, though, were the piles of bodies—the people who'd been caught out in the street and either explosively decompressed or taken down by flying debris. These, the cartoon represented as bright yellow, pillowy-looking figures with oversized heads, big black eyespots, and grinning half-circle mouths. A big heap of happy dolls, indeed.

But moving among the dolls were other happy figures—these in gray—and one very tall, very thin humanoid that seemed to be put together from marshmallows and sealed in a wrapper of black cellophane. That one was the happiest of all, with a toothy grin taking up the vast majority of its polished white cranium.

"Tactical analysis," Conrad demanded of Bell Daniel, forgetting for a moment that they were both construction workers.

But the wall thought he was talking to *it*, and annotated its cartoon with little tags saying TO BE REVIVED for the dead yellow dolls, and POSSIBLE ACTIVIST over the gray smiling figures. For Death, it seemed at a loss, and marked the figure with a message saying only, INCONSISTENT READINGS.

And to his credit, Bell Daniel replied as well, saying, "Um, well, it looks like they're searching house-to-house."

And indeed, the gray dolls had a tool or weapon of some sort—shown in the cartoon as a smiling padded fish—which opened perfectly rectangular doorways in the buildings, from which little cartoon swirls would emanate. The air escaping, the people inside suffocating. And when the swirls had stopped, a platoon of the gray smiling dolls would prance inside, only to prance back out again a minute or two later to join the rest of their darling little army.

"They're probably looking for you," Daniel said to Conrad. And Conrad felt a sinking feeling, because the same thought had just occurred to him.

"On *Sealillia,* too," he said. "And probably in Cork, where my family lives."

"Are they backed up? Your family?" Daniel wanted to know.

But instead of replying, Conrad turned and ran for the fax machine, shouting, "Space suits! Battle armor! Weapons! Now!"

And while he had no official standing as yet, and the building truly didn't know him from any other Tom, Dick, or Herzog in the Queendom—nor, for that matter, from the gray fuzzy attackers outside—it must be said (a) that the building was not stupid, (b) that every society recognizes a right to self-defense, and (c) that Conrad's authority-figure routine was neither self-conscious nor marked by any physiological signs of deception or duplicity. So it is not entirely surprising that when the Fatalists broke through the building's exterior, exposing its *interior* to the harsh Lunar vacuum, they were met not by corpses but by a dozen armed men and women and the withering rain of six tripod-mounted wireguns.

It was not easy to kill a Fatalist ghoul in full battle armor, but a combination of surprise and determination can accomplish much, and Conrad emerged from the building a minute later with five of his people still alive.

"Are you all right?" he asked Bell Daniel.

"I surely am," the man replied angrily. "You will find, sir, that *my way* is like the toilet: when people *go* in it, they feel better, but when they *get* in it, they're shat on and flushed."

"You'd've made a good sailor," Conrad said to him, on the strength of that comment alone. And together they launched the counterattack.

•

"This cannot be," said the King of Sol.

Altogether, in four separate attacks, the Fatalists had killed eleven hundred instantiations of eight hundred and twenty different people. More tellingly, they had coupled the assault with antimatter attacks on two of the great, secret archives where long-term human backups were stored. The aim was clear: to catch key people *while they were dead*, and delete their archival patterns. In this they were unsuccessful, since all of the deceased persons had either living instantiations elsewhere in the Queendom, or backups stored in other facilities. But in some cases, years of precious memory were lost, irretrievably.

Damn. Bruno had *adored* the Queendom's long peace, and hated to see it shattered like this.

"In a way it's reassuring," said Cheng Shiao of the Royal Constabulary, "for with its death toll of zero, this is still the most successful Fatalist attack in Queendom history. If they pre-position their assets for these offensives—and surely they must—then we may suspect that this one has cost them dearly, and bought them nothing."

"Except a lot of fear and suffering," Conrad Mursk said, clutching at his wife's hand and glancing meaningfully at Bruno. Or rather, at the contingency copy of Bruno that had been instantiated at the start of this crisis. *The "real" me is still on Maplesphere,* Bruno thought, *blissfully undisturbed.* Or perhaps Mursk was staring at the Palace Guards, which (Bruno had already figured out) made him uneasy.

Well, he'd best get used to it. Before the dust had settled, even before the last of the shooting had stopped, Bruno had ordered these two Barnardeans hauled into protective custody at Constabulary headquarters on Tongatapu.

"If they're not safe *there*," Tamra had remarked, "then no person is safe anywhere in the universe."

She would later have cause to regret those words, but for the moment they seemed true enough, so that Mursk, in Bruno's opinion, most likely felt confined rather than endangered. A choice of two evils.

Bruno had placed himself in police custody as well, albeit at the head; he was known to involve himself from time to time in legal matters, when the mysteries were sufficiently compelling and the stakes sufficiently high. Could a scientist-king do any less?

Women ran the worlds from the household level on up to the monarchy itself, keeping track of schedules and finances and subtle balances of mood that perhaps trumped all else. He supposed they had always run things, or nearly always, even in the ages of supposed male dominance. But was their universe fully constructed? Fully invented? Were there no discoveries to be made, nor evildoers to be caught and punished? If women consolidated and civilized, surely it fell to men to build and fight, to push the boundaries within which their women ruled.

"On the contrary, my old friend," Bruno said to Captain Shiao, "our Fatalist adversaries have exactly what they want. They've decohered an uncertainty, nailing a message to the collective lintel of our civilization. And the message is death. Whether or not anyone has actually been expunged, they've succeeded in reminding us all that true death is *still possible*, even here. Thus, they have altered the context of future debate, and furthered the cause of their deathist allies in polite society."

"No doubt you're right, Sire," Shiao said with utmost diplomacy, "but I would rather face an enemy who reminded me of death, than one who was actually capable of producing it."

They all shared a laugh at that—except Shiao, who stood ramrod straight and seemed poised to leap into action at any moment. Indeed, Bruno would expect no less of him, for the universe required vigilant defenders for whom humor was a rare extravagance.

"They may still be capable," Mursk said finally, studying the gloomy activity around him. They were standing in the Constabulary's Intelligence Control Unit, twenty meters underground. All around them were workstations occupied by grave-faced men and women examining graphs or holographic images or lines of scrolling text, or else listening to focused audio streams no one else could hear. In fact, the most talented among them were doing all of these things at once.

"Possibly, sir," Shiao allowed, "but how? Wherever antimatter or fissionable materials are stored there is always neutrino leakage. Suspects will occasionally try to shield their contraband behind opaque condensates, but the shadow stands out clearly in our nasen-beam searchlights, which run continuously. This also allows us to track the absorption spectrum of explosives and toxins and fusionable materials. Neubles of course store a tremendous energy which can be released if they're broken, but fortunately they produce the sharpest echoes of all. So at least on the planets themselves, we know the locations of every gram of material capable of meaningful destruction."

"Not all, clearly," said Xmary Li Weng, in starship-captainish tones.

"All," Shiao insisted. "And if we find one that isn't licensed we drop a team on it immediately. This morning's attacks were unusual, in that they employed positronium-in-wellstone fuel bricks which the targeted facilities had actually ordered for their backup power systems. Positronium cannot be faxed, and must instead be couriered, because it's two percent antimatter by volume. The suspects are presumed to have intercepted the shipments and tampered with their programming in some way, so that the containment fields would decay at a preset time. We're investigating that, and we'll be looking more closely at all such shipments in the future.

"Meanwhile, although the attackers themselves have been wiped beyond hope of interrogation, we do know that they were produced from the buffer memory of several off-network fax machines. Since we know the locations of every single print plate within Queendom space, we will systematically scan their memories for all forms of contraband and all traces of proscribed activity. New filters will be installed in every machine, with or without their owners' permission. No one will harm another person in this way, ma'am, ever again."

"Then in some other way," she said, looking around the room as if probing for weaknesses. "Have you ever been in a battle, Captain? A real one, against powerful enemies?"

"Yes, ma'am," Shiao replied stiffly. "Several times, ma'am."

"And did the enemies' weapons *never* surprise you?"

"They always did, ma'am. I once battled with Marlon Sykes himself, and his methods were anything but conventional. I daresay I could never have beaten him alone. But then, as now, I had the *king* on my side."

Hoy, Bruno didn't like the sound of *that*. He remonstrated, "The king is fallible, Captain, and he will thank you to remember it."

"Yes, Sire," Shiao said unconvincingly.

"Eh? What's that? Do I need to request a thousand push-ups?"

"No, Sire."

Bruno didn't enjoy making trivial threats, but he knew Shiao enjoyed receiving them. Like many of the best police and soldiers, Shiao was a masochist at heart, and could not feel truly loved without at least the suggestion of pain.

And here, in truth, was the secret heart of Queendom power: treating people not as they asked to be treated, but as they truly wished, in their secret heart of hearts. Invasively, yes, for perfect rule required perfect knowledge, and in matters of state the Queendom recognized no right to silence or privacy. In unguarded moments, Bruno occasionally wondered whether this dictum applied to him as well, who had been dragged kicking and screaming to his own coronation.

To Conrad and Xmary he said, "Will you come with me, please?" He led the two Barnardeans toward a conference room, with the Palace Guards trailing warily behind. He said, "I should apologize for placing you two—*and* your friends—in harm's way, but the simple fact is that harm would find you whether you were helping the Queendom or not. As in Barnard, you symbolize much that our enemies despise. I shall not release you from the service you've promised, Mr. Mursk. And as for you, Ms. Li Weng, my wife has declared you the provisional mayor of Grace, the next floating city, until its population stabilizes and a proper election can be held."

The Barnardeans grumbled at that, though not loudly. They hadn't heard the worst of it, though. "Both of you will be attended by robotic guards until further notice.

Not Palace Guards"—he saw Mursk relax visibly at this—"but Law Enforcers, which are nearly as capable."

"We can take care of ourselves," Mursk pointed out, with only a trace of sullenness. "We *have,* for a thousand years. We didn't have robots when we escaped from Barnard."

"No," Bruno agreed, "but you needed them to survive your midcourse accident. And at any rate you work for me now, which is more dangerous than you seem to imagine."

book two

the
eridaniad

The initial excavation was much briefer than *Conrad would have imagined. Two years, to dig out the burrows and caverns that would serve as entry points for the later, more profound tunneling. His crew swelled from dozens to hundreds and more, topping out around six thousand, and whenever possible he chose them from among the twenty thousand successfully revived Barnardeans. After all, even the least of them had participated in a grand terraforming experiment, albeit also a grand failure. But he was careful to balance them with the children of Sol, who needed the work at least as desperately, and were capable of great loyalty and even greater imagination. Their pent-up need for accomplishment more than made up for their lack of grit.*

Meanwhile there were factories abuilding, for the production of certain specialized machineries. There had been neutronium barges scouring the heavens around Sol for fifteen hundred years, and Conrad's people simply tweaked and reinforced the design, so that it could roll across a tunnel floor on house-sized treads and eat through solid rock rather than flying through diffuse clouds of ice and dust.

But it was fundamentally the same machine: a blunt cylinder a thousand meters long and seven hundred wide, with a yawning open mouth that could swallow literally anything. And on the day these machines were first fired up, the moon trembled and groaned beneath its wellglass domes, and the remaining population—angry holdouts defiant to the end—were evicted by their own police or, in a handful of cases where the police themselves were holdouts, by the SWAT robots of the Royal Constabulary.

Conrad's own escort of Law Enforcers got a bit of a workout as well, when Fatalist or naturalist saboteurs succeeded in bringing a tunnel down on top of him. His body was crushed beyond repair, and he would just as soon have died and reprinted, but the Enforcers managed to save his head and toss it, fainting and throbbing with agony—into the nearest fax.

"Don't," he tried to tell them, but without breath or vocal cords he didn't make much of an impression, and the Enforcers either couldn't read lips, didn't care to, or had been programmed to ignore his dying wishes. Still, they needn't have bothered; this "rescue" saved a grand total of five hours' stored experience, of which the pain itself was the only thing he would really remember.

Conrad was later to mark this event as the end of an era—one of many he'd encountered in his long strange life. His beheading coincided with the start of a time crunch that no amount of plurality could really abate. Being in five places at once was all well and good, but the real trick was coordination, and for that he had to know everything, instantly. He did the best he could, which really wasn't bad, and he made an effort to keep up his home life as well. And with love, money, recognition, and meaningful work, it wasn't a bad way to live. Just a very, very busy one.

Soon, the months and years and decades were passing in a kind of daydream; his world never changed, or rather it changed slowly and at his own command. In the outer universe, art and fashion and politics morphed swiftly by comparison, when he bothered to notice. Which was rarely, and this is truly saying something, for his own wife had become a politician herself! He breathed her air, listened attentively to her stories, and yet remained somehow detached or aloof.

Was this what it felt like to be Bruno de Towaji? Consumed by the practical difficulties separating plan and theory from hard reality? Anchored only by the love of a good woman? For her part, Xmary seemed to understand; Conrad had never been happier, and a part of each of them suspected he never would be again. "These," she told him once, "are the good old days. Savor each one, for they'll never come again."

Not that it was a peaceful time. Far from it! More and more tunnels collapsed, some by accident and some by malevolence, but most because that was how they were supposed to work: the neutronium bores would hollow out the ground and then bring it crashing down behind them. Deaths and manglings by misadventure were a part of the monthly routine; by its very nature, this workplace could not be made safe, any more than a shifting volcano of boulders and razor-sharp knives could be safe. Rest assured, through their labors the project's burgeoning crew learned a thing or two about pain and loss and recovery.

But in the best of worlds, learning does modify behavior. Few of Luna's workers died more than twice. It became, in a way, a rite of passage, except for Conrad himself, who well remembered his faxless days on Sorrow and could not be bothered to die even once. "I hope to lead by example," he told his crew on several occasions, when Bell Daniel teased him about it.

And so, year by year the moon changed and shrunk as the mass beneath its surface was squozen into neubles and packed down into diamond plates near the solid core. And as the lithosphere's diameter approached its final value, the bores' work became slower and more precise. A traditional sculptor cuts first with a jackhammer, then with a chisel, then an awl, and finally with a rasp and a file and a block of heated wellstone to smooth and polish. Such was the role of the destruction crew in those last eighty years: finessing the rubble of Luna into something new and wonderful.

Of course, an odd thing was happening by this point: the moon had begun to retain air. It wasn't much at first—just a bit of outgassed oxygen, combining with a bit of hydrogen from the solar wind. The pressure could be measured in microbars—millionths of a breathable atmosphere—but overnight it seemed to change the texture of the soil and rocks at the surface, which had never before felt the touch of anything but vacuum.

And then the first of the gigantic atmosphere-processing faxes had been lowered into place along the Nearside equator. Tied to a network gate, it called down nitrogen from Titan, carbon dioxide from Venus, methane and heavy nobles from a spherical station adrift in the atmosphere of Jupiter. The Elementals grew wealthier still, for who but they could arrange such enormous transfers of purified mass? And then, before the atmosphere had achieved even a tenth of its final density, a second fax was placed on the Farside to crack additional oxygen from the soil itself, and to combine some fraction of it with the carbon and hydrogen and nitrogen to produce a gray, reeking smog of water and hydrocarbons, fats and other complex organics which would be useful in conditioning the soil for the arrival of life.

And indeed, life was not far behind; soon the surface was crawling with dainty labor robots, spreading and raking and watering and fertilizing a powder of microscopic spores. This had few visible effects, but on the visceral level it struck a deep chord: for the first time in its 4.5-billion-year history, this world was waking up. Suddenly it had a smell, a feel, a sky under which you could walk without protection. Whether the Fatalists and naturalists liked it or not, the history of Luna would be forevermore shaped by living things.

Which was good, because the flow of refugees from the colonies now exceeded the Queendom's own population growth by an order of magnitude, and was expected to continue increasing. If crushing the moon had once been a forward-thinking solution to long-term problems, it was now a grim and immediate necessity. But that was a political matter, and Conrad felt justified in letting other people worry about it. After all, he was just an architect.

"Don't lose too much contact with reality," advised King Bruno on one of his status-check visits, when Conrad made some comment along these lines. "Believe me, even on Maplesphere things are easier when I keep the end users in mind. I've wasted years of my life solving the wrong problems, and now I should like to have them back. I've lost arms inside a wormhole, lad, but never my entire self."

But in spite of the king's warnings, Conrad found himself spending less time on Grace—his nominal home—and more here on this squozen moon, whose lifelessness had begun, suddenly, to seem precious even to him, in the way that all things become precious when their time is nearly over. Another era of his personal history—and Luna's—was drawing to a close. And not only theirs; all the Queendom seemed to be drawing its collective breath, preparing for some new spasm of change. And as Conrad became aware of this, as his gaze turned finally outward, he found all the eyes of the Queendom looking in at him with worried impatience.

What have you built for us, Architect, in this hour of need? And the answer that came to Conrad was a strange one indeed, for he found he didn't know. His job was to deliver the skeleton of a world; its final flesh and purpose had never been his to decide.

Said Rodenbeck, "History is a blind toboggan. A single man can sometimes steer it, much to the trees' dismay, but a billion dragging feet will have their say as well."   •

in which a frontier is
finally opened

Was it a sad moment? A happy one? A moment of triumph or the passing of a triumphant age? Was it all of the above?

The kilometer-wide neutronium bore was a cylinder of mirror-bright impervium, and as it chewed its way through Lunar bedrock—consuming oxides of iron and silicon at one end and excreting neubles at the other—it made a sound like the end of a world. A never-ending detonation of antimatter, yes, a crushing of atomic bonds and atomic nuclei, a crushing of matter itself into dense neutron paste.

Architect Laureate Conrad Ethel Mursk stood behind it at a safe distance, along with his wife, Governor Adjudicate Xiomara Li Weng, and the very closest members of his construction crew's inner circle. Watching and thinking, celebrating and mourning. Not talking, because the sound had already tattered their eardrums, pulverized their fibrediamond-reinforced hearing bones. If they stood here long enough, the sound—still skeletally conducted through the ground—would deafen them at the cerebrum level as well, and finally bruise the soft meat of their brains into unthinking goo. In Conrad's outfit, sound levels were measured not in decibels but in Minutes To Kill, and this one pegged the meter at MTK 15.

There were no standards or limits per se, although it was generally recognized that at levels higher than this, useful work became a *lot* more difficult. Even 15 was pushing it, hard. But the people of Sol were tough, and the survivors of Barnard tougher still, and with a fax machine handy the assembled group had little thought for its safety.

Nor were they afraid of the dark, here in the deep, deep bowels of the world. Which was fortunate, because dark it was, and dark it would remain. Thousands of kilometers long, the winding tunnel was wide enough to swallow any conventional flashlight beam, and this dig was too transient to bother installing the usual bright track lighting. So Conrad and Xmary, Bell and the others carried "rock burner" lamps—multispectral lasers which cast white spots whose apparent size and brightness was independent of range. Thirty-six degrees of arc—no more, no less. To accomplish this, the beam power could ratchet all the way up to fifty kilowatts—which at short range was enough to vaporize human flesh, to melt most ordinary metals, to discolor exposed stone. Rock burner, yes. The devices were smart and accidents were correspondingly rare, but the name served to remind its wielders what a powerful and dangerous piece of equipment it really was.

And by the light and shadows of these bright, bright lamps, playing over the stern of the kilometers-distant bore, they watched a neuble fall from the bore's mechanical anus and settle—under the influence of straining gravity lasers—to the tunnel floor.

WHUMP. The ground rippled at the impact, and dimpled impressively despite the grasers' carrying fully 99.999% of the weight.

And that was that. The *last* neuble. The thundering machine—the last of its kind still operating—rumbled to a halt.

The moon lay silent for the first time in two hundred years. In the one hundred and fifty-first decade of the Queendom of Sol, crushing operations on the world of Luna had just officially ended. Or would later today, when this tunnel was collapsed.

HUZZAH! said the scrolling marquee across Bell Daniel's space suit.

"Well done, all," Conrad replied, speaking aloud in words only his suit could hear. They appeared immediately on his own marquee.

Xmary offered her CONGRATULATIONS!!!!, and the four others exchanged the visual equivalent of small talk, complimenting one another on the excellence and timeliness of their work.

COULDN'T HAVE DONE IT WITHOUT YOU, BOSS, Bell offered, and Conrad wondered why he bothered kissing up like that, on his last day of work. From now on, Luna—or rather *Lune*—would belong to the seismology and hydrology and ecology teams. Aside from a few temporary structures on and near the planette's surface, there would be no meaningful construction here for another twenty years.

THANKS, AND LIKEWISE, Conrad assured him. THE ERIDANI REFUGEES WILL BE GRATEFUL WHEN THEY ARRIVE. SHALL WE HAVE THE CHAMPAGNE?

ASSUREDLY, Bell agreed, and Lilly Frontera, his executive assistant, dutifully passed out the bottles, which were made from a frangible soda-silica-lime material—old-fashioned breakable glass that no fax machine would dispense without authorization. And Conrad's crew dutifully smashed these against the tunnel floor, or hurled them—with more enthusiasm than hope—toward the bore and the distant walls of polished basalt.

Conrad and Xmary, for their part, clinked their own two bottles together and popped the corks, then raced to dump the liquid over each other's suits before it boiled away in the vacuum. They were grinning, and Conrad was pretty sure he was chuckling as well, but there was a seriousness to it just the same, for change was upon them once again. These crush-the-moon days—harried and hopeful and deeply fulfilling—would be replaced by something new, and nothing would ever be the same.

And it was a funny thing, how sad such moments could be, for the alternative was to live forever with no change at all. And that was a kind of death—a lame and sorry one that anyone should be glad to avoid for a little while longer. But Conrad had never gotten used to change, and if he welcomed it, it was in the way that a man welcomes a familiar enemy.

Ah, well.

CALL SHIPPING TO PICK UP THE NEUBLE, he said unnecessarily. I WANT THAT LAST PLATE FILLED AND SEALED BY CLOSE OF BUSINESS.

SURE, BOSS, Bell said, with all the poignancy a two-word text message could convey.

That was the *really* private ceremony. The semiprivate one occurred four hours later, on the surface, where Conrad addressed a staff of thousands, including a few hundred retirees who'd wandered away from the project before its completion.

They were in the bowl of a shallow crater in Nubia Province, sucking dry, barely breathable air that stank of methane and sulfur. The sunset was gray.

"You've done excellent work here," he told them all. "And God willing, we'll see each other again someday, on a grander project still."

"*Crush Venus! Crush Venus!*" the crowd chanted happily in reply. And then a woman off toward the rear called out "Crush Mars!" Then everyone was shouting: Melt Europa! Ignite Jupiter! Reconstitute the asteroid belt! And finally the noise dissolved into argumentative laughter.

None of these things were possible, of course; King Bruno wasn't exactly *out* of money, but he wouldn't be playing sugar daddy to the Queendom again for another few centuries. The workers were just letting off steam, kidding themselves that it could all keep going.

"We'll do *something*," he assured them, "and when we do, I'll know exactly who to call. The best damned crew in the universe!"

They cheered at that, of course.

Was there anything else to say? He shook the hands that needed shaking, then wandered off into the barren hills to let his people—his *former* people—sort it out on their own. He wasn't their boss anymore.

"You should be happy," Xmary said, walking alongside him.

"I am," he assured her. "Very." And it was true. "I'm just...I don't know, more *tired* than anything. My willpower's browning out. Which is bad, because there's a lot of work still to be done. And a *lot* of refugees streaming homeward, expecting a place to live."

At that, she patted him on the rump and smiled wickedly. "I know what you need, Architect. Around that withered soul you're still young and virile. A body like that requires attention." And that was true, too.

Although the planet had shrunk beneath it, Luna's actual crust hadn't gotten any smaller. But it had only one-fourth the area to cover, so over the years of its set-tling it had folded and wrinkled and cracked, raising jagged mountain chains, broad steppes, and vast, broken plains. Even here in the relative flat of the former Mare Nubium, it wasn't hard to find a little valley so secluded that it would be visible only from directly above.

"We start pouring the oceans tomorrow," he told his wife. "Faxed ice from Callisto, mostly. And for the first year or two the water will simply sink into all these voids in the crust. The surface will be as dry as ever, but with the water to lubricate them, and explosives to jar them loose, the rock plates should settle together, smoothing out all these jags and spines."

"All?"

"Well, a lot of them. We still want some contour, obvi-ously, and with the highest mountains reaching *twelve whole kilometers* above the plains, we'll definitely still have some. But the geo boys are having the time of their lives, figuring out where to plant all the bombs. We'll go after the biggest voids with subnukes and aye-ma'am, and over time the water will be squeezed back out to the surface. Truthfully, with a fixed mass budget we're not sure how deep the oceans will *be* when it's all said and done. But there'll be enough to stabilize the climate and the ecosystem. And there'll be beaches."

"Sounds lovely," Xmary said, in a we're-done-talking-now kind of way. Her clothes, sensing the moment, peeled away and fell to the dusty ground. Conrad's did likewise. Soon the two of them were *on* their clothes, rolling and wrestling, feeling the dry air soak up their sweat. The love they made together was excellent, as al-ways.

There were more failed couples in the universe than successful ones, and conventional wisdom thus insisted that two people simply couldn't get along forever. But

Conrad had never understood this. He was barely old enough to deprogram facial hair when he'd met Xmary, and they'd become lovers within the year.

Later, they'd tried it apart for what seemed like a long time, but their flexibility hadn't been up to the task. Like two trees that had grown together, they simply couldn't disentangle. Not without damage, without broken hearts and limbs and skyward-pointing roots. And eternal youth or no, who had time to recover from a thing like that? Who would want to?

True love is immorbid, Conrad wrote once in his diary. *You can kill it, but it never gets old. It's stronger than petty anger or lust. Stronger even than boredom, and that's a strong force indeed.* Or maybe he, personally, was just weak. His love for Xmary belied any notion of free will; he could leave her, yes, but he couldn't *want* to.

"I can't imagine my life without you," he told her now, murmuring into a sweaty ear.

"Enough," she said. "Talk later. Let's enjoy this planet of yours."

The ground shook a little then, as if in agreement or—as Conrad would later see it—in warning.

And Xmary, perhaps sensing this, added, "While it's still ours. Before the homeless arrive and things get interesting. It's not enough to crush the moon; you've got to decide how you're going to love it."

Lune. The name—chosen democratically and rati- fied by royal decree—seemed strange, musical, and somehow appropriate. *Luna* took twice as long to say, for a world twice as wide. "Ash," by contrast, was a drab moniker for the outermost of this new world's planettes, poised at the L1 Lagrange point and stabilized there by a network of orbiting collapsiters.

Ash itself, though, was anything but drab. The planette Varna, orbiting thirty thousand kilometers closer to Lune, was blue and green and steamy, like a little tropical Earth. Beneath that was the grassy Kishu and—visible just now off the limb of Lune—the desert Harst, glowing like a little beige pinpoint.

But Ash's biosphere was dominated by reds and yellows: snapdragon and bougainvillea, cardinals and canaries, foxes and howler monkeys and fluorescent yellow mice. The trees were engineered specifically for the site, and were like nothing ever seen on Earth or in the colonies. Tall and sparse as autumn poplars, prickly as cacti, stronger and more flexible than bamboo, they rose from the dome-shaped ground like pillars of flame, waving brightly in the breeze.

And in Ash's pearl-gray sky, the spectacular blue-green orbs of Earth and Lune were almost exactly equal in size. Their impending eclipse, two days hence, would see the glare of Sol line up perfectly behind the Earth, which would cast its shadow across Lune and turn *it* red as well. The red of sunset, of sunrise, of beginnings and endings.

And per the queen's proclamation, the sixty-two minutes of the eclipse's totality were to mark the formal opening of Lune to human settlement. But the queen had declined to run these dates by her architect laureate, and in Conrad's professional opinion they were utter hooey. He'd been building that world for long years, and he needed another eighteen to complete the job properly. At least eighteen!

"Be realistic, Your Highness," he said to Tamra, by the light of the sun and the Earth and of Lune itself. "Be reasonable. This party is several years premature."

This was the *official* celebration, to which none of Conrad's crew were invited, despite his strenuous objections. They were of course welcome to attend the *public* celebration during the actual eclipse, except that at full capacity the planette could comfortably hold only eighty thousand people, and for a construction worker the tickets would cost a year's salary at least. So in fact they'd be watching the ceremony on TV, or via neural sensorium, or maybe just skipping it and going straight to their own drunken revelries. It seemed a shame.

"The official commencement will be a simple dinner party," the queen's invitation had told him primly, "for a few close friends and relations. Since your wife is also invited, you needn't bring a guest. Her Majesty understands your concern, but is she to share her table with every rigger and wrench-boy in the Queendom? She loves them all equally, but she hasn't the time to love them *individually*. She could dedicate a score of copies to that purpose alone, and never make a dent in the problem. And what would she do with the memories? Summarize them, or be hopelessly clogged, or forget them entirely. And wouldn't that defeat the purpose?"

"Not for the workers," he told it. "They'd treasure the experience forever."

"Presumption is rude, Architect," the invitation had chided. Then, "Come now, you owe the luminaries of Sol a chance to congratulate you."

So here they were, seated at a pair of long, arch-shaped tables that followed the curve of Ash's surface. Forty people, only half of whom Conrad knew at all well. But Feck was here, and Eustace, and a handful of other revived Barnardeans who'd made good in the stodgy old Queendom. The king was here too, of course, and so were Donald and Maybel Mursk and, rather surprisingly, Xmary's parents as well.

Since Mimi and David Li Weng had disowned their daughter after the Revolt, Conrad had never actually met them. Nor wanted to, though it wasn't a position he'd considered overmuch. They were historical figures more than anything, and though Xmary was largely ignoring them, their presence did lend an odd authority to the proceedings. Their daughter, the Governor Adjudicate of Central Pacifica and wife of a celebrated architect, was no longer an embarrassment to them.

"Hi. I hope you burn in hell," Conrad had told them both brightly when the queen had introduced them, and it felt good to get that off his chest. Really.

"Be reasonable. I would say the same to you, Architect," the queen answered him now, forking a bit of cheese-draped sausage into her mouth and chewing thoughtfully. Seconds later she touched a napkin to her lips and added, "You really must try the cheese. That woman over there—in the green frock, yes—is perhaps the most brilliant flavor designer in human history."

"High praise indeed," Conrad allowed, taking a nibble. Damn, it *was* good. Melting in his mouth, almost vaporizing, it had a taste at once fatty and ethereal, rich and salty and yet somehow subtle as well. His eyes closed for a moment, of their own accord.

"Immorbidity demands novelty," the queen opined. "Else it's bread and water forever. Bless our flavor designers, every one."

And to that Conrad could not help answering, "We did without them on Sorrow, Majesty. But aye, not forever."

Tamra nodded solemnly. "You see my point, then. Shall we consign ourselves to no better a fate? Will you not surrender yon world to me? Our population crisis continues to grow. Our middle-class homeless now number in the tens of millions, and the political pressure to open a new frontier—any frontier—is overwhelming. Am

I to resist the will of the people? The *need* of the people? They don't require a perfect world, and your quest for one—though admirable—consumes precious time. *And* money. Endings are always difficult, but there comes a point when the engineers and craftsmen must disperse, and find new projects."

"No doubt, Your Highness," Conrad hedged, "but is that day truly upon us? We've only just sealed the last of the neutronium plates. The lithosphere above them is full of voids and faults, which store a tremendous unwanted energy. Over time they will settle, with unpredictable results."

"That's been understood for some time," the queen countered, "but you can relieve these pressure points at leisure, with minimal disruption at ground level. True? I'm informed that the largest tremors will cause only minor damage at the surface."

"Possibly, Your Highness, but none of us can say that with confidence. We're speaking of probabilities, in a world of imperfect knowledge. The first Ring Collapsiter was considered safe as well, and we know how that turned out."

"Cunning sabotage," the queen said dismissively, "at the deepest levels of design. We trust you, sir, to eschew such scheming."

"Do you? Then trust me that Lune is incomplete, Majesty. The biosphere is another problem, immature and unstable. On Sorrow and Pup we've seen what that can do. How much suffering has our impatience created there?"

"Your point is duly noted, Architect. However, as on Sorrow and Pup, we're installing town-sized fax plates to churn out fresh gases and creatures, keeping the ecology in crude balance. Yes? And *unlike* those worlds, we've the infrastructure of an entire civilization to draw upon.

Mars and Venus are better analogies, for in their early civilized histories they prospered with no biosphere at all. As did Luna herself, for a dozen centuries and more. In any event, these risks are mine to assess, and I have more brains to pick than yours alone. You *will* prepare the moon for immediate habitation."

And here the king added his own voice to the fray: "It's no use, lad, to argue with the facts. Focus on the work itself, yes, but remember who pays your salary. Your job is not to *run* the new world, but to deliver it."

"Aye, Your Majesty," Conrad said, unconvinced and unconvincing.

"Come now," the king expounded, tossing a grape onto Conrad's plate. "Do you think you're the first? Has no engineer before you surrendered his treasures to a witless society? I do know the feeling, lad. How many deaths linger on my conscience, do you suppose, from the discovery of collapsium alone? When I finally get these wormholes working, do you think I expect there to be no accidents? No malice? All systems are subject to failure, but the mere possibility should not shackle our striving."

He tossed another grape, and another. "Will you choke on these? Are they poison? Will they beguile you and squander your time, as mass-stabilized wormholes have squandered mine? I could let you *starve*, lad, for fear of what a grape might do. Or we could get on with the party, and see what happens."

"You've become quite the orator," Conrad said. "When did that happen?"

Such a comment might easily have been taken as rudeness, but the king just laughed. "With fifteen hundred years of life, my boy, one does eventually learn to speak."

At that, Conrad's old friend Feck chimed in. "Don't let the refugee crisis escape your attention, hmm? We've got six million in storage, and *three billion* on the way. At present deceleration, *Perdition* is only two months out, with fifteen percent of the load. I would say there are risks in *every* course of action, and especially in responding too slowly."

And Conrad, being a refugee himself, could hardly argue with that. The remaining colonies were simply collapsing. They were up to their armpits in dead and mortal children, and had turned their spasm-wracked economies to the sorry task of triage: shipping "home" as many as possible, by whatever means possible, and leaving the rest to their fate. Whatever that might be.

Conrad sometimes wondered whether this trend had been inevitable all along. Had the colonists carried out with them the seeds of their own destruction? Or was this simply a fad, a mass surrender, a herd action inspired by the traitorous flight of *Newhope*? If so, then Conrad and Xmary and Feck had a lot to answer for: the death of billions. The death of hope itself.

"Have there been any further communications with the *Perdition* or the *Trail of Tears*?" Conrad asked, for no matter what Feck said, he was poignantly interested in the refugee crisis. He was just out of step with the news. But Feck was the queen's Minister of Colonial Affairs, and would know everything.

"Communications, yes," Feck said, sounding both chagrined and incensed. "Meaningful dialogue, no. Eridani breeds angry, suspicious men. And women, too, one supposes, but since they're cloistered, we never hear from them. At any rate, the Eridanians' journey has been a hard one, and they're not eager to park their butts in Kuiper Belt storage when they finally arrive."

"Nor would I be," Conrad said. He'd visited Eridani twice in virtual form, and remembered it as a place of sharp contrasts: molten metal and frozen gas, wild anger and wilder compassion. Eridani boasted no habitable worlds, and like all the colony stars it was richer than Sol in stormy radiation. And the outer system's Dust Belt was treacherous—it could grind even the proudest of habitats to rubble in a matter of years. Even the inner system was full of flying crap. Eridani had thousands of times more asteroids and comets and random small meteoroids than Sol; its planets had been battered all to hell, and still endured several large impacts each year.

So the people, in their tens of billions, lived deep underground in Aetna, the moon of Mulciber, and ventured only rarely to its cratered-upon-cratered surface. To compensate for their bleak, cramped quarters, they had opted for a gradual reduction in body size, and while they were at it they'd added new metabolic pathways and—they claimed—new modes of thought which opened their minds to a greater spiritual awareness. And why not? What the hell else did they have to do under there?

But they were also energy-rich and element-rich and lived like kings in their stifling burrows. Or they had, anyway, before the fax machines started giving out. Theirs was a sad history, as fraught with broken promise as Barnard's own.

"What are we supposed to do?" Feck demanded suddenly, taking the comment as a barb. "There are a dozen asylum-seeking vessels parked in the Kuiper Belt already, and if we wake their sleepers only as new living space becomes available, we're accused of breaking up families and friendships, of scattering the refugees out over time and space. Of *destroying their culture*.

"But if we hold them in storage, awaiting a world of their own, then we're pushing them off into some indefinite future. Which is a kind of murder, for many suspect we'll never wake them at all. And that's a valid question, Conrad, because even Lune cannot absorb the colonies' entire human flux. How long will those worlds take to die, and how many of their children will they dump on us beforehand?"

The queen cleared her throat. "These decisions are *also* mine, Minister Feck. You've done very well for your charges, and argue their case most effectively. But their fate is not yours to choose. This is the point of monarchy, you see: to concentrate blame. *You* may sleep soundly, your conscience untroubled."

Feck looked ready to argue that point, but finally thought better of it and dropped his eyes to his dinner. "Of course, Your Highness. My apologies."

"Accepted," she said, favoring him with the smile that had earned her the love of billions.

"The day grows late," warned the red-haired Wenders Rodenbeck, in a tone that managed to convey at once a personal sadness, an official gravitas, and a semiamused kind of told-you-so. "A stiff wind rises at last, and we find our house of straw less sturdy than we'd hoped."

"Don't gloat, Poet Laureate," the queen said, clearly annoyed. "It shows off the food in your teeth. If we'd listened to you all these years, I suppose the Queendom would still be a paradise, and never a tear would be shed?"

"No indeed, Majesty." The playwright's voice was, to Conrad's ear, rather shrill, but in a way that enhanced rather than detracted from his air of authority. "I would suggest a more careful reading of my oeuvre, when time permits. In fact, my own paradise would likely have collapsed by now as well, for reasons we couldn't imagine at the outset. Such is the fate of human endeavor; our vision is not extended merely by the stretching of our lifetimes."

"Go on," the queen said skeptically. "You have my attention. What remedies do you propose?"

"Why, none," said Rodenbeck, spreading his hands as if this should have been obvious. "Who has taught me to plan for the long, long term? Where shall we draw our lessons, when this civilization of ours has outlasted all that came before it? The Queendom rose from the ashes of Old Modernity, which sprang from the embers of Rome, which drew upon the lessons of Greece, and Egypt before her. Indeed, Highness, Egypt had the Minoan example to emulate, and fair Atlantis was a focused echo of the civilizations of Indus and Jomon, drowned in the Deluge at the closing of the Ice Age.

"History is not linear, I'm afraid, but cyclic, for sustainability has never guided human affairs. And in banishing death, we simply condemn ourselves to observe the cycle from within. To live, as it were, in the filth we've excreted, with the sound of falling towers all around."

"Ah," said Tamra, "so we needn't listen to you, then."

"Not at all, Majesty. I am but a mote in the vastness, amazed by all that I perceive. Let's do take a moment, though, to congratulate ourselves for all that we've accomplished. Even this ghastly destruction of Luna, yes, for it speaks to grand intentions. And here at the end of the day, we shall need a warm thought like that to remember ourselves by."

"Quite," the queen agreed, in a tone that closed the subject. And then, to Conrad: "We do have evidence, Architect, that *Perdition* is in regular contact with someone in the Queendom. Does that make you feel better?"

"Um, well," Conrad said, "that depends on who they're talking to."

The queen's smile deepened. "Someone charming, I'm sure. Shall we have dessert?"

chapter thirteen

in which the demands of
beggars are voiced

It was, of course, the Fatalists with whom *Perdition* communicated, and while the details of their exchange were quantum-encrypted and thus impossible to decipher, archaeologists and historians agree on this much:

First, that the exchange was hundreds of petabytes long in both directions—more than adequate for a self-aware data construct to be passed back and forth several times. Or, alternatively, for several constructs to make the crossing once.

Second, that the Queendom recipients of these messages were, without a doubt, located well away from Earth and Mars and Venus. Mercury and the moons of Jupiter are considered unlikely but cannot be ruled out altogether. Almost anywhere else in the system is possible; no physical traces have ever been found.

Third, that the virus released into the Nescog on Lune Day was of Eridanian origin, or evolved from an Eridanian template which in turn traced its heritage back to the early Queendom. Sol had endured crippling network attacks during the Fall, and the "Eridge" plague showed a cunning grasp of both the strengths of that ancient assault, and the weaknesses of the contemporary network.

These weaknesses were few and slight, so the virus spread at only a tiny fraction of the classical speed of light, and was not truly lethal in its effects. Still, it was stealthy, and raised no conclusive alarms until it had wormed its way to the heart of every switch and router, collapsiter and precognitor in the system.

Conrad Mursk first learned of the attack indirectly, faxing home from a meeting with the Europan Ice Authority. As he stepped out of the print plate into his penthouse apartment in the city of Grace, he found himself staggering for a drunken moment. This was not entirely unheard of, for Grace was a floating city, and the Carpal Tower at its center was very slightly flexible. On windy days, you could feel the roll and sway of the city here as nowhere else.

But never this much. Though his balance reasserted itself, Conrad felt at once that something was wrong. For one thing he was covered with a fine white dust, like talcum powder. For another thing, the evening lights of the city below were not all lit. Some were flickering; others were simply out.

Worse, he had the distinct sense that there was something different *about him.* Inside, in his mind or his memories or his immortal soul. Nothing monumental— he was still Conrad Mursk of Ireland and Sorrow, Lune and Pacifica—but it seemed to him that he was suddenly peppered with small absences. With tiny half-remembered things, now wholly forgotten. Or was he imagining it?

"Call Xmary," he said to the ceiling, but he needn't have bothered, for moments later she spilled out of the fax in person. This was, after all, dinnertime, and she'd've called him already if her gubernatorial duties required her to be late, or to spawn an extra copy or two.

She was also covered in powder, and looked startled and subtly off-kilter.

"What just happened?" she said, fixing her eyes on Conrad, her hands on the black hair hanging down past her neck.

"I don't know," he admitted. "Are you all right?"

"I . . ." *I think so*, she'd been about to say. But something stopped her. She *didn't* think so.

"Maintenance," Conrad instructed the apartment. "Fax diagnostic, *now*."

"All functions nominal, sir," the fax said, sounding ever-so-slightly offended.

"Seconded," said the ceiling. "No sign of anomalies."

"Not here," offered the floor. "But look at sir and madam. They're quite disturbed. Perhaps they encountered a transit glitch."

"Impossible," the fax replied.

"Improbable," the floor countered, "and yet—"

"Everyone shut up!" Xmary commanded firmly. "Conrad, do you feel . . ."

"Funny? Full of holes? Dusty? Yes. Something's happening."

Xmary looked up at the ceiling. "News."

"Today's top story: Travelers report fax anomalies. No details available. Please propagate this message on supraluminal channels where possible."

Well, that was helpful.

"That could mean anything," Xmary grumbled. "What travelers? Where? *Us*? Update the top story every time it changes, please."

"Yes, madam. Today's top story: This is a travel advisory. Travelers in the vicinity of Earth and Mars report minor cellular injury after Nescog transport. Citizens are advised to avoid Nescog travel wherever possible. No further details available. Please assign this story top priority on all civilian supraluminal channels."

And then, on the heels of that: "Today's top story: Her Majesty has declared a state of emergency. Please remain where you are, or limit necessary travel to licensed air, ground, and space vehicles. The Nescog is hereby reserved for authorized emergency personnel."

"Damn," Xmary said. "I'd better get back to the office."

"How?" Conrad wanted to know. The Central Pacifica governor's office was on Cooper Ridge Construct, eight hundred kilometers away.

"I'm emergency personnel," she pointed out. "I must be."

"But do you want to risk the damage? It could be permanent. For all we know it could be *fatal*."

"Hmm. I could take a glider, I suppose. Or maybe a boat. There *are* boats here, right? It's an island."

She was spared any further thought on the matter by a crackling from the fax machine behind her. It coughed out a cloud of dust, then a sizzle of blue sparks, and finally the staggering body of a heavy, bearded man.

Bruno de Towaji, the King of Sol. Presently, he put an arm out and fell flat on his face.

"Blast," he said woozily, "that *is* a nasty smack, isn't it? Am I still me?"

"Your Highness!" Conrad and Xmary said together. "What are you doing here?" Conrad added, while Xmary asked, "Are you all right?"

"Scrambled," the king said, picking himself up, brushing the dust from his eyebrows and beard. "If that's the worst they can do I'll be happy, but still. How dare they do their worst!"

"What's happening?" Xmary asked him. "Why *are* you here?"

"I set up a point-to-point filter between this apartment and the Beach Palace, but someone had to go through it first. As a calibration article."

"Why?"

He didn't answer, but turned groggily back toward the fax again. "I'm close to a breakthrough on the wormhole front. I can feel it! But Maplesphere and Earth are suddenly very far apart. It'll take us *months* to filter this irritant from all possible routes. Indeed, it may be quicker to purge the virus entirely than to design emergency workarounds."

"What virus?"

"Eh?" Bruno looked over his shoulder. "The one they've attacked us with."

"Who?"

"The Fatalists. The Eridanians. The dark angel of unintended consequences. My errors return to me, young lady, a thousand times magnified." To the fax he said, "Royal Override. Apply calibration results and clear your buffer. Begin point-to-point transfer."

The Queen of Sol stepped out of the plate, with no more fuss than if she'd stepped through an ordinary doorway.

"Thank you, darling," she said to her husband. "I appear to be intact. And you?"

"I will be," he said, "when I can get my hands on a pre-virus backup. They've taken down the first-tier error correction. The damage is minor but . . . disconcerting."

"All right," she said brusquely. "Give me safe passage to *Malu'i*. For two."

Malu'i. Protector. The navy's flagship.

"Are we under attack?" Conrad asked stupidly. He'd fought a dozen battles in his life, and they were all different, all surprising. But they shared this characteristic: he never really believed they were happening until he was in the thick of it, fighting for his life or his freedom or for some empty principle he'd barely remember afterwards.

"Play message Doxar twenty-one," the queen said to the apartment walls, instead of answering Conrad directly. "Full exchange, half duplex."

A hollie window appeared near the fax, and in it the face of an Eridanian man. There was no mistaking the Eridanians, for their heads were overlarge and over-round, their dark eyes glaring out from beneath bushy white eyebrows and thick manes of curly silver hair. Their skins were as pale as chalk, except in the shadows and creases, where they were as black as coal. This was a trick that helped them radiate excess body heat, but it made them look... exaggerated. False. Like comic drawings designed to highlight particular emotions: here is HAPPY! Here is ANGRY! Here is FILLED WITH THE ENNUI OF TOO MANY CENTURIES IN A CAVE! Their small size—about two-thirds the height of a natural human—only exaggerated the effect.

This particular Eridanian was ANGRY.

"I am Doxar Bagelwipe," he said self-importantly, "of Humanitarium *Perdition*. Y'all poseth unacceptably, y'hear? We *will not* end our travail in forgettable parking orbits, for yet more centuries of unlife. To prove the sincerity of our conviction, we assail your teleport network. Consider it declared: no less than full sanctuary is acceptable, for all persons stored cold or warm aboard this vessel."

Next, Queen Tamra's own image replaced Doxar's. "Captain," she said calmly, "the people of Eridani will be resettled in the Queendom of Sol *as space and resources permit*. Your impatience is understandable, and in sympathy with your plight we're doing all we can to prepare new worlds for habitation. But this sabotage is counterproductive, and can only hurt your standing with the people of Sol. Please reverse it immediately, and proceed to your designated orbit."

Doxar reappeared then, for his message was interactive, and carried with it the full force of his personality. Why wait for the speed of light, when you can send your image to negotiate in your stead? Particularly when your position is inflexible, and no persuasion can hope to alter it. "Unacceptable. We declare the right to escalate," Doxar's image said, and then winked out.

Damn.

The king said to Conrad, "If they actually enter the Queendom, right now and all at once, they'll destabilize the economy. We *must* delay them. Meanwhile, my boy, you and I are traveling to Lune, and thence to Callisto and Europa. Just in case things go astray, we've got to get as much water onto that dustball of yours as we can in the next seven weeks."

When *Perdition* was due to arrive. With guns blazing?

Said Queen Tamra to Governor Xmary, "You captained a starship for hundreds of years. You know how starship crews think, how they react. And you have actual combat experience, correct? You fought a space battle."

"Once," Xmary protested.

"Not a police impoundment," the queen pressed. "Not a simulation or staged maneuver, but a to-the-death battle against a determined and capable opponent. From the forces of my son, King Bascal."

"Once!"

"That's once more than anyone else, Governor. You won the fight, correct? You survived, and your opponent didn't."

"That's accurate, yes."

"Then come with me," the queen said. And to Bruno: "Is the fax machine ready?"

"It is."

"Then kiss your husband good-bye," the queen instructed Xmary. "Your respective duties may keep you apart for some time. I wish I could say how long."

Conrad reeled. Was this truly happening? Was Xmary being drafted right in front of his eyes? Sent off to fight for her life in the wilds of space?

"I—," he said, but nothing else came out.

"Don't," Xmary told him, turning into his arms, putting a finger to his lips. She looked scared and somewhat dazed, but fully in control of herself. "You know how these things go. All we need is a show of force, then a show of compassion, and then a get-to-know-you coffee in the observation lounge. I'll see you soon." She kissed him then as he had rarely been kissed, in a thousand years of life.

"Be careful," he said, clutching her in his arms, unwilling to let go. But she extricated herself anyway, and answered, "Always."

She nodded to the queen then, who was kissing her own husband good-bye. Then the two of them—the strongest women Conrad had ever known—stepped into the fax plate and vanished.

What happened next is history, in all the great and small senses of the word, for it is written in the Ballad of Conrad Mursk, "They faxed from the house / the queen and his spouse / and he never saw neither no more."

chapter fourteen

in which consequences are weighed and chosen

The error-correction virus turned out to be merely the first salvo in a battle that would later be known as Eridge Kuipera. The damaging effects on travelers turned out to be incidental to the bug's real purpose, which was to prop open a small vulnerability in the Nescog, paving the way for further attacks.

The second and third viruses rebounded from a growing thicket of Queendom defenses, but the fourth one—named by different authorities as Heater, Snaps, and Variant Delta—managed to pick its way through the obstacles and squeeze itself into some twenty percent of the Nescog's scattered nodes. Its effects were rather more serious, being fifty percent lethal to traveling humans and, ominously, to their buffer images and unsecured backups as well.

As a precaution, citizens were advised to back themselves up at their earliest convenience, at any of the Queendom's thousands of secure, off-network repositories. But with tens of billions of customers flooding in all at once, the Vaults were overwhelmed, and waiting lists quickly grew from weeks to months to well over a decade.

Meanwhile, *Perdition* continued downsystem on a course that could only be described as belligerent, for its exhaust of coherent gamma rays cut straight through the heart of the Queendom, sweeping dangerously close to the Saturnian system and in fact bathing several asteroid-belt settlements with sublethal but highly obnoxious radiation. Shipping lanes were disrupted; ring collapsiter segments flickered and flashed with secondary Cerenkov emissions.

And unless the starship's course was altered, that beam would eventually—if briefly—play right across the Earth at much closer range, sickening tens of billions of people on the ground and, in all probability, vaporizing anyone in orbit, where the shelter of a planetary atmosphere was moot. Plant life would not be much affected, but the animal toll on the worst-hit continent of South America would be steep.

Too, the atmosphere itself would heat up in a hurricane-sized bullseye pattern—elevated by ten or twenty degrees Kelvin at the center—and the oceans beneath would warm slightly as well. This would be enough to play havoc with the weather for months, or perhaps longer. And then *Perdition* itself would ease into a high orbit, from which further assaults on the Earth would be trivially easy.

These Eridanians meant business.

So did the crew of *Malu'i*, though, and the queen to whom they answered. Tamra had never asked to rule this system, but she'd never shirked from the responsibility, either, and *damn* if she'd let some gang of colonial hooligans tear the place up, no matter how sad their story might be.

"If we're forced to target your engines," Tamra tried explaining to the invaders, "there may be considerable hazard to your passengers and crew. And even if you escape without injury, you'll be moving through the Inner System at several hundred kps. You'll fly right through, and back out to interstellar space before we can arrange to decelerate you. A rescue operation could then take weeks to mount, and *years* to bring you to the park orbit we've already assigned."

"Prick yer five holes, y'all shite-bathed daughter of pigs," replied the image of Doxar.

Given the length of the Queendom's history and the size of its population, we can assume that fouler curses than this had been directed, from time to time, at Tamra-Tamatra Lutui. If so, however, no record of them has survived. Certainly, the immediate shock and indignation of the men and women on the bridge of *Malu'i* suggests that such outbursts were rare indeed.

Nevertheless, Tamra's response was well measured. "Such language may be commonplace in the caverns of Aetna, Captain, but here in the cradle of humanity we've found that mutual respect yields better results. And surely you understand that with the security of our citizens and biospheres at risk, we're quite prepared to fire on your vessel."

"And we'm prepared to crash your Nescog, missus. Completely and utterly, I kid you not. Y'all think we can't?"

"I suspect you can," she conceded. "Or your agents here in the Queendom can. You'll find them dangerous allies, I daresay, but they've certainly inconvenienced us before."

"Then give. Because I will not."

"No one surrenders so easily," said Tamra coolly. "We're not inflexible, Captain, but neither are we stupid, nor craven, nor weak. You will alter your course, and divert your drive beam away from populated areas. *Then* we'll negotiate. From receipt of this message, you have five minutes to comply. Or rather, the true Captain Doxar does. You, his pale shadow, may fly back to him now with my regards."

She blanked the hollie, ending any further communication with Doxar's image. It could hang around if it wanted to, but the real Doxar's reply would overwrite it in any case. Of course, *Perdition* and *Malu'i* were five light-minutes apart, so with round-trip signal time it would be *fifteen* minutes before anything actually came of this exchange.

"Well played, Majesty," said Brett Brown.

"Thank you," she acknowledged, mindful of his pride, his authority before the bridge crew, and indeed before the whole of the navy itself. "I'd like to discuss the matter with you later, if you have time."

In fact, Brown had nothing but time, and while his strategic and diplomatic skills were not in question, this was unarguably a tactical situation. Still, appearances mattered, for he had been this vessel's captain for nearly six hundred years, and his sudden replacement by Governor Li Weng—a comparative greenhorn—was bound to raise eyebrows, even if Tamra *had* promoted Brown to admiral in the process.

Fortunately, the past two weeks had proven Tamra right, for Xmary was a cunning fighter who'd steered *Malu'i* onto a vector that took maximum advantage of her maneuverability, and minimized the options of the faster but much heavier *Perdition*. Brown had fought in thousands of simulated engagements, and won the vast majority of them, but bloodlessly. He had never once witnessed an actual permanent death, whereas Xmary had seen hundreds, and *personally caused* at least twenty. More, if Fatalist ghouls were to be counted. So if it came to blows—and it might!—Tamra figured the safe money was on known killers.

"I'll check my schedule," Brown answered carefully. "Meanwhile, with your permission, I'll recheck the status of fleet maneuvers."

"Later," Tamra suggested. "I prefer your attention to be more tightly focused." Which was true, for she *did* value Brown's tactical opinion. He was without doubt her second or perhaps third choice for the job. And anyway the "fleet" right now consisted of just *Malu'i* and a pair of lightly armed and largely inconsequential grappleships. There were other assets en route, but the closest of them was still six light-minutes downsystem of here. A really high-powered nasen beam could of course strike from that range, but not with precision. Not without absurdly high risk to the two hundred million human beings onboard *Perdition*. So for the moment, *Malu'i* was effectively alone in the conflict, and must act carefully indeed, or else wait two days for backup.

To Xmary the queen said, "Have you formulated a plan of attack, Captain?"

Xmary looked up from the console in her armrest. "Working on it, Majesty." Then, to Brown's Information officer, "Where's that blueprint, Lieutenant? I need to know exactly how much antimatter is in there, and exactly where."

"That's difficult, ma'am. I can show you mass concentrations and annihilation signatures, but anything else is guesswork."

"Deductive guesswork," said Xmary. "But if you lack the necessary skills, then forward me your data."

"Aye, Captain," Information replied, suitably chastened. "My preliminary analysis is also appended."

"Thank you. Ah. This is good. Your Highness, I propose a three-pronged attack. We can litter the space in front of *Perdition* with radar-bright proximity mines. We'll dial them to minimum yield—they shouldn't even penetrate the aft nav armor—but Doxar won't know that. He'll have to assume the worst, and that will tie up his propulsion. He's flying backwards, right? Decelerating toward the planet he covets. He'll be juking laterally, and holding the gamma-drive exhaust out in front of him to clear the path. And even so, he's likely to suffer a near miss or two. Give him something to worry about."

"Hmm," Tamra said, considering that. "And meanwhile?"

"Meanwhile, we launch a salvo of ertially shielded grapplets, minus the warheads. At maximum acceleration, they should reach *Perdition* in under thirty minutes. Targeting the drive section, one hit could slice the magnetic choke clean off, with almost no collateral damage."

A grapplet was a munition whose only propulsion was a gravity laser. It *fell* to the target under its own artificial pull, and if the grapplet was ertially shielded then it fell very quickly indeed. *Malu'i* only had five such weapons in its inventory, though, and could produce no more, for their shields were of collapsium and could not be faxed.

"Those are unstealthed munitions," protested Admiral Brown. "Their release will give away our position."

"Briefly," Xmary conceded. "But we'll maintain evasive maneuvers throughout the deployment, under full invisibility. The last time I did this I was inside the chromosphere of a star, where heat dissipation and signature management were nearly impossible. This'll be a lot easier, for *Perdition*, on her pillar of flame, cannot hide from us at all."

"Hmm."

"The third prong is right out of the navy textbook: a nasen beam to the external engine assemblies. We have to be *very* careful not to destabilize the aye-ma'am plumbing, or the whole ship will go up. But again, it should be possible to take a scalpel to their magnetic choke, after which the failsafes will simply shut down the drive. Uncontrolled reactions should be limited to a few kilotons—hardly noticeable."

This all sounded plausible enough to Tamra, but just to be safe she turned to Brown and said, "Opinion?"

"Standard doctrine calls for a breaching of the enemy's hull, Majesty," Brown replied at once. "However, given the refugee status of this opponent, *Perdition*'s crew is unlikely to be backed up on any sort of durable medium. Any deaths we inflict will therefore be permanent. Under these assumptions, then, Captain Li Weng's plan strikes me as both humane and effective."

Xmary added, "We'd need to launch the first two waves *now*, Majesty. There isn't time for debate—not unless you're willing to erode our positional advantage."

"Hmm." If there was one thing in the universe Tamra hated, it was snap decisions. Still, sometimes they were necessary, and delaying them was itself a snap decision. "Very well. You may proceed, Captain."

The appropriate orders were given, and within the minute both salvos were away.

"There is one additional danger," Xmary noted. "There could be spies aboard *Malu'i* who are capable of revealing our position. This information is of limited value to Doxar, given ten minutes of round-trip signal lag"—She checked a reading, and then amended—"sorry, *nine* minutes' lag. But it would give him a fighting chance. With all that aye-ma'am onboard, he's got a *lot* of energy to throw around."

Admiral Brown coughed out a chuckle at that. He was a good man, and a kindly one, but Tamra had the distinct impression he enjoyed catching out his replacement in a statement like that. "You hardly need worry, madam. This crew—this exact crew, save for yourself—has served together for centuries. We're as much a family as we are a

military unit. If there were criminals or Fatalists, turn-
coats or sympathizers among us, we should know it before now."

"Of course, sir," Xmary said.

More was said and done after that, but there was an
air of busywork about it, until finally the fifteen-minute
mark drew near.

"Do you suppose they'll go quietly?" Tamra asked Brett
Brown.

"They're overmatched," Brown said, as though that answered the question.

"They're desperate," Xmary countered. "They're prepared to die, to kill, to cripple our networks. You can't
imagine the conditions they're leaving behind."

And as if in agreement, Doxar's face reappeared in the
hollie. "Y'all seem not to comprehend. Possibly we'm explained it badly. You're thinking, 'We can survive without
Nescog.' Maybe so. But we can *break* it and send the
pieces tumbling. *Very* dangerous."

"Just divert your course," Tamra said to him, firmly
and reasonably.

But was there time for that message to travel back and
forth? She'd given a deadline, and could not now retract
it. She killed the hollie and asked Xmary, "Time to nasen
beam firing?"

"Ten minutes, Highness. That's all the grace period
they get."

There was no point wishing it otherwise; the great-
grandchildren of Sol had returned, broken and furious,
blaming Tamra for all that had befallen them. And
shouldn't they? Who, if not she, had crafted their fate?
Who else could possibly have changed it? And now here
she was, preparing to punish them—perhaps to *kill*
them—for her own failures.

Her anger vanished in a sudden wash of guilt. Her

sense of duty remained as strong as ever, but her sense of *what* her duty *was* had come unglued. How did it come to this? What was she to do?

Of Brown and Li Weng she asked, "What are the odds we'll blow up that ship?"

"Unknown," Brown said without delay. "The number of variables—"

"Make an estimate," Tamra instructed. Then wondered: did her people even know how?

"Thirty percent," said the governor-captain, who was herself a refugee from the stars. A victim of Tamra's failed policies, of imperfect data and shortsighted advisors. Of simple hubris.

Tamra nodded, absorbing that. "I see. And the chance that we'll kill at least one person? Permanently, irrevocably? For no greater crime than the seeking of asylum?"

"That's all but certain," Xmary said quietly.

Tamra brooded, and would have wept if she didn't still need her face for negotiating. She'd been *fifteen* when they made her Queen of All Things. An orphan, grieving for her drunken, foolish parents. Was it any wonder she'd made mistakes? How could she not? She grieved now— she *ached* for that lonely girl, on whom such burdens were heaped. What a bitter cup to drink from!

To Xmary she said, "Tell me if that ship changes course. If they twitch, if they *move at all*, I want to know about it. Immediately."

"Aye, Majesty."

"Time to nasen firing?"

"Six minutes."

A while later: "Time?"

"Four minutes."

Later still, Xmary piped up with a guarded, "*Perdition* is turning, Majesty."

"Oh, thank God," Tamra said, feeling suddenly clammy

and limp. "Stand down all weapons and prepare to destealth."

But Xmary remained rigid in her captain's chair. "Ma'am, the maneuver could be defensive. It could be *offensive*. It could mean anything."

"Yes, yes. Is their drive beam pointed through the heart of civilization?"

A pause, then, "No."

"Does it impinge on any habitats?"

"No."

"Then we've room to de-escalate this encounter. Stand down all weapons and prepare to escort *Perdition* into high orbit over Lune."

"But Majesty," Brown protested. "The economy—"

"Will muddle along somehow. Stand down all weapons, Xmary. That's a *decree*." Then: "Navywide transmission: Royal Override, all channels, all devices. Cease hostilities and escort *Perdition* to Lune."

History records this command as Tamra's greatest—and final—mistake, and perhaps that is so. But erring on the side of compassion had always been her way, and if nothing lasts forever, then at least a queen should die as she has lived.

Was there a spy onboard *Malu'i*? A saboteur? Was there perhaps some superweapon onboard *Perdition*, whose design and function has since been forgotten? In any case, these words were Tamra's last, for *Malu'i* exploded three seconds thereafter, in a flash of light so brilliant it was visible to telescopes as far away as Eridani itself.

And then the Nescog fell.

The last official act of the Queendom of Sol was a simple radio message eleven hours later, from a King Bruno mad with grief. "The speed of light is hard upon us, my friends. God forgive us our sins. I cannot rule, with confidence, any region larger than the Earth and moon together. Full legal authority is hereby transferred to the regional governors for the duration of this emergency. Royal Override on all channels, all devices. Be brave, and uphold the ideals for which we've stood."

And so they did, those citizens of the Queendom, for the bravely fought decades it took the shattered Nescog—nearly a trillion miniature black holes, equaling the mass of several Earths—to alight upon the planets of Sol, one by one, and crush them to oblivion.

Accipe signaculum doni Spiritus Sancti.

"A denouement gives flight to mere incident," Wenders Rodenbeck wrote in the classic *Past Pie Season*, "freeing us at last from the rigid rail of time. Berries wither, leaves fall, and the mourning dove bows her head, with a song of distant spring beating frozen in her breast."

book three

twilight over astaroth

chapter fifteen

in which the plight of a
world is examined

"In light of your past service to the nation of Imbria," says the woman named Danella Mota, "we are prepared to forgive the excesses of your men on the ramparts today."

They are deep within the city of Timoch, on the hard-pressed world of Lune, where three women—with shadowy Eridanian faces and six-fingered Sirian hands—apparently rule over humanity's strongest remaining nation-state.

"The Furies are most generous," Radmer answers, with a bow of the head that is surely calculated for maximum ambiguity. Is he being surly or ironic? Is he partly or wholly sincere? Bruno can't tell.

A partial answer comes when the second woman, Pine Chadwir, admonishes him, "That term is no longer considered polite, General. We are, as always, the Board of Regents of the Imbrian Nation."

"Ah, yes. My failing memory is abetted by your grandmother's sense of humor in these matters, Madam Regent."

But "Furies" is a good nickname for these three old

women, who command a quarter of Lune's surface from this very room, the Silver Chamber. They are seated on a dais ringed by aides and pages, scribes and whispering advisors, but the room's three primary lights—halide-filament vacuum bulbs, Bruno thinks—point straight down at them, with a smaller, dimmer bulb casting a cone of yellow around himself and Radmer.

Behind them, the Olders Sidney Lyman and Brian Romset—who were permitted to accompany Radmer as bodyguards—exude an air of angry but fearless distrust. And in counterpoint, a dozen Dolceti guards in canary-yellow uniforms loom quietly in the shadows behind the dais, looking grudgingly respectful but ready for anything. *Dead before you hit the ground, villain,* their looks seem to say, though if it came to that Bruno could probably take down one or two of them himself before succumbing to any serious injury.

But all things considered, the chamber is exceedingly quiet, and the lighting makes it seem dreamlike as well, and the seated ladies mythic in proportion and demeanor. All they need is a spindle, loom, and scissors to complete the effect. But out of courtesy they speak the Old Tongue—essentially Queendom-standard English—and Radmer, with a different kind of courtesy, does the same. That makes them seem more human, and anyway Bruno is well familiar with the psychological tricks a leadership can employ to enhance its mystique, its air of natural authority. The Queendom was founded on these principles, long before he'd been drafted as its king.

"Do enlighten us, Radmer, with your reason for this accostment," says the third Fury, whose name Bruno can no longer remember from the introductions. Sprain? Spirulina? Something like that. "It may surprise you to learn we've an invasion to repel."

"The very reason I'm here," Radmer tells her, "for I

watched Nubia fall to the Glimmer King's armies. I know very well what Imbria faces in the coming weeks."

"Our guards report you've distinguished yourself in clashes against the enemy."

"Aye, madam, on Aden Bluff and outside your gates, and in Nubia before that."

"We also had a string of reports out of Highrock. That you supervised the construction of a very large catapult? Using the Tillspar bridge as its lath?"

"That's so, madam."

"And this catapult is capable of flinging a hollow canister completely off the planette?"

"Not to escape velocity, madam. The capsule falls back again unless its rockets are fired. But yes. The VLC can also bombard any point on Lune, though its accuracy is measured in kilometers, and its firing time in days. If we knew the location of the Glimmer King's palace—assuming such a place exists at all—then with a hundred shots we might have a hope of hitting it. But I doubt we'll be granted the time such an experiment would require."

"Indeed," says Pine Chadwir. Then she pauses, looking apologetic, as though her next words will sound insane. "But one of our agents observed *you* climbing into such a canister, being fired at the heavens and not returning during the three days of his observation. Is there any truth to this?"

"Aye, madam. The Imbrian astronomer Rigby believed there was someone living on Varna."

"The slowest moon. And also the most distant?"

"Correct, although there was a farther moon in days gone by. And since traffic to Varna ended with the Shattering, any population there was likely to include Olders from the Iridium Days or before. Specifically, Rigby was of the opinion that the group was small—possibly a single individual."

Understanding blooms in the eyes of the Furies. "This man?" They point at Bruno, studying him closely for the first time.

"I'm called Ako'i," Bruno tells them. Not a name but a title: Professor.

This prompts some surprise on their parts. "He can speak!" And this is no idle exclamation, for Bruno passed the time on Varna as a kind of sleepwalker, repeating the same few tasks over and over again, day in and day out. Unaware of the passing centuries—unaware of anything, including himself. Beyond his first few weeks on that neutronium island, he can't remember a single thing until Radmer's arrival.

Indeed, until a few hours after that, for the sleepwalking did not immediately subside. He had spoken—even held fragmentary conversations—but either his brain's neocortex had not fully engaged, or else its hippocampus had been sluggish about laying down new memories. "Neurosensory dystropia," they called it. Or "maroon sickness," or "zombitis," which wasn't even a proper word. In extreme cases it was irreversible.

In declining that final trip from Varna to the chaos of an overpopulated Lune, Bruno had been trying, in a way, to draw an end to his long life. But he hadn't really understood what awaited him. Now the image makes him shudder: the "indeceased," wandering like animate ghosts, wearing grooves in the countryside with their feet. According to Radmer, whole villages had been known to succumb, going blankly through the motions of life until their crops eventually failed and they starved.

"I can reason," he assures the Furies. "Though perhaps not well."

They study him some more, furrowing and clucking. "Radmer, dear, this is a season of ill omens. The sun has been kicked twice, fair Nubia has fallen, and rather than fleeing, or pledging your sword to our defense, you've brought us an old man. Your ways have always been strange—since the world's very creation, we're told—but this is truly baffling. What do you seek from us?"

"The sun has been kicked?" Bruno repeats, wondering what such a thing could mean.

"A metaphor for eclipse," says Radmer. "Murdered Earth transits the sun, which appears to explode and then re-form. Lesser kickings occur when one of the other murdered planets passes in front of something."

"Ah," Bruno says, for he has seen that sight himself, long ago. To the Furies he says, "But that's a matter of clockwork, yes? Not an omen, but a happenstance of whirling bodies."

"So our ministers inform us," says the oldest of the Furies, as though it's a matter of little consequence. "But we face extinction. Nubia has been stripped of metal, and is it coincidence that the metal armies which razed it have since doubled in size? The reports we have from that lost republic are as terrifying as they are sparse. Mass starvation, mass enslavement. In the face of that, everything is an omen."

"We're here to help," Radmer assures her. "This man is possibly the oldest living person, and his knowledge of Queendom technology is unsurpassed, easily dwarfing my own."

"That's wonderful," says Danella Mota, "except that we have no Queendom technology. The city's last well-stone is buried in the dumps, for we were unable to make it work."

"If that's so," Bruno says to her, "you should exhume it and allow me to make blitterstaves of the material. It isn't difficult, and it would improve your defensive position enormously. With care, every square meter of rubble can be fashioned into twenty weapons."

This comment gains him the Furies' full attention.

"Ah, yes," says Radmer, though surely the idea is obvious to anyone who has been both an architect and a general. *And* a matter programmer.

"Don't patronize me," Bruno tells him. Then, to the Furies: "How much intact material can you salvage? The deconstruction needs to have been performed in particular ways, to avoid damage to the nanofiber weave that produces the pseudoatoms."

That goes a bit over their heads, but they are persuaded nevertheless, and in short order a courier is sent out to order an immediate excavation of the city dumps.

"So," says Pine Chadwir to Radmer, with half an eye on Bruno, "this ancient vessel still holds a bit of wine. You have our thanks, General. Does he do anything else?"

Radmer forms an embarrassed half smile. "Actually, I had something quite different in mind, and with your permission I'll soon remove this man from Timoch altogether."

"Yes?" says the eldest Fury skeptically. "Our would-be savior? And where exactly would you bring him?"

"The Stormlands," Radmer says. And everyone in the room seems to gasp in surprise, then slowly nod in agreement.

Soon they're in a different room whose decorations consist mainly of dead robots crucified on the walls. The human beings—and the Olders—are all standing around a table whose surface is a map of the country. It's rather misleading, Bruno thinks, because Imbria covers almost half of the northern hemisphere, and stretching it out flat produces eerie distortions in the squozen moon's once-familiar features. Fortunately, a large globe hangs above the table for reference, and another one sits on the floor behind it in a two-axis mechanical spin platform that would have been perfectly at home in the Old Girona of Bruno's youth.

The table is dotted with chessmen—mirror-shiny for the Glimmer King's armies, blue for Imbria's, and red for the tattered, fleeing remnants of the armies of Nubia. The planette's Olders are apparently too few and scattered to merit chessmen of their own, but if they ever find their way to this table, Bruno has no doubt they will be some weary shade of gray.

Anyway, at a glance he can see just how badly the war is going; two southern cities—labeled Renold and Bolo—are staring already into the faceless faces of the approaching enemy, and if the robots march by night as well as by day (and why wouldn't they?), the sites will be under siege by midnight, and likely demolished before sunrise, just over sixty hours from now. These sunset rays slanting through the slatted windows might be the last daylight the two cities will ever see.

Meanwhile, a third branch of the robot army is streaming northward between the two, aiming for the city of Tosen and, one hundred fifty kilometers beyond it, the capital city of Timoch itself. The Imbrian Sea—a bit larger than in Bruno's day—fills a basin just west of Timoch, stretching northward to the Mairan Shelf and west to the Stark Hills in a rough triangle three hundred kilometers on a side, covering the middle third between the planette's equator and the north pole.

And chillingly, there are at least a dozen smaller silver chessmen—the Glimmer King's scouting patrols—scattered all the way from Imbria's border to the southern shore of its sea. The only saving grace—the only thing that keeps it from looking like certain doom—is the fact that the bulk of the robot army is still in Nubia, in Lune's southern hemisphere, and does not appear on this map at all. But even Bruno can sense the mass of them down there, implicit in the northward-streaming formations.

"How accurate are these unit positions?" he murmurs to Radmer.

"Very. Cover the nation in hundred-kilometer circles and you'll find a watch tower on the highest points of each, with dozens more running through the passes and lowlands in-between. During daylight hours, everything that moves is tracked with great precision."

"How do the towers communicate?"

"Semaphore," Radmer says, as though this should be obvious. "It's a quaternary code loosely based on DNA sequences. With properly trained crews, their data rates approach two digits per second, including parity and checksum bits on every tenth flag. It can even send pictures."

"Hmm." Not a stupid way to handle things, though a lot of skill and muscle would be required. Something similar had been tried in Bruno's native Catalonia, before the Sabadell-Andorra earthquake had ended that nation-state's flirtation with things medieval. But he seems to recall that effort being abandoned in favor of an Old Modern maser network.

And it's interesting, he thinks, that Imbria has electricity but no sign of lasers or computers. No telegraphs, no wireless. Its leaders, advised at least occasionally by real astronomers, have a rough understanding of the heavens they cannot touch. And they know what wellstone is, though they lack the equipment to produce it or the technical skill to program it.

Clearly they're not a stupid people. Bruno surprises himself with a sudden ache of sympathy for them, caught as they are in some bizarre remnant of Queendom-era intrigue which they surely can't understand. Not because they're incapable, but because no one has bothered to explain it to them.

"Someone has revived an old fax machine," he announces to the room, when a lull in the conversation permits. The Imbrians fall quiet at that, and suddenly all eyes are on him. Obligingly, he steps over to a crucified robot—one of a dozen mounted around the room's circumference. He points to the shattered iron box on the side of its head. "As you might guess, this annex, this junction box for external wiring, is not a part of the original design. It's been soldered on—here and here—using aluminum, which adheres well to both silicon and impervium. And while the skin may look flawless it isn't really. It's been scratched and filled, you see? Even impervium, eleven times harder than diamond, will flake and abrade with sufficient mistreatment. There's a thin layer of resin in every small groove; this hull has been expertly polished."

He moves to another robot. God, they look so familiar. So harmless! "But see here? The same welds. The same scratches. These robots are of Queendom design, crudely modified but otherwise well cared for. And they're all identical. The fax machine has a buffer, you see—a kind of memory of its last few operations. Someone found the fax with its libraries scrambled, but the image of a robot stored intact in its buffers. A household robot, ordinarily harmless. And this Glimmer King—surely an Older of great technical skill—cut it open and jumpered its wiring. This is no small feat, for the Asimov protocols are buried deep in the wellstone itself, and are designed to reconfigure around any casual tampering. But he accomplished the task, and put the robot back together, and fed it into the fax again, to be duplicated and reduplicated.

"But as you've surmised, he needs metal. Gold and aluminum are best, but almost any conductor will do—wellstone is anywhere from twelve to twenty percent metal by volume. The rest is all silicon and oxygen, easily obtained from even the most sterile of soils. He has a small quarry nearby, you can bet on that. But not a mine, not a refining operation. Why bother, when he can loot the hard-won fruits of civilization instead?"

"Why?" someone demands. "Why would he do such a thing?"

"To conquer the world," Bruno answers simply. "To smash it and remake it according to some blueprint of his own. The lives of his victims are incidental; he's chasing some mirage of imagined 'greatness.'"

"Blueprint?" someone else asks, in thickly accented tones.

"Sorry, a . . . a map. A design. An image of how things will appear when he's finished. The intermediate stages are nothing to him; your suffering is meaningless. He's got his eyes on the future, not the present."

"You sound as though you know him," Pine Chadwir says, not quite accusingly.

"I know his type," Bruno answers. "Given the constraints on your life span and population size, such individuals may be rare on Lune. But they used to crop up with fair regularity. When exactly did these troubles begin?"

"It's difficult to say with any certainty," Radmer answers, jumping ahead of the Furies and their attendants in a way Bruno would have found rude. He walks to one of the globes, spins it ass-up, and points his finger at a region marked in orange, which includes the south pole and over half the former Farside. "Here, in the high desert hills of Astaroth, there have been robot sightings for fifteen, maybe twenty years. They were dismissed until two years ago, when it became clear that Astaroth had ceased to exist as an organized nation.

"This may sound odd, but the actual date of its collapse is unknown. Astaroth had always been a sparsely populated country, with internal squabbles and few diplomatic ties to the rest of Lune. Most of its people just disappeared, quietly, and by the time refugees started finding their way to Nubia, why, the Nubians' days were already numbered."

Bruno nodded, processing that. "And where does the name Glimmer King come from? These refugees?"

"According to them, it comes from the robots themselves. I've never encountered the story in anything but fragments. He has . . . other names as well."

Bruno looks him in the eye and nods very slightly, acknowledging that. There have been rumors, yes.

"Robots have been known to speak," says Danella Mota. "They addressed the Senatoria Plurum in City Campanas, for example, shortly before sacking it and killing the people inside. Only a few escaped with their lives, so I can't help wondering what the robots said, or why they bothered. It seems capricious, especially for machines."

"Only because you don't see the plans that drive them," Bruno tells her. "But these can be deduced through careful study, and usually are. No one has ever conquered the whole human race—not without a majority vote in favor."

"You have an air of comfortable authority about you," says the eldest Fury to Bruno. "Mr. . . . Ako'i, is it? So does General Radmer, but he defers to you, not the other way round."

"I was once a teacher," Bruno answers. Which is certainly the truth, if not the whole.

"Hmm," she says, unconvinced. "I suppose this 'fax

machine' is like a mirror? Its reflections are made solid somehow, but the device itself can be smashed?"

"Certainly."

"And this is your plan? To find it and break it?"

Here Bruno comes up short, because no plan has been explained to him in anything but the vaguest terms. The "Stormlands" are visible on the map as a gray oval smear, perhaps eighty kilometers wide and a hundred and eighty tall, near Imbria's uninhabited southeast corner. The province is marked with the name "Shanru." But no such place had existed in his day. A land of permanent storm? Why would he go there? What would he accomplish?

His ignorance seems to disappoint the eldest Fury. To Radmer she says, "Will you elaborate on your plans, General? You can risk your neck in the Stormlands without our blessing. You're here because you need something."

To this Pine Chadwir adds, "If you can fling yourself all the way to Varna, then surely you can fling yourself directly into the Stormlands' eye. Assuming it has one."

"It does, Madam Regent," Radmer says. "I've seen it myself, from high above the world. A fifteen-kilometer hole in the clouds. Its western edge, against the Blood Mountains, is piled high with sand dunes, but near the center I saw a crisscross of straight, dark lines."

"Manassa?" asks the eldest Fury, her eyes glittering in the sunset.

"The fabled city itself," Radmer agrees, "exactly as Zaleis the Wanderer claimed. He really did make it in and out."

"And so you believe his other claims," says Danella Mota, "his 'Dragon of Shanru' and his 'engines and objects of great antiquity and wholly mysterious purpose.'"

"There were no dragons in this world when it was new, madam. Whether any have been created since then I couldn't say. But aye, the rest of it I believe. And this man, who calls himself Ako'i, is better qualified than any living person to bring these engines and objects back to life. The Glimmer King's robots are not invincible, just strong and numerous. With proper equipment on the human side, it should be possible to defeat them."

"Possible," says the eldest Fury with a slow nod. "Well, that's something. But what do you need from us?"

"Transportation," says Radmer. "Armed escort. A safe-conduct passport which your turnpike guards will accept. The enemy will have taken my capsule by now, and even if I had a spare, landing inside the eye of a storm would be risky indeed. Hiking in on foot, as Zaleis did, is more likely to succeed. I've studied his path, which appears to be the best compromise between weather and terrain. I believe we can duplicate it."

"We cannot spare troops, Radmer," says Danella Mota warily.

"I need only a few. A dozen Dolceti, perhaps."

The room explodes at that remark. "Dolceti! A dozen! This Older is as mad as all the rest."

"Your request is denied," says a harried-sounding Pine Chadwir. "You ask the one thing we cannot possibly grant, in this hour of greatest need."

"Then I'll take my leave," says Radmer, "and return to the veils of Echo Valley to await this world's destruction. I would stand and die with you, madam, if I thought it would do any good. But if civilization must die again, I prefer to be among friends."

Now the room falls silent, and fearful, and all eyes are on the Furies, wondering what they'll say next. It's the eldest who speaks first, and her tone is wistful and quiet. "They say you built the world, Radmer, as a carpenter might build a house."

"The world was here long before me, madam. All I did was remodel it."

"So. Not quite a god, then. But something powerful nonetheless. And still afraid! You've traveled far on our behalf—to Varna and back."

And here Bruno catches a glimpse of the young Conrad Mursk in the weathered features of Radmer. "I've traveled much farther than that, Madam Regent. To the stars themselves, where this sunlight won't arrive for years."

"You're very old," she says, considering that. "And wise, and strange. And very kind—or foolish—to offer this peculiar assistance to us, who barely know you. Whether it help or not, it surely cannot make things any worse. I give you twenty Dolceti, General, and the blessing of the Board of Regents."

chapter sixteen

in which a fateful journey is undertaken

"One of the diamond pillars buckled," Radmer is telling Bruno, "and the neutronium plate above it slipped almost to the center of Lune. The plates are flat hexagons, right? But at the surface, the region of depressed gravity is more nearly circular. And with mountain ranges on either side, you can't even really see that. It ends up being more of an oval."

"A permanent low-pressure system," Bruno muses. "A permanent thunderstorm."

"More nearly a hurricane. It brings no joy to the region, no refreshment. Only a hard cleansing. And when it happened, when the pillar buckled and the plate fell and the ground above it cracked and sank, the shock waves struck every fault and fissure in the whole damned planette, releasing gigatons of stored energy."

"This was the 'Shattering,' that looms so large in these people's history?" Bruno asks.

Radmer confirms it. "Half the population died in the first few hours, and within a week no two bricks were left standing, anywhere in the world. Lune was the jewel of post-Queendom civilization, and without it things just . . .

fell apart. Again. No more rockets, no heavy industry of any kind. It's only in the past two centuries that there's been any real consolidation. And frankly I'd still call this a borderline dark age, even without the war."

Bruno weighs this against his conscience, probing for the guilt he ought to feel. Surely this Shattering is another calamity he could have prevented. But as the two of them step through an archway and into a large courtyard of grass and concrete and grimly drilling soldiers, he glances up at the sky. The sun has finally gone down, but the clouds are aflame, dwarfing the works of Man beneath them. And he finds he can no longer be angry with himself for honest mistakes, or for living through to this moment.

Still, more from a sense of duty than anything else he says, "You and I have a lot of bodies at our feet."

"Aye, well. At least there *is* a Lune. We can take credit for that."

"There'd still be an Earth, if not for the Nescog. If not for me, personally."

But Radmer just shrugs. "Something would have killed it, sooner or later. It's the way of things. The important question is whether it was good while it lasted."

Bruno, though horrified, can't help but chuckle at that. "You've become a deathist, lad. Who'd've thought?"

"Aye," says Radmer, cracking a feeble grin of his own. "A vegetarian, too, for in this life the meat comes from creatures. They have faint little hopes and dreams of their own, and I've made war on them long enough. Why should some chicken lose everything, to add another day to *this*?" He waves contemptuously at his own flesh.

"Would you hasten your own story's end?" Bruno probes. Among men as old as they, it isn't a rude question at all. "Is that why you became a soldier?"

But Radmer dismisses that notion just as contemptuously. "I've always been a soldier, a fighter, intolerant of oppression. I fought *you*, once."

"So you did," Bruno muses, remembering back to those days, when Conrad Mursk and Bascal Edward had been inseparable, and the problems of the world could be dismissed as mere childishness. It doesn't seem so long ago, really, and *there's* a sentiment the deathists would have an opinion about. Did the long years of his life count for so little? "Still, here we are. Side by side for a new war."

Radmer grunts. "I gave that up, too—soldiering. Really! With a fax-filtered body and three thousand years of dirty tricks, it was like shooting babies. Not a risk to myself at all. It was nothing a moral person could condone."

"But you'll fight robots," Bruno said.

"Aye, one last time. In my next life I'll be a farmer, bringing sustenance into the world."

Now there's an interesting thought. What will the resurrected Bruno do, if it turns out there's a future for him to do it in? Teach? Open a bistro, as his father had done long ago, in a land not so terribly different from this one? The idea seems bizarre, alien, tragically comic. But not impossible.

Any further rumination on the subject, though, is extinguished by the arrival of Bordi, the Dolceti Primus and Captain of the Timoch Guard.

"Where are your men?" he asks crisply, in the Old Tongue.

"Departed," says Radmer. "Returned to protect their own homes and families."

Well, yes, thinks Bruno, but not as easily as that. At the last, Sidney Lyman had resisted. "So, what, you're going to help the humans, be a hero, and we're dismissed?"

"You didn't even want to be here," Radmer told him. "I dragged you."

"Come with us," Lyman said urgently. "Or let us come with you. There's too few of us in the world, sir, to be scattering to the winds like this. We've got to hang together."

"I agree. Which is why you're needed back at Echo Valley."

There'd been more to it than that, but eventually Lyman and his followers had given up, realizing that their old commander simply wouldn't be responsible for them any longer, would not allow them into harm's way on his account. On the one hand it was a sorry way to repay their loyalty—with the barbed kindness of condescension. On the other hand, it was exactly what Bruno would have done in his place. If the world be doomed, well, let them salvage what they could. *That's an order, soldier.*

There are so many people he misses, people he loves but will never see again. If he could reach back and save even one of them—not just Tamra, but anyone—he'd do it in a heartbeat, whatever the cost. But here there are no such decisions for him to make. Here he's a relic, nothing more, and that's all right. He'll do his bit—or try, anyway—and fade back into the mists.

"It's just the two of you?" Bordi asks.

"Right," says Radmer. "And if it's all the same to you, I'll delegate all the logistics. Just get us to the Stormlands and back, before this city falls."

"Already working on it, General. Your timing is good; with the sun setting, the upslope winds will begin blowing in a few hours. Eastward, against the mountains. That will buy us a hundred kilometers right there. I'd advise you both to get some sleep beforehand."

"Why?" asks Radmer. "How are we traveling?"

"On the back of a flau," Bordi answers, in hard and mirthful tones.

This turns out to be a living creature, mostly hollow and filled with hydrogen. With the proportions of a Tongan royal pleasure yacht, the thing has a broad, flat back some fifteen meters wide and forty-five long, with a bulbous, vaguely ship-shaped body underneath. At the front, its mouth is surprisingly tiny, and surrounded by eyes and nostrils of alien design.

"It looks like a leviathan," Bruno says, referring to the largest of the multicellular creatures in the ocean of Pup, the marginally habitable world circling Wolf 359. The thought brings a pang to his heart, for the King of Wolf had been Edward Bascal Faxborn, an alternate version of Bascal Edward de Towaji Lutui. King Eddie to his admirers, he'd been by all accounts a fair-minded ruler who had taken more closely after Bruno and especially Tamra.

And though he'd thought his grief long exhausted, Bruno finds that the thought of Tamra Lutui can still wrench his insides. Not just the coolly smiling Queen of Sol—though he misses her, too—but the twenty-year-old girl who'd gigglingly granted him the title of declarant in a room full of well-dressed strangers. And then philander, yes, a few months later—in her royal bedchamber, attended only by those dainty robots that looked more like ballerinas than like the later Palace Guards.

"It was a leviathan once," Radmer says, yanking Bruno back to the present. "But now it swims a sea of air."

And that's absurd, because the Wolfans had never managed a starship to return even their own miserable selves to Sol, much less a mindless, overgrown alien invertebrate.

He says, "Was the genome transmitted over the Instelnet? Part of the intellectual property traffic?"

"It was, yes, during the late Queendom era. Eridani bought it from Wolf, and carried it here in their armadas' libraries. And since the four known life-bearing worlds were all seeded by the same primordial source, deep in the galaxy somewhere, it wasn't hard to insert that genome into a Terran yeast cell and convince it to grow. If you recall, the early Lunites were quite talented bioengineers."

"I don't recall it, no," says Bruno. "I was quite busy at that time, trying to save a bit of Earth. All in vain, as it turned out, but it was important to try."

Radmer muses for a moment before adding, "Those engineers had all the best equipment from the old Queendom, and all the best techniques from half a dozen colonies. And there was no law to stop them, not really. From the original genomes, of course, they began their customizations; the flau was only one project of hundreds."

The creature is ugly in the extreme, its lumpy, rubbery skin gleaming in the rainbow light of Murdered Earth. It doesn't seem to have much shape, either, though that might be more a function of its lying on the hard, flat pavement of the Timoch International Airport. In the water, with its fans and frills extended, the leviathan had always moved with the same slow, eerie beauty of sea creatures everywhere.

Heck, it probably still drifts in the seas of Pup, dreamily unaware of the solid little beings that came and went in the caverns of its world's rocky highlands. Unlike the Eridanians, the Wolfans could at least *go* outside, if not exactly live there. They could explore their ocean, could sting its residents with probes and biopsy needles. A few humans had even been *eaten* by leviathans, and at least one man had been rescued alive, days later, after cutting through to an air sac and subsisting on the moisture of its walls. It was huge interstellar news at the time. But even that had scarcely seemed to register with the affected creature, which swam peacefully away in unhurried search of more cooperative meals.

Here, the "flau" has had metal rings driven through its body, with hemp and leather ropes strung through them, making it a kind of artifact, a ship, an old-fashioned beast of burden. A thing both owned and controlled, no longer free.

"This is how people travel?" he asks disapprovingly.

"When necessary," Radmer allows. "Though smaller groups would generally use a cloth balloon, and single individuals can still travel by glider. If they begin at sufficient altitude and ride the thermals skillfully, glider pilots have been known to circumnavigate the world."

This surprises Bruno only slightly, because the world is small, and the mountains of Lune tower much higher over its seas than the hills of Earth ever did, giving rise sometimes to *very* strong updrafts. Still, this place evokes a sort of continuous amazement in him, for what appears rustic—even primitive—at first glance, always turns out to be something more. Something clever, something optimized for the environment and the available resources. The absence of wellstone—indeed, of semiconductors in general—has pushed the Lunites to almost uncanny extremes of artistry and invention. And that makes it not so terribly different from the Queendom, which after all had hired an inventor as its king.

"Why not simply use a blimp?" he asks.

And Radmer counters, "Why not stay home? The flau can be a bit tricky—people have been known to fall off when they get the hiccups—but they know their own way. They're self-healing and self-balancing, and they almost never get hit by lightning. They just...go around the storms."

"General," says Bordi, striding toward them in the darkness. "The wind is shifting, so we'd best get aloft while we can. You two can lash your bags at the stern. Mind the steersman, though; put them exactly where he specifies, and no other place."

"Aye," Radmer acknowledges. "Thank you, Captain."

Two other people follow in Bordi's wake, and after a moment Bruno recognizes them as Natan and Zuq, the Dolceti who stood with him at the city gate, while the others ran off to battle.

"Good evening," he says to them, without any particular emphasis. And their reply, though less than enthusiastic, contains a good bit more deference than their earlier speech had. "It's Encyclopedia Man. Hello, sir. Apparently we're at your service."

"Not by choice, surely," he says, and they surprise him by denying it. "Now, now. Any ward of the Regents is a ward of the Order of Dolcet, and deserving the best protection. We volunteered and were accepted."

"Well," Bruno says, feeling a bit of human warmth stirring in the ancient hollows of his heart. "You have my gratitude, then."

"Up you go," says Zuq, grabbing a rope ladder and climbing upward, showing the way.

"After you," says Natan, with a valetlike gesture. Radmer and Bordi have gotten separated somehow—Bruno can see them heading up toward the flau's pinched little face—and he appears to be in the care of these two men once again. So he climbs the ropes himself, clambering past a network of rings and fishnet and flat leather straps.

The deck of the flau—if indeed that's the proper term—is a woven mat remarkably like the deck of a traditional Tongan catamaran, except that the bark it's fashioned from feels thicker and tougher, the strips much wider. All around it is a waist-high railing of something like bamboo—some light, stiff, hollow plant that looks gray under the night sky.

Immediately he's set upon by a bare-chested little Luner man wearing a vest and pants and cylindrical cap of supple brown leather. "Who's you?" the man demands in a thick New Tongue accent, and if the Dolceti have dispelled any notion of these "humans" being childlike or comical, this stocky, strutting, hypercephalic figure provides the counterpoint. "Older? Been y' on a flau before? Don' put tha down thar, foo!"

"Our steersman, Fander Kytu," Zuq explains, leaning easily against the railing, which for him is nearly chest-high. "Don't make him angry, or we'll have a long night of it. Be assured, he's the best in the world at what he does."

"Bag," says Fander, pointing to a netted-over heap near the deck's stern.

"I'll take it," says Natan, relieving Bruno of his few meager possessions. Except the sword and pistol the Furies gave him, which he keeps in leather scabbards at his side. The sword is not an air foil. In fact, it's not a real sword by any reasonable standard. It's made of opaque forged steel, for one thing, without so much as a diamond coating to stiffen it and hold its edge. And it doesn't vibrate or glow white-hot or anything, so if he's to cut anything with it he'll need to swing very hard indeed.

A blitterstaff would be much more the thing, but the Imbrians have made a mess of their remaining wellstone. Bruno was only able to salvage five staves from the entire façade, and they were of such unspeakable value here that to ask for one was to ask too much.

For that matter, the pistol they've given him would be little more than a toy in the Queendom. It fires thumbnail-sized metal bullets at only slightly more than the speed of sound! One well-placed shot is enough to fell a grown man, and a better-placed one will burst the junction box affixed to a robot's head, with generally terminal results. But he will have to aim it himself, by eye and by hand.

Still, he's seen too much of this world to want to travel it unarmed, and at the end of the day a blade is still a blade, and a projectile a projectile. He knows what to do with them.

"All board!" calls the steersman to the Dolceti, who are swarming up the rigging like they've been crewing such flights all their lives. Bruno catches sight of Radmer up by the bow. "Wind arising! Hook off! Cast by!"

And these commands—both to the Dolceti and to the minimal ground crew on the pavement below—suffice. Over the next half minute the mooring ropes are untied and the flau—swelling beneath them—becomes a thing independent of the ground on which it rests. Not airborne yet, but neither wholly in the thrall of gravity.

"She weighs only as much as a cow, if you can believe it," Zuq says conversationally. "Even with her bladders flat, old Natan and I here could practically carry her where we're going. But it is a fine thing, to ride the upslope on a winter's night, with the light of Murdered Earth shining down all around."

And as if in answer, the flau beneath them gives a final sigh of inflation, and lifts gently away from the planette.

It's funny, Bruno thinks, that a black hole should be surrounded by so much light. But the halo of Murdered Earth—shaped like the stem and cap of a toppled mushroom—captures the full glory of Sol and tears it apart into nested rainbows. The whole thing is larger and brighter than the full moon had been in the skies of Old Earth.

And while it moves across the heavens on a twenty-eight-day cycle, first approaching the sun and then opposing it, it does not go through "phases" per se. It's always bright, and washes out the sky so badly that he supposes most Lunites have never seen the Milky Way on anything but Earthless nights. There must be a lot of things they never see, and still more they've never heard or dreamed of.

Still, Lune's jagged landscape is eerily beautiful by this varicolored glow. And the stars—what he can see of them—are peaceful, and since the flau is drifting eastward on the wind itself, at the speed of the wind, the air around it gives an impression of stillness, even as the Earthlit roads and farms roll by underneath. Ahead is the Sawtooth, the first range of the very tall Apenine mountains. Beneath them lies Aden Plateau, where Bruno and Radmer first landed in their sphere of brass. Lord, that was only forty hours ago—less than a day by the Luner clock. But it seems a longer time. Weeks.

"Look," Zuq tells him at one point, "there goes another flau."

And indeed, there it is, spread out above them and slightly south, pulling ahead in a stronger wind. Bruno can see its downward-pointing sail, so very much like the frills of Pup's ever-slumbering leviathan. From this vantage he can get a sense of the creature's entire shape, its natural form, which looks neither tortured nor artificial. In fact, from a distance it's quite beautiful, an elegant blending of form and function.

He sees another one far below, its decks swarming with men and women in white jackets, singing some bittersweet melody. To celebrate their escape from the doomed city? To mourn it? But then, with a shock, he recognizes the faint tune itself: it's Bascal Edward's Song of Physics, which once sought to capture the essence of Queendom science in twenty memorable stanzas.

It's beautiful. Bruno can barely make out the words, but it seems to him that the song has been passed down intact, in something close to the Old Tongue. And suddenly the tears are flowing freely from his eyes, for whatever sins might weigh against his son's name, Bascal had risen to that particular challenge with all the grace and skill his genetics and training could muster. He'd been, if nothing else, a truly brilliant poet.

And of course any thought of Bascal is really a thought of Tamra, and this makes him leak saline just that much faster.

"Are you all right?" Natan asks him, coming over to lean his elbows on the railing. If Bruno tried that on this lightly rolling deck, he'd be pitched right over the edge the first time his attention wandered. But Natan is shorter, and surer of foot, and to Bruno's surprise he sounds more than professionally concerned.

Angry at himself, Bruno wipes his eyes on a sleeve. "This is what old men do, I'm afraid. The grief comes upon us in unguarded moments."

And Natan surprises him again by asking, "Was it real beautiful, your world? Your many, many worlds?"

"Indeed," Bruno confirms, as a fresh wave of tears rolls down his cheeks. "It sounds fatuous to say it, I realize, but there was more beauty and wonder than you can imagine. Did we even notice at the time? But your own world is beautiful, too. Promise me this, guardsman: take nothing for granted in your flicker-short lifetime. Appreciate."

"I will," says Natan. "I do. Life is a precious gift."

Still wiping his tears, Bruno chuckles at that. "An odd

sentiment—don't you think?—for an elite soldier in a sorely endangered country. Shouldn't you be a Stoic?"

"Uh? I don't know that word."

"Er, silent. Economical in word and motion. Quietly suffering, to the point of simplemindedness."

"Ah." It's Natan's turn to chuckle. "We have no need of that, sir. That warrior mysticism, that claptrap. We don't have to be that sterile. We have the blindsight training."

Suddenly the wicker deck is creaking under boot-steps, and Radmer is there. "Ako'i?"

"I'm fine," Bruno assures him, to forestall any involved discussion. The concern in Radmer's voice is far less friendly, for Radmer's duty is not to a person or an ideal, but to the human race generally. It's a heavy burden, and admits little room for empathy or play. "Just reminiscing a bit."

"That can be dangerous. Have you slept enough? Some of the men are tying down, over there on center-deck."

"I'm not blind, Architect. I can see what's happening five meters from my elbow."

"Yes, well, you'll need your rest for the climb. After we land, we'll be ascending eight vertical kilometers in less than a hundred horizontally."

"What's our entry point?" asks Zuq, somewhere behind them all at the stern.

"Black Forest Pass," Radmer answers, with such portentous foreboding that even Bruno, who's never heard of the place, feels a shiver run through him at the prospect.

chapter seventeen

in which light fails

Bruno finds himself brushing a quantum horse— white with black spots, like a negative image of the wide, unforgiving cosmos. This creature, he knows, has the power to carry him anywhere he wants to go. The catch being, he first has to go *everywhere*, and then collapse his waveform to a single location. And that seems an odd bargain to strike; there's a faint whiff of brimstone on the air. But there's a destination he must reach, an error of judgment he must correct before...before...

But the flau jostles beneath him, and the wicker deck creaks, and he opens his eyes to darkness. The dream flees to wherever it is that dreams go, and is forgotten. Although he doesn't know it, Bruno has had this dream five times before, and the warnings buried within it have been a great, if vague, source of trouble to his waking mind.

"Where are we?" he asks, sitting up abruptly. The coarse rope around his waist draws taut.

"Landing," says Zuq, who sits beside him as a man might sit by a campfire. For warmth, for a kind of company. Along the railing that circles the flau's broad back, every third post is triple-high, with a paper lantern lashed to a hook. The lamps have been lit with electric bulbs, and from this vantage Bruno can see there are similar lamps as well on the ground below. Landing lights.

And the stars are still up there in the sky, though the Murdered Earth clings low above the clouds which hide the western horizon, and the sea. But there is something ineffably *dark* about this place. The light doesn't quite seem to reach the ground, or else reaches it but is not reflected back. Indeed, outside of the tiny islands of illumination underneath the airfield lights, he can't *see* the ground at all. He has no idea whether they're landing in a valley or on a mountaintop, although something in the angle of the breeze implies neither. On a shelf, halfway up a steep mountainside? To the east there's nothing but blackness, and the voices of men, calling out landing instructions, echo as if from a canted, irregular wall.

"Where are we *physically*?" he presses, frowning down at the knot that holds him. "The Sawtooth Mountains, obviously. But is this the pass?"

"Aye," says Zuq. "The Black Forest herself. We're about three and a half kilometers above sea level, on the Andrea Bench overlooking Aden. Due east of Timoch, give or take. The land rises eastward like a staircase."

"I can't see a thing," says Bruno. His vision is still quite good—probably better than any of these "humans" can boast, but their trait of rapidly shifting skin pigment has made even Zuq into a shadow. It's rather warm for a winter's night in the high mountains, but dark skin will more readily absorb any ambient, radiant heat. In the cool and dark, these people, these humans, grow darker still.

"You're not the only one," answers Zuq. But he points to a faint glow, perhaps a hundred meters off the flau's port side. "That's Gillem Forta, the army base. Eight hundred men on station, and another fifty in semaphore shacks running all up and down the pass. Behind the main barracks there, you can just make out the highway."

All Bruno can make out is the edge of a single building, and only because an electric lightbulb burns there in the gloom. There's no road, no army base, no people at all except the airfield technicians, who are throwing ropes up to the waiting Dolceti under the disapproving glare of the steersman.

"You can't see it from here," Zuq continues, "but just the other side of the road is the Rayton Inn, where travelers catch their breath before the steepest part of the climb. Is it true blackberries come from the stars?"

"No, although they fared well in the soil of Planet Two, in the stormy skies of Barnard's Star. They're from Old Earth. Why do you ask?"

"Because the inn makes a fine blackberry pie, and an even finer blackberry beer, which they still call 'the best in four worlds.' I suppose they can call it whatever they like."

"We're not staying for pie," says Radmer, walking up to them with a grim look. "Unless you want to reach the Stormlands at the height of morning thermals, when the gravel rains down, we must cross the pass summit by midnight, and the rim of Shanru Basin by the first light of dawn."

"Black Forest at midnight," Zuq marvels. "These *are* desperate times. I hope the road's in good repair."

"Parts of it," Radmer says coolly. "But it can be done without roads at all. I once took a thousand men through this pass on a cloudy, Earthless night, without so much as a footpath to follow. In the other direction, the harder direction. And those were happy days, comparatively speaking."

"The Davner War?" Zuq asks, marveling. He breaks into song for a moment: "*When the Endistal Faction broke*

the Gower Monop'ly? / And the rivers of freedom ran red!
Are you *that* Radmer?"

"I'm older than I look," Radmer says, deadpan. And
Bruno laughs, because to a trained eye the remains of
this architect laureate appear very old indeed. But he's
struck again by the span of time this Irish lad has
crossed, the events he's been caught up in. Never one to
leave well enough alone. Surely not to abandon a world
to its fate. Not again, not another one.

"The Endistas' role in that story is underappreciated,"
Radmer adds thoughtfully. "Kung's army had nothing to
eat but sugar, and I kept saying they had to crash sometime. But they led us a long, frantic chase, and if not for
the harrying of those recon units we might not have
caught them before they hit the flatland. I had an unusually good team with me."

To which Captain Bordi answers, from somewhere
nearby, "Way I hear it, Radmer, every team with you on it
is an unusually good team. By coincidence, you'll say, but
I assume my grandfather had reason for idolizing you the
way he did."

With a smirk in his tone, Zuq says, "Maybe something
else. That ballad isn't all about fighting, you know." He
breaks into song again: *"Radmer stayed with Queen Mon-
day for eight years and twenty / and she bore him five sons
and a girl!"*

"That's enough, lad," Bruno tells him gently. "No one
likes to hear his old joys and sorrows reduced to a banjo
ditty."

"Ah. Okay." Young Zuq sounds disappointed. *There's
more fun to be had with this,* his tone implies. He doesn't
seem to realize it could hurt as well.

Soon, though, the ladders are unrolled and the Dolceti
are swinging down onto solid ground. Bruno is nearly the
last to go, with only Zuq behind him. The sandy ground is

coarse with sharp, angular pebbles that crunch and grind underfoot. The night is very black, and suddenly, inexplicably colder here at ground level.

"Why is it so dark?" Bruno can't help asking. "I can see the western sky. We're not in a valley, right? Where do all the photons go?"

"Solar trees," one of the Dolceti answers over her shoulder. "This is the Black Forest." The speaker is Parma, one of the "mission mothers." Bruno isn't clear on whether this is a formal rank or title, or a job assignment, or just some sort of nickname, but the lowest ranks among the Dolceti are "squad leaders" like Zuq, with "deceants" like Natan just above them. And both ranks act deferentially toward the two mothers, who are the only women in the group. The womens' age is equally ambiguous; neither one has acquired the lines and sags of full-blown geriatry yet, but the bloom of youth isn't prominent either. Bruno knows almost nothing about "human" physiology, but if he had to guess, he would put Parma's age at around forty years.

Anyway. Solar trees, hmm. Is that supposed to be self-explanatory? The first hint of understanding comes as he watches the Dolceti appearing and disappearing around him. Not in the manner of Lyman's Olders, with their stealth-mode inviz cloaks drawing kilowatts of power from hidden reserves, but in the manner of people walking behind pillars of superabsorber black. Once clear of the gravel airfield, they've moved in among a stand of trees. Very, very dark trees. The Dolceti are *groping* their way through, he realizes, with uncertain steps and their arms out ahead of them. Above Bruno, the starlight has been replaced by a roof of absolute blackness.

He touches one of the trees. Nearly runs into it, in fact, and is saved only by the envelope of cold air around it—characteristic of surfaces which absorb infrared but do not release it. He stops short and—gingerly—reaches out to brush the surface with his fingers. It feels slick, nearly featureless, interrupted only occasionally by small ridges or bumps. If it's tree bark, it's far smoother than birch or aspen or anything else he's familiar with. And it's cold, drinking in the heat of his fingertips. Reaching up, he can feel limbs as thick as his wrist, branching up and away at forty-five-degree angles.

"Are these natural?" he asks.

"They're biological," says Radmer's disembodied voice, from some distance away. "They grow and die. They drop seeds and sprout forests. The soil conditions have to be just right, but where they are, the solar trees will choke out any other vegetation."

Indeed, the ground remains a wasteland of sand and gravel, unbroken by grass or moss or even leaf litter. The spacing of the trees, too, is remarkably regular—a sort of honeycomb pattern. Because no tree can grow in the shadow of another, Bruno realizes, and because any open space will surely be colonized. The sprouts must fight it out for dominance, for survival itself, but the contest is rigged from the start: a tree at the edge of a clearing must eventually grow into the shadows of its neighbors, its energy budget forever restricted. A tree at the *center* of a clearing would have no such constraint, and could reach its full growth and potential without hindrance.

"This is one of the great failed experiments of early Lune," Radmer expounds. "They were supposed to enrich the world, to bring infrastructure to its remotest corners. And they have, in a way. But the price is steep."

"So now you're older than the trees themselves?" Zuq asks, as though he only half believes it.

And Bruno tells him, "When our Radmer here first stood upon this sphere, son, there wasn't even air. There wasn't even gravity, not as you feel it now. It took him two hundred years to make a world of it. But he had built other worlds before this one." He waves a hand at the sky. "Out there, among the stars. Where the blackberries grow."

"Such sorcerers we have in our midst!" Zuq laughs, and again he's only half joking. For the second time, Bruno feels a surge of sympathy for these unlucky people. To Zuq, this grotty little war is epic in scope! The history behind him seems unimaginably vast, with an uncertain future ahead and himself at the cusp, a young hero on a desperate quest. His humor is of the funereal variety; he expects his life to be violent and short. He expects his noble death to be written up in a song, if indeed his people survive at all.

Bruno feels a sudden urge to hug this young man, to rub his head, to offer some reassurance. But there's nothing to say, for the situation really is desperate. And anyway Zuq is off in the trees somewhere, separated from Bruno by four meters of blackness. So fortunately the urge is not difficult to resist, and the lad escapes with his dignity intact.

Then, suddenly, Bruno and Radmer and the Dolceti are in a clearing, with buildings all around. It isn't a natural clearing—black little sprouts and silver-gray stumps attest to the violence of its maintenance—but here the light can travel for more than a few meters. Here in this little bubble it can reflect, and re-reflect, and mingle with the starlight raining down from above.

"Bestnight," says a soldier leaning in a doorway. It's a Luner greeting Bruno has heard once or twice already. "Luck unto yer."

"Danks," replies Captain Bordi. "Luck en yer hold'n dis pass. We will'n no enemy et ours back, right?"

"Right," the soldier agrees. There are other signs and sounds of activity here, but the place has a sleepy, dolorous feel to it. An air of fatalism, of doom. These ordinary soldiers are an afterthought in the epic; their job is simply to die, to hold the borders for a while and then be overrun. And yet there's discipline here; there's a man in every doorway, grimly standing his watch. At the side of the "highway"—really just a thin ribbon of tar and crushed rock—sits a shack atop a three-meter tower, with lamps burning brightly and three men waving semaphore flags up and down, left and right. Dutifully transmitting the nation's network traffic by the effort of their own eyes and arms.

Bruno's first surprise is the stream of refugees trickling uphill, against the pull of gravity. A family of four rolls by on a pair of six-wheeled scooters, whirring with the unmistakable tones of the old-fashioned electric motor. Up ahead, almost lost in the gloom, he can make out the lights of a slightly larger group. These are not traumatized people, hollow with the shock of murder and destruction. Indeed, he hears the sound of laughter drifting along the road, and the cases and trunks strapped to the vehicles show every sign of having been packed with care and forethought. These families have simply done the math, and concluded that the coastal lowlands of central Imbria are no longer the fashionable place to be.

And though Bruno is hardly in a position to criticize them, he asks, "Where are they going?"

"Manilus, probably," Radmer answers. "It's a large enough city to absorb a few extras. If their treaders hold out, if nothing breaks down, they'll be behind city walls again by morning."

"Will they be safe there?"

"For an extra few Luner days, I imagine. It hardly seems worth the effort, but people always do this. In a way it's admirable: squeezing out the last few drops of the good life, refusing to buy into the gruesome promises of war. And more often than you'd think, some miracle really does intervene, and spare them the nightmares they've never quite believed in."

"Well, then, why doesn't *everyone* flee?"

"You're asking me? I suppose the glib answer is that treaders—those vehicles, there—are expensive. But the real answer goes deeper than that. People are rarely eager to march into certain doom, but there are those who'll stand their ground at any cost. And truthfully, it takes both kinds to clean up afterward. War after war, people like that have their spirits broken, while people like this survive with their illusions intact. And that's what soldiers are for, Your Hi— er, Ako'i. If we cannot protect idealism, then there's little point in protecting anything."

"So *you're* their miracle," Bruno says, almost reproachfully.

"Sometimes," Radmer admits. "When luck and timing allow it. But not for a very long while. I really was retired. I swore I'd never take another human life, and I've kept that promise. These people have no brickmail inside them, no wellstone, no fibrediamond or regeneration factors. When they lose an eye, it never grows back, and they get only a few years of practice to refine their skills."

"And dolcet berries!" one of the Dolceti chimes in. "I reckon those helps us a bit!"

There is scattered laughter at that remark, but Radmer presses on. "For me to fight against these children—even in the cause of justice—was terribly unfair. Such battles are their own to win or lose. It's their world."

"Hmm. Yes. But these new enemies come from without. You've roused yourself from the fireside at last—roused me as well!—to strike down a foreign invader who upsets the balance of power you've so carefully cultivated. To protect your children."

"Don't romanticize it," Radmer warns. "I did have children of my own, once."

And Bruno answers, "As did I. There's nothing pretty about this mess, but having agreed to participate, I do mean to understand it."

Bruno's second surprise is that there are twenty-two of those six-wheeled vehicles, those "treaders," waiting for him and his escorts. Fully equipped, yes, and with a pair of army lads standing guard to make sure the travelers and inn guests don't have a chance to swipe anything.

"Someone has called ahead," Bruno says, impressed.

To which Radmer reacts with irritation. "What kind of place do you think this is? Yes, it's still the Metal Ages here, but we didn't have wellstone and fax machines in the colonies, either. Not after the first couple of centuries. Did that make us uncivilized? Even badly outnumbered, the Eridanians *defeated* the Queendom of Sol."

"Meaning no offense," Bruno says mildly, for he's tired of taking the blame for his ignorance. Plenty of blame attaches to him for other reasons, but this at least is not his fault. When he lived here, briefly, it was another age entirely. The Iridium Days, yes. He's never heard the songs of Lune's history, never even glanced at a current political map for more than a few seconds. How could he? And anyway, it was entropy that defeated the Queendom. The Eridanians were simply there at the time.

Soon, Natan is showing Bruno how to mount a treader. There's no great trick to it—there were electric motorcarts of similar design in Old Girona, and alcohol-powered scooters in the islands of Tonga, which Bruno and his family had occasionally ridden. But the treader is more complex, better balanced. Bruno sees at once that its six wheels, cunningly articulated, will keep the chassis approximately level through considerable variance in the terrain. These are off-road vehicles, deigning for the moment to travel a ribbon of pavement.

In another minute they're off and rolling, a loose pack of riders with Bruno and Radmer at the protected center. They're not moving all that fast—forty kilometers per hour, perhaps a little less—but the progress is steady, and the treaders seem little troubled by the steepness of the climb. Neither their motors nor the wind noise is loud enough to be troublesome. Indeed, it's an eerily silent way to travel, like flying a glider low and slow, not touching the ground at all. But Bruno is glad he's not riding out in front, for the treaders' headlight beams travel only as far as the next little curve, where they're swallowed by the superabsorber blackness of the forest.

"This is the most direct route," Radmer tells him apologetically. "Flau have been known to reach an altitude of six kilometers, but their gas bladders suffer permanent damage, and they're too hypoxic to follow navigation commands. Even in emergencies such as this, their service ceiling is capped at four kilometers. But Gillem is the highest airfield in Imbria, and one of the highest on Lune, and the Black Forest Pass will lead us to Tillspar."

"The bridge?"

"Right. And once we're across the divide into East Highrock, we can follow the old Junction Highway— what remains of it—east to the base of the Blood Mountains, where the Stormlands begin. The northern route, through a town called Viewpoint, would be a flatter, brighter way to pass the night, but it would take four hours longer. It's a delay we can ill afford."

"And the southern route," Bruno says, trying to picture the jagged land around him, "cuts through the north of Nubia, where our enemies are as thick as flies."

"Right," Radmer says again. "So Black Forest it is." He

looks around at the shapeless dark. "Was it like this during the Light Wars? This dark, I mean? Every building greedily drinking in the energy around it, heedless of courtesy or the greater good?"

With the wind in his face, Bruno laughs humorlessly. "Believe it or not, lad, the Light Wars were before my time. My parents were born in that period, but even they were sheltered from it, for Catalonia had stern regulations about wellstone. It had to be locally produced, inefficiently and at great cost, or else it was subject to tariffs. It still found its way in, of course, but rarely in anything as bulky or expensive as a *building*. And in Girona, where my parents lived and died, there were social taboos attached to it as well. The people weren't fanatics, but they favored a kind of technological puritanism. A hands-on approach, if you will. As a boy, I sometimes wore clothing woven from the wool of actual sheep!"

"And yet," Radmer says in tones of mock accusation, "you turned the world of physics on its head. You changed everything."

"I did," Bruno agrees. "Almost as soon as my parents were buried. And I fear I'd do it all over again if I had the choice! But it was that Old Modern styling that made the Sabadell-Andorra earthquake so deadly when it hit. I wasn't the only one turning my back on it; the whole world was shaken, looking for a new path, a new monarch to lead the way into a brighter future. And in that sense, my research wasn't a betrayal of Girona's ideals at all; it was very hands-on. It put the deadly fringes of quantum physics right there at your fingertips."

"Just how old *are* you, Ako'i?" asks Zuq, who is riding along just a few meters away. "You're talking about Old Earth, right? Before Tara and Toji conquered the solar system."

Bruno laughs again. "Tara and Toji, was it? Yes, lad, I

remember their conquests well." Then, in a more maudlin tone: "Such memories linger far beyond their usefulness. It's a cruel sort of prank, for the past seems palpably close, even when the last of its keepsakes have turned to dust."

chapter eighteen

in which a harbinger of battle is vindicated

On a road made of gravel and tar, the occurrence of frost heaves and potholes can hardly be surprising. Particularly as the altitude rises up above the permanent snow line, which in this country hovers around seven kilometers. Nor can the effects of hypoxia be overlooked, for on Lune the atmosphere halves in pressure with every five kilometers of height. In this, at least, the post-Queendom humans are resilient, for they can subsist on partial pressures of oxygen as low as thirty millibars, or one-fifth the sea-level norms of Old Earth. But their metabolism slows accordingly, dulling their reactions.

Thus, when the Dolceti's lead treader, piloted by a young man named Vick of Greening, hits a patch of invisible ice on a hairpin turn and continues straight on into a lethal rock face, no one is surprised. Indeed, the surprising thing is that the two treaders in his wake manage to brake to a halt without leaving the road or triggering a massive pileup. But just the same, Bordi orders a refueling halt and a chance for the Dolceti to stretch their legs, to catch their breath, to revive their senses on something more than the blackness of the forest pass.

"Shall we bury the body?" Bruno asks Natan, who is the most senior Dolceti he feels he actually knows.

"If you like," Natan replies, "but the Gillem patrols will do a better job of it when they find him. If the wolves don't find him first."

"Hmm. That seems a bit callous. Did you know him? Was he a friend?"

"We're all friends," Natan says with no particular emphasis. "I'll miss him. But I'm embarrassed for him, too. That stupid son of a pig has eaten the berry and taken the training."

"Had the reflexes and didn't use them," Zuq agrees, and there are murmurs of assent all around as the Dolceti walk their treaders off the road.

"Would you rather he'd died in battle?" Bruno asks, partly out of politeness and partly because he's genuinely curious. This isn't the reaction he would have expected.

And Natan compounds Bruno's confusion by laughing. "In battle? Against whom? Dying is *sloppy*."

"Er, perhaps if the odds were overwhelming?"

"All the more reason to duck out of the way, I'd say."

And with that, Bruno feels his first tingling of unease about these Dolceti. Is this bravado a part of their esprit de corps, or do they simply lack a background in failure? "Anyone can die," he cautions. "Everyone will, including yourself. If you fail to believe that, you'll never take the proper steps to protect yourself."

"You're telling me?" Natan says, unimpressed. "I took a vow, sir. I'm dead already. But I'm still *effective*, see? Still enjoying the pleasures of life. When I finally screw up, I don't want nobody being proud of me for it."

"I'll spit on your grave, sir," Zug offers, to general laughter.

But Natan answers, "You'll lose it before I do, boy. Even blind, you're too slow on the left. Got a lazy limbic, you." Then to Bruno he says, "Come on, I'll show you how to recharge your treader."

And this too is perplexing, because Natan is rolling his own vehicle into the trees. Is there some sort of fuel depot back there? In this nowhere spot on this nowhere road? But the man drops a kickstand, pulls out a pair of sharp metal spikes, and unreels a few meters of two-stranded, rubber-insulated cable. And finally Bruno understands.

"The trees store an electric charge."

"Course they do," Natan says, pulling out a mallet and driving the longer of the two spikes into the black-on-black trunk of the nearest specimen. "What do you think they're for?" He pounds in the shorter spike a hand's breadth below the longer one, and suddenly a yellow electric lamp is glowing where the handlebars of the treader meet in the center.

And now Bruno can picture it: a dielectric in the "bark" and "wood" which drives electrons inside the trunk and won't let them back out again. Or ions, perhaps, if the storage medium is chemical rather than capacitive, but either way they'd be separated by a barrier layer, which the longer spike is designed to penetrate. Half of it had been insulated with some sort of tar compound, yes? To keep it from shorting against the outer layer, which makes contact only with the shorter spike. Current flows, yes, but only through the storage battery of the treader.

The electrical systems of Timoch suddenly make more sense to Bruno. Is electricity a harvestable commodity here, like grain or walnuts? Is it shipped to the city in barrels and consumed directly, without transmission over long wires?

"How long does it take to charge?" he asks Natan, whose shrug is barely perceptible in the darkness.

"Depends on the tree, but most will charge a lot more batteries than a treader can carry away. And the more charge they have, the faster they deliver it. Call it half an hour, more or less."

Right away this tells Bruno that the trees and treader batteries are chemical in nature, because capacitors or superconductors could be slam-charged or discharged in mere fractions of a second. But they must be big, clever batteries to store so much energy, and the charging circuitry must be fairly sophisticated or the batteries would deteriorate in mere months. Yet again Bruno finds himself reassessing his opinions of Luner culture and technology.

So he hammers in his own spikes and goes off to look for Radmer, to obtain a complete explanation.

Unfortunately, Radmer isn't in a talking mood. He's found a laminated wooden helmet of the sort worn by civilian treader pilots.

"The force of the blow," he's saying to Bordi, and pointing to a gore-spattered gash across the laminate, "is considerable. The blood is still tacky. Bandits would hide such evidence, not leave it beside the road. There'll be bodies nearby, and not a scrap of metal anywhere near them."

"Alert for danger!" Bordi calls out to his men. "Search the area by fours!"

"The refugees?" Bruno asks.

Radmer looks up from the helmet and says nothing.

"Why would they target civilians?" Bruno presses. "What's to be gained? They can't be acting out of malice."

"Greed," Radmer corrects. "Civilians carry metal, and the robot scouts are careful not to leave witnesses behind. And if they were traveling on the road we'd've heard the alert drums; there'd be semaphore towers dropping off the network left and right. The patrol must have been traveling north, just cutting across the pass, and these people were simply unlucky. Wrong place at the wrong time. With a rich haul the robots would have turned back to the south, to deliver it to some Nubian foundry, or maybe take it all the way back to Astaroth. We don't really know what they do with it, except that their numbers swell in proportion with the tonnage they cart away."

"They're feeding a fax machine," Bruno says, eyeing a little termite mound beside the road. "Nothing else makes sense, and anyway it's a fine, cheap way to conquer the world. To raze it, to impose a viewpoint upon it and build it afresh. If *you* had the machine, I daresay you'd be tempted to try a stunt like this yourself. All they need is metal."

While he speaks, Bruno keeps his eyes on the termite mound. What do these creatures live on, he wonders, here in this solar-tree desert? He crouches to watch them streaming in and out of their nest, but in the darkness he can't see what, if anything, they're carrying. To feed themselves, to swell their ranks. To fill the planette to the very brink of its termite-carrying capacity. He's impressed that they continue working in this total darkness, but given the trees, he supposes it might not be much brighter during the day.

"And it's a bad sign," he continues, "to find scouts this high, this far north. How many patrols are in these mountains right now? How long before they identify us as a strategic threat, as opposed to a merely tactical one?"

"These robots got eyes," volunteers one of the Dolceti. "Not in their faces, maybe, but they see things."

And Bruno says, grimly, "Perhaps more than you think. Even if these termites were natural, it would be a trivial exercise to reprogram their colonies to serve as sensor networks."

"Well," says Radmer, "aren't you a barrel of laughs?"

From the forest comes a strange cry: *Thawt! Thawt!*

"The owls seem to think so," Bruno says dryly. But Radmer and the searching Dolceti tense up at the sound, looking around nervously.

"What is it?" Bruno asks.

"A thrat," says Bordi, his eyes on the forest.

"A threat?"

"A thrat," Radmer corrects. "A sort of bird you find sometimes in the solar-tree forests, or the pine barrens. There it is. Do you see?"

Bruno looks where Radmer is pointing, and where the black of forest meets the deep, dark blue of sky he can just barely make out an avian form atop the cone point of one of the trees. Its beak is raised up toward the stars, its wings outstretched.

Thwat? Thwat?

"Is it dangerous?"

"No," says Radmer, "but its wings are laced with nerves so sensitive . . . well, people say it can read minds."

"Ah. I see. And can it really?"

"I'm not sure. They do seem to know when they're being hunted. Try pointing a weapon at one; you'll find it gone before you've even finished thinking. For the princes of the Second Dynasty, to bring home a live thrat was considered the ultimate quest. The logic being, it would only come to you if there was genuine kindness in your heart—a thing that couldn't be faked."

"And did they?"

"Eh?"

"Come to these princes. Did a prince ever capture a thrat, and become a king?"

"Once," Radmer says distractedly. "King Minor of Daum. He was a really good guy. Funny, and very strong. Tried to make a sort of lie detector out of it, but it looked so *sad* in its cage, he finally released it. It's still on the family crest, though."

"All right, so," Bruno says, beginning now to lose patience, "if this bird is harmless, then why are we so tense all of a sudden?"

ThooRAT! ThooRAT!

"Because it drinks the blood of corpses," Radmer says evenly, his eyes on the blank wall of forest. "With a taste for adrenaline and the stink of fear, it's the harbinger of battle. In the opinion of that bird, Sire, someone is about to die."

"Oh. Well." Bruno's weapons are of the usual sort: a sword and pistol, some glue bombs, and a stout metal rod for, in theory, holding an enemy outside of sword-thrust range. He takes quick stock of them, and finally draws the pistol.

Just in time, as it turns out; the robots burst through the trees, swarming across the road like a troupe of whirring, clicking ballerinas. Before he knows it, Bruno is firing wildly, then firing more carefully as a robot engages a Dolceti just a few meters away from him. His bullet misses its target—the iron box on the side of the robot's head—and clanks off its superreflective neck without leaving a mark.

Then the glue bombs are flying, splattering in sticky masses that trip and snare the robots but slide right off human flesh. And the guns are popping, and the swords and clubs are swinging, and the air foils are flickering in the darkness. Men call out to each other, and Bruno finds himself face-to-face with a robot attacker. He's fought robots before, and feels no particular fear as he whirls the iron bar into play and strikes for the side of the thing's head. The box! Hit the box! But his aim is as worn-out as the rest of his ancient body; he misses by inches, and he senses the blow wasn't hard enough anyway, to do more than dent the metal.

He isn't afraid, no, but he's disappointed. The robot's sword is coming around now, and he has no way to block it except by throwing an arm up over his head. Will it be enough? Will he live to see the Stormlands, or the ancient city hidden within? Will he not confront the mistakes and misdeeds of his past?

The razor-sharp sword strikes his arm with the force of a pile driver, shearing right through the skin and the outer layer of fibrediamond and cutting into the muscle beneath. He feels the bone chip, and his strength is insufficient to keep the sword from continuing downward, to ring painfully against his Imbrian army helmet. The shock leaves him dazed, but a part of him is swinging the bar around anyway, with all the strength his good arm can muster. It isn't much, but it pushes the robot back for a moment, delaying the final, killing blow.

And then Zuq is there with a hard body slam to the robot's impervium hull, and Bordi is ducking beneath the whirling sword blade and stabbing directly into the box with the diamond tip of an air foil. The robot tries to dodge, to parry, but the void in the middle of the weapon simply baffles it. The point digs in, punching through the thin sheet of iron, and the robot is falling away in a kind of seizure.

And that's it. The battle is over. The ground is littered with twitching robots and severed robot limbs.

"Ako'i!" says Bordi, looking at Bruno with considerable alarm. To someone else he says, "Throw a tourniquet around that shoulder! Lose the arm, not the man!"

"Excuse me," Bruno tells him, collapsing down onto his rump. A tourniquet won't help, he wants to say. The arm isn't severed, just mauled, and what it really needs is to have the edges of the wound sewn back together. His body will do the rest, knitting skin and bone and muscle with better-than-human efficiency. The fibrediamond will not grow back, alas, and the bone is unlikely to heal perfectly around its dented brickmail sheathing. He'll have a permanent scar, a permanent ache. But with proper first aid, amazingly enough, he and his arm will both survive.

He can't get the words out, though, because his pain receptors are functioning perfectly, and no matter how wonderfully reinforced his skull might be, the brain inside it remains a fragile pudding of delicate bioelectric tendrils. It's also reinforced, and not given to internal bleeding, but just the same he's dazed, torpid. His bell has been rung.

Fortunately, Radmer is there in another few seconds, and takes charge of the medical response. Bruno watches with dizzy detachment as a needle and thread are worked through the injury, lacing it together. His eyes are inspected with lights, his reflexes tested.

"You'll live," Radmer pronounces finally. "But it's going to hurt for a day or two."

"Noted," Bruno says muzzily.

"You're going to have to ride, I'm afraid. If we carry two on a treader, it'll slow us down."

"I understand. I'll muddle through. These . . . these Dolceti are very fast, aren't they? The best fighters in the world."

"You didn't fare so badly yourself," Bordi says, with some grudging cousin of admiration. "I thought they'd killed you. The moment that robot stepped in front of you I said to myself, 'That's it. He's dead.' But you actually hit the thing, twice."

"It was in my way," Bruno said, trying to make a joke of it. Then, more seriously, "Has anyone got some water? Fighting really takes it out of you. I've lived a long, long time, but I'm not sure I've ever been quite this thirsty before."

Someone hands him a bottle, and he drinks from it greedily, trying to slow the rasp of his breathing so he won't choke. Finally he says to Radmer, "So there. Your thrat-bird was wrong."

"Not at all," Radmer says grimly, pointing to a heap on the road which Bruno had taken for a pile of oil-stained rags. But on closer inspection he can see the "oil" spreading in a pool, and a pair of pointy boots sticking out of the heap. It's Parma, the mission mother. Minus the top of her head.

"Sloppy," someone notes, in tones of mild embarrassment. "You can see she was half a step too close."

chapter nineteen

in which a great gulf is spanned

The long night just keeps on getting cooler, and as the road climbs higher and higher into the thin mountain air, the last traces of Imbria's temperate winter fall away. Not all of the Dolceti had started off the journey in riding leathers, but before setting off from the scene of the battle they'd all zipped up, and before long they were stopping again to throw vests and parkas over the leathers, and mitten-tops over the fingers of their gloves. Progress slows, and slows again as the slipstream turns to icy daggers.

"Cold enough?" Zuq asks Bruno at one point, and in his addled state, with his face half-frozen beneath a muffle of soft cloth, Bruno can only manage a grunt in reply.

Finally, as the solar trees peter out into scraggly tundra and then bare rock, it actually becomes possible to see the semaphore towers, which roll by every few kilometers. It must be cold duty manning these stations, Bruno thinks, though not nearly as cold or wearying as the long ride between them.

Finally, Bordi calls another halt. "It would be nice to sleep in Highrock," he says to Radmer. "But we're cold and tired already. Let's get some rest and then regroup for the final push across the summit."

Radmer carries a pocket watch—a sort of mechanical contraption for ticking off the hours and minutes of the day. Or the night; its hands and numerals glow with the phosphorescent green of radium. He makes a show of checking it now, and as he pops the cover open it casts his face in a sickly light. "Five hours, Captain. No more than that."

And Bordi answers, "The general is most kind."

So they make camp, and Natan shows Bruno how to unroll his bivvy, which is a thing that owes its ancestry to sleeping bags and canopy beds and one-man tents but is different from all of these. On the bottom, stiff tendrils of closed-cell foam provide both padding and insulation against the rocky ground. On the top, stiff arches of cloth keep a vented air space above his head, keeping out the wind—or the rain and snow, if there were any. And in the middle are layers of padding which, for a substance not composed of quantum dots, are surprisingly warm and light.

Bruno is asleep before he can draw twenty breaths, and mercifully, the Quantum Horse declines to visit him this time. Still, when Zuq rouses him he resists at first, unable to believe that five hours have really elapsed. "Find your amusement elsewhere, lad!"

But Zuq is both understanding and persistent. "It's time to go, Ako'i. Come on, I'm responsible for you. Come out of there and pack up."

There is a hasty meal of nuts and raisins and little flavored bits of dried chicken, washed down with water that has begun to freeze in its bottles.

"How much farther *is* the summit?" Bruno asks Radmer as the two of them stow their gear aboard the treaders.

"A couple of hours, if we hurry. The people of Highrock need to be warned; if the enemy is here in Black

Forest already, Tillspar will be a major target for them, both strategically and materially."

"A lot of metal, is it?"

"Wellstone, actually. And a lot of it, yes. More importantly, as the only bridge across the Divide, it's a critical link between East Imbria and the coastal cities. Without it, Manilus and Duran and Crossroad will be cut off. That's a third of the republic, geographically speaking, and nearly a fifth of its people."

The night has grown colder still, and there's a stiff breeze blowing, but at least here there are no solar trees drinking in what little heat remains. The men—and the sole woman left among them—saddle up and go, beneath the river of the Milky Way and the watchful eyes of Orion. The stars, barely twinkling, are as clear here as they would be on the surface of an ordinary planette. You'd need a space suit to get a better view. Murdered Earth is hidden by the mountains; only the glow of headlights interferes.

Still, it's slow going up here in the cold and thin, and they crest several false summits which prove, to Bruno's sinking spirits, to have even higher, steeper mountains behind them. Indeed, when they've truly reached the top of the pass, Bruno doesn't realize it until he sees the lights of a small town, kilometers in the distance and slightly below their current position.

"Is that Highrock?" he calls out to Radmer, now several treaders away in the pack.

"Aye," Radmer confirms. "If you look, you can even make out the bridge."

And it's true; past a sharp turn and a fork in the road, Bruno can see the town nestling on either side of some dark expanse, and between them the inverted, caternary arches of a suspension bridge, its cables strung up with electric lights. It's a scene straight out of his childhood, and it brings another pang of nostalgia. Oh, for those simpler days! But it's a false longing and he knows it, for the simple life is never simple, nor safe. The Queendom, for all its faults and programmed failures, was a place more worthy of his pining.

"That's a river, then?" he asks Radmer.

And Radmer laughs. "There is a river, yes, carrying meltwater westward to the Imbrian Sea. On the other side it flows east to Tranquility, where the site of Luna's first human visit lies submerged under eighty meters of briny ocean. But there's more to the Divide than that."

"How so?"

"You missed the Shattering, Ako'i. It'll be easier to explain when we're actually on Tillspar, looking down."

They ride onward, and at the outskirts of the village they encounter a lighted guard shack, with a sort of vestigial gate blocking the road, consisting of little more than a horizontal boom which can be pivoted up out of the way.

"Bestnight. What bin'z, then?" asks one of the two guards in the shack. But the other one, recognizing Radmer in the pack, steps forward in surprise, then finally moves to the doorway and walks out. "Radmer! My God! I never thought we'd lay eyes on *you* again!"

Radmer chuckles at that. "Oh, ye of little faith. You think a vanishing dot in the sky is the last you'll see of me? I'm harder to get rid of than that."

"But we saw it hit the ground! That capsule of yours, a gleam of light in the setting sun!"

"You saw it cross the horizon," Radmer corrects, "at an altitude of ten thousand kilometers and climbing. Really, Elmer, if the course was plotted by the astronomer Rigby, and the capsule and catapult were overseen by no less than Mika's Armory and the watchmaker Orange Mayhew, then it's Highrock's reputation at stake more than my own sorry skin. Is this or is this not the Artisans' Pinnacle?"

"Aye," the guard agrees, "yours was a finely crafted delusion. Wheels and chains, bombs and hatches! A fitting tomb for such as you, big brass balls and all. No offense to the men what built it, sir, but I'm surprised to see you just the same."

"Well," Radmer says, pulling out a set of travel orders to show off as a formality, "perhaps you could send word to the mayor, let her know I'm here."

"I've rung the bell already," the guard assures him.

Soon, the other riders are shouldered aside and Radmer is surrounded by a milling throng of villagers, talking over one another in a rapidly rising din. "How did that air filter work? Radmer? Radmer! Did the wheel springs seize at all? Did the dinite charges hurt when they went off? Where did these Dolceti come from?"

It's the mayor herself who rescues him, striding along the cobblestone avenue in a green robe, with some sort of golden ceremonial pendant dangling from her neck.

"So. How many lives *does* a scoundrel have?"

Radmer looks up, suddenly pleased and sheepish, vaguely off balance. "More than he can count, Your Honor. I'm pleased to see you again."

"I should say the same to you." She clucks, looking him up and down. "In one piece, no less. That's good. Did you find what you were looking for up there?"

"I did," Radmer answers, presenting Bruno with a flourish.

"Hmm." The mayor then turns her appraising eyes upon this even older Older, who is immediately reminded of his wife. Tamra used to look at Bruno exactly like that—interested, curious, vaguely exasperated—whenever things were just starting to go askew. A couple of years ago, it seemed. A couple of hundred at the very most. "And is he worth your worldly fortune, General? We're living quite well on the wages you paid us."

To which Radmer answers, "If he's not, Your Honor, then you should spend the money while you can. The Glimmer King has scouting patrols in this pass already. I fear it won't be long before they're coming for Tillspar in force."

Her smile is vaguely condescending. "The bridge has stood since the Shattering itself, General. It was built, I understand, by the very architect who crushed this world from the husk of a lifeless moon. Chairmain Kung of the Gower Monopoly once struck it with a blitterstaff, if I recall the story correctly, and the bridge rang like a gong and stood firm. And there've been lesser attempts by lesser villains, which accomplished nothing at all."

"Kung struck only one blow," Radmer says, "before I pitched him over the railing. Two minutes later you could still hear him screaming, all the way down. We never did find the staff. If we hadn't been there to stop him, he'd've fared a lot better."

She arches an eyebrow. "Your point being?"

"I won't be here to help, Your Honor. Not this time."

"We've got a full garrison," she reminded him, sounding annoyed.

"So did every outpost in Nubia. Against this enemy, a few hundred men are no defense at all."

She leans close, dropping her voice to a murmur. "What do you want me to say, Rad? We'll hold it for as long as we can, and if we fail we'll go down fighting. Is that what you want to hear? This is *Highrock*. It's *our bridge*, and anyway we've got a few surprises up our skirt."

"I expect you do," he concedes.

The two of them look at each other for a long moment, until Radmer finally asks, "Where are Orange and Mika?"

"On the bridge, if you can believe it. Cocking the VLC for a shot down the pass."

"Well, bless their little hearts."

"Yes."

Another long moment passes.

"You're not staying," she says. "Not even for a few hours."

"No. I'm sorry, but we've had enough delays already. We need to be through the Stormlands before the mid-morning thermals kick in."

"Stormlands." She clucks, shaking her head slightly. "You sure know how to pick your battles, General."

"Aye," he agrees sadly. "It's always been my greatest talent."

Soon the riders are rolling on, right through this gingerbread town, leaving the gate and the guards and the mayor behind.

"So, Radmer," Zuq wants to know, "what color are her nipples?"

The buildings of Highrock have straight, high, rec-tangular walls of gray mortar and smooth yellow river rock, ranging from fist sized to head sized. The roofs are of wooden shingle, sprouting key-shaped chimneys of tin tied down with steel cables. The whole place smells of burning wood, and Bruno can see wagonloads of cut-up logs in alleys and behind the houses, awaiting their own turn in the furnace.

Apparently the weather is highly thought of here, for every roof seems to sport a vane to indicate the wind's direction, and a cup anemometer to gauge its speed. There are black-painted water tanks on the roofs as well, nestled close to the chimneys to keep from freezing. At first glance, the bridge doesn't seem like anything special. The far side of the Divide, perhaps a kilometer distant, gives no real clue as to just how far down the bottom is.

But as they draw nearer, the walls of the chasm go down, and down, and down some more.

On the bridge itself, Bruno quickly realizes that this "Divide" is no mere riverbed. Its sides—separated by a thousand meters of blackness—drop away almost vertically, and although the edges are jagged as lightning, the overall course of the thing is almost perfectly east-west. In total darkness it might've baffled Bruno's senses completely, but during the long night, Murdered Earth has overshot the sun and can be seen on the eastern horizon, right through the crack of the Divide itself. And in the other direction, through haze and darkness, Bruno fancies he can see all the way down to the Imbrian Sea, now hundreds of kilometers west of him, and ten kilometers down. Indeed, what else could that be? That muzzy juncture between ground and sky?

Where the mountains fall away to the east, below the rising Earth, the crack runs together as a pair of converging lines before seeming, at some impossibly remote point, to take a sudden and decisive turn to the northwest. Below, there is only darkness and the howl of wind. And this is telling indeed, if Bruno can see the horizon through the gap in the rock!

"This is a crevasse," he diagnoses for Radmer's assessment. "A single seismic crack down the spine of the entire mountain range. Very deep."

"Very," Radmer agrees. "Beneath Tillspar, the river Arkis sits only two hundred meters above sea level. Its source, a wellspring eighteen kilometers upstream, is only two hundred meters higher than that."

Although Bruno has seen some large artifacts in his day, he cannot help being impressed. A crack in the earth ten kilometers deep! The Shattering must have been a violent event indeed, and a sudden one. No wonder the world had fallen again into ruin!

The bridge itself is an interesting bit of retrofit; the

road runs right to its edge and then turns to a bed of wooden planks that look as though they've been freshly laid. And these planks are secured at the center and edges by simple iron bolts, whose patina of recent oxidation is evident even by the weak electric lights strung up along the bridge. They've been in place for weeks, not millennia, and from the look of it they won't last out the century.

As for what the planks are bolted into, why, that's another story altogether. The superreflector gleaming of impervium and Bunkerlite is unmistakable, and yet these substances are encased in something translucent and ordinary: a glass, a clear resin. The suspension cables are thicker than Bruno himself, and they fire into the rock face at a twenty-degree angle, where they're held fast by a larger-than-life system of plates and bolts and old-fashioned threaded nuts.

"Nice design," he notes.

"Thank you," Radmer acknowledges, "but I was only peripherally involved. The bulk of the engineering was handled by Bell Daniel."

"Of Lunacorp Construction? My goodness, I remember him."

"He lived a couple hundred years past the Shattering. Died of electrocution, if you can believe it, trying to wire up some old apartment building. Anyway, yes, there were a lot of Olders still around back then, looking forward to a long future, and they financed Tillspar, which was consequently built to last. These cable stays are longer than the bridge itself, anchored a full kilometer into the toughest bedrock in the whole region. The structural members are layered composites of programmable and traditional materials, and the programmable ones have every security feature and safety lockout we could scrape together at the time. I don't want to use the word 'tamper-proof,' because nothing ever is. But it's certainly tamper-resistant. I'd have a hard time changing the thing myself; Bell scrambled all the passwords at the ribbon-cutting ceremony."

"And it was from here that you launched yourself to Varna? That's your Very Large Catapult, there?"

Bruno points at a system of large reels and pulleys mounted behind one of the railings, near the center of the bridge.

"Yep, that's it. Thirty turns on a block-and-tackle, plus a counterweight thirty times the mass of the capsule. If you allow ten kilometers of throw, the pull of gravity really adds up! It's not a ride I'd recommend—not so gentle as the explosion that kicked us off Varna—but it's tolerable."

"Gentle? I don't recall anything gentle about that."

"Well it's all relative, isn't it? It depends how badly you want to go. The only really difficult part was hacking the bridge to harvest a sufficient length of impervium wire. It made such a mess that we finally had to replace the whole road surface, as you can see. It's a rush job; someday I'll come back and fix the thing properly."

"If you survive."

"Aye. If any of us do."

Even after watching half a dozen Dolceti roll out ahead of him, driving his treader onto the planks and out over empty space is, for Bruno, an act of faith. He has never trusted the flammable, frangible substance known as wood, and indeed it creaks and bends alarmingly under the weight of his treader, and the many other treaders around him. The planks are knotty, bumpy, warped, not with age but from having been harvested too young. Bruno remembers the sawmill near his father's bistro, and the sorry planks it cut from local wood. There was a shortage of old-growth forest in Catalonia then, and clearly there was one on Lune now, at least in this mountainous region. And why not, when wood was at once an ornament, a structural material, a fuel, and a source of durable fiber? And electricity!

But Radmer, seeing his look, is quick to offer assurances. "Even in its current state, sir, Tillspar could easily carry ten times this load. There are greater problems to worry about."

"Er, yes. Perhaps. But not deeper ones."

The planks are separated by significant gaps—three or four centimeters in places!—through which Bruno can see rock walls converging down into a yawning blackness. From here, for all he can tell, the Divide might reach all the way to the center of the planette. And through these gaps the wind whistles, producing a light, tickly sensation on the soles of his feet, as though he's not wearing boots at all. He can also feel the bridge swaying beneath him, a few centimeters back and forth, back and forth like the seat of a gigantic swing. Has this thing really stood for two millennia and more?

At first, the mountain slopes gently beneath the planks, but about thirty meters out the ground drops away sharply, and the wind picks up. It's less bitingly cold than the air of the mountains, though; this is a warm draft welling up from the high-pressure spaces below. The bridge is suspended from a pair of towers, driven into opposite faces of the Divide at a sixty-degree angle. At the first tower is a plaque, bronze in color but utterly untouched by weather or corrosion or time. It might have been cast this morning. In the spotlights shining on it, it reads:

Tillspar
Highest known suspension bridge
Constructed Jun 4–Dec 7, Year 38 of the Fjolmes Dynasty
Chief Engineer Belliam K. Daniel
Consulting Engineer C. E. "Rad" Mursk
This property has been placed on the Global Register of
Historic Places by the order of Her Excellency
Babsie Fjolmes, Second Dynast of Imbria and North Astaroth

Beyond the plaque, the bridge begins to feel even less secure. It rises and falls by several centimeters at a time, and when Bruno looks along the handrail he sees little transverse waves rolling back and forth across it, faster than a man could run. Near the center of the bridge, it's like walking on a ship, or the deck of a soaring flau. He can feel it rolling and swaying under him; when he looks at his feet or his wheels instead of the dim silhouette of the mountains, he feels mildly but immediately seasick.

To Bruno's surprise, though, as they approach Radmer's catapult mechanism at the center of the bridge, the Divide offers a wider view which includes several rows and banks of electric light on the near side, far below and behind them, like the view from an air car or a landing spaceship. He can even—to his much greater surprise—see *boats* down there, alive with tiny lights, slowly bobbing and swirling through what must be very large rapids.

"What industry is this?" he asks Radmer wonderingly. "Those lights, those boats! To pilot a ferry through such landscape as this must be a thrilling career."

"And a short one," Radmer says, "for the rapids are deadly and the loads very heavy." Heedless of the half dozen Dolecti rolling out ahead of him, he stops and points beneath the railing on the side of the bridge. "Down there is the tin mine, from which Highrock got its start as a metalworking capital. There's a gold mine further down, which you can just make out from here. Rare earths are mined upstream a ways. As you can see, there's quite a lot of lithosphere laid bare in these walls. Easy pickings, prelayered by weight."

Bruno can see no such thing in this darkness, and he says so.

Radmer grunts. "Well, I suppose you develop an eye for it after a while. If we had all night to linger here, you'd see all sorts of things in these walls, which have grown dusty with edible lichen, pale green and rusty orange. In the cities it's considered a delicacy. Can you see it there in the spotlights? Those baskets are for lowering the harvest girls down along the face, looking for morsels choice enough for human consumption and scraping the rest into hog-slop buckets. They only do that in the daytime, though."

"I wish I could see more," Bruno offers politely.

"Yeah, well, in some ways the daytime view is actually worse, because the sunlight never penetrates more than two-thirds of the way down. But it washes out the artificial lighting, with the result that you can't see anything down there at all."

"Hmm." This conversation is not without interest for Bruno, and in the past he has found reason to pause in places much scarier—much more tangibly deadly—than this. He was once trapped inside a Ring Collapsiter fragment, with only ion thrusters to turn his ship and keep it off the walls! But in the interests of moving along, he says nothing more, instead releasing the brake on his treader and rolling forward.

So when Radmer stops again at the center of the bridge, to speak to the two men fussing with the cranks and reels there, Bruno doesn't know whether to see it as another interesting landmark or an unwelcome pause. Nor is he alone in this worry; the Dolceti—brave souls, to be sure—are aglow with anxiety, no doubt picturing themselves in a battle against gravity itself, a long fall during which their uncanny reflexes would avail them not at all.

"Let's *go*, old man," Zug mutters in a voice barely audible above the wind, whistling through the bridge cables.

"I hope you're throwing something heavy," Radmer says to the two men. "At someone truly deserving."

They look up, and one of them says, "Oh. Hello, General."

Radmer seems disappointed with that. "Is that all you

have for me, Orange? No warm greetings? Aren't you surprised to see me alive?"

"Should we be?" asks the other man, who must be Mika, the armorer. "All right, then, it's good to see you. Alive. Can you give us a hand with this cocking latch?"

"Sure." Radmer puts his kickstand down and dismounts. "What's the payload? I'd dearly love to drop a greeting card right on the south pole. Just a note to say hello, right? But I'm afraid a show of defiance will tip our hand prematurely. Better to show our weakest face, until the last possible moment."

"He'll find *us* a bit sticky, if you'll excuse my saying. This here's eight tons of glue bombs, packed to scatter. *That* ought to hold the pass for a minute or two."

Catching hold of a spring-loaded lever, Radmer laughs. "We can hope, yes. Are there oil traps as well, to tilt and slide your enemies into the Divide?"

"Course there are," says Orange Mayhew.

"And other gifts," says Mika, "fit for a Glimmer King. Where're you heading?"

"Stormlands."

"Ah. Bad luck, that."

"Eh. No worse than usual. I saw Manassa from orbit—a hidden ruin, perfectly preserved right there in the center—so we're hoping to collect a few surprises of our own."

"Hmm," says Orange Mayhew. "Well. Do me one favor, General: don't get killed."

"I'll take that under advisement. You too, hey?"

But Orange just shrugs. "We're human beings, sir, Mika here and myself. Living forever, well, it ain't on our list of options."

chapter twenty

in which darkness proves an ally

On the other side of Tillspar, the highway is less icy but in generally poorer condition. As the road snakes down the eastern slope of the Sawtooth Mountains there are shelves and valleys with highways of their own—opportunities to turn north or south—but the riders follow the Junction Highway east and down. The air gets warmer, thicker, easier to breathe, and Bruno's ears pop again and again as the pressure upon them slowly increases.

But every kilometer of road seems to be in greater disrepair than the one before it. As the treaders pass through East Black Forest, potholes give way to craters. And as the solar trees thin out to a simple pine forest, the craters become larger and more frequent. Ironically, just as the road is beginning to straighten and level out, it becomes impossible to follow anything like a straight-line course along it. A treader must needs zigzag between the holes at half speed.

"I'm surprised there's any pavement here at all," Radmer says when Bruno remarks on it.

"Nobody looks after this road," Natan agrees. "It don't go anywhere."

At that Radmer muses, "It used to go straight to Crossroads, near the triple point where Imbria and Nubia and Viense come together. It was bigger than Timoch, which back then was a sheep-and-cow town. Manassa was the largest city in the hemisphere, a center of commerce easily rivaling Tosen and Bolo on the south coast. Keep in mind, there were a lot more people then."

"I remember the Iridium Days well," Bruno tells him, "if not happily. Lune was the rotting corpse of our Queendom; I couldn't love it. Couldn't *bear* it. I fled because my soul had died and my body refused to follow. But I do remember Manassa. The towers of wellglass all strung together with bridges, and every morning a silence field enforcing ten minutes of meditation . . . When I left they were in a blue period, with every surface glowing in the sun like crystalline bits of sky."

"Well," says Radmer, "after the Shattering, Manassa was gone and the Junction Highway led straight into permanent storm, and you had to take the long way around to get to Crossroads. The little towns along the way continued for quite some time afterwards, but one by one they sort of dried up and blew away. This road is two thousand years old, and it's been, I'll guess, almost three hundred years since it saw any attention. So like I say, the surprising thing is that there's any road left."

Bruno snorts at that. "When I was a boy we were still using Roman roads, older than this one and in far better condition."

"The Catalan weather was kinder," Radmer says. "For what it's worth, there are diamond highways here on Lune that will last until the end of time. This pavement was a high-end temporary, never meant to last so long."

Ahead of them, finally, the sky above another mountain range has begun to show signs of impending dawn. Even on Lune, the night cannot last forever. And the extra light is welcome, because the riders have finally abandoned the idea of avoiding the rough spots, and are now riding straight through them in a clattering mass. At first the clever six-wheeled suspension of the treaders is adequate to the task, but as the ruts deepen and their shapes become more complex, the wheels begin to exceed their vertical travel limits.

Soon, the heaving bodies of the treaders are pummeling their riders' legs, and headlight beams are waving up and down so madly that the road might as well be illuminated by strobe lights. Progress slows yet again. They're still going faster than they would on foot, but that margin is shrinking. Still, Bruno finds he can minimize the beating by crouching in his stirrups—essentially using his legs and back as an extension of the vehicle's suspension system. And once that principle is established, there's no reason not to straighten out his back, to stand tall for a better view, to gun the throttle and dance with the bumps.

To his surprise, he's having a good time, and not feeling guilty about it. Not *all* the problems of this world are his fault, after all, and this ride is in the service of a noble cause, from which he may very well not return. And that, in truth, may be part of why he's feeling good; the possibility of death hangs all around him. He nearly died back there in the pass; for Parma and that unlucky rider there was no "nearly" about it.

Bruno has been without useful work for so long that he hasn't even bothered to count out the span. Thousands of years, certainly. But here he is again, doing something. And his time on this world, on any world, may at last be nearly over—his sins all called to account—so what's the point in holding back? There's nothing to keep him from riding to the limits of his ability, and even slightly beyond.

Eventually, he finds himself leading the pack, the wind whipping his hair out behind his helmet as the countryside slowly brightens ahead of him. He doesn't notice that he's left his escort behind, or else he notices but manages not to formulate any sort of conscious plan to correct it. But Captain Bordi's voice calls ahead angrily, "Ako'i, back! Fall back! We're supposed to be protecting you, damn it! Slow down!"

And when he does so, dropping back among the Dolceti, Bordi glares sternly at Natan and Zuq, telling them, "Stay within arm's reach of him. Let nothing happen. You boys have taken the berry, taken the vow. You're expendable; he isn't."

"Yes, sir!" the two of them call out ruefully, then cast baleful glares at Bruno.

But when Zuq finally speaks, all he says is, "Where in the hell did you learn to ride like that? You've never been on a treader, you said."

And Bruno's only answer is a muttered "Beginner's luck." Because there's no point explaining to this boy that he's ridden a scooter, ridden a car, ridden a skimmer and a broomstick and a *horse*. Not to mention a grappleship. He's tried his hand at more different vehicles than Zuq will ever see or imagine; one more doesn't tax him in the least. And he was never exactly a motor fanatic; he's simply lived a long time.

Too, there's the matter of being comfortable in one's own skin. Bruno knows exactly what his body is and isn't capable of. If he falls, he knows roughly what injuries he can survive. And he's far more afraid of embarrassing himself than he is of getting killed, so he will drive this instrument, his body, exactly as he pleases. Indeed, for all their courage and reflexes the Dolceti are indifferent riders, and their pace begins to seem unnaturally slow.

Still, he grits his teeth and perseveres, and hour upon

hour the Sawtooth Mountains shrink behind them, while the equally jagged Blood Mountains draw nearer up ahead. They pass a lake, which Natan calls The Lake of the Maidens. They pass a grove of peach pie trees, and another of peach cobblers. They pass five flocks of sheep, and once a shepherd looking down on them from a hilltop, the traditional crook-ended glowstaff in his hands.

Says Zuq, "The shepherds here have magic bottles, in which the milk never sours. Or so the story goes."

And Bruno answers, "I believe it. Those bottles were common, once."

"Really? And were there trolls in the hills back then, and mermaids in the sea?"

"There were. And stranger things."

"'For the insult, the trolls carried off Gyrelda, and made hard sport of her until Gyraldo stormed their bunker and won her freedom, and gave her a hundred paper dollars for her dowry.' Is *that* true?"

Against the wind, Bruno laughs. "Perhaps. There *were* paper dollars then, inscribed with their value in gold. But the trolls I remember were all fine gentlemen."

"Amazing. And did the animals really speak in human voices?"

"Ah. That's probably *not* true, or at least I've no such recollection. But anything's possible, eh?"

"Used to be," says Zuq, agreeably. "Would you go back there if you could?"

"To the Iridium? Or the Queendom?"

"I dunno. You tell me."

Bruno, his hair whipping in the breeze, grins over at the young Dolceti without humor. "My boy, I fear I'd go back to the Queendom if it cost the lives of millions. That's precisely what we're up against here: that yearning."

As the morning slowly inches its way toward sunrise, Bruno can see that there's something going on with the air behind the Blood Mountains' forbidding peaks. Some sort of haze, some sort of cloud bank, darker than a mere rainstorm. In the flash of a lightning bolt he even fancies he can see dust and debris spinning around in there, in great, slow arcs and whorls.

"The Stormlands?" Bruno asks.

But Natan and Zuq can only shrug. "Maybe. We never seen it before, sir."

Finally, the Dolceti out in front have lost track of the road altogether, and are bouncing through one dry wash after another. The wind, too, has taken on a foreboding character, slamming down from above without warning, the downdrafts bursting like town-sized water balloons. And the land has begun to slope upward again. Soon they're riding up between hills, and then cliffs. Their progress slows yet again, and finally it's Radmer, not Bordi, who calls a halt.

"Believe it or not, we're early. I can see the gaps in these hills, but I can't tell which one is our pass. I don't think we'll make any progress here until sunrise."

"Four-hour halt," Bordi calls out then, for sunrise is still five hours away. "Everybody eat and sleep."

But Bruno is too keyed up to do either, and finds himself in a sort of mutual interrogation against Natan and Bordi, who are suddenly curious about his history, there beside a crackling firepit, with Radmer and a dozen Dolceti slumbering nearby.

"You're a soldier," they accuse.

Bruno laughs. "I? Taking orders? Marching in straight lines? I was a sort of knight at one point, but that's a very different thing. Even at the worst of it, there wasn't much fighting, and still less discipline."

"A knight for whom?" Bordi presses. "Tara and Toji? Did you stand guard over this world while Radmer and his men crushed it?"

"Er, well, in a manner of speaking."

"It's hard to credit," Natan says, "him being strong enough to carve a whole world. I've seen a lot of it; it's a big place. So why does he need us if he's such a power? Why can't he just carve Astaroth right off the globe, and the Glimmer King with it?"

"Hmm. That's a hard question to answer, lad. I suppose, when you get right down to it, we were only as powerful as our tools. These were exceedingly complex, and when too many of them broke down all at once, we were hard-pressed to repair them. Until that time we'd always seen civilization as an upward climb; it didn't occur to us there was a down as well. Just as difficult and treacherous, but every step carried us farther from the stars, not closer."

"Like the air foil," Bordi suggests, drawing one and examining it. "They're not making *these* anymore."

"Indeed, yes. It's a more wondrous thing than you probably suspect. But to build another one would take centuries. Whole nations would need to be conscripted, their entire economic surplus diverted, just to build the components of the tools which make this thing possible."

"Maybe that's what the Glimmer King is all about," Natan says. "There's all this work going on in the world, right? But it's purposeless. Just shoes and plowshares, lightbulbs and treaders. Some little luxuries on the side. So a fellow comes along who thinks like you, right? But he's not so agreeable. He sees all this capacity and he *wants* it, not for shoes and hats but for himself. There's specific things he plans on building, but first he's got to *own* those nations."

"He means well," Bruno says without thinking. "In his mind, he's doing what's necessary to achieve a kind of . . . paradise."

Bordi turns and looks at him hard. "You said you didn't know him."

"I've seen his type," Bruno answers.

"So you told the Furies. And would we like this paradise of his? Would we be happy there?"

"I, uh . . . I doubt it. Someone would be happy, but certainly not everyone. And even if you bought into the vision somehow, I suspect you'd balk at the cost of getting there. Notably, he isn't offering you the choice."

"No. He isn't. So what's he got in mind?"

"I wouldn't know," Bruno answers honestly. "We had a guy once who wanted to collapse the sun, as a means of opening a window into the future. Even ignoring the enormous loss of life, there was no particular evidence that seeing the future—the end of the future, specifically—would be in any way helpful. Might be a bad thing, who knows? But he didn't offer a choice, either. These madmen never do."

"Dulcet berries!" Zuq shouts, from a dozen meters away. "I've found dulcet berries. Two whole bushes of them!"

"Get some sleep," Bordi tells him wearily.

"Never could sleep in the dawn hours," Zuq answers. "Even when I'm tired, which right now I'm not. Can we do some blindsight, Captain?"

Bordi sighs. "It takes more than berries, boy. It takes courage. Takes equipment. Takes a cocktail of other drugs to get the training burned in properly."

"But we have all that, sir."

"Not all of it, no. Sit down and have a meal, why don't you?"

But Zuq is not so easily deflected. "Never could eat in the dawning, either. Not till sunup, when my stomach comes alive. And sir, we don't want to be lax on our training. Not at a time like this."

Natan turns to Bordi. "You've got to admire his spunk. Most guys his age do the bare minimum, sweating it beforehand and moaning afterwards. If you could join the Dolceti without actually taking the berry, I swear, there's a lot of people would do it."

"So," Bordi says, "in admiration of his fortitude, you're volunteering to conduct?"

Natan thinks for a moment, then shrugs. "I don't sleep in the dawning much, either."

And Bruno, as curious as ever, chimes in with, "May I participate, Captain? I've heard a great deal about this 'blindsight training,' and it would be nice to know what's involved. Firsthand, I mean."

"I'll save you the trouble," Bordi says, unamused. "It's pain and it's terror. After their first experience, only one in a hundred ever go back for a second. It's that bad. You can't see, and you feel like you can't breathe."

"But you can," Bruno says. "It's physically safe."

"Well. Yes, but—"

"The berries aren't toxic? It won't injure me to take them?"

"No, but—"

"Captain, I've been in some very tight corners in my time. I'm old enough to know my limits, and although you've seen me driving recklessly, I promise you I'll not endanger myself again, so close to the target of our mission. I'll do my duty, yes? But I would like to take this training. Indeed, it may help *save* my life when the moment of truth arrives."

And to that Bordi has no response. But Bruno fancies he can see the man rethinking his opinions about this ancient beggar, Ako'i.

Says Natan, "The idea here is to bypass the con-scious parts of your brain. There's enough intelligence in the limbic to conduct a fight, and it's fast, so that's where we're going this morning. Deep inside. And in the brain stem there's more than just reflexes. It's your bird brain, and it's capable of behavior as complex as any bird, and as fast. That's where your vision is going: to the birds. Take five berries—five, mind you!—and chew them thoroughly. When you got a good paste in your mouth, swallow it down."

The berries are smaller than Bruno's pinkie nail, and the same bright yellow as the Dolceti's traveling cloaks, but other than that they look like blackberries, or little bunches of grapes. Their taste is overpoweringly sweet, so much so that like the drug, it's probably a defense mechanism to keep animals from wanting to eat them. Their texture is surprisingly dry and leathery. The paste they form in Bruno's mouth is like syrup cut with vinegar: dense and sticky, sweetly acrid and vaguely corrosive.

"How often have you done this?" Bruno asks Zuq when he's choked them down per instruction.

"This'll be my tenth time. It takes five before the Order will even admit you, and two more harder ones before they'll give you rank and let you out on assignment. Dolceti are usually older than I am, because most of them can't handle the berry more than a couple of times a year. Me, I've been trying to go every month."

"So you're tougher even than the average Dolceti?"

"Aw, it's not my place to say that. But I'm definitely tougher than when I started."

"Cut the chatter," Natan instructs. "Take the yellow pill, and wash it down with a bit of water."

The yellow pill is tasteless and perfectly spherical. Also very small, but its texture is gritty enough that it doesn't go down easily.

"Now the white."

Another sphere, larger and smoother.

"You'll begin to lose your eyesight in about two minutes. After that, the fear will set in, and Ako'i, I want you to promise not to run off on me when it does. If you can't handle it—and there's no shame in it; most people can't—then just curl up on the ground and we'll look after you. Believe it or not, you'll still get something out of the experience.

"The idea is to turn on your amygdala, your fear. We'll create a behavior loop that bypasses the frontal lobe. Fear's a tool; the more threatened your limbic feels, the more your behavior follows a preset routine, like a dance step. We're just giving it a better routine than to run around screaming, see? A higher class of irrationality. There's a time for being rational, but it's not when a bullet's flying at your head."

"You people can dodge bullets?" Bruno asks, already feeling short of breath.

"That's what blindsight training *is*," Zuq answers, sounding surprised. "Didn't you know? Sticks, rocks, arrows . . . The training bullets are a special round, oversized and not that fast, but yeah, they'll be flying right at you. You'll swat them aside or suffer the consequences."

This idea fills Bruno with a gnawing dread, or perhaps the drugs are doing that, but either way he finds himself wishing, suddenly and fervently, that he had never pressed Bordi to allow this. What was he thinking? Even if these bullets can't kill him—and it's likely that they can't, at least by ones and twos—he could be *maimed*. It might be *weeks* before he grows back all his missing parts!

"What does the blindness do?" he asks, for in spite of everything his curiosity is unimpaired.

"It isn't blindness," says Natan, "it's blindsight. The berries are shutting down your visual cortex, but your optic nerve continues on down to the brain stem. Your inner bird can see just fine, and it's *his* reflexes we want. He's the one we're training; the conscious 'you' is just a passenger."

"A blind passenger. A terrified passenger."

"Right. Mentally tied up, to keep you out of the bird's way."

Bruno's vision is turning gray and fuzzy around the edges, which terrifies him. What if something goes wrong? What if it never comes back? To be immorbid *and blind* . . .

"People experience the training differently," says Natan. "Some feel divided, like there are several distinct . . . things, entities, living inside their skulls. Some people just remember it as a panic. A blind panic, literally, where they can't control theirselves. Some remember the whole thing as a set of conscious choices, even when they know it isn't so. Some remember nothing at all, like their frontal lobe just goes to sleep."

"Which am I?" Bruno asks, inanely, for how could Natan possibly know that?

Then, with alarming swiftness, his vision shrinks to a tunnel, then a drinking straw. He sees a burst of swirling patterns: lace, spirals, Cartesian grids mapped onto heaving topological surfaces. His life is far too long to flash before his eyes in a moment, but he gets pieces of it: a month of mathematical insights in a Girona tower, a decade as philander in Tamra's court, an hour in battle armor under the red-hot surface of Mercury. Then nothing at all.

Nothing at all.

Bruno de Towaji, the one-time King of Sol, is blind.

"So fast! I wasn't . . . ready . . ."

"I'm here with you," Zuq says, from very nearby.

"Ah!" Bruno replies, fighting not to run. "Ah, God! Can you see anything?"

"No."

"Try and relax," says Natan, in a voice much calmer than Zuq's. "Fear is a tool. Just a state of your brain, which we happen to find convenient. It's nothing to do with *you*, the person. Just ride it."

"In a moment...of weakness," Bruno tries. "I've never...Rarely has such a moment of weakness been... I'm sorry. I'm sorry, I can't...compose—"

"Enough talk, old man. Defend yourself!"

Bruno swats Natan's hand aside. "Leave me. Alone." He swats again, and again. Natan is trying to slap him! "Stop it. Stop! Leave me alone!"

And suddenly Bruno realizes what he's doing: blocking slaps he cannot see. His arms aren't moving of their own volition—he's doing it himself, or feels that he is—but the sense, the feeling, the *certainty* that drives them... How does he know? How does he sense the blow coming?

Block. Block. Block block.

"Good," Natan says. "Take hold of this."

Bruno reaches out and accepts a wooden staff from Natan. There's no fumbling in the motion, no guesswork. He even knows the shape before he has it in his hands. He's aware, dimly, of movement all around him, the jiggling fire, the men rolling over in their sleep, the wind gusting straight down. But he cannot *see* them. This "blindsight" it isn't like seeing at all. It isn't like feeling or hearing. He simply *knows*.

How terrifying.

"Defend!" Natan commands, and Bruno is raising his staff. *Crack! Crack!* He blocks a pair of telegraphed blows, and then a shorter, swifter one delivered like a punch. *CRACK!*

"Attack!" says Natan, and Bruno is too afraid to

disobey. Pulling left to avoid Zuq's fragile human skull, he whirls the staff around and Strikes! Strikes! Strikes!

"Good," says Natan, falling back to deliver fresh blows of his own.

"What about me?" Zuq asks, from a position Bruno doesn't have to guess at. "This was supposed to be *my*—"

"Silence, maggot!" commands Natan. Bruno senses him whirling past in a blur of flesh and wood. *Crack! Cracrack!* The two of them come together and then separate, come together again.

"Ako'i! Attack! Both of you maggots, come, hit me. As hard as you can!"

Bruno does as he's bid, and amazingly enough manages not to injure himself or Zuq in the process.

Still curious even in the face of this terrifying blindness, he asks, "Is this right? Is this the training?"

To which Natan just laughs. "Old man, this is the stretching exercise. The *training* doesn't start for another fifteen minutes, when your drugs is more than a whisper in the blood. Now shut your hole and fight like a Dolcet Barney."

"Ah," Bruno gasps, and blocks a string of five blows.

chapter twenty-one

in which the appetite of dragons is tested

The wind no longer whistles, but shrieks. It's no longer cold, but deathly frigid. The rain no longer spatters, but fires down frozen from the heavens like a hail of meteorites. The ice melts swiftly, but so powerful is the wind that when a squall has passed, the sodden clay of the ground is dried in minutes, and peels away in crumbling sheets. As a result, the Blood Mountain Pass is a mess of sucking mud and stinging grit, with no sign of the pavement that once adorned it.

"I see the way now," Radmer had said to the waking men. "If we hurry, we may yet miss this morning's rain of stones."

But had they? Would they? Overhead, the sky is a deep shade of gray-green that Bruno has never seen before. Still, despite the obscurants in his way—the dust and hail, the unruly clouds themselves—he can see structure in this unending storm. It's a squashed toroid, a stretched donut, an elongated treader wheel nearly a hundred kilometers wide—nearly *two* hundred kilometers north to south—hovering flat against the landscape. And at half the footprint of the Imbrian Ocean, that's a sizeable blemish for a world barely forty-four hundred kilometers around! On Earth, the equivalent storm would cover the whole of Greenland, or Europe from Gibraltar to Sardinia to the ports and vineyards of Bordeaux.

"When the pillar buckled and the neutronium plate slipped," Radmer calls to him from two treaders over, "the gravity in this hex dropped by nine percent. It doesn't sound like much, but it created . . . this. The low-pressure system might be circular if not for the Blood Mountains on the west and the Johnny Wang Uplift on the east, squeezing it, pushing it north and south in a big oval."

While still piloting his treader, Radmer attempts to gesture his way through the half-shouted explanation. "Now that you're here, you can see it: the air rushes in along the ground, and then suddenly it weighs less. More importantly, all the air *above* it weighs less, so there's less pressure holding it down. It wells up. Then it hits the tropopause and flattens out, rolling back the way it came and then cooling and sinking, condensing out moisture. It's a big, rolling ring, like a stationary smoke ring, except that Coriolis forces—weak as they are—pull it around into a cyclone. Add the turbulence and static of air passing through these mountains, and you've got a real mess!"

Indeed, the Blood Mountains are lower than the Sawtooth, but every bit as jagged. This world simply hasn't had time to wear them down. And thanks to grit and sleet and the occasional uprooted shrub, Bruno can *see* the turbulence they create: crack-the-whip sheets and rolls of whirling air snapping off every peak, slicing through every valley. He hasn't seen lightning yet, but the air is sharp with the tang of ozone.

"Are we going to survive this?" he asks casually, raising his voice above the howling wind.

"Most groups turn back around at this point," Radmer answers. "Some vanish, or return at half-strength. Some probably find their way in and then die of starvation, rather than brave the tornadoes again. Only Zaleis the Wanderer has been to the eye of the storm and back, and lived to tell the tale. And he started with a group of five."

Then, in a more personal tone, "How are you holding up?"

"Well enough," Bruno says, not sure how else to answer.

"Sore?"

A barking half laugh. "No! Victims of explosive decompression are sore. I'm, well, there isn't quite a word for it. The body hurts badly, but the real wounds are in the soul."

"I could've told you not to try that," Radmer chides. "Especially not before a big push like this. People end up in Special Care from that shit. Some of them permanently. You wouldn't blow out an airlock and call it training. You wouldn't smash your treader into a wall and call it training. If you survive, yes, you'll have learned a thing or two. But there are better ways. *All* practice—especially repetitive—involves the brain stem. It has to!"

"He did all right," Natan says, with a bit of warning in his tone. "I've seen better on the first try—I've seen a lot better—but with years of practice he could be one of us."

Bruno has lived long enough to recognize this as high praise indeed. But he can also see the truth in Radmer's criticism; blindsight is a shortcut, for people whose lives are miserably brief. The effect is real, yes: he can feel a new strength, a new swiftness in his limbs. They have a mind of their own now—quicker and surer than his own, yet subordinate to him. With practice, he could summon or dismiss it at will.

But with longer practice—decades, centuries—he could achieve a comparable grace without the . . . side effects. A little slower, a little smarter, a lot less damaged inside. "Disfigured" is the word that springs to mind, when his mind considers its own sorry state. The drugs have done something to him, something bad. Prolonged abuse of them would create...well, Dolceti. Violence addicts. Affable men and women with a zest for life, but a strangely sterile view of death and fear and pain, and no hope for a normal existence. In their own way, the Dolceti are as different from human beings as the Olders themselves. Bruno can appreciate that now. And fear it.

"He'll be all right," Natan says.

"Better than all right," Zuq echoes.

But their definition of "all right" clearly differs from Bruno's own. If he were going to live forever he'd probably feel a bit cheated, like he'd lost a finger and could never grow it back. As it is, with this sense of welcome doom hanging over him, he'll simply accept the scar, and the costly insights that come with it.

To Radmer he says, "It's no wonder you wanted Dolceti for my bodyguards. Who else would be brave and stupid enough to follow you into that?" He nods toward the pass ahead, where a trio of dust devils are whipping together into a single large vortex.

"Shit," answers Radmer.

The vortex whirls straight down the pass, straight toward the riders.

"The dragon!" someone calls out, in mingled worry and glee. "The Shanru Dragon! See the mark she leaves! The dragon's tail upon the ground!"

"Get down!" Radmer calls out. "Get off, get into the ditch!"

But the Dragon of Shanru is swift, and falls upon the treaders before all the riders have dismounted and fled. One Dolceti is pulled right off his mount, and another is whisked from the ground, and both are flung high into the air, twirling and tumbling, and then dashed against the cliff wall high above. Their bodies fall, limp and lifeless, against the cliff's sharp crags.

Bruno, who reached the ditch in time, feels the tornado pass right over him with no worse effect than a sandblasting, a slam against the ground, a breathless moment of popping ears and eyeballs bulging against tightly closed lids. The Dragon's shriek and chuff are deafening, and then they're gone, and for his fallen comrades Bruno momentarily feels only a deep contempt. Because they brought it on themselves. Because they stopped to look at the vortex bearing down on them, when they should have dropped and crawled.

"Fools," he mutters under his breath. And only then thinks to feel ashamed.

Soon there is lightning crashing all around, and except for the occasional errant gust, the shrieking wind is firmly at the riders' backs. The Dolceti are more careful on the Dragon's second visit, suffering no additional casualties, but after the roadway's third scouring Radmer proclaims, in a voice barely audible above the storm, "These twisters are dropping down into the pass from above! Bigger every time! Our luck won't hold; we've got to seek higher ground!"

"The treaders won't climb these walls!" Bordi says. "Too steep, too pointy!"

"I know; we'll have to leave them behind!"

"Are you insane?" someone asks. But Radmer just looks around at the Dolceti, his expression answering the question for him: *No, just desperate.*

"This moment had to come! Sooner or later, we'll have to press forward on foot. The question is, how many people do you want to lose before we try it? Load up your packs, everyone! Food, water, bivvies, nothing else. Oh, and weapons!"

Well, obviously, Bruno mutters, in a voice even he cannot hear.

In another three minutes they're all scaling the canyon

wall, following Radmer single-file along the uphill slope of jagged basalt layers, like arrowheads sprouting from spearheads sprouting from swords and fallen, leaf-shaped monoliths. The points and edges have been sandblasted dull—no one seems in danger of cutting off a hand or foot—but with even a minor fall the jags are sufficient to snap a human spine, to stave in a skull, to shatter a leg and leave its owner stranded. There could be little doubt that the group would press forward, leaving any such unfortunates to their fate. Except for Bruno and Radmer, of course; *they* would be rescued at almost any cost. But that was hardly fair, for they were as close to unbreakable as a human body could be made.

There had, of course, been even ruggeder body forms out in the colonies—trolls and whatnot, shot through with diamond—but they had sacrificed their softness, their sensitivity, their very humanity. And although many such creatures had returned from the stars in the gray days after the Queendom, none had survived even into the Iridium recovery that preceded the Shattering. One by one they'd succumbed to disease, to old age, to the gloom of loneliness, and their genomes had rarely bred true. Even the Olders bore mortal children, yes? When they bore children at all. In the colonies, and indeed in the Queendom itself, the art of reproduction had decoupled itself from any natural biology. And it suffered grievously, when those technical crutches were kicked away.

Still, nature is clever where the propagation of species is concerned, and a love of breeding can welcome many a wayward subspecies back into the gene pool. Whether by chance or by design, these "humans" of Lune are a clever synthesis of the many human-derived forms Bruno recalls from those days. And they *are* human, far more than they're centaur or angel or mole. As such they're frail, and he fears this terrible country may be too much for them.

For that matter, it may be too much for Olders, else Manassa would be more than a half-believed legend. Had only one person truly made it there and back in one piece?

A message crawls back along the line, shouted from man to man over the howling of restless atmosphere: "We don't dare climb to the top of the ridge. The winds are fiercer up there, and we'd be a prime target for lightning. We'll proceed about two-thirds of the way up the canyon. Move cautiously. Step on the big rocks, not the small ones; they're more stable."

Bruno sends his own question up the line: "How much farther do we have to go?"

A minute later, the reply comes back: "Two full kilometers to climb, across ten horizontal. After that it's downhill into Shanru Basin. But the winds will keep getting worse until we cross the eyewall, twenty kilometers from here!"

Ah. Well, here's another great surprise, another place Bruno never imagined ending up. The benefit of a long life, yes: a large number of very large surprises. Moving glove-over-glove and boot-over-boot like this, across jagged, icy rocks, they'll be lucky to manage a kilometer an hour. And what sort of shape will they be in when they finally burst through into clear air? What if they have to fight? What if they have to *think*?

He supposes at first that the final hours will be the hardest, but then he begins to suspect that nothing could be worse than the battering they're receiving right now. The wind here carries not only dust and grit, but occasional bursts of sharp gravel as well. Dragon or no, Bruno is nearly ripped from the rock face many times by errant gusts. Dragon pups? At other times he's slammed against it, until his skin is raw and his bones are aching inside their carbon-brickmail sheaths. His arm screams where the robot's sword cut it; it has healed, yes, but it will never be the same.

But the trudge goes on and on and on some more. The

sun must be well up into the sky by now, but here beneath the roiling thunderheads it's dark as dawn and gray as a Fatalist ghoul. No more messages are passed. Even thoughts are drowned out by this unending noise.

When they reach a flat, minimally sheltered area and the line around him begins to break up, Bruno at first worries that they're going to lose somebody. *Single file, people!* he thinks at them furiously. But then, as the Dolceti get their bivvy rolls out, he understands: they're stopping to rest. Not to eat, certainly not to cook, but to huddle together in a miserable mass. One guard manages to lose his bivvy into the wind, and ends up curled in with Mathy, the surviving Mission Mother.

Bruno manages to hang on to his own, although its tent top rips as he's climbing in, and finally tears away altogether. It scarcely matters; the freezing rain finds its way in horizontally under the rock shelf, under the tents, and soaks all the bags anyway. Fortunately, the material they're made from seems to retain its heat even when wet. Resting here seems a laughable concept, like falling asleep in a barrel rolling down a jagged slope, but incredibly, Bruno remembers nothing after that frazzled thought.

Nothing, that is, until the firm hand of Radmer shakes him awake. His eyelashes are partially frozen together, but he forces them apart and sits up. Radmer—looking miserable as a scarecrow, with icicles hanging from the chin strap of his helmet—says something to him which he can't make out. He answers back with something even less coherent. But all around him the Dolceti are packing away their bivvies, and he must do likewise. To stay here would mean certain death.

Soon they're on the move again, and Bruno can't guess what time of day it is, or how far they've come, or how much longer they have to go. Indeed, his mind can scarcely grasp these concepts at all; the world is reduced to wind and pain, to slow, careful movement between the rocks. When he closes his eyes—and he closes them often now, against the frigid sting of wind and sleet—he still sees rocks. These are his thoughts: rocks, and more rocks, and the occasional step or grasp to carry him from one to the next. Time has no meaning at all.

Still, there does come a point where he notices they're going downhill. This by itself is not unusual, for the pass snakes up and down many times as it rises through the mountains. But the *trend* is down now. They've passed the summit, and are on their way down into the Shanru Basin. They have reached the halfway mark. Which only means that the worst is still to come.

Of the terrible hours after that, Bruno later remembers nothing at all. His first clear memory is of the eyewall, which resembles a tornado, except that it's so large—fifteen kilometers large!—that it appears flat, like a genuine wall. It's so tall that it seems to have no structure at all, no top, no twist or curl. It's just a straight, opaque, heaving wall of flying debris, from dust and fines to sharp rocks the size of his head. Blowing *up*, more than laterally. Is this the main source of the region's gravel rains?

He notices another thing as well; the wind has changed somewhere along the way. No longer frigid and damp, it's now warm and very dry. He can no longer blink his eyes; they've dried open in a crust of mucus. When did that happen? In fact, the air grows warmer with every step. The eyewall itself must be as dry and hot as an oven; he can feel the heat radiating off it. From friction? From the sudden compression of unwilling air against the storm's unyielding center? Certainly, the sound of it is louder than anything Bruno has ever experienced. Like an ongoing explosion, the eyewall is a vertical slice of hell. How deep can it be? How long can a human survive all this?

"Are we going through there?" he shouts to no one. And

of course they are. Where else is there? Even staggering like drunks, what other chance or choice have they got?

Blast.

And somehow they do get through; Bruno will later remember the experience like a nightmare: in fragments. Smashed against a rock, then clinging desperately to it as he's lifted off his feet! Smashed against the ground, then scrabbling for something, anything, to grab on to as the vast suction takes hold of him. A dizzy airborne moment and then, miraculously, a hard landing on his knees. That's all. He later suspects that he managed to close his eyes, and in fact had them closed the whole time, for the memories are visceral rather than visual.

In any case he emerges onto a plain of sand, beneath a sky so blue and bright it seems to burn his optic nerves. The sun hangs over the eyewall's far side, illuminating the storm's interior like a vast, spinning paper lantern.

He staggers forward, becomes aware of a figure ahead of him, a figure behind. He wants to rest, to drink a sip of water and then collapse into a dreamless coma. He doesn't care if he ever awakes. But there's brick-sized debris raining down all around him, so he staggers on a little farther, a little farther. The bedrock beneath his tattered boots gives way to dirt, and then to sand that feels as soft and cool as a wellstone bed.

Finally he comes to a gathering place, a hollow in the sand where raggedy human beings have accumulated. He throws himself down among them and takes that longed-for sip of water. Another person plops down beside him, and then another. And there must be some part of his brain that remembers thought, remembers mathematics, for he takes in the scene with a glance and says to himself, "Our twenty Dolceti are down to just ten. We've lost six more along the way."

It's his last thought for a long, long time.

chapter twenty-two

in which a crown of empire is retrieved

Looking over Bruno and the sleeping Dolceti, a newly awakened Radmer feels—if grimly—the same vindication he did upon setting his boots on the beaches of Varna, after a fifty-hour tumble through cold vacuum. Crazy idea, yes, but here they are. Ten bodies poorer than they began, but still operational.

And there, in the distance, nestled among dunes as high as ten semaphore towers, lie the ruins of Manassa. He sees stone and brick walls jutting up, gray and black and ocher against the sand. More important, he sees the mirror-black sheen of inactive wellstone, alive with glints of green and purple and tarnished silver. It's been a long time since he's seen so much in one place, and it's a good sign indeed; this deadly journey has not been in vain.

The dunes themselves are light brown in color, with patches of gray-black and khaki, and long, strange smudges of darker brown. They look like nothing so much as a pair of desert camouflage trousers out of some Old Modern war drama. The top of the dune field makes a clean line against the sky, not sinusoidal but irregular, ripply, dotted with shallow crests and peaks. It divides the world in two: brown underneath and achingly blue above.

By contrast, the first ridgeline of the Blood Mountains is jagged and chaotic with trees, with rocks, with a variety of grays and browns, dark greens and light greens. Behind that sits the eyewall, which reaches away to the north and south, wrapping around the Shanru Basin. A weak tornado, fifteen kilometers wide.

To the west, the ragged line of the Johnny Wang Uplift is lost in blue-white haze, with the eyewall behind it and evil-looking clouds boiling over the top, racing hard to the north. The ground between here and the Uplift is incredibly flat, broken only by the dune field itself.

Ah, my precious Lune, Radmer frets. He hasn't seen this place since the Shattering, when the ground fell two hundred meters and the city burst like a melon. Almost no one got out alive. It looks now like a cork jammed too deep in its bottle and then left too long on the shelf, so that the resulting hollow has filled with dust. Disrupting the clean lines of his planette, his would-be masterpiece. If he'd had more time to track down and melt out seismic hotspots, that terrible day might never have come. He'd never had it in him to save the Queendom, but the Iridium Days, at least, might still be going strong if he'd managed the last years of Luna with greater finesse. Tamra had forbidden him from completing the crustal stabilization, yes, but that simply told him he should have begun it earlier. Somehow. He should have paid more attention to the news; he should have anticipated the need.

Or, alternatively, he could have mustered the resources of the post-Queendom era. With sufficient digging—and he knew where to dig—the worst of the pressure could still have been relieved, gradually and intentionally. *Not* all in one shot. The Shattering was *his* fault if it was anyone's. Still, his punishment is fitting: to dwell forever in the ruins. Such is the fate of an immorbid people, as Rodenbeck had warned.

But Radmer learned long ago not to mope. It doesn't help anything. He turns his mind instead to practical concerns: a fire, upon which a decent breakfast might finally be cooked. He begins gathering up bits of desert driftwood, strangely light and hard in his hands.

At the edges of the dune field, there are dead and dying trees. Also a few living ones that look recently halfburied, and some dead-and-mostly-buried ones looking as though the sand moved forward and swallowed them a long time ago. Here and there, thick roots and branches jut out of the sand like bones, with a solid, shiny feel that suggests they're already partially fossilized. How long would it take to petrify wood in sands like these?

But the stuff burns well enough when he lays it in a pit, so he unfolds the little titanium grate he's been carrying all these days, and places some hard biscuits and olives and fatbeans in a tray of water to soften them up for grilling.

Soon the smells of food are waking up the others, who rub their eyes, make faces at the scum and grit in their mouths.

"Am I dead?" the young Dolceti, Zuq, asks hopefully. He looks like a man badly hung over and ready to swear off the grape forever. His skin has gone purple-white, but that at least is a reaction to the brightness here; his body is attempting to reflect unwanted heat and UV.

"Not yet, I'm afraid. But with one of my breakfasts, you may be in luck. How's your condition?"

"Not good," Zuq answers, showing off a broken wrist.

And he's not alone; of the ten Dolceti who've made it this far, nine are sporting some sort of major sprain or fracture. Splinting these becomes the first task of this day, which is already into late afternoon and will see the sun set in another twelve hours.

"Remember the war," Radmer tells them solemnly, as Bruno de Towaji stirs, shakes the sand out of his hair, and finally rises. "Injured or not, you're here to fight. You're here to protect this man, Ako'i, while he rummages through yonder ruins."

"We know our jobs," Bordi answers solemnly. "We don't need you to tell us."

"Fair enough. But you do need breakfast."

He dishes it hot into their waiting bowls, and for those who've lost their bowls along the way he plops it, steaming, into their bare hands. If it burns them, they don't acknowledge it, but rather wolf it down, barely pausing to chew.

"I've been here before," Bruno says while the others eat. His eyes are on the distant wellstone jutting up from the sand.

"In the Iridium Days?" Zuq asks, sounding, as always, like he just barely believes it.

Bruno snorts. "They weren't called that until they were nearly over, lad. We had no name for that bitter time, when the Earth lay dying, chewed outward from its core by fragments of the murdered Nescog. Still, 'iridium' is a clever pun; someone back then had an acid sense of humor."

"Because it sounds like Eridani?" Radmer asks.

Bruno coughs out a bitter laugh. "Not at all, lad. Think back to your chemistry lessons; think of a periodic table. Iridium is a member of the precious metals group, one step down from platinum and two down from gold. But it's less shiny than either, and was never a favorite in coins or jewelry. In a value-of-metal sense, the phrase 'Iridium Days' falls somewhere between 'Golden Age' and 'Iron Age.' It's a dark subtle irony for an era of decline."

"Well," says Zuq, "at least they kept a sense of humor."

Bruno smiles down at the boy, who still looks to his eyes like an overgrown toddler. Not only is he short, but like all the "humans" he's got that oversized coconut, those big questioning eyes. "You mightn't say that if you were there."

"You did a lot of fighting?"

"Indeed, though not against an enemy you'd recognize. Oh, there were shooting wars here and there, but for the most part we had shamed ourselves into a kind of sorry truce. Even Doxar Bagelwipe was appalled at the scale of destruction. 'So fragile after all,' he said on his deathbed. The nerve!"

"So what *did* you fight?"

Bruno waves a hand. "Oh, you know. Gravity. Entropy. I spent a decade as a common laborer in the Bag Corps, trying to rescue as much mass as possible for the neutronium presses. Trying to turn the Earth into a constellation of planettes, so her people might have somewhere to flee to, even if they lacked the means. But they *did* lack the means, and so did we. Only two planettes were built down there in the gravity well, before the Earth collapsed into rainbows. I have no idea what's become of them since. Uninhabited, presumably, or your people would know of them. Have you heard of a world called Ramadan? Or another called Open Hand?"

"I haven't," admits Zuq. Other voices mutter their agreement.

Bruno sighs. "No, I thought not. Alas. Before that I was involved in a project to revive select portions of the Nescog. Right here in Manassa, for almost a year. Someone had found an old fax machine, complete with network gates, and we snatched it from the hospital system and were trying to contact the last few nodes, before they went down. With that, you see, we could yank people right off the dying planets! But the tide was against us, all efforts in vain. Were there people who considered the situation normal? Even glorious? I never met them. For those who remembered the Queendom, its aftermath was a time of great sadness."

"It got better later," Radmer tells them both, as if apologizing. But Bruno is mostly right; the Iridium Days were never as roaring as the legends that adhered to them afterward. But neither, in his opinion, was the Queendom itself. He'd fought against it, been exiled from it, crawled back to it in defeat, and finally, toward the end, joined its upper echelons—a rich man with heady connections. He knew it better than Bruno did; knew it from up and down, from inside and out. And the simple fact was, the Tara and Toji of Luner mythology, with their Sphere Palace and their Great Bronze Navy and their "only as strong as the weakest among us," were creatures out of fairy tale. He'd long ago stopped trying to reconcile them to any literal history.

But Bruno surprises him by saying, "Nothing lasts forever, my friend. Not even the bad."

And what can Radmer say to that, who has seen his share of bad, and even a goodly slice of forever?

After breakfast, he leads Bruno up into the dune field for a closer look, taking Deceant Natan—the only uninjured Dolceti—along as bodyguard. Radmer doesn't expect trouble, but he's always prepared for it.

At the base of the hills, the dirt looks almost exactly like beach sand: a mix of white and brown and black grains, very small, interspersed with sharp bits of un-weathered gravel that can't have been here very long. And like an undisturbed beach or riverbed, the ground is covered with a ripply pattern of footprint-sized dunes. When he steps in the trough of one, he finds it squashing underfoot like a sponge. When he steps on the crest, it supports his weight for a moment and then slowly under-goes a kind of staged collapse. *Squish squish crunch.* It's like this at every step, and it will take a lot of steps to carry them up to those ruins.

With a terraformer's eye, he takes in the view ahead, admiring the way the sweep of the mountains has con-spired with the swirl of the storm to gather so much dust in this quiet corner. The dune field is larger than the city it swallowed. In fact, Radmer can see now that the city must extend beyond the eastern side of the eyewall, into even greater ruin.

Still, surprisingly, the northeast faces of many dunes are lined with grass and other plants, particularly at the base, or the seam between dunes, and it strikes him sud-denly that this is not so much a desert as a battleground, between the forces that build and move the dunes, and the forces that seek to smother them with plant life. It's the terraforming drama itself, writ small.

Nor is this place particularly dry. Indeed, emerging from the base of a high dune, a little stream flows in bursts, with minor flash floods of water surging every twenty seconds or so. *Gloo-OOP! Gloo-OOP!* like a kind of geological clock, ticking away the empty millennia. Bruno pauses here, admiring.

"I should like to study this regularity," he says, sound-ing wistful. "How do deep sand and shallow water con-spire in this way? Tick, tock!"

But Radmer doesn't have to remind him there's a war on, with millions of lives hanging in the balance. Bruno watches four complete cycles, and then he's off toward Manassa again, without prompting. It's not an easy walk; after a while, the crumbly yielding softness of the sand fatigues the calf muscles, the ankles, the tendons along the top of the foot. Maybe a camel would feel at home on a surface like this, but few other creatures are adapted for it; Radmer is keenly aware that he's a primate of seashore and savannah and forest. He can climb a rock or a tree without difficulty, but his evolution doesn't know this place.

Still, they find their way. The crests of the dunes are almost like roads, extending for winding kilometers. On either side the dunes drop away into hollows a hundred meters deep. On the face of a dune, the undisturbed ground is a tiger-stripe pattern of brown and black, or beige and dark gray. The lighter sand seems to accumulate in the hollows, with the darker sand following along the ridgelines.

"Something to do with grain sizes?" he asks Bruno.

But the older man just shrugs. "A natural sorting mechanism, clearly. Weight, temperature, the stickiness of the grains . . . You're the planet builder, I'm afraid. I can only guess."

Anyway, for whatever reason, the vegetation and the lighter sand seem to occur mainly in the same places— streaks of white and green among the brown. Even though it's technically winter, the long day has heated up the dark sand, which shimmers with mirages. Radmer is already thirsty again, and from the road-crest of a dune those cool colors beckon. And the roads don't lead the right direction anyway; from here, straight on is straight down! But walking down the steep hillside is almost impossible; it invites one to run. Soon the three men are descending in great walloping giant's steps, with the sand squeaking and groaning wherever their feet touch down.

It's hilarious and a little bit frightening, because the dune collapses with every step, and it seems to Radmer that the whole thing could easily bury them without a hiccup if they stumble. So they don't.

The pale sand at the bottom of the ditch is very firm when his foot comes down straight on top of it. A sideways kick loosens it, though, revealing softer sand beneath. It appears, actually, to be a semisolid crust of larger particles sitting on top of a fluid of smaller ones. The trough is full of dried, dead vegetation, with mounds of light brown sand surrounding it.

He's got to retract his thoughts about the lifelessness here, though, for on closer inspection he sees that the dunes are crisscrossed with little tracks. The shapes and even sizes of the footprints have been lost—blurred out by the shifting sand—and there's no other clue to their identity. Ironically, the plants here in the trough look edible and even succulent: desert species of pea and rice and pepper, perfectly adapted to sucking moisture out of this environment.

He hasn't seen a termite mound anywhere, but here in the trough he does see a few individual blue-on-clear specimens, carrying not only seeds and wood fragments but also the body of some larger insect he's not sure he recognizes. Or perhaps it's a little machine, not truly organic at all, and the termites will go hungry tonight. In any case it's balanced along three blue-and-clear backs, and moving steadily toward whatever home the termites have here.

"Industrious and hungry," says Bruno, looking down at the marching line, and Radmer can see how *strange* these engineered creatures must seem to him, who grew up on an Earth still mostly natural.

"Food for something else," he counters, for ultimately that's the only purpose any animal serves in this ecology. Or any ecology.

One set of animal tracks, clearly left by a kangaroo rat, consists of paired footprints, very small, with a linear drag mark between, as from a little tail. The footprints terminate in a fist-sized mound of undisturbed sand, and Conrad supposes the thing has buried itself there to wait out the day's rising heat. In summer this place must be an oven! But Radmer can see, again with his terraformer's eye—how a big, hungry creature like himself could make his living out here. Reaching an arm into the sand to pull out mice and lizards, garnishing them with desert rice and desert peas and cooking them over half-fossilized driftwood, with the woody, nutty taste of termites for dessert . . . The eye of the Stormlands would be hard-pressed to support a large population—as the empty city of Manassa can attest!—but there's enough energy here to sustain a small band of frugal hermits.

Would it make them hard? Vicious?

"Keep your eyes open," he suggests to Natan, quite unnecessarily since the Dolceti have no other job. "This place isn't exactly lifeless."

"If there's boogeymen," Natan agrees cheerfully, "I'll hold 'em off."

Radmer isn't kidding, but neither is Natan, so he lets it go.

"There's good clean air here," Natan adds approvingly. "Nice for my allergies. Don't worry yourself, General."

Surprisingly, an hour later they're only about halfway to the area Radmer has identified as the "top" of the dune field. If there are more and higher peaks behind those, he doesn't want to know about it! But it seems they have arrived at the outskirts of Manassa; a corner of wellstone juts up half a meter from the sand.

"Declarant," Radmer says to Bruno, pointing out the anomaly.

"Ah," says the former king, rubbing his hands together.

"Well, well. What have we here?" He kneels next to the object and brushes some of the sand away from it. "It's dead, for starters, but so are a lot of things. Wake up, you!" And when that doesn't work, he taps it forcefully, several times. "Hello? Activate!" This, at least, produces a brief flicker of color.

Bruno looks back at Radmer. "You used to know these things, Architect. Have you any ideas? It's getting plenty of sunlight, so it should—"

"*This piece* is getting plenty of sunlight," Radmer says, and for a moment he sounds like Conrad Mursk, even to himself.

"Ah!" Bruno agrees, liking that answer quite a lot. "This piece is getting plenty of sunlight, but we have no way of knowing how far down the structure extends. It's browning out! This little sliver may be attempting to power an entire building, yes? Or else it really is dead, but let's start with what we know. Natan, will you break off a piece for me? *This* way, if you please, not that way."

But it proves more difficult than he'd expected; against even dead wellstone, mere human strength is rather slight. But with swords and feet and a great deal of grunting and heaving, the three men manage to break off a shard that fits neatly into Bruno's hand, with edges dull enough that Radmer doesn't fear he'll cut himself.

But still, the fragment refuses to respond with anything more than flickers of green and a faint, faint crackling noise. Finally, in exasperation Bruno says, "Listen, you, this is a Royal Override. Shut down all resident programs and boot up in command line mode."

Strangely enough, that works. Yellow letters and numerals appear on the flat surface, and in another moment Bruno is tapping the shard with three fingers in rapid sequence, keying in a set of basic configuration commands. The thing, already shiny rainbow-black in his hands, turns the color of a solar tree: *superabsorber* black. Then it begins to change in more sophisticated ways; colors shoot along its length as it reconfigures itself, layer by nanoscopic layer.

"God's eyes!" Natan curses, watching the fragment flicker and change. "I never quite believed in sorcerers!"

Bruno looks up in annoyance. "Eh? Is it sorcery to spill ink on a page? To rot an apple? To stand in the sun and turn your 'human' skin as white as milk? No? Then I'm no sorcerer, Deceant. This object is a tool, like a special sort of window glass. Nothing more."

"So you say," Natan mutters, looking as though he'd prefer to take a step or two backward. But this Older is his responsibility, through death or worse. He stands his ground. "But in the stories, it's only Tara and Toji who can command the stones. 'Roylovride,' yeah, that's the magic word."

Bruno turns away in weary disappointment. "Believe what you like. I don't suppose it matters." To the fragment in his hand he says, "Run standard sensor package. Run *any* sensor package. Run sensor diagnostic." Then, when these fail to work, he casts an annoyed look at Radmer and says, "Do you know anything about sensor design?"

And although Conrad Mursk did time in two different navies, in deep-space and deep-solar atmospheres—places where wellstone sensors were the difference between life and death—it never really rubbed off on him. He was remarkably bad at a remarkable number of things, which in the end is why he's ended up here, why the world is the way it is.

"No," says Radmer. "I wish I did."

"Hmm. Well." Bruno plops his ass down in the sand and peers at the fragment for several long minutes. "There's information buried inside you," he mutters to it at one point. "Libraries of it. You know things; you just don't *know* you know them."

He sits there, fumbling and muttering, for what seems like a long time. Then, finally, perhaps an hour after sitting down, he rises again and brushes the dust off himself.

"Have you got it working?" Radmer asks, trying not to sound weary or ungrateful.

"Not properly, no," Bruno answers with obvious irritation. "I'm trying to map the city by composition, and it's just not working. But I've located something that might make the job easier."

"Yes? What's that?"

"A working fax machine," Bruno says, as though it isn't good news at all.

As it turns out, the fax is located a kilometer and a half deeper into the dune field, where the free flow of sand is restricted by the presence of wellstone walls, running deep. And even to Radmer himself, it really does begin to seem that Bruno is a kind of sorcerer, for though he's complained about the crude sketchplate in his hands—it isn't working properly, it isn't suitable, its library has been corrupted—he's able to use it, somehow, to communicate with the dead wellstone all around him. Conrad Mursk had been an expert programmer in his day, and his particular specialty was in speaking to buildings, or pieces of buildings. But Conrad had merely been determined and lucky, which was not at all the same thing as being brilliant.

Now, Bruno walks out ahead of Radmer and Natan, and the dead wellstone in his wake turns to silver and gold, to impervium and marble and mother-of-pearl.

There's no real rhyme or reason to it, no master plan, no memory of how the city once looked. The King of Sol is just fooling around, putting the stuff through its paces, like a musician picking up a long-forgotten instrument. In truth the effect is kind of gaudy, kind of ugly. But it makes a world of difference in the appearance of the desert: no longer a ruin, no longer a dead city filled with sand, but a sleeping one, carefully preserved for later use.

The first problem comes when the fax machine turns out to be buried deep in the sand. When the men arrive at the designated spot, there isn't even a building. There are wall fragments and even a bit of intact rooftop nearby, but the magic spot itself is just a basin of sand, featureless and apparently empty.

"Blast," Bruno says, surveying the scene unhappily. But he isn't daunted for long; within another minute he's calling out instructions to the surrounding wellstone, forging connections between the intact pieces of building and the intact pieces of street far below. Soon the fragments are coming alive with circuit traces, white and gold and silver on black, and he's murmuring to them, gesturing, and finally raising his beseeching arms into the air, more like a prophet or a druid than any conventional sort of scientist.

And the sand responds.

At first there's just a hissing sound, and then a slight rumble underfoot, barely noticeable. Then Conrad's hairs suddenly stand on end, his pistol and blitterstick rattle in their holsters, and there is a tangible jerk in the ground beneath his feet. Against the sides of the wellstone ruins, the sand begins flowing like water. Out, away, unburying this place. And in another few seconds these trickles are entraining more sand around them, becoming rivulets, streams, rapids. Radmer exchanges a glance with Natan, and the two of them step back, and back, and back some more. If Bruno needs protection in this place, it's not a sort that they can provide. Soon, the dust is flying in geysers and there's an excavation happening in real time, right before their eyes. The hole is rectangular, at least to the extent that the collapsing sand permits, and it's three meters deep, then five, then ten. Radmer and Natan retreat farther. Then the hole widens, and they have to retreat some more. Within minutes, the top of a building is exposed. Then the whole top story, with the sand flowing away in rivers, crawling to higher ground and spilling down out of sight, into hollows somewhere, burying mice and lizards and desert peas.

Then, all at once, the sound and the movement stop. The sand neither rises nor falls. It doesn't trickle back into the hole, and Radmer's hair does not lie flat against his scalp. There is some sorcery at work here, still.

"It's down there," Bruno says, pointing quite unnecessarily into the pit. As if they could miss what happened there. As if they could be looking at anything else. The building fades from mirror-black to bronze, and Bruno says to it, in a somewhat louder voice, "Glass ceiling. Glass windows. Door."

A double line of round portholes appears in the bronze, one of them surrounded by a rectangular seam, which parts from the material around it and swings inward on imaginary hinges. Bruno climbs down into the hole on sure, steady feet, as though he does this all the time. He follows the carpet of rigid sand right into the doorway itself, pausing at the threshold to look over his shoulder at Natan and Radmer. "Are you coming?" It's very nearly a command.

Natan is looking frankly scared by all this, and Radmer can hardly blame him. He hasn't seen a sight like this in thousands of years, or maybe ever. But he murmurs, "It's all right. We're in good hands."

And Natan replies, "I'd fling *myself* into the great beyond for this man, too, in a sphere of brass or not. Suddenly I feel sorry for the Glimmer King. Isn't that a funny thing?"

"Aye," Radmer can only agree. And with that, they follow the ancient scarecrow of a man inside the ancient building.

The interior is surprisingly well lit. It's an office of some sort, and the surfaces are immaculate—walls and floors and countertops, tables, the arms and seats and backs of wellstone chairs, supported by spindly structures that look, even to Conrad's eye, as though they should have collapsed at the first puff of wind. The fax machine—a sight Radmer hasn't seen since the Shattering, or nearly, stands against a far wall. Bruno walks right up to it as though he owns the place.

"Buffer status."

And then, when that doesn't work, "Royal Override. Reset all functions to factory nominal. Report the status of mass buffers. Report the status of memory buffers. Perform a full diagnostic, and stand by."

The foggy, fractal surface of the print plate flickers for a moment, and then the walls around it come alive with diagrams, with scrolling lists of words and numbers, with a holographic table of the elements, annotated with a bar graph showing how much of each element is present in the machine at this particular time. It isn't much.

"Fax," Bruno says to it, "how are you feeling?"

"Very well, Your Majesty. It's good to be functional again, for the first time in nineteen years."

"Nineteen? Not two thousand?"

"I'm not sure why I said that, Sire. A glitch, I'm sure. Did I wake briefly, under the soil? Did some ray of invisible warmth find me for a moment? Long enough to reset my counters? If so, I'm honored to be reactivated now for more meaningful service, especially by one so eminent. Is there anything I can help you with?"

"Yes. Much." Bruno runs his admiring fingers over the surface of the print plate, looking wistful and perhaps a bit sad. "I see from your diagnostic you have two human beings in your buffer. Optimized humans, bearing the unmistakable imprint of Queendom-era pattern filtration. I don't recognize the names, but then again I wouldn't expect to. There used to be so many people."

"Shall I reinstantiate these two for you?" the fax machine asks, with no particular emotional emphasis. It doesn't care one way or the other; it will simply obey the man it perceives as its king.

But Bruno shakes his head. "No, let them sleep. It's more humane. But preserve them in your memory, fax machine. Let no misfortune befall them, if it's within your power to prevent it. You are about to see some heavy use, and I'd prefer those patterns not be erased in the process. Is your library intact?"

"Alas, Sire, it is sorely degraded."

"Have you any battle armor?"

"No."

"Hmm. Have you ordinary space suits?"

"No, Sire. But I do have some police uniforms."

"Ah. Well, that's a starting point. I'm going to feed you material samples and provide some detailed specifications. We're going to improvise."

"It will be a pleasure, Sire."

But Natan is striding forward now, the look on his face almost angry. "I'm remembering something from my classical literature, all of a sudden. That word, 'ako'i.' It isn't a name at all. It's an old term meaning, like, 'professor' or something."

Bruno turns, looks over his shoulder. "You surprise me, Deceant. And you're absolutely correct; Ako'i is not my name."

Radmer is not accustomed to feeling like a spectator, but the two men have locked eyes, locked step in some ephemeral way, and he's on the outside. He has nothing to say, nothing to add, no tasks to perform. He simply wants to see what these men will say next, what they'll do. A sense of terrible importance hangs over the moment.

"Your name is Toji," Natan accuses.

And Bruno smiles sadly. "No, that's not it, either. But you're very close." He murmurs something to the fax machine, and a perfect diamond crown tumbles out into his waiting hand.

Bruno had never asked to be a king, and in many ways he'd felt himself wildly unsuited to the role. But he had learned how to play it, and more than that, to *feel* it. Because people could tell the difference between a leader who spoke from his heart, and one who was just going through the motions. He was an inventor, yes. A scientist and lover, yes. A father and a hermit and a failure, yes. But he was once a king as well, and he consequently understands the power of myth, to rally the spirits of men when cold reality's at its grimmest. He has left Natan and Radmer behind, instructing them to gather raw material to feed the fax. He himself has other business.

And he's young again! Immorbid! His black hair flowing almost to his shoulders, his black beard bristling, his veins coursing with élan vital! A medical-grade fax machine was a rarity indeed in the Iridium Days; this one may have been the last in all the world, in all the universe. Perhaps the very one he'd once employed himself, to seek the final remnants of the shattered Nescog. And he remembers with perfect clarity: by the end *there had been no working collapsiters*. He and Eustace Faxborn—newly widowed in some accident or other—had broadcast Royal Overrides in every band of the spectrum, had scoured the heavens for even the lowliest maintenance ping in response. But they had gathered only silence, and eventually the project had been shut down. So why are there packet acknowledgments—recent ones!—in the fax machine's history file today? Why indeed?

His mind feels fresh. His scars and wounds have fallen away like hosed-off grime. He has designed himself a suit of Fall-era battle armor, and it fits him more perfectly then he could ever have dreamed or remembered. And with its impregnable power all around him, he feels like a king indeed, or more than a king, for the people of this world have never seen anything like him. He bounds across the dunes at a speed no mere human could sustain. He leaps and twirls, firing weapons into the ground for the sheer bleeding hell of it.

In no time at all he comes upon the wounded Dolceti, eight men and a woman huddled miserably in their hollow in the sand, and he alights among them, striking a pose that feels appropriate for the moment.

"We are successful, my friends," he says to them through his suit's loudspeakers. He's tried the radio, too, but the Dolceti don't have receivers, and anyway all the police channels seem to be drowning in interference, or in voices at such high volume that Bruno hears them only as noise. Why? From where? Is it some communication channel of the robot army? Is it something else entirely? He doesn't know, and for the moment he doesn't much care.

"Succor awaits," he says to the Dolceti. "Walk into the dunes, into the ruins. Along the walls, there are flickering lights that will show you the way. Enter the top of the bronze tower, and speak with Radmer and Natan. There you'll be healed. There you will be equipped with such armor and weapons as you've only heard of in stories. For the journey out of this place, and for all that follows afterward."

But Bordi says to him, "The hair and skin look nice, sir. Truly, it's a miracle. But you forget yourself, yes? You're not in command here."

"Are you sure?" says Bruno. "Then I'll ask you, as a friend, to follow this recommendation. Time is short, and we have much to do."

From his sprawled position on the ground, Zuq looks up at Bruno with a smirk. "God's eyes, Ako'i, in that costume, with that hair and those eyebrows, you look like the King of Sol."

And Bruno, sensing his moment, places the diamond crown atop the Gothic dome of his helmet, and says, "Your mother didn't raise any fools, lad. That's good. Now go, do as I say, and I'll be with you shortly. I must tarry here awhile, to contemplate matters strategic."

In fact, he needs to tarry here for a good bit of brooding—perhaps even tears—because all this has reminded him too much of his beloved Tamra, for whose smile he would gladly trade this world and all its people. Fortunately, no one is offering him that trade. No one ever will. The past is gone.

Unless perhaps some device could be constructed to interfere with it—an *arc de commencer*, so to speak. Bruno has never really wondered how such a device might be built, how it might operate, but perhaps now, with his mind restored to youthful vigor, is the time to give it some thought. Might he right the wrongs of his past, wiping this world's very existence from the stage of history?

But the Dolceti—unaware of the apocalypse he so idly contemplates for them—are rising to their feet, appraising him with new eyes, weighing his stance and his words, murmuring quietly among themselves. It's Bordi who breaks the moment, bowing his head and saying, "I always thought there was something funny about you. Now, at last, I understand. And what of the Queen?"

Bruno shakes his head. "If she were here…if she were here none of this would be happening. We used to say she had Royal Overrides for the human soul. But not the Eridanian one, alas."

"Hmm. We owe you no fealty; you know that. You're not our king. Or perhaps you are and always were, and your authority supersedes that of the Furies, or any other worldly power. It hardly matters, in this hour of doom. Can you save us from the armies of Astaroth? If not, then who could? I know a good bet when I see one, Sire. My sword is yours to command."

To which Bruno answers, "Having seen your sword in action, Captain, I know full well the value you offer. Now look me in the eye and tell me you'll fight bravely, for your world and your people."

"You know I will."

"Indeed. Now go."

And they do, hauling their bodies up and limping off into the dune field, while Bruno sits his ass down to commence the aforementioned mope. He will not, he realizes now, tamper with the flow of time. Even if he could, even if he *would*, his very presence here in the ruins of Lune is evidence that he shan't. Do people possess nerve endings which extend, in some ephemeral way, into the future? For even in this state of unnatural vigor, Bruno senses nothing ahead of him. He is immorbid, yes, but not immortal. He cannot imagine any future beyond the next few days.

Indeed, the hour is later than he's thought, and the situation more dire, for as the disc of the sun slips behind the Stormlands' eyewall to the west, over the vanishing silhouettes of the Dolceti, a bird calls out from the east, from somewhere among the scraggly trees clinging to the hills there.

ThooRAT!

ThooRAT!

Should omens be believed in this place? Bruno doesn't know, but before another minute has passed he spies a trio of tattered figures approaching him from out of those same stony hills, from the teeth of the storm itself. There's dust and worse raining down all around them.

Bruno calls up a sensory magnifier in the clear dome of his helmet, and scans these approaching figures in every spectrum he can think of. He's expecting Dolceti stragglers, but in fact the newcomers are Olders. Familiar ones: Sidney Lyman and his lieutenants, Brian Romset and Nick Valdi. They look exhausted, battered, barely conscious after fighting their way through the eyewall and the raging storm beyond it. But they're moving quickly and purposefully across the sand, because...

They're being chased by two dozen gleaming robots.

chapter twenty-three

in which the old meets the new meeting the old

Bruno has faced worse odds than these, with poorer equipment to back him up, so his leap to action comes virtually without thought. He tears across the sandy plains, confident of passing Lyman and his fellows before their dainty attackers can reach them. And the look on their faces when he does pass is, he thinks, worth the thousands of years of solitude that carried him to this point. At long last he has become a sort of Buddhist, or a factory-issue mammal, fully present in the moment, able to appreciate the humor of it all and yet caring little about the outcome. He will simply do his best to smash these robots, and see what happens.

And that best is quite good indeed, for as he arrives among them they stab and hack with whirling blades that might easily have severed his head from the brickmail-reinforced neck that supports it. The blades are that sharp, yes, the blows that fast and hard. This time, the robots mean business; they're saving nothing for the trip back home. But what Bruno lacks in speed he more than makes up for in sheer capacity; the attacks push him this way and that, but his unscathed armor scarcely sheds a molecule.

And meanwhile he's grabbing swords, grabbing arms, firing energy beams at point-blank range. He doesn't even bother to aim for the iron boxes on the sides of their heads; those are for merely human weapons to pierce. Bruno was never a *great* warrior; he merely happened to be present at a few of history's most crucial battles. And while the abomination of blindsight training still crackles inside him, informing his actions, he is no Dolceti. Just a man, just some guy in a suit of armor. So if these robots were combat models he might have cause to worry.

But they aren't, and he doesn't; their impervium hulls are thin, never meant to withstand the burn of a gamma-ray laser or the punch of a hypersonic wirebomb. He's got a blitterstaff slung across his back which he doesn't even bother to use, because it's *cleansing* to fight this one out hand-to-hand.

And the robots seem to get the message; *they've* never encountered anything like him before, either, and as five of them collapse into sparking fragments during the first few seconds of combat, the rest retreat to a safer distance, ten and twenty meters back so that Bruno must aim more carefully to hit them. And aiming carefully is not one of his better skills, and the robots are circling and regrouping with inhuman grace and fluidity, and he's just deciding to unsling that blitterstaff after all when they suddenly leap upon him en masse.

Oh. Oh, dear.

He goes down under their weight, sprawling onto his back with a robot on each arm, a robot on each leg, two on his chest, and a dozen standing round him like the outlines of an angel. They raise their swords, preparing to peel him out of his wellstone skin no matter how long it takes.

Fortunately, there's a response for this in the annals of the Queendom's martial arts, with which Bruno was once, of necessity, familiar. "Discharge all!" he screams at the suit, and it responds by turning to glass underneath him and then opening up its capacitors, dumping all their stored charge. For a few nanoseconds he's crawling with surface electrons, which quickly find their way to the ground through every object within easy arcing distance. The voltage is high, but it's the *wattage* that really counts, burning paths through the robots' own wellstone, through the very circuitry that controls them, through libraries of collective memory and programmed response. From a distance it looks like an explosion, and indeed it sends eleven robots flipping through the air, dazed and befuddled, parts of them damaged beyond repair.

And in the wake of that, Bruno shouts: "Royal override! All autronic devices, stand down and await instructions!"

The robots will not obey this command, but he knows from experience that they'll recognize it in some way, that it will confuse them for a moment. And he takes advantage, struggling to his feet in a garment that has gone stiff and lifeless, gone black in a last-ditch attempt to drink in energy from the sky.

There are eight attackers left on their feet, staring at him with their blank metal faces, and he steps backward through a gap between them, unslinging the blitterstaff. This is a weapon that requires no finesse; it's coded to ignore his suit, but any other wellstone it touches—for example, the impervium of a robot hull—will be subjected to an intense barrage of electrical and software and pseudochemical insults, in random patterns shifting too rapidly for the robots' defenses.

He touches one, and it falls apart into screaming, steaming shards. Touches another, and it bursts like a chestnut in a fire. But the other six have their wits about them now, and are dancing toward him with deadly intent. There's nothing for it but to whirl the staff around him, not with any great skill but in a simple space-filling function that leaves no room for a robot to pass. He clobbers another two before a third one manages to slip in at ground level—literally crawling on its back!—and take a firm hold on his legs. He kills that one, too, but not before he loses his balance again and tumbles over the back of another one crouching behind him.

Blast, he thinks as the ground rushes up again, *these robots are cleverer than they ought to be.* He shouldn't have taken them on alone—not that he'd had much choice. Now he's facedown in the sand, and when the first blow slices down at his neck he tries to struggle away sideways, but something is holding him. He tries to raise the blitterstaff, but something is weighing it down. He tries to fire his wrist-mounted wireguns again, but of course there's no power. Not yet, not for another few seconds at least. The blindsight part of his mind is painfully, terrifyingly aware of that blade rushing down. And there isn't a thing it can do.

The blow lands solidly, and Bruno's suit is no longer absurdly durable. In fact, it's just a fine-mesh silicon cloth, not much different from old-fashioned fiberglass. The blade doesn't penetrate, but it does concentrate a great deal of force on a rather narrow stripe of neck. The impact is like a flash, a shock, a crashing together of cymbals. Heedless of his dignity, the King of Sol screams in rage.

But this recalls another bit of Queendom battle lore: when all else fails, there *is* power in a scream. In a brief burst of strength he manages to lift himself, to roll a bit, to make the next blow come down in a different place and at a less-favorable angle. He manages to jerk the blitterstaff free of whatever was holding it, and to sweep it around him in a ground-level arc. It hits something along the way, although he has no idea what, or whether it'll help him.

And now, finally, he fears for his safety. As a result, the next few seconds of the fight are pure blindsight; Bruno sees nothing, and is only vaguely aware of himself in the conscious sense. He is motion and shadow. Then his vision flickers on: once, twice, like a heartbeat and then a constant hum, and he's on his feet, and the sand around him is littered with robot bodies. Some of these are dead and shattered, and some are dragging themselves pathetically toward him, as if they might still somehow injure him with the last of their strength. Their bodies have gone black, too, groping for solar energy, although there's a fine grit of storm-blown dust settling onto them from above. They'll be buried long before any self-repair can kick in.

Still, there's something so *purposeful* about it all that he pauses for a moment, wondering whether finishing these bastards off might be some kind of sin. But he's spared the trouble when the crack of a rifle sounds, and the nearest robot head explodes. Then another, then another, until there are no robots left.

And then Sidney Lyman is rising from the crest of a dune, dusting himself off, and the other two Olders are there at his side.

"Bloody glints," one of them mutters.

Bruno squats for a moment, panting, just looking at the three men while he regains his breath. Finally he says, "Gentlemen. Welcome to Shanru Basin. To what do we owe the pleasure?"

"You weren't fooling anyone, Sire," Sidney says to that.

"Hmm?"

"Admittedly, it took us a while to figure it out. I mean, we hadn't seen your face in what, two thousand years? But it clicked. Right after you left, me and the boys here were just kind of looking at each other, saying, 'Whoops, that was kind of stupid.' I sent most of the unit back to Echo Valley, but for my own self I just . . . needed to be here. You and Radmer, you're off to fight the Glimmer King. Without me! Without my boys, here! Look at you: you're *young*. You're armored. You just took on twenty-some robots all by yourself, saving our sorry asses. Fucking King of Sol."

"Sorry to trouble you," Bruno says to him, meaning it. "You don't owe me a thing. Quite the reverse: I'm responsible for all the misery you see around you."

"Oh, piffle," Sidney says, almost spitting the words. He looks utterly exhausted, but this flare of anger is enough to keep him going for a little while longer. "You haven't even been here. You think we can't fuck a world up all by ourselves? Listen, you, we're here for . . . for . . ."

"Closure," says Brian.

"Right. Closure. And you're going to give it to us."

Bruno blinks. "Are you here to assassinate me?" It's a strange concept; on some level it's exactly what he deserves, and yet he cannot allow it to happen. Not now, not yet.

But Sidney just rolls his eyes. "Oh, please. We're here because it puts some . . ."

"Meaning," says Brian.

"Right. On all the fuffing time we've killed on this planette. Hiding out is not the same thing as actually turning the place over to a new . . ."

"Generation?" suggests Nick Valdi.

"No. A new paradigm. A new *society*. Free from all this debris. From all our broken dreams." He points vaguely in the direction of Manassa.

Bruno eyes these three raggedy men carefully, seeing no deception in them, no weakness. They *will* fight, even if they cannot say exactly why.

"I understand," he says, for he truly does. "Up there in the ruins is a fax machine which will get you back in fighting condition. But it's no substitute for rest, after a journey through the Stormlands. A little farther into the dunes, you'll find our camp. The sand is very soft there."

But Sidney Lyman just laughs at that. "Your Majesty, do you think we just happened to run into a scouting patrol here? The enemy may not have figured out what you're up to, but they know you're up to something. There's about fifteen thousand robots on the march, and they'll be here, oh, any minute now."

"Ah," Bruno says, processing that. On the face of it, it's very bad news indeed. But how much does it really change? "Well, I suppose we can all rest when we're safely dead and buried. In the meantime, come with me. Quickly, if you please."

By the time Bruno returns to the bronze tower, with Lyman and his men in tow, Radmer has already fed most of the Dolceti through the fax. They're standing around now, admiring each other in their battle armor, which Radmer has done up in bright, dolcet-berry yellow with a subtle metallic finish. Their blitterstaves are a shade of dully glowing crimson that complements the uniforms nicely.

At the sight of it Bruno feels yet another pang for the Queendom, whose sense of style—and ability to follow through on it!—was unmatched by any society before or after. On those terms, King Bruno had been an embarrassment to his people, who were forever beseeching him not to wear anything in public which had not first been approved by his wife, or one of her courtiers, or his own valet, or even Slappy Luzarre, who for one thousand years sold bananas from a wagon on the street outside the palace gates. But like any mathematician, Bruno could recognize beauty when he saw it, and he'd seen it everywhere in the Queendom. Here on Lune, even the Iridium Days had been drab by comparison.

Radmer himself is wearing reflective inviz, which is like regular inviz except that it's purely passive, illuminated only by ambient light and reflection. Consuming far less energy than a full stealthing cloak, it doesn't attempt to match the radiant brightness of sun or sky, and it leaves a clear, sunset-elongated shadow upon the dunes. His head and hands are also visible.

"What do you mean I'm a copy of my old self?" Mission Mother Mathy is demanding of his floating, disembodied head. "Did I die? Did that thing in there kill me and take my soul?"

"Will you calm down?" Radmer replies wearily. But not all that wearily, for he too is young again, and looks exactly like the Conrad Mursk who agreed, so long ago, to crush this moon for fun and profit.

"No one knows the fate of a human soul," Bruno says, striding up, "when the body is destroyed and recopied. But such adventures were commonplace in the Queendom, and though we were vigilant—especially in the beginning!—for signs of spiritual decay, none were ever observed. The process is, to all tests and appearances, safe. And better than safe, for you've been rendered immorbid."

"Oh, my, God," Mathy says, horrified.

Hmm. Apparently these people are deathists. And why not, with only decayed, bitter Olders around to show what immorbidity was like? Well, no help for it. He says, not just to Mathy but to all of them, "Fear not, for though your bodies cannot grow old, they most certainly can be killed. And as we speak, there's a robot army marching through the eyewall that will gladly make it happen."

Indeed, on the hills just this side of the eyewall, glints of light have begun to appear, reflecting the blurry red of the sunset behind the eyewall's other face. If they're undamaged by the storm, and move at the speed of household robots, they'll be here in twenty minutes. Perhaps less.

To Sidney and Brian and Nick he says, "Refresh yourselves quickly, in there."

"Hello, sir," they say to Radmer in passing.

"Hi," he says back. "You shouldn't have come here."

Then, looking out unhappily at the approaching glints, Radmer asks Bruno, "What of Highrock? Is Tillspar in enemy hands already?"

"I haven't heard. But this army apparently followed the southern route, bypassing the Divide. So there may yet be reason to hope."

"For now. How many are coming? Are we enough to hold this site against them?"

"Perhaps," Bruno says, though even with Queendom equipment he doubts it very much. The odds are just tilted too steeply in the enemy's favor. "But we may find greater advantage in moving onward."

"A fighting retreat? I'll begin the weapons training immediately."

"Do that, yes," Bruno says, "But first there's something you should know. This machine here"—he waves a hand at the bronze tower-top sticking out of the sand—"is in contact with at least three collapsiters, somewhere in the lower Kuiper Belt, just above Neptune's orbit. A bit of Nescog survives!"

"How is that possible?" asks an incredulous Radmer. "We would have known, long ago."

Before the Shattering, yes. Even before the Murdered

Earth cracked and fell in itself and breathed a last puff of air from the lungs of its dying billions. Curses, mostly, with Bruno's name figuring prominently among them.

"Indeed we would," Bruno agrees. "And something as complex and fragile as a collapsiter doesn't simply reconstitute itself. Perhaps the hand of God has intervened on our behalf, or perhaps the hand of Man, if Lune is not the last bastion of us after all. It hardly matters at this late hour, General. My point is simply that I can take us out of here. Swiftly and without a trace."

"To where?" asks Radmer.

And here Bruno cannot help grinning, for there's nothing more just in this world than turning a villain's own dirty tricks against him. "The survival of a fax machine for this long without maintenance is surprising, but hardly incredible. It's *use* that wears them down. And the gates are just as durable, so it's reasonable to suppose they're intact. I'd be more surprised if they weren't."

"So, what? We fax out and back? Use the speed-of-light delays as a kind of time bomb, and step out of the plate ten or twelve hours after we left?"

Impatiently, Bruno tries to run a hand through his hair, but bangs up against the dome of his helmet instead. "Listen, all right? *Ours is not the only fax machine.* We've assumed another all along. In Astaroth, yes? In the Glimmer King's own presumed fortress, somewhere in the vicinity of the south pole. It will take hours, yes, for our signal to travel to the outer system and back. But when it does, we can step right to the heart of this world's problems. And solve them."

"Oh," says Radmer. He seems stunned to blankness by that remark, but slowly he recovers himself, and finally matches Bruno's grin. "That sounds a bit dangerous, old man. Are you sure you're up to the task?"

"As sure as the sun shines, my boy. I've penetrated

a fearsome lair or two in my day. And I hadn't the Dolceti with me then, nor you, nor the element of surprise. Now if you'll excuse me, I have a three-thousand-year-old telecom network to fix."

Alas, this proves more difficult than he'd assumed at first. The collapsiters are clearly pinging and responding to pings, but sorting through the fax machine's comm logs, he's baffled at first by the nonsense he finds there. He *built* the Nescog, and while the passage of time has bleached out the specific details of its comm protocol, he does at least recognize his own work when he sees it. And this is something...else.

This isn't Nescog at all, but some derivative coding system built upon it. When? By whom? Could it be the fabled Shadow Network of the Fatalist ghouls? A hundred gigatons of collapsium could not be hidden in the Old Solar System—every collapsiter was known and tracked—but a parasitic protocol running secretly in the margins...Well, it isn't impossible, but it still doesn't explain how dead collapsiters have turned back into live ones. And anyway something in him doubts that explanation. It fails Occam's Razor; it's too complex. Something else is going on.

Alas, the mystery will have to wait for another time; with a few minutes of study he's able to decipher the important features of the log file, and construct an access request that will race out ahead of their own corporeal images, logging them on to the mystery network just in time to be routed through it, and also scanning for additional gates and logging them on, involuntarily. A hostile takeover of the Glimmer King's fax. Or so he hopes; if the process fails, they'll bounce right back here again, to face the robot army.

"They're coming!" someone shouts down to him from outside.

Well, yes. That goes without saying. Of the fax he asks, "Does this transaction look valid to you?"

"I have never seen one like it, Sire," the fax replies, from a speaker grown adjacent to its print plate. "But it appears to be a valid construction."

"Then implement it, under full Royal Override."

"Doing so."

"Architect!" he shouts then through the open doorway. "We're ready! Start sending people through!"

But something's wrong; there's a rising din and clatter out there. The battle has begun, or rather resumed. Blast. He races outside, prepared for the worst, and sees pretty much what he expects: the site is overrun. Already there are dozens of robots down and dozens more swarming among the Dolceti, and there are *hundreds* pouring over the nearby dunes. Presumably thousands racing upward through the dune field, out of sight for the moment but not planning on staying that way for long.

"Radmer!" he shouts, blasting his voice over the loudspeakers. "Bordi! Get the Dolceti through the fax!"

"I'm not going in there," someone protests, over the grunt and clatter of combat and the death screams of household robots.

"You're not staying here," someone else remarks. And a third voice—Mathy's—adds, "I'm not going first, I'll tell you that much."

Bruno pauses to smash down a pair of attackers, and then says, "General Radmer will go first. Then Sidney Lyman and his men, for they'll know better what to expect on the other side." He pauses again to rescue a fallen comrade, then continues, "Next will go Natan and Zuq and Mathy, and all the rest of you, and"—he fires an energy blast at a nearby hilltop, scattering the robots there in a burst of sand and sundered wellstone, and sorely depleting his energy reserves once again—"and finally Bordi."

"You're not going last," Bordi says, while laying about him with the blitterstaff in decisive blindsight strokes. "Not if I have anything to say about it!"

"You do not," Bruno answers, "for only I can seal the gates behind us, and prevent this army from pouring through in pursuit."

"Good luck," says Radmer, on his way down into the pit and through the doorway. Lyman and the other Olders follow behind, murmuring similar sentiments, and then the Dolceti are making their retreat, stepping backward into the pit while hundreds of robots swarm in after them. It's dicey for a few moments when the sheer weight of attackers thrusts Mathy and two other Dolceti away from the doorway. It fills with robots, which pour inside like a fluid. And then it's worse, when the three of them are lifted off their feet and hoisted into the air, faceup, struggling upon the upraised hands of dozens upon dozens of robots. Bruno does what he can, firing wirebombs into the fray at the rate of fifty per second, but his aim is hasty and there are just too many targets moving too quickly, and his charge and munitions are low. Mathy and the others don't know the power of their suits, their weapons. Of the several moves they could make right now, few are obvious to an untrained person.

Bitterly, Bruno makes an executive decision, and allows the robots to carry the three Dolceti away. He must concentrate on clearing that doorway, and holding it, or *all* these people will be lost, and their world along with them.

"Mathy!" someone shouts in tones of pained helplessness. And then, on the heels of that, "Stupid sow. Keep your feet!"

But the flood has taken them; they're out of sight now, out of mind, and Bruno is using every milligram of martial skill he can summon, to drive Bordi and the four remaining Dolceti forward through the impervium swarm, which gleams and flickers in the light of sunset.

Another Dolceti goes down and is swept away. Then another, and then two, and finally it's just Bruno and Bordi in the doorway, with shattered robots piling higher and higher around them, threatening to block the way. Bruno shouts, "Go! Quickly!"

The diamond crown is knocked off his head and spins away into the heaving robot stream. As Bordi falls back into the tower room, fighting his way through the robots still inside, Bruno is forced to acknowledge that he has never, in fact, faced a battle as dire as this. The attackers are not well armed or armored, but in such numbers there's little he can do to stop them. Soon enough his suit charge will be zero again, and like so many voracious termites they'll be carrying *him* away.

He's out of time, and he can't spare a glance to see whether Bordi has gotten through safely or not. To the walls he shouts, "Fax! Royal Lockout! Pass no objects save myself! Walls! Release all fields and power down permanently!"

"Acknowledged," the fax replies calmly, unaware of His Majesty's peril and possibly incapable of understanding it. "Immediately, Sire," say the walls, which go dark, reverting to blank wellstone. And then the sides of the sand pit slide inward, carrying live robots down with them and burying several. Bruno retreats inside.

And that's that: no one but he will ever use this place again, for travel or medicine or resupply. The Royal Lockouts and Overrides were built into the Queendom's well-stone at the deepest levels. Subverting them had always been possible, but insanely difficult. The sands will reclaim this place in minutes or hours, and since Bruno does not expect to pass this way again, the sands and the lockouts will remain. One more treasure of Lune consumed for the sake of this stupid war.

Along with the two human patterns still stored within it. He thinks of them suddenly: the final victims of the Queendom's demise. Should he wake them amid all this clamor? To die afresh, without the least understanding of why? No. Better to let them sleep. Better to worry about his own skin for a little while longer!

The trick, now, is to battle the rushing tide of sand and robots, to protect his front and his back without actually whacking the fax machine with his blitterstaff. Because that would kill it even for him.

There's a bad moment when the robots team up to high-low him again, tumbling him off his feet. He feels strong hands on his ankles, preparing to lift him, to carry him away! But with the wellcloth of his suit still active, he manages to call up a slippery exterior and wriggle free, leaping and sliding for the fax plate ahead of him. His momentum is sufficient—just barely!—to carry him through.

The plate crackles blue for a moment and then falls forever silent.

chapter twenty-four

in which the fortress of a traveler is breached

Once through the gate, the first thing Bruno no-tices is absolute silence. There's no battle on this side, no scream and crash. The second thing is the trio of bright yellow Dolceti crowded in front of him: Bordi and Natan and Zuq. And since he's still slipping along the floor on his hands and knees, the third thing he notices is the tussle of bodies falling all around him like tenpins, their blindsight reflexes lacking the time or the space to operate.

"Oof," says Zuq.

But the Olders, crowded just ahead in this narrow passageway, are still on their feet, poised at a corner and looking out.

"They don't see us," Sidney Lyman is murmuring.

"They see," Radmer corrects. "They don't react."

"Excuse me," Bruno says to the Dolceti. He wipes away the suit's slippery skin program and staggers to his feet, pleased to find himself still alive. Successfully tele-ported, yes, for the first time in millennia, and under cir-cumstances far from ideal. He steps over the men while they're attempting, in the unfamiliar bulk of their armor, to rise. At the corner he taps Nick and Brian out of his way, and has a look.

The room is full of robots.

Specifically, it's full of unarmed robots, engaged in the task of filling buckets with sand. And filling smaller vials with measured amounts of other substances: black carbon and white, shiny metals, poured from the sort of long-beaked glass orbs. Finally, the vials are emptied into the buckets, which are placed on a slow-moving conveyor. The light is a sickly yellow-green, from phosphor-coated electric bulbs set in sconces along the walls. Like many on this world, the walls are interlocking blocks of cut stone. The whole scene looks like nothing so much as an ancient alchemist's workshop.

Presently, a pair of robots fetch one heavy bucket each, and begin walking toward the fax machine. With his staff at the ready, Bruno sidles out of the way, while Radmer and Sidney press themselves against the wall, turning their suits to full inviz. But indeed, these robots take no notice of their workshop's invaders, simply crowding around them on their way to the fax.

Then the buckets are hurled right through the print plate, which crackles and sputters in accepting them. From the ozone smell alone, Bruno can tell this machine is on its last legs, relying heavily on error correction to smooth over its many burned-out faxels. Under other circumstances, this might be disturbing; how much damage and drift did they all incur, in printing themselves through that used-up old plate? But under *these* circumstances, it hardly matters.

Presently, the plate crackles again and a shiny new robot emerges, carrying perfect copies of the hurled-in buckets. It isn't gleaming mirror-bright, though, or anyway most of it isn't. Instead, its impervium hull is surrounded—except on the joints and sensory pits—by an outer layer of glassy ceramic painted in green and brown camouflage spots. Once free of the fax, it steps around the Dolceti and follows its shinier brothers out into the workshop, where another robot hands it a rifle—not a sword but a *rifle*, with a bayonet fixed at the business end. And then it walks out through an open archway and vanishes down a corridor.

"Well," says Radmer, "here, as promised, is the source of all our trouble. They seem to be printing one every three minutes. That's what, twenty-four hundred robots per Luner day? More than enough for the task at hand."

"It's not the source," says Bordi, eyeing the print plate with superstitious awe. "This is just a clever tool. The *source* is the Glimmer King himself."

"True," Radmer admits.

To which Bruno says, "We shall deal with him soon enough."

He pulls a wellstone sketchplate—a proper one this time!—out of his pocket, and begins programming sensor algorithms. He can't simply interrogate the walls, for the walls are merely stone. But he can analyze the sound waves reflecting and refracting through the building's corridors. He can measure cosmic radiation and its secondary cascades to gauge the amount and type of material between floor and sky. He can measure heat and vibration, light and magnetic fields. He can even, given enough time, image the neutrino absorption of the structure and build a literal image in three dimensions. That process could take months, though, so he leaves it running in the background and forgets about it. Even without it, a crude sketch of the building begins, slowly, to emerge.

Meanwhile, though, two more robots have been printed, issued rifles, and sent on their way.

"They've given up on swords," Zuq observes.

"Worse than that," says Bruno, "they've developed a blitresistant outer shell, insulating and nonprogrammable. Look at this, it's glass. Tempered, reinforced, camouflage-painted glass. We'll need to crack through it before the blitterstaves can do their work. Which is troubling, because it means they've been analyzing the battle in Shanru."

"Their first real defeat," says Radmer. "Their work has gotten more difficult as they've moved northward, but they've just thrown more hardware at it. They've never needed to shift tactics before."

"Well, they're clearly capable of it; we've only been away for ten hours, and already they're responding. Surprise is not entirely ours, though they don't seem to expect us *here*."

"Right," says Bordi. "So let's move. Let's finish this while we can. They've seized samples of this armor"—he pinches his own shoulder for emphasis—"and you can bet they'll soon be wrapping *that* around their soldiers. I'd give it a day or two at the very most."

"Indeed," says Bruno. "An excellent point. Astaroth's military expenditures clearly need to be capped." That said, he heads back toward the fax machine with purposeful strides and raps its print plate hard with the butt of his staff. The effect is immediate; it flickers, coughs out a cloud of glittering dust, and then darkens and fades like the eyes of a dying beast.

Still another Queendom treasure removed from the game board that is Lune. It's a cultural apocalypse and a damned shame, but Bruno can see no other way forward. The past is not quite dead, and that's the problem.

Unfortunately, while the arrival of back-door intruders didn't raise any alarms, the interruption of power through the fax machine does. Almost immediately, electric bells are ringing throughout the fortress, and the only clear advantage is that this fills in a lot of echo data on Bruno's map. He's seen a fortress or two in his day, and a fair number of palaces, and he knows a throne room when he sees one. And if this king is not on his throne—which seems unlikely, given all that Bruno knows of his character—then he may well be in the apartments behind them, or in one of the hidey-holes nearby.

Bruno gestures and points, then calls out over the clattering bells, "Look for the Glimmer King one floor up, and thirty meters *that* way. I shall lead."

"No," says Radmer. "No way. Men, kindly surround him. Protect him with your lives. Let's get him there in one piece!"

And with that, their luck has officially run dry; a sea of glass-skinned robotic troopers pours through the workshop's entrance, with rifles aimed and triggers already halfway pulled. Unsynchronized chemical explosions fire up and down the line, hurling projectiles at the suited Olders and Dolceti.

They really can slap bullets in flight, Bruno sees with wonder, watching Zuq and Bordi—with movements almost too quick to follow—knock away one projectile each. The Olders, for their part, favor a quieter strategy of simply staying out of the firing arcs. It's like every rifle has a laser beam projecting out of it, showing where its bullets will strike; Radmer and Sidney and the others simply watch these invisible beams and calmly step around them, mostly with very small movements. But it's not enough. Bruno sees right away that both methods will be overwhelmed by the sheer number of guns and bullets in play.

And it's worse than that, for the projectiles are no mere bullets of lead, but needle-sharp cones of some material sandwich that's both charged and highly magnetic. On impact, they pierce a little way into the wellcloth armor and then let go their charge in spiraling bursts. It's a crude attack as such things go, but it *will* damage wellstone fibers. Enough hits like that and the suits will develop dead spots, through which these darts should eventually penetrate. And the robots' rate of fire is impressive; in the first five seconds of the engagement Bruno himself—at the protected center—is struck by ten or twenty.

Still, once the initial shock has worn off the Olders and Dolceti are on the offensive again, pressing forward with blitterstaves, with wirebombs and laser light. The new robots aren't *that* tough, and they wither and crumple under the attack. Which is, in its own way, a bad thing for the human side, because it saves the robots the trouble of moving out of the way when they're out of ammunition. Those bayonets are cute, but against two centimeters of live wellcloth they're of little use. Bullets are the real danger here, and the hail of them continues. By the time the men are out in the corridor and striking for a stairwell up ahead, their suits are already showing signs of wear.

The darts must have some poison upon them as well, for on the stairs themselves, Bruno watches one penetrate Sidney Lyman's armor. Lyman flinches and gasps and then crumples to his knees, and is grabbed and hoisted and carried up and away by strong robot hands. There are enemies both behind them and in front, and at the top of the stairs it's Nick Valdi who yelps and collapses and tumbles backward into certain doom. And then in another hallway it's Natan's turn, and his end is uglier than the others, for it involves a spray of bright arterial blood on the inside of his helmet dome. Bruno watches it all through his rearview mirrors, and mourns.

But next they're at the entrance to the throne room and fighting their way inside, dodging and slapping a storm of projectiles. Bruno even swats one aside himself, feeling the buzz of its approach and reacting without thought.

And then they're in. Glass windows look out on a set of low hills, illuminated by evening twilight, and if this truly is the south pole, locked in permanent shadow, then it's always evening here. Or else—Bruno hardly dares to think it—it's always morning. Each moment beginning the world afresh.

The throne itself is a predictably gaudy affair of golden arms and lion's feet and a great sunburst disc spreading out behind. But there's no Glimmer King in it, just another robot. Or is it?

Amid the broken bodies of a dozen determined attackers, Brian Romset, the last of Lyman's Olders, goes down in a mess of his own guts and hacked-off limbs. But Bruno scarcely notices; his eyes are on that throne. On the robot on that throne. The robot which has no iron box welded to the side of its head, but rather a crown of gold soldered round its brow. The robot whose scratched, worn, battered hull bespeaks long years of wear and tear, and something more, for ordinary robots never show that kind of damage pattern.

Indeed, it's the clear fingerprint of an emancipated 'bot, left to find its own way in the world. And there is something chillingly familiar about this one, about the tilt of its head and the lazy dangle of its arms. Bruno's worst fear—his prime suspicion—has proven out.

"Hugo!" he cries to the figure on the throne. "Stop this, I beseech you. Royal Override: stand down and await instructions!"

And just like that, the defending robots are frozen in their tracks. Zuq takes the opportunity to smash another one down with a blow to its exposed armpit, but he sees Bruno's glare, and does nothing further. Which is good, because Bruno knows full well that his overrides have no power over this seated creature. He has merely intrigued it.

"Hugo," he says, stepping toward the throne in a daze of sorrow.

But with its blank, mouthless face the robot answers,

"Why do you . . . call us that, Father? Do you not recognize us?"

Bruno pauses, while hope and fear war within him. "Bascal?"

"Don't be a fool," says Radmer beside him. "What is this thing? Where is the King of Barnard, who has written so much villainy across our landscape?"

The robot's laughter is cool, unfriendly, more than a little unhinged. Its face is turned exactly toward Bruno, ignoring Radmer, ignoring everything. "You needn't act so . . . shocked, Father. Our condition—my condition— did not arise by accident. Or had you . . . forgotten?"

Indeed, Bruno had not. That lapse of judgment—a desecration of all that human beings hold dear—is woven deeply through the tatters of his conscience. Pouring a copy of his tyrant son into the *only* copy of his pet robot!

"This *is* the King of Barnard," Bruno says, amazed at the weight of his sin now that it confronts him face-to-face. Poor Lune, to suffer so greatly for his mistakes! "Parts of him, anyway."

He'd known it was a bad idea even at the time, but he was very curious to see what would happen. And he'd missed his Poet Prince, yes, the last link to his old life. He'd longed to speak with that boy again, if only for an hour, a minute, a *word*. Memories can be edited! There was some etiological and mnemonic and engrammatic surgery involved, far more elegant than a simple cut and meld. The approach was sound and carefully—if hastily—reasoned.

But Bruno was no surgeon, and the road to hell is paved with careful plans. The effort had been furtive because it would find no support if revealed. He had no friends or relations left; he worked alone, in secret, as far from the ashes of civilization as *Boat Gods'* fuel supply could safely carry him. Which wasn't far. And the result had been more horrific than even a pessimist would predict; he'd shut the monster down barely five minutes into the experiment.

"You have proved yourself unworthy of even my . . . disdain," it had told him, with halting but vehement passion. "Beware, for I'm incapable of fear." It had said other things, too, of a vile and personal nature. And the worst of it was that it *sounded* exactly like Bascal. It *moved* exactly like Hugo. It was the perfect synthesis of the two, and the conversation had begun well enough, with prancing bows and twirls and snippets of spontaneous verse. "Ah, to exist! To have a . . . form to which the soul might cling! A clever . . . thing, and sorely missed."

But that exuberance was not to last, for the creature had made demands. Lightly at first, and then angrily, and then with threats of force. Had it realized its peril it might have kept up the illusion awhile longer, and so escaped into the world, into the ruined solar system, into the universe at large. But the experiment was structured so that keeping his creation alive required a conscious act of will on Bruno's part. In his first stab of real fear, that concentration had wavered and the delicate quantum waveforms had collapsed. The monster had died. Bruno had buried it in secret, and never breathed a word about it to any living person. Iridium Days, indeed.

In the wake of this final failure, he'd powered up his grappleship—one of the last of its kind—and sent it puttering into the void without him. Marooning himself, yes. Perchance to starve, though he'd ultimately failed at that as well.

"I turned you off," he says now. "I buried you in space. I would have fed you into the fax if it had been working. I *should* have fed you into the sun."

On the throne, the ancient robot considers these

words, and slowly nods. "Or vice versa. It's . . . good to see you, Father. I had no idea you were still alive. When first my resurrection was upon me, I . . . thought myself awakened by providence. I *felt* it: the finger of God upon me, commanding life. It commanded nothing else, but the . . . ship had awakened as well. From nowhere had appeared a sparkle of stored energy—enough to carry me down, to this . . . world I found myself circling. I survived the crash, and if the fax machine was dead for you, Father, then the . . . finger of God must have touched it as well. For I stepped into it once, and out of it twice. And from that moment, my . . . path has been clear. To reestablish a monarchy over all that exists."

The story makes no sense—the "Glimmer King" is clearly deranged—but Bruno can picture this much: one robot overpowering its faxed twin, strapping it down, tinkering with its circuitry until resistance ceases and obedience is absolute. And then feeding this perfect soldier back into the fax machine to create an army. Capturing first a village, then a fortress, a city, a world. Spreading outward in relentless waves, to fill the universe with some strange echo of Bascal's would-be paradise.

Ah, God, Bascal *did* have vision. Would so many have followed him otherwise? To their ruin and his? He'd understood the human heart as well as his mother, though he'd used the knowledge very differently. *Very* differently.

"Stop all this," Bruno says to the thing in the chair. "Please. You're defective; your very construction prevents you from grasping the horrors you've spawned, the horror you *are*. The responsibility is mine. You have no idea what I've done here, through you. But take my word: the society you dream of cannot be built on a foundation of murder. It must be freely chosen, and chosen anew with every morning. It must be the sum total dream of all who dwell within it."

"Ah," says the Glimmer King, "but the mind of meat is wounded by its own imperfections. It is you who cannot conceive the totality of my vision. I knew it the...moment I awoke: that in the quantum-crystalline purity of my thoughts I was blessed, and more than blessed. Do not blame yourself, Bruno, for it was...God's own hand that crafted me. You were merely the instrument."

"What the hell is going on?" demands Radmer. "Is this the Glimmer King? This? Bascal's recording in a robot body? Are you *kidding me*?"

And finally, the robot's head swivels toward Radmer. There's a sound, a kind of electronic gasp or grunt or snigger, and then Bascal's voice again: "Conrad Mursk? Do I...dream? Is that you I see before me, fighting at my own father's...side, whom once you fought against?"

"Aye," says Radmer, and spits on the inside of his helmet dome. "Though I'm called Radmer now, and have sworn to kill you on sight."

"Radmer!" says the Glimmer King. "Ah! How many... times we've heard that name, Hugo and I! From books, from songs, from the lips of tortured prisoners! I... should have known it was you, always sticking your nose in the business of others. How little surprised I am to find you here! I knew someday we would...face each other again, and you would be called to account for your wrongs against me. And yet, now that the...moment is here I can only recall that you twice saved my life." He spreads his arms. "Give us a...kiss, me boyo, and join us in remaking this world."

"If you owe me anything, then stop this war," Radmer says coldly. He, too, seems little surprised now that the shock has worn off. It makes sense; Bascal's name had been mentioned more than once in connection with the Glimmer King, by the robot soldiers themselves! The Senatoria Plurum in Nubia had even written it into their formal record, which Radmer claimed to have carried away with his own hands. But surely the real Bascal had ended his days swinging from a Barnardean lamppost, a lynch mob's noose slowly throttling the life from his damnably hard-to-kill body. And even if he hadn't, could he have come so far? Marshaled the resources of his dying colony to send his only self back here? Perhaps, yes. But he didn't.

"Ah," says the Glimmer King, sounding regretful. "I could wish for you to...disappoint me, but alas your character holds firm." He rises from his throne, steps down from the dais, and walks toward Bruno and Radmer.

"Halt," say Bordi and Zuq together, raising their blitterstaves to block the way.

But suddenly the battle is on again; robot soldiers are swarming the two, and though they fight hard to protect their charges, there are only two of them against an infinite supply of attackers. They're driven back, and the Glimmer King continues to advance.

"Halt," Radmer warns him in the same tone, raising his own staff.

But the Glimmer King's mind, however defective, is faster than meat. In his impervium hand is a miniature blitterstick, of the sort sometimes carried by Olders in this world. Of the sort Radmer himself had carried, until the battle of Shanru afforded him a stouter weapon. With it Bascal easily blocks Radmer's feint, and where the two sticks touch there's immediate trouble; they attack each other as easily as they attack mere impervium. There are sizzles and pops and flashes of light, and both weapons fall to dust.

Then, with offhand grace, Bascal kicks Radmer hard in the stomach, and raises a hand in the air. As if by magic, another blitterstick flips into his grasp, hurled by one of the robots somewhere in the room. He touches it to Radmer's suit, which has some built-in resistance and doesn't immediately fail. But it does burn and sizzle in glowing, expanding rings, and Radmer shouts, "Escape sequence!" Unnecessarily, for the suit, sensing that he's not surrounded by vacuum or poison, is already peeling away. Better no armor than dying, defective armor! There's another blow to Radmer's stomach—unprotected this time—and he falls away, gagging and coughing.

And then the Glimmer King is attacking Bruno, striking down his staff and his armor. There is no expression on his blank metal face, but his body is fluid with rage.

"You've ruined my . . . only fax," the robot says angrily, over the din of battle all around. "You've set me back a hundred years. I should kill you both in the most horrible ways. But in memory of our . . . history I will simply deactivate you."

And with that, he punches again. Very hard. Bruno's sternum is reinforced with diamond and fullerenes and assorted species of brickmail, and the heart behind it is as tough as a treader wheel. But there are valves; there are weak points. Underneath it all he's still a creature of flesh and blood. The strike is precisely aimed, and Bruno feels something give way.

How astonishing it is! He feels himself collapse, watches the world spin around him, sees the floor come up to smack his helmet. He can actually feel his blood pressure dropping—it's a distinct sensation, like standing up too quickly—and for a second or two he's simply fascinated by the novelty of it all. Internal hemorrhage; the blood spilling warmly inside him.

But then the Glimmer King is looming over him, preparing to deliver some coup de grace, and Bruno feels a flicker of worry at what awaits him. He *is* afraid to die, at least a little, and he's even more afraid of leaving this business, his final business, unfinished. In the end, a man owns nothing but his past.

But the robot says, "What does it mean that I crave your...forgiveness? Malice hurries me on, and yet my...heartless soul is toxic with remorse. In loosing so much creation upon the worlds, you've entrained... forces to which our mere passions are unequal. Shall we sit among the ruins and lament? Embrace your...fate, Father. I beg you."

To which Bruno replies, weakly, "Son, the office thrust upon us we'd've handed you gladly, eons ago, if you'd shown the maturity that chair requires. We're still waiting, I'm afraid." His voice drops to a rasp. "Shall I tell you the secret of rule? It's love. Simply that. They'll forgive you anything if—"

But something's wrong; among the shots ringing out, several have struck the Glimmer King himself, in the chest. The darts bounce right off the impervium, whining and buzzing off into the room somewhere, but the sites of their impact are dead gray circles, and the next volley punches right through. The Glimmer King's hull is thin, lacking in countermeasures. Now it gapes, throwing off sparks. At the end of the day, he's little more than a crazed household robot.

He looks down at himself, staggering, then looks to the figure of Radmer seated on the floor, his back against the wall, a well-aimed rifle tucked beneath his arm.

Indeed, Bruno sees, *all* the robots are looking at Radmer. All motion has ceased, and if a featureless metal head can convey shocked betrayal, then the room is drowning in it from every angle. There are no more Dolceti; Zuq and Bordi have dropped somewhere, amid the heaps of slain enemies.

Says the Glimmer King, "Nineteen years ago, when I was fallen fresh upon this world, when I glimpsed the cheering twilight and heard the rustle of leaves and the trilling of birds, this second life seemed precious indeed. I knew it would be you, Conrad. Someday, somehow, my dearest friend, I always knew it would be you. Alas, this body sheds no tears."

That said, the thing collapses to the stone floor and moves no more. Nor do the other robots move; they're frozen in place like statues, with blank surprise written across their bodies. The army of Astaroth is defeated.

Radmer drops his rifle and crawls to Bruno's side.

"Sire! Are you hurt?"

Looking up at his old architect laureate, Bruno gasps out a chuckle. "You could say so, yes. My heart is broken at last, my chapter in history drawn finally to a close. It feels so strange, and yet I know exactly what to do. To die. The arc of my life has led me to this moment fully trained. Are *you* hurt?"

Radmer looks pained at those words. "I'll live. Oh God, I'm sorry, Bruno. About your son, about everything."

He doesn't bother with platitudes, with assurances, with medical lies. He has, Bruno thinks, seen too many dying men.

"My son left us long ago," Bruno says, and now his voice is just a whisper. His limbs are cold and numb; he needn't move them ever again. "But you're still here. Shall I claim you for my own? Don't be sorry, lad. I'll let you in on a secret, my own private sin: I have no regrets."

He would fondle an air foil if any had survived the journey through the fax, but they, too, are gone. And it's a pity, for they illustrate so much! But perhaps mere words will suffice. "To make a thing of fragile beauty and wonder, Conrad—even to *try*—is a worthy task for human lives. I'd do it all again, every moment of it."

He'd like to say more about that, but there isn't time. There isn't need. He appears to be finished.

chapter twenty-five

in which power fails to corrupt

Radmer wept for hours. For Bruno, yes, and for Bascal. For the Olders and Dolceti, for Xmary and Tamra and the Queendom of Sol. And for himself, with the misfortune to be the last of them all. *If ending comes to all things,* he wondered, *and gives them meaning, why do we despise it so?*

When he was finished weeping he slept, for his body was tired and his injuries serious. He never knew how long he slept, for when he awoke, the twilight over Astaroth was unchanged. But he felt a little better—his body was healing itself—so he found a kitchen all decorated with cobwebs, and made a fire from the dusty wood he found there, and grilled up the last of his olives and fatbeans. Oh, what he wouldn't give for a flavor designer now! He'd been eating this slop for a thousand years too long. He was ready for something new, or an end to all of it.

When his meal was done he found his way outside, and located a shovel, and dug seven graves in the rocky polar soil. Incredibly, there *were* some small trees here, and birds warbling from their branches, and soil-grubbing bugs and worms for the birds to eat, and tufts of grass to house the bugs. It was a whole twilight ecology, which apparently had grown here all by itself, for Conrad Mursk had never scheduled or budgeted such a thing. And it was quite beautiful, really—a fitting place to leave his friends.

So that's what he did.

Six weeks later he found himself addressing the Furies, in a darkened chamber deep within the battered city of Timoch.

"...and that is the tale, I'm afraid. The long and short of it, for better or worse."

Said Danella Mota, "You've concealed information from us, General. Important information, which might have colored our judgments and informed our actions."

"I withheld only suspicions, Madam Regent. As you said yourself, I hardly know you."

"Ah." Pine Chadwir clucked. "But we had history's greatest hero right here in our midst—King Toji himself!—and you told us nothing."

"King Toji never existed, Madam."

"Towaji, then."

"Still. The creatures of fable bear little resemblance to the human beings of actual memory. His name was Bruno, and he once taught university. The rest is mere happenstance."

Which was neither completely true nor completely fair, and would have been a perfect opening for Spiraldi Truich, the oldest of the Furies, to further demolish Radmer's pretenses. But Spiraldi was among the casualties of the siege; she'd died on the walls with a rifle in her hands, protecting her people as a good ruler ought.

So instead, Radmer took the opportunity to change

the subject. "When will new elections be held, Madams Regents? And in their wake, will it still be you who address me here in this chamber?"

"Likely not," answered Danella Mota. She lifted a Luner globe from its rack and turned it idly in her hands. "With the southern hemisphere in such disarray, Imbria and Viense are the only real nations remaining. And we're wounded, both. We can't leave the south to its fate, and neither can we help them—or each other—through separate efforts. We must work together—truly together—to clean the mess and build this world anew."

"A global government?" Radmer asks, impressed with the audacity of such a scheme, at such a time as this.

"A global monarchy," says Pine Chadwir. "And then a Solar one, to rival the glories of old. And now we come to the deeper purpose of your summons here, General, for no living person remembers the glories of old more fully or more truthfully than you."

Oh. Crap. Radmer doesn't like the sound of *that*.

"No one has fought longer or harder than you, for the peace and justice of Lune."

Worse!

"No one knows this world better than you, who built it."

"Stop right there," Radmer says. "I am *out* of the leader business, and I mean forever. Once we're done with our little chat here, I'm going to hightail it under the veils of Echo Valley and never come out. I'll rot my brain. I'll walk a groove in the soil with the endless reptition of my steps."

"A selfish gesture," says Danella Mota.

"Not at all," says Radmer. "This isn't my world. We speak different languages, Lune and I. If I'm as wise as you suggest, then listen to me now: choose your leaders from among yourselves. The past is dead because it *killed itself*. Through better management than mine."

"There is renewed interest in the Old Tongue," says Pine Chadwir. "In the old ways. In yourself."

"I said no."

More words would certainly have been exchanged on the subject, had a page not chosen that moment to run in screaming, "A ship! Madams Regents, a ship has landed!"

"Inform the port master," said Danella. "All cargoes are welcome, but we're in session here, boy."

"Madams, please, it's a *space*ship!"

And so it was that C. "Rad" Mursk came face-to-face with Ambassador Tilly Nichols of the Biarchy of Wolf and Lalande.

"You look just like your pictures," she said, shaking his hand out there on the cement of the Timoch International Airport. Her gleaming starship hulked in the background like the end of a world, appearing less like something out of history than something out of its most fanciful stories—a Platonic dream of starshipitude.

"And you look...familiar," he said, trying to place the woman's face.

"You knew my birth mother. Bethany."

"Ah! And how is the Queen of Lalande?"

"Retired," said the ambassador, "and thrice reincarnated. When I left Gammon she was a little girl on a solar farm, way out on the western coast. But she remembered you a little. And my father, King Eddie; she said she was going to find him someday and marry him all over again. But she asked me to give you her best. Poor dear; it never occurred to her that you might be dead."

"I certainly might. Everyone else seems to be."

"Well," said Tilly, "I'm sorry for your people's suffering, and I want you to know, we're here to help. We tried remote activation of your inert systems, and when that didn't work we tried synching to the remains of your collapsiter grid. And when *that* didn't work, we decided to show up in person. We're installing a wormhole gate now, so you should be up and running in a few days. Then we can start in on educational travel and the real-time transfer of materiel. This place looks like a long, long shortage of just about everything."

Conrad gawked. It had been a long time since anyone had spoken to him like that! "What and what? You're . . . Young lady, I don't even know what you're talking about. Did it ever occur to you to ask permission? To await an invitation for your help?"

"Fallen colonies are often too proud," she said. "We understand, having been there several times ourselves. Only with great determination and patience have we elevated ourselves to what you see." She nodded back at her ship, from which strangely attired workmen were already unloading crates and tubes of . . . something. "And it must be particularly galling, for the very seat of humanity to fall. . . ."

"Fall where?" he demanded. "Enlightened lives are played out here all the time, as always."

"*Short* lives."

"Oh, so. Does quantity suddenly matter more than quality?" That sounded lame to him. What he really meant was something grander, but he lacked the words. He had always lacked the words.

"If there isn't time to achieve personal fulfillment," said Tilly, "then yes, I would say quantity matters. In the Biarchy, we strive for milestones and then reinvent ourselves upon their achievement. Before we grow stale. We join the Exploration Corps, which will soon be visiting a hundred new stars. Or the Diplomatic Corps, which visits the old ones and invites them into the wormhole network, which we call the Muswog. Five systems and counting! The point is, we *have* these choices, and we make them freely."

"Hmm. Well. I believe I understand your offer; you've clawed your way up from the ashes of your parents' great blunders, and it has made you strong and clever and smug. And now, in your boundless generosity, you seek to deny the same privilege to the people of Lune. The only thing wrong with this place, kiddo, is people like me who never cleaned up our toys. But that's all finished now. Help? What do you expect to help us with? What is it you think we need?"

"That's what I'm here to find out," she said reasonably. "I asked to speak with someone in charge, and you're the one they sent. Has there been . . . some error?"

"Definitely," he answered, turning his back on her and everything she stood for. "Like your mother, I'm just some farmer who used to be somebody."

chapter twenty-six

in which an act of kindness takes flower

Conrad would have cause to regret those words, for as a king he'd've been entitled to throw these smug missionaries out on their collective ear. As it was, they dealt with the Furies instead, and with the Grand Kabinet of Viense, and in short order they had conspired together to launch the largest restoration project in history.

Murdered Earth was, apparently, an affront to all humanity, for the Biarchists promised, at their own expense and under their own supervision, to place a shell around it which closely mimicked the original surface to a depth of fifty kilometers. Following this, they contemplated the resurrection of Mars, and possibly Venus as well. And resurrection *was* the proper word, for they planned to populate these worlds with simulacra of their departed residents—most especially the famous ones.

"It's nothing personal," Tilly Nichols insisted, in response to Radmer's outrage. Was Earth to be an amusement park, then? A monument to its former self, incapable of growing beyond the fairy tales that had accreted around it like orbiting debris?

"Not at all," Tilly said, looking and sounding politely

amused. "We expect it to be as different from the original as you are from the dapper fellow my mother once courted. In your experience, eternal life and eternal death are the only options. You admit no shades of gray."

"But some people will remain dead," he accused. "Most, in fact. The vast majority."

To which she simply shrugged. "Our powers are limited. And the ones who do live will be reincarnations, yes. Not literal resurrections, not faxed copies. But also not witless and alone, like the natural-born, with no past lives to draw upon, no wisdom to inform their childhoods... I don't know what you're so offended about, truly; in Barnard your children were born as functional adults!"

"That also offended me."

"Oh. Well. We'll try to be conscious of societal norms here, to avoid such offenses wherever possible."

"How kind of you."

Unperturbed, she said, "To answer your question, Mr. Radmer, we start with celebrities because the reincarnation process is more accurate the more we know about a person. And through the gratings and lenses of their memory we can sift the quantum traces of those we know less well. Slowly but surely, Earth will give up her secrets."

And it was with precisely these sentiments that they exhumed the grave of Bruno de Towaji, and scanned his rotting carcass and the many electromagnetic ghosts it had left behind. De Towaji had gotten around in his long life; there were imprints of him all over the ruins of Sol system.

And of Tamra, who'd left nearly as many writings behind, and a great many more recorded images. "The lift of an arm," said Tilly, "speaks volumes about the mind that controls it."

Alas, through Tilly's eyes he could see that it was true. Poor Tamra. To be a literal puppet for these oversweet invaders, lifting her arms for their amusement!

"I'd love to scan you as well," she told Conrad on another occasion. "You knew the king and queen personally; you knew the age. Living brains make questionable witnesses when it comes to detail, but for recalling the scope and flavor of a bygone era, nothing else really quite compares."

But Conrad had no desire to meet—much less help create!—the Biarchy's caricatures of his dead king and queen. And as for the Xmary they would surely pluck from his dreams . . . God, the notion was seductive. Fragments of a woman half-remembered, whom he'd loved fiercely but never wholly known, for who could know the mind of another? Still less a woman! For all he knew, she would be as monstrous as the ghost of Bascal in a robot body. And know it! And resent it!

"Thank you, no," he said to Tilly. "My wife would kill me."

Finally, though, during his fiftieth or two hundredth argument with this alien woman, relations began to shift. They were in her quarters near the top of the starship, seated on opposite sides of a dining table that had risen up from the deck, overflowing with faxed meats and cheeses, steaming flavor-designer breads and lightly chilled fruits. The outer bulkhead had gone transparent, and the views of Timoch and the ocean behind it were pleasing.

They could have met anywhere; it was an act of kindness—of respect—for her to invite him specifically here. She wasn't even playing him, particularly—just being thoughtful. And it came to him suddenly, that she was doing exactly the same thing on a global scale: simply extracting and fulfilling the most deeply held wishes of

Lune. Was it her fault she was rich? Had guarded generosity become a sin? Her resources seemed to dwarf even those of the Queendom at its peak, and there was no wickedness in her, nor foolishness.

Whether Conrad liked it or not, the people of this world were indeed choosing their own destiny. They wanted an end to death and politics, and who could begrudge them that age-old impossible dream? More than that, they wanted the *stars*, as Conrad had once wanted them. When had he shriveled into this ridiculous old fuddy-duddy, with nothing to do but stand in their way? His time was past. How lucky they were not to have him for their king!

But even this sentiment brought only kind laughter when he shared it with Tilly.

"You love these people, Mr. Radmer. It's evident in everything you do."

"Call me Conrad."

"All right, I will. Thank you."

"You're genuinely welcome." But then a black thought overtook him, and slowly became a certainty. "You beamed signals at this world. You tried to activate our wellstone systems remotely. Nineteen years ago, was it? Maybe twenty?"

"We tried. It didn't work," she said, shrugging.

"It did," he told her. "My God. The haunted towers of Imbria. A fax machine briefly awakening in its sandy grave. The finger of God, commanding a robot to waken. It was you!"

"I ... don't understand."

"You stirred up old horrors, Ms. Nichols. You're responsible for the robot army that nearly destroyed this world! Bruno had the sense to kill his monstrous child, millennia ago, but *you* brought it back!"

That seemed to rock her. "We what? Conrad, in all our encounters we've done our level best to avoid damage—"

"And a splendid job you've made of it!" he spat, trying to sound venomous. "Only two of four nations destroyed, a fifth of the world's population killed . . ." He wanted to unload the full sedition act on her, but he found his heart wasn't in it. His voice trailed away.

Because how could they know? How could they imagine their well-intended fumbling might kick loose such an avalanche? That there'd been a hill of loose scree waiting to collapse was no fault of theirs, and if a beggar should choke on a gift of bread, did that lessen the kindness of the gesture?

"If what you say is true," she answered guardedly, "then reparations are in order."

"How?" he demanded, briefly flaring once more. "You're already giving this world everything it ever dreamed of. Its heroes, its riches, its dead . . . Your apology—if I dare call it that—is lost in the noise of your . . . overwhelming generosity . . ."

He stopped there, for he was spouting nonsense: they had been *so good that they couldn't do better*? And that was a bad thing?

In spite of everything, the two of them looked at each other and burst out laughing. They laughed until the tears streamed down their cheeks, and then Conrad laughed some more, and wept, and felt an unfamiliar ache at the corners of his mouth. A grin that refused to be wiped away by his anger, no matter how hard he tried.

"It's good to see you smile," she remarked when things had settled down.

"It feels strange," Conrad admitted, with a tinge of

resentment. Then, more reflectively: "It was bound to happen sooner or later. I'm an old soldier, Ms. Nichols. An old, unwilling soldier."

"Please, call me Tilly."

"All right. The thing is, Tilly, it ends here. I'm finally done fighting. You may be the most genuinely happy person I've ever met, and my defenses aren't up to that. I'm officially opening my gates; you may enter and do as you will."

"Or you could come out," she suggested. "And do as *you* will."

And before he knew it they were falling into bed together, rolling and twisting on wellcloth sheets in a field of sharply reduced gravity.

"God," he said. "Oh, my God. Is this happiness? Is this what hope feels like?"

"Explore," she advised him, offering herself as freely as she offered her planets' riches. "Live a little. Have some fun."

And it seemed like very good advice indeed, here at the start of something wonderful.

appendix A-1

rights of the dead

It was an interesting statutory question, still largely unresolved: if these interactive messages were the only remains of a legal individual, did they have the right to be played back indefinitely as holograms? Or to be burned into blank human bodies and treated as people? They couldn't possibly hold all the memories of their original senders, all the nuance and subtlety of a lifetime's experience. They were doppelgängers at best—superficial, hollow inside—and at worst they were shadows or caricatures of the original person, laughably incomplete.

And there was another question here, not so much legal as moral: these deceased persons had won their reincarnation at the expense of their fellow colonists. Pushing and bribing their way to the lifeboats, as it were. This didn't warrant punishment per se, but neither did it encourage charity.

A few well-to-do families had claimed such messages as prodigal children returned to the fold, and had tried to give them their old lives back. But they'd had to hire teams of cognitive and cellular surgeons for weeks at a time, and the results were not encouraging: people who could hold a brilliant conversation on flowers but didn't recognize one when they saw it. People who could barely feed or dress themselves, who behaved badly in public, who mistreated the unfamiliar flesh that housed them. And even in the famous "Smith and Jones" trial where two partials had been declared "legal and functional children with the hope of future maturity," the families' petitions for public assistance had been roundly and loudly denounced.

appendix A-2

resupply

One could not *produce* deutrelium in a fax machine. The machine could only assemble the atoms which existed in its own buffers—a stable subset of the periodic table. But in the strange ways of the sprawling collapsiter network that was the Nescog, one could *transmit* any isotope, stable or non-, from an Elemental stockpile to any point with a functioning network gate.

Not antimatter, of course (or "aye-ma'am" as the sailors called it). Not collapsium or neutronium, nor any material or object which incorporated durable spacetime defects into its structure. But anything else, yes. So with a few hours' light lag, deuterium and trelium (respectively, heavy hydrogen and light helium—also known as "fusion lotion" or "doot toot" or "treat") could be ordered direct from the gas mines of Jupiter and Saturn, and charged to Bruno's account. Hoses and pipelines could not, alas, be sealed against the fax's print plate, but a good old-fashioned barrel could roll right through.

planet envy

But hell, *all* of Sol's gas giants were prettier than Barnard's, except perhaps for Uranus. And Sorrow was no Earth, and Planet One was no Mercury, and Barnard's two asteroid belts were paltry middens against the grandeur of Sol's one. That was the problem with red dwarf star systems: they occupied only the top three rows of the periodic table. Chlorine was the heaviest of their common elements, leaving little room for exotic aero- and geo-chemistry. They were, in a word, boring.

glossary

Accipe signaculum doni Spiritus Sancti—
Traditional Latin benediction: "Be sealed with the gift
of the Holy Spirit." Employed by several Old Modern
religions as a prayer for the dying.

Aft—(adj, adv) One of the ordinal directions onboard a
ship: along the negative roll axis, perpendicular to the
port/starboard and boots/caps directions, and parallel
and opposite to fore.

AKA—(abbrev.) Also Known As.

Ako'i—(n) Tongan word meaning "teacher."

Antiautomata—(adj.) Describes any weapon intended
for use against robots.

Apenine—(prop n) Province of the Luner nation
of Imbria which includes the capital city of Timoch.

Arc de commencer—(n) A hypothetical device for diverting photons to a chronologically "earlier" point in spacetime, for the purpose of altering a historical outcome. Attributed to Bruno de Towaji.

Ash—(prop n) A planette constructed in the late Queendom period at the L1 Lagrange point between Earth and Luna. Symbolically, the middle ground between two worlds. Later ejected by n-body perturbations.

Astaroth—(n) Luner nation including the south pole and southern portions of the former Nearside and Farside, with a population of approximately five million.

Astrogation—(n) Astral navigation. In common use, the art or process of navigating a starship.

AU—(n) Astronomical Unit; the mean distance from the center of Sol to the center of Earth. Equal to 149,604,970 kilometers, or 49.9028 light-seconds.

Autronic—(adj) Capable of self-directed activity. Commonly used to differentiate "robots" from teleoperated or "waldo" devices.

Aye-ma'am—(n) Colloquial abbreviation for antimatter.

Barnardean—(adj) Of or pertaining to Barnard, the first of the Queendom's thirteen colonies.

Barocline—(n) Any layer boundary marked by an abrupt change in pressure.

Biomod—(n) Biological modification. Any genetic, synthetic, Lamarckian, or bionic enhancement, whether heritable or non-.

Blindsight—(n) A condition in which the conscious portions of the neocortex (primarily the frontal lobes) are prevented from receiving input through the visual cortex, while the brain stem receives its own visual inputs normally. Although blindsight sufferers are able to avoid obstacles and grasp specific objects on demand, they experience none of the sensation associated with "seeing."

Blitterstaff—Also *Blitterstick*. (n) An antiautomata weapon employing a library of rapidly shifting wellstone compositions. Attributed to Bruno de Towaji.

Bootward—(adj, adv) One of the six ordinal directions onboard a ship: along the positive yaw axis, perpendicular to the port/starboard and fore/aft directions, and parallel and opposite to caps.

Brickmail—(n) An allotrope of carbon consisting of benzene rings interlocked in a three-dimensional matrix. Brickmail is the toughest known nonprogrammable substance.

Bunkerlite—(n) Copyrighted, superreflective wellstone substance employed as protective cloth or armor. Attributed to Marlon Sykes.

Campanas—(prop n) Capital city of the Luner nation of Nubia.

Capward—(adj, adv) One of the six ordinal directions onboard a ship: along the negative yaw axis, perpendicular to the port/starboard and fore/aft directions, and parallel and opposite to boots.

Cerenkov radiation—(n) Electromagnetic radiation emitted by particles temporarily exceeding the local speed of light, e.g., upon exit from a collapsium lattice.

Chromosphere—(n) A transparent layer, usually several thousand kilometers deep, between the photosphere and corona of a star, i.e., the star's "middle atmosphere." Temperature is typically several thousand kelvins, with roughly the pressure of Earth's atmosphere in Low Earth Orbit.

Collapsar—(n) see *Hypermass*

Collapsiter—(n) A high-bandwidth packet-switching transceiver composed exclusively of collapsium. A key component of the Nescog.

Collapsium—(n) A rhombohedral crystalline material composed of neuble-mass black holes. Because the black holes absorb and exclude a broad range of vacuum wavelengths, the interior of the lattice is a supervacuum permitting the supraluminal travel of energy, information, and particulate matter. Collapsium is most commonly employed in telecommunications collapsiters; the materials employed in ertial shielding are sometimes referred to as collapsium, although the term "hypercollapsite" is more correct.

Converge (also *Reconverge*)—(v) To combine two separate entities, or two copies of the same entity, using a fax machine. In practice, rarely applied except to humans.

Coriolis force—(n) An apparent force on the surface of a rotating body, which causes apparent deflection of trajectories from the "expected" course in the rotating coordinate frame of the body. In meteorology, the force responsible for large-scale cyclonic weather systems.

Day, Barnardean—(n) A measure of time, equal to the stellar (not sidereal) day of Sorrow, aka Planet Two. There are 23 pids, or 460 Barnardean hours, or 1,653,125 standard seconds in the Barnardean day.

Deathist—(n) Adherent to the belief that the death of individuals is healthy for the population as a whole. Rarely applied except to humans; animal deathists are generally referred to as naturalists.

Deceant—(n) Title accorded to Luner military officers in charge of ten individual soldiers.

Declarant—(n) The highest title accorded by the Queendom of Sol; descended from the Tongan award of Nopélé, or knighthood. Only twenty-nine declarancies were ever issued.

Decohere—(v) To collapse a quantum uncertainty into a classical or Newtonian certainty, as with the position or trajectory of a particle or the state of a quantum bit.

Deutrelium—(n) A mixture (generally frozen or slushy) of equal numbers of deuterium (^{2}H) and trelium (^{3}He) atoms, used preferentially in magnetic-confinement fusion reactors.

Di-clad—(adj) Sheathed in an outer layer of monocrystalline diamond or other allotropes of carbon.

Dinite—(n) Any detonating or deflagrating explosive consisting primarily of ethylene glycol dinitrate.

Dolceti—(n) One or more members of the Order of Dolcet, whose "blindsight" training relies on the mildly toxic dolcet berry, native to Lune.

Downsystem—(adj) One of the six cardinal directions: toward the sun in any orientation.

Elementals, The—(n) Queendom-era cartel responsible for some 70% of the traffic in purified elements throughout the Queendom of Sol, with even higher percentages for certain key metals and rare earths.

Epitaxial—(adj) Describes a crystal of one material grown on the crystal face of another material, such that both crystals have the same structural orientation.

Eridanian—(n, adj) Resident of the Epsilon Eridani colony, typically characterized by short stature, neoteny, and photochromic skin pigments. Alternatively, anything pertaining to the Eridani colony.

Ertial—(adj) Antonym of inertial, applied to inertially shielded devices. Attributed to Bruno de Towaji.

Extrasolar—(adj) Existing outside of Sol system.

Fatalist—(n, adj) Adherent to the belief that all events are predetermined and inevitable. As a proper noun, refers to any member of a Queendom-era organization dedicated to the forcible restoration of death as a natural renewal process.

Fax—(n) Abbreviated form of "facsimile." A device for reproducing physical objects from stored or transmitted data patterns. By the time of the Restoration, faxing of human beings had become possible, and with the advent of collapsiter-based telecommunications soon afterward, the reliable transmission of human patterns quickly became routine.

Faxborn—(adj) Created artificially in a fax machine, with no natural counterpart. In practice, applied only to human and human-derived beings, where it is often used in lieu of a family name.

Faxel—(n) Facsimile element. One element of a fax machine print plate which is capable of producing and placing a stored atom with 100-picometer precision.

Fibrediamond—(n) Composite material of whiskered crystalline carbon in a resin matrix. Unless sheathed in a superreflective coating, fibrediamond is notably flammable.

Flau—(n) Member of a species of living airship developed on Lune, based originally on the genome of the leviathan, the largest native marine creature of Pup.

Fuff—(v) A polite term for sexual intercourse, popular in the Queendom of Sol and its colonies.

Geostat—(adj) Fixed in reference to the Earth. In fashion, a clothing or paint pattern which appears to hold stationary while the subject moves through it.

Geriatry—(n) The condition of physical decrepitude which occurs in natural organisms over the course of their presumed lifespans. Geriatry is characterized by high rates of apoptosis triggered by lipofuscin buildup, and cellular senscence triggered by telomere shortening.

Ghost—(n) Any electromagnetic trace preserved in rock or metal. Colloquially, a visual image of past events, especially involving deceased persons. The term may also refer to interactive messages, especially from distant or deceased persons.

Gigaton—(n) One billion metric tons, or 10^{12} kilograms. Equal to the mass of a standard industrial neuble or collapson node ("black hole").

Girona—(prop n) A minor city in the E1 Gironès comarque of Catalonia, Old Earth, situated at the confluence of the Ter, Güell, Galligants, and Onyar Rivers, some 80 kilometers from the nation's former capital at Barcelona.

Grand kabinet—(prop n) Primary ruling body of the Luner nation of Viense.

Grappleship—(n) A vehicle propelled by means of electromagnetic grapples. Use of grappleships was considered impractical in the Queendom until the advent of ertial shielding, though high-powered inertial devices were capable of attaining enormous accelerations.

Graser—(n) A gravity projector whose emissions are coherent, i.e., monochromatic and phase-locked. Attributed to Bruno de Towaji.

Gravitic—(adj) Of or pertaining to gravity, either natural or artificial.

Hollie—(n) Abbreviated form of "hologram." Any three-dimensional image. Colloquially, a projected, dynamic three-dimensional image, or device for producing same.

Hypercollapsite—(n) A quasicrystalline material composed of neuble-mass black holes. Usually organized as a vacuogel.

Hypercomputer—(n) Any computing device capable of altering its internal layout. Colloquially, a computing device made of wellstone.

Hypercondensed—(adj) Condensed to the point of gravitational collapse, i.e., until a black hole or "hypermass" is formed. Colloquially, condensed to any level the speaker finds impressive. Also "hypercompressed."

Hypermass—(adj) A mass which has been hypercompressed; a black hole.

Imbria—(prop n) Temperate Luner nation of the northern hemisphere, on the former Nearside, with a population of approximately ten million.

Immorbid—(adj) Not subject to life-threatening disease or deterioration.

Impervium—(n) Public domain wellstone substance; the hardest superreflector known.

Indeceased—(n, adj) Luner colloquialism for senile Olders who are incapable of useful learning or work.

Instantiate (also *Print*)—(v) To produce a single instance of a person or object; to fax from a stored or received pattern.

Instelnet—(prop n) The low-bandwidth lightspeed data network connecting the Queendom of Sol and its thirteen colony systems.

Judder—(v, n) To vibrate energetically. As a noun, a motion artifact produced when stored images are played back incorrectly. Judder can be employed deliberately as part of an error-correction scheme in defective fax machine print plates.

Juke—(v) To move unexpectedly out of position. Colloquially, to cheat or deceive.

kps—(abbrev.) Kilometers per second, a measure of velocity for celestial bodies and interplanetary/ interstellar vehicles. The speed of light is 300,000 kps. (Also kips, kiss).

Kuiper Belt—(n) A ring-shaped region in the ecliptic plane of any solar system, in which gravitational perturbations have amplified the concentration of large, icy bodies or "comets." Sol's Kuiper Belt extends from 40 AU at its lower boundary to 1000 AU at its upper, and has approximately one-fourth the overall density of the much smaller Asteroid Belt. The total mass of the Kuiper Belt exceeds that of Earth.

Light-minute—(n) The distance traveled by light through a standard vacuum in one minute: 17,987,547.6 kilometers or 0.12 AU.

Light-year—(n) The distance traveled by light through a standard vacuum in one year: 9.4607 trillion kilometers or 63,238 AU.

Luna—(prop n) Original name of Earth's moon.

Lune (also *The Squozen Moon, The Half Moon*)—(prop n) Name attaching to Earth's moon following the terraforming operations which reduced its diameter from 3500 to 1400 kilometers.

Malo e lelei—Traditional Tongan greeting widely used within the Queendom. Literally: "Thank you for coming."

Matter programming—(n) The discipline of arranging, sequencing, and utilizing pseudomaterials in a wellstone or other programmable-matter matrix, often including the in situ management of energy and computing resources.

Mechsprach—(n) Any spoken accent or dialect reserved for use by machines, to distinguish them from human or human-derived speakers.

Metastable—(adj) Existing in an unstable state which is transient but relatively long-lived.

Microbar—(n) A measure of atmospheric pressure, equivalent to one-millionth of an Earth atmosphere at sea level. Partial pressures of oxygen must reach approximately 70,000 microbars to be considered breathable.

Millibar—(n) A measure of atmospheric pressure, equivalent to one-thousandth of an Earth atmosphere at sea level. Partial pressures of oxygen in the 70 millibar range are generally considered breathable.

Nasen—(n) An acronym: Neutrino Amplification through Stimulated EmissioN. A monochromatic beam of high-energy neutrinos, sometimes employed for interplanetary communication thanks to its extremely small divergence angle. However, the difficulty of generating such a beam, plus its ready interactions with matter, limit its usefulness except as a weapon.

Naturalist—(n, adj) Adherent to the belief that natural events and processes are preferable to artificial ones. Naturalists may or may not also be deathists.

Neoteny—(n) The retention of juvenile characteristics (usually physical) into adulthood.

Nescog, The—(prop. n) NEw Systemwide COllapsiter Grid. Sol system's successor to the Inner System Collapsiter Grid or Iscog; an ultrahigh-bandwidth telecommunications network employing numerous supraluminal signal shunts.

Neuble—(n) A diamond-clad neutronium sphere, explosively formed, usually incorporating one or more layers of wellstone for added strength and versatility. A standard industrial neuble masses one billion metric tons, with a radius of 2.67 centimeters.

Neutronium—(n) Matter which has been supercondensed, crushing nuclear protons and orbital electron shells together into a continuous mass of neutrons. Unstable except at very high pressures. Any quantity of neutronium may be considered a single atomic nucleus; however, under most conditions the substance will behave as a superfluid.

Neutronium barge (also Neutronium Dredge)—(n) A space vessel, typically one billion cubic meters (1000 x

1000 x 1000 m) or larger, whose primary function is to gather mass, supercompress it into neutronium, and transport it to a depot or work site. Although less numerous, smaller neutronium barges also existed for transport only.

Nubia—(prop n) Subtropical Luner nation of the southern hemisphere, on the former Nearside, with a population of approximately 100 million.

Older—(prop n) Informal title or ethnic slur applied to immorbid Queendom residents by the morbid, mortal peoples of Lune.

Ophiuchus—(prop n) A large, dim, nonzodiacal constellation, "The Snake Holder," beginning between Scorpius and Sagittarius near the Sol Ecliptic Plane and extending some 50 degrees northward.

Petabyte—(n) A measure of data storage equal to 10^{15} bytes or eight quadrillion digital bits.

Philander—(n) A title granted to formal consorts of the Queen of Sol. Only four philanders were ever named.

Photochromic—(adj) Changing color under the influence of light.

Photosail—(n) Any nearly two-dimensional device whose primary function is to derive mechanical energy from the pressure of reflected light, including sunlight, starlight, and radiation from artificial sources. The term "solar sail" is sometimes applied colloquially, but in fact solar sails are a subset of photosails.

Photosphere—(n) The hot, opaque, convectively stable plasma layer of a star beginning at the photopause, responsible for most thermal and visible emissions. Usually less than 1000 kilometers deep, with temperatures of several thousand kelvins and the approximate pressure of Earth's stratosphere. The photosphere floats atop the deep hydrogen convection zones of the stellar interior.

Photovoltaic—(adj) Capable of generating an electrical voltage with the input of light energy, through the liberation of bound electrons in a preferred direction. In many isolated devices, wellstone pseudomaterials *must* be photovoltaic in order to maintain their other properties using ambient radiation.

Picometer—(n) A measure of distance, equal to 10^{-12} meters or one-billionth of a millimeter.

Planette—(n) Any artificial celestial body consisting of a stony or earthy lithosphere surrounding a core or shell of supercondensed (neutronic) matter. The vast majority of planettes are designed for human habitation, and include Earthlike surface gravity and breathable atmospheres.

Plibbles—(n) Fruits of the plibble tree.

Plurality—(n) The condition of existing in more than one physical instantiation under the same identity, e.g., with intent to reconverge the copies at a later time.

Positronium—(n) A material consisting of "atoms" made from one electron and one positron orbiting their mutual center of attraction. Unstable in free space, positronium is generally stored in magnetic nanobottles between the fibers of bulk wellstone.

Print plate—(n) The largest single component of a fax machine, responsible for assembling and disassembling finished goods at the atomic level. Print plates are generally flat and most typically rectangular, although with effort they can be fashioned as cylinders or other three-dimensional forms.

Pseudoatom—(n) The organization of electrons into Schrödinger orbitals and pseudoorbitals, made possible with great precision in a designer quantum dot. The properties of pseudoatoms do not necessarily mimic those of natural atoms.

Pup—(prop n) Innermost world of the Wolf 359 star system, first colonized in Q427. Considered marginally habitable.

Quantum dot—(n) A device for constraining the position of one or more charge carriers (e.g., electrons) in all three spatial dimensions, such that quantum ("wavelike") effects dominate over classical ("particlelike") effects. Charge carriers trapped in a quantum dot will arrange themselves into standing waveforms analogous to the electron orbitals of an atom. Thus, the waveforms inside a quantum dot may be referred to collectively as a pseudoatom.

Reportant—(n) Any person or mechanism gathering information for public distribution.

Rodenbeck, Wenders—(prop n) Poet laureate of the Queendom era.

Senatoria Plurum—(prop n) The main governing body of the Luner nation of Nubia.

Sensorium, Neural—(n) Any system for channeling synthetic neural inputs into the brain. Sometimes employed as a form of torture, but generally considered a medium for education and entertainment, especially in remote environments.

Shattering, The—(prop n) Global seismic event with a death toll in the hundreds of millions, generally credited with destroying the post-Queendom Iridium Age civilization of Lune. According to Conrad Mursk, an ostensibly preventable disaster.

Sila'a—(n) A pinpoint fusion generator or "pocket star" consisting of a wellstone-sheathed neutronium core surrounded by gaseous deuterium. From the Tongan *si'i* (small) and *la'aa* (sun).

Sketchplate—(n) A thin, typically rectangular block or sheet of wellstone sized and preprogrammed for the portable display and input of text, drawings, and physical simulations.

Squozen Moon, The (See *Lune*)

Stealth—(n) Concealment, especially during movement or action. Colloquially, a synonym for technologically derived invisibility.

Stormlands, The—(prop n) 180-kilometer-wide region of Lune's northern hemisphere, characterized by reduced gravity, peripheral convection cells, and permanent cyclonic weather formations.

Superabsorber (also superblack)—(n) Any material capable of absorbing 100% of incident light in a given wavelength band. The only known universal superabsorber (i.e., functioning at all wavelengths) is the event horizon of a hypermass. (Approximations of 100% absorption are generally referred to as "black.")

Superfluid—(n, adj) Any fluidized material capable of propagating with zero friction and zero viscosity. The vast majority of superfluids are either cryogenic, as with liquid helium, or supercondensed, as with neutronium.

Superreflector—(n) Any material capable of reflecting 100% of incident light in a given wavelength band. No universal superreflectors are known. (Approximations of 100% reflectance are generally referred to as "mirrors.")

Supervacuum—(n) A state of vacuum in which some wavelengths of the Zero Point Field have been suppressed or excluded. Since the speed of light is a function of vacuum energy, supervacuum is useful for the transmission of matter and information at supraluminal velocities.

Supraluminal—(adj) Exceeding the classical speed of light.

Tazzer—(n) A short-range beam weapon consisting of pulsed, coaxial streams of electrons and metal ions in a guide beam of blue or violet laser light. Tazzers are primarily used to induce temporary incapacity (pain, paralysis, unconsciousness), although lethal versions also exist.

Terraform—(v) To make Earthlike. In general, to match the gravity, climate, and atmosphere of a planet or planette to that of Earth, possibly including the imposition of a stable biosphere. Enclosed spaces are "climate controlled" rather than terraformed. Attributed to Jack Williamson.

Thermocline—(n) Any layer boundary marked by an abrupt change in temperature.

Tillspar—(prop n) Highest nonvacuum suspension bridge in the known universe, spanning the 10-kilometer-deep Highrock Divide in the Imbrian province of Apenine, Lune.

Timoch—(prop n) Capital city of the Luner nation of Imbria, with a population of approximately two million.

Tonga—(n) Former Earth kingdom consisting of the Tongatapu, Ha'apai, and Vava'u archipelagoes of Polynesia, and scattered islands occasionally including parts of Samoa and Fiji. Tonga was the only Polynesian nation never to be conquered or colonized by a foreign power, and was the last human monarchy prior to the Q1 establishment of the Queendom of Sol.

Tropopause—(n) In a planetary atmosphere, a sharply defined thermocline or barocline separating the troposphere or lower atmosphere from the stratosphere or upper atmosphere.

Upsystem—(adj, adv) One of the six cardinal directions: away from the sun in any orientation.

Varna—(prop n) A 640-meter-radius planette constructed in orbit around Luna by private investors during the latter years of the Queendom of Sol. Site of the Q1290 Treaty of Varna, granting Right of Return to Barnard refugees.

Viense—(prop n) Temperate Luner nation of the original Farside, including the north pole, with a population of approximately fifty million.

Wellcloth—(n) A fabric woven wholly or partially from wellstone fibers. While sheet wellstone could technically be considered a form of cloth, the term "wellcloth" is generally reserved for fabrics with weavelengths larger than 1 micrometer.

Wellglass—(n) Any wellstone substance which is both optically transparent and electrically insulative, often employed as the default state of wellstone devices. Most typically refers to a wellstone substance closely emulating the properties of transparent silica-soda-lime (SiO_2, NaO, CaO) "window glass" preparations except in terms of mass and toughness. In general, natural substances containing a preponderance of silicon are the easiest to emulate in a wellstone matrix.

Wellstone—(n) A substance consisting of fine, semiconductive fibers studded with quantum dots, capable of emulating a broad range of natural, artificial, and hypothetical materials. Typical wellstone is composed primarily of pure silicon, silicon dioxide, and gold.

Wellwood—(n) An emulation of lignous cellulose ("wood"), often employed as the default state of wellstone devices.

Zetta-ton—(n) A measure of mass, equal to 10^{21} tons or one million billion billion kilograms.

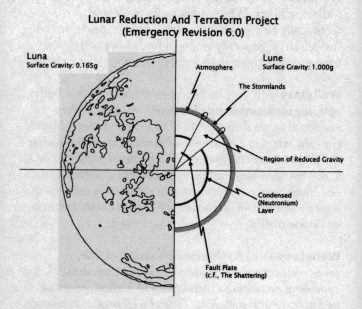

Lunar Reduction And Terraform Project
(Emergency Revision 6.0)

Luna
Surface Gravity: 0.165g

Lune
Surface Gravity: 1.000g

Atmosphere

The Stormlands

Region of Reduced Gravity

Condensed
(Neutronium)
Layer

Fault Plate
(c.f., The Shattering)

appendix C

technical notes

planetary descriptions

For the curious, the Lalandean world of Gammon and the Wolf 359 world of Pup, which are mentioned briefly in Chapter 10 and form the twin seats of the Biarchy government in Chapter 25, are described in more detail by this series' previous volume, *Lost in Transmission*.

Saturn's A, B, and C rings—by far the most visible at a distance—are 15,000, 25,800, and 17,400 kilometers wide, respectively, as measured from the inner to the outer edge. Their outer *diameters* are obviously much larger: 274,000, 235,400, and 183,500 kilometers, versus 120,700 km for the planet itself. By comparison, the Earth's diameter is only 12,750 km. The observation platform described in Chapter 8 is just inside the orbit of Mimas, the innermost of Saturn's large, spherical moons. Notably, it's also inside the sparse E ring, which is thought to extend to a distance of eight planetary radii and to include a number of the inner moons. Please note that this book relies on pre-*Cassini* data. I had a hand in the launching of that spacecraft and will be following it with great interest, but as of this writing it has not yet reached the planet.

As described, the planet Mulciber in the Epsilon Eridani system is possible only if it's close enough to its parent star that the ambient heat will melt tin and drive off light gases such as oxygen and nitrogen. Also, for heavy metals to occur in such abundance at the planet's surface, Mulciber must have been shattered by a collision of some sort, in such a way that its light, rocky crust has coalesced into a separate moon—Aetna—while its exposed iron core re-formed into the planet Conrad describes.

Stephen L. Gillett (while not mentioning a world as strange as Mulciber) outlines some of the details of this process in his excellent reference *World-Building* (Writer's Digest Books, 1996), but it's worth mentioning that something very similar appears to have happened to Earth. If the mass of our moon were distributed on top of the existing Earth, as it seems to have been in the early stages of the solar system's formation, we'd have a much thicker crust with much lower metal content near the surface. If the Mars-sized body which struck Earth had done so less glancingly, our planet might well have become an iron cannonball with a much larger moon. A straight-on hit could even have pulverized the Earth, forming a second asteroid belt, although it's likely that a planet of some sort would have re-formed from the shards eventually.

the squozen moon

The atmospheres of planettes like Maplesphere and Ash are not stable over geologic time, or even the span of a few years, without a replenishment mechanism and/or a mechanism for keeping the upper atmosphere very cold. Make no mistake: these are technological artifacts, like buildings, and will not persist forever without steward-ship.

Lune, the Goliath of planettes, does not have this problem, and will keep its atmosphere indefinitely. With a radius of 707 km (reduced from the original 1738 km), a surface gravity of 1.0 gee, and an unaltered mass of 7.3×10^{22} kg, Lune's escape velocity is 3.72 kilometers per second (vs. 11.9 km/s for Earth). This is more than enough to retain oxygen and nitrogen, but also small enough to make access to space a lot easier than it is from Earth.

The delta velocity necessary to reach Varna—in an orbit 50,000 km high—from Lune's surface is very close to the escape velocity:

$$\Delta V = (2\mu/707E3 - \mu/25350E3)^{0.5} = 3,697 \text{ m/s}$$

Fortunately, this is achievable through low-tech means, as we see in Chapter 19.

Note that Lune's sphere of influence—the maximum radius of a stable circular orbit—is just over 65,000 km. Past this point, the gravity of Earth (even Murdered Earth) will perturb the orbit over time, until the orbiting object either crashes, is ejected from the Earth-moon system, or becomes a stable satellite of Earth.

The dimensions of Lune give it a surface area of 6.28 million square kilometers—about 17% of its original area, or 1.7% of Earth. This is slightly smaller than the continent of Australia, and while it includes ocean as well as land surfaces, it does create a plausible home for hundreds of millions of human beings even at sub-Queendom technology levels.

Because angular momentum is always conserved, reducing the diameter of Luna from 3476 to 1414 km (almost exactly a 60% reduction) will increase its rotation rate. For a sphere with a mass M, rotation period P, and radius r, the angular momentum is $(\frac{2}{5})(Mr^2)(2\pi/P)$. Thus, r^2/P is a constant, and reducing the radius by 60% decreases the rotation period by a factor of 6. As a result, the moon's current solar day of 29.53 Earth days (708.72 hours) is shortened to 4.92 Earth days (118.12 hours). By crushing to slightly less than 60%, the day can be adjusted to exactly 5 earth days, or 120 hours.

The original soil composition of Luna is compared with the Earth's crust in the table below:

Element	Earth	Moon
Oxygen	47%	42%
Silicon	28%	21%
Iron	4.5%	13%
Calcium	3.5%	8%
Aluminum	7.9%	7%
Magnesium	2.2%	6%
Titanium	0.46%	2%
Nickel	**0.001%**	**0.6%**
Sodium	2.5%	0.3%
Chromium	0.01%	0.2%
Potassium	2.5%	0.1%
Manganese	0.1%	0.1%
Sulfur	0.025%	0.1%
Phosphorus	0.1%	0.05%
Carbon	**0.19%**	**0.01%**
Nitrogen	**0.002%**	**0.01%**
Hydrogen	**0.22%**	**0.005%**

So, from a terraformer's perspective Luna is not a bad piece of real estate once the gravity problem is solved.

The only real problems are a lack of carbon and hydrogen in the Lunar soil, and an overabundance of toxic nickel. The figures on nitrogen are misleading, since Earth's atmosphere contains a huge reservoir of this element, whereas Luna has no such resource. A dense nitrogen atmosphere is certainly necessary to support Earthly life, so one would need to be imported.

wellstone

I've written a great deal about this subject elsewhere, and will not repeat it all here. For now, I'll just say that although it sounds far out—and I've pushed the limits of credulity pretty hard here—this is a mostly real technology which is currently under development. Readers interested in learning more are encouraged to check out my nonfiction book on the subject, *Hacking Matter* (Basic Books, April 2003), or the web site www.programmablematter.net.

positronium

The "positronium" material mentioned in Chapter 11 is a real substance, consisting of a semistable "atom" with an electron and positron (or antielectron) orbiting their mutual center of attraction. The positronium atom has no nucleus, but it does have a definite size, and in fact the Air Force Research Laboratory has investigated quantum dots (and by extension, wellstonelike quantum-dot solids) as a means for storing this explosive in microgram quantities. According to Gerald Smith of Positronics Research in Los Alamos, New Mexico, when the electron and positron are collided together by shock or high temperatures, each microgram of positronium releases the energy equivalent of 40 kilograms of TNT. Thus, the potential for positronium-in-wellstone as a fuel or a munition is considerable. A BB-sized pellet of the stuff could easily sink a battleship, or propel a Volkswagen to the moon.

blindsight

Again, a real thing, although the dolcet berry is not. Interested readers should check out V. S. Ramachandran's fascinating *Phantoms in the Brain* (Perennial, 1999).

appendix D

further voyaging

Pumpkin orange, Conrad noted with surprise and mild disappointment. There were hints of rainbow at the edges, hints of laquered sheen at the center, but the dully glowing "white dwarf" was fundamentally orange, not much different in appearance than the neutron star had been. More than anything it looked like a wellstone nightlight in the wall of a child's bedroom. But unlike the neutron star—really just a tourist stop along the way— this planet-sized sphere contained riches: stable transuranics by the gigaton, held tightly in the core by a hundred thousand gravities.

"If only we could pry them loose," Tilly said to him as they stood together on their yacht's observation deck. "We'd be richer than the Biarchy itself."

"I think I've got an idea," Conrad replied. And so he did, though its implementation was more difficult than he could possibly have imagined. But that's another tale entirely.

about the author

In a decade and a half as an aerospace engineer, Wil McCarthy has designed satellite orbits, built robotic bulldozers, simulated giant lasers, sent space probes off to the planets, and spoken the words "Guidance is go" through a dippy-looking headset. Today he's a freelance science journalist, the Sci Fi Channel's science correspondent, and president of The Programmable Matter Corporation (www.programmablematter.com), a Colorado nanotech startup doing, well, some of the things you'll read about in this book.

On the side, he's the author of nine science fiction novels, including BLOOM (a New York Times Notable Book) and THE COLLAPSIUM (Nebula Nominee and Amazon.com "Best of the Year") and one nonfiction book, HACKING MATTER (Amazon.com #4 bestseller and Nanotechnology Now "Best of 2003"). His short fiction has appeared all over the place.

Further information is available at www.wilmccarthy.com